W9-BPK-417

FORGE OF THE
TITANS

FORGE OF THE
TITANS

STEVE WHITE

FORGE OF THE TITANS

A Baen Books Original

Baen Publishing Enterprises
P.O. Box 1403
Riverdale, NY 10471
www.baen.com

ISBN: 0-7434-3611-3

Cover art by David Mattingly

First printing, June 2003

Library of Congress Cataloging-in-Publication Data

White, Steve, 1946-
 Forge of the titans / Steve White.
     p. cm.
 "A Baen Books original."
  ISBN 0-7434-3611-3
  1. Titans (Mythology)—Fiction. 2. Telepathy—Fiction. I. Title.

  PS3573.H474777F67 2003
  813'.54—dc21

                                                        2003006196

Distributed by Simon & Schuster
1230 Avenue of the Americas
New York, NY 10020

Production by Windhaven Press, Auburn, NH
Printed in the United States of America

10   9   8   7   6   5   4   3   2   1

To Sandy, who has her own kind of magic.

AUTHOR'S NOTE

In the common tongue of Khron, final vowels are always pronounced—"Quire" rhymes with "why ray." The next-to-last syllable is normally stressed, with the exception of words with the "-uo" ending (meaning "people of" and pronounced as "yew-oh"); in these words, the last syllable before the ending is stressed. Otherwise, readers are on their own.

CHAPTER ONE

In Virginia, summer is the only reliable season: you *know* it's going to be hot and humid.

Otherwise . . . well, Derek Secrest's boyhood recollections of winter included Christmas days outdoors in shirtsleeves, but also of freezing his butt off shoveling two feet of blizzard out from around his dad's car in latitudes where you weren't supposed to need a garage except perhaps as a glorified tool shed. Likewise, spring and autumn could be a damp misery of drizzly chill that lent the tourist ads every quality of a joke except humor.

But sometimes those ads told the truth—and less than the truth. Autumn really could fulfill all the promise of Indian summer for a few days when old memories crowded around and you wanted time to stand still. And spring, at its best, seemed to justify the universe by sheer, throat-hurting beauty.

Today was that kind of day: past the full glory of azaleas and dogwoods, for this was mid-May, but still partaking of that fragile, fleeting perfection.

So, wondered Derek with twenty-two-year-old impatience, *what the hell am I doing indoors?*

He knew the official answer, the reason they'd given him when he'd been ordered up here from Pensacola: *research.*

1

It told him precisely nothing. As far as he could see, the only research he was doing was determining experimentally whether it was possible to be literally bored to death.

Cruelly, he could even glimpse the gorgeous day through the window of the waiting room where he sat—and sat, and sat—with an assortment of other uniformed people. It would have been a lovely view if he'd been in the mood to appreciate it. Not all of the northern Virginia landscape had vanished under endless rows of gratuitously undistinguished townhouses containing government employees who hadn't yet stolen enough of the taxpayers' money to afford something more pretentious. And this installation, to which he'd been bused after landing at Andrews Air Force Base across the Potomac, was pretty out of the way. In fact, he wasn't clear on just exactly *where* it was—and this was not unfamiliar territory to him. Curious.

Actually, there was a lot that was curious about this whole business. Naval Aviation Officer Candidates like himself were used to participating in experiments on a voluntary basis— *really* voluntary, for there was never any shortage of volunteers. Why should there be? As long as you were sitting at a keyboard performing some routine task as fast as you could while occasionally being stung by a harmless but irritating electric shock, or doing something else equally idiotic, you at least weren't getting yelled at by your drill instructor.

This time, though, they hadn't asked for volunteers. . . .

The outside door of the waiting room opened, derailing Derek's train of thought. He had to fight his impulse to stand up and come to attention, for the man who entered wore Navy short-sleeved whites like himself—but with the two gold stripes of a full lieutenant on his shoulder boards, rather than the tiny gold anchor that adorned Derek's. *You're not at Pensacola, dummy!* he reminded himself. *And this guy doesn't work for Training Command.*

The lieutenant looked around, saw an empty chair beside Derek, and walked over. "This seat taken?" he asked in a vaguely Gulf Coast-accented baritone.

Again, Derek had to restrain his leg muscles from propelling him up out of his chair. "Oh no, sir!"

The lieutenant gave a lazy smile as he eased himself down. "Hey, relax, Candidate! I'm not here to dick you over."

Derek really did relax. The lieutenant's smile had that effect. He even found himself able to look past the rank insignia at individual details.

The lieutenant's name tag read "Rinnard." He wore pilot's wings on his left breast above a row and a half of ribbons. (Derek grew painfully aware that he wore only the red-and-yellow ribbon of the National Defense Medal—the "walk-and-talk ribbon.") Normally, those golden wings would have inspired an awe that transcended even their wearer's exalted—to an NAOC, anyway—rank. But Derek found himself looking beyond even that, and wondering why he did.

Granted, the lieutenant was tall, well-built, and handsome in a dark swashbuckling way. But there was something beyond looks—something hard to define. It probably had to do with that smile. But, for whatever reason, the lieutenant oozed a quality that drew every eye in a room as surely as though by magnetism or gravity. Maybe it was what people meant when they spoke of "charisma."

Lieutenant Rinnard had evidently been studying him as well. "You must be just back from Tyndall." He indicated the four tiny gold bars above Derek's name tag. "Congratulations."

This guy had been through Pensacola—that much would have been clear even without the evidence of his pilot's wings. He knew Derek had completed land survival training at Tyndall Air Force Base, north of Panama City, and thereby cleared the last real hurdle before commissioning. He also knew what the four little gold bars meant: Derek was of above-average "candidate officer" rank in his last week in NAOCS, just barely below the godlike level of the Marine drill instructors in the terrorized eyes of the "poopies," as the new arrivals in the hell of Indoctrination Battalion were called.

"Uh, thank you, sir. Yes, but . . ." Military propriety struggled with the urge to blurt out the confidences that this man seemed to invite. "Yes, only I'm . . . that is . . ."

"Only you're here instead, and missing your chance to dump

on the poopies like you got dumped on," the lieutenant finished for him sympathetically.

"Yes, sir. And also missing the chance to graduate with my class." There, he'd said it. He wasn't sure this hotshot would understand. He wasn't sure he understood it himself. *Sergeant McManus is a sadistic, semi-literate redneck,* he thought savagely. *So why does it mean so much to me to be able to march out of that hall with Class 22-14, wearing ensign's shoulder boards, and have him standing there at the foot of the steps, and take my first-ever salute from him?*

But the lieutenant did understand. "Well ain't that a shit sandwich? You'll have to get commissioned with a later class. You must have been ordered here like me."

Derek emerged from his self-pity into an embarrassed awareness that he might, just possibly, not be the only one here against his will. "Yes, sir. I wasn't told anything about it. Does the lieutenant know—?"

"Lighten up! You're not at Pensacola!" The same inhibitions-dissolving smile flashed.

"Uh, no, sir, I'm not." Derek swallowed before pronouncing the forbidden pronoun. "Do *you* know what's going on here?"

"Haven't a clue. I was aboard *Reagan*, off Rosie Roads for an operational readiness exercise, when I got my orders. Even the skipper of my squadron—that's VF 98—said he didn't know what it was all about. And I believe him. He was ricocheting off the walls at losing one of his pilots just before an OPREDEX."

Derek's jaw dropped. VF 98 was one of the first squadrons to have gotten the new advanced two-seat fighter, just arriving in the fleet to replace the obsolescent F/A-18F. "So you fly the F-39, sir?" he asked in awe.

"Yep. Is that what you want to pilot?"

Derek's ardor slumped a little. "Actually, sir, I'm in flight officer training. My eyesight—"

"—Isn't quite absolutely perfect," the lieutenant finished for him.

"Twenty-forty in one eye," Derek confirmed ruefully. "But I do want to be a radar intercept operator in F-39s."

"Listen, we need RIOs just as much as we need pilots. Mine's a damned good man. I only hope the Ops officer will be able to schedule some flight time for him while I'm here doing whatever it is we're doing. Oh, by the way, I'm Paul Rinnard." The lieutenant extended his hand.

Derek took the proffered hand gingerly. "Derek Secrest, sir."

"Anyway, I don't think it's just a coincidence that my orders came just a few weeks after we were given those new tests—you know, with the weird helmet gizmo they put over your head, and the pills that make you feel woozy the rest of the day."

"But I thought that was just part of the induction physical at Pensacola."

"Nope. Word is that everybody in the fleet has been getting it. And, I suppose, not just the fleet." Rinnard indicated the rainbow of uniforms in the waiting room.

The inner door opened, and a harried-looking Air Force technical sergeant emerged, consulting a clipboard. "All right, you're next. . . ." He looked slightly askance at Derek's shoulder boards. "Er, Midshipman Secrest."

Derek gritted his teeth at the common but mortifying error. Midshipman indeed! He remembered when they'd brought some fourth-year Naval Academy pukes—they were *undergraduates,* for God's sake!—through Pensacola for aviation orientation. He'd personally taken great satisfaction in running their supercilious butts into the sand on the cross-country course.

But the tech sergeant was—for another week, at least— his senior by one grade, and he just had to take it. "Here," he mumbled, getting to his feet.

Lieutenant Rinnard looked up slowly. "That's *Candidate* Secrest, Airman," he corrected in a very quiet, very smooth voice—a voice which held something below the level of sound, something of which everyone in earshot was conscious, judging from all the raised heads.

Sweat popped out on the tech sergeant's brow. "Ah . . . that is . . . of course, sir. This way, if you please, sir."

It took a heartbeat for Derek to realize that the second "sir" had been addressed to him. He gave Rinnard a look that held something more than mere gratitude, then followed the tech sergeant through the door.

Derek didn't waste his breath kvetching about his presence here to the severe late-middle-aged woman in the white lab coat, whose office name-plate read *Rosa Kronenberg, M.D., Ph.D.* She was a civilian, and would never understand.

"First of all, Mister Secrest," she began, surprising him with a correct form of address, "I must emphasize to you that everything you are going to see or hear in this installation is classified Top Secret."

Hope flared in Derek. As an NAOC, he wasn't cleared for Top Secret. "Actually, ma'am, there seems to have been some mistake. I'm not—"

"Yes, you are." Kronenberg slid a paper across the desk. It looked impressively official. "You would have been ordered here sooner, but the background investigation took a little while."

Derek's curiosity would no longer be denied. "Ma'am, may I ask what this installation is, and why I'm here?"

"No, you may not. That's on a need-to-know basis, and all you need to know is that you're under orders to cooperate to the fullest with certain tests that will be administered over the next few days. If necessary, I can bring in a senior Navy officer to give you those orders verbally. But I don't think that will be necessary. Do you?"

"No, ma'am." Derek decided he didn't like Doctor Kronenberg very much. And her "next few days" language was a stake through the heart of his last hopes of rejoining Class 22-14.

"The tests," Doctor Kronenberg resumed, "will be harmless and painless, although I can't promise a total absence of discomfort. And now I'll turn you over to an orderly who'll conduct you to your quarters—you'll be sharing a bunkroom with three others. The personal effects you brought are already there. You won't need your uniforms, though; you'll be issued clothing. Report back here at 0800 tomorrow morning. We may be seeing each other again from time to time during the tests."

Be still, my beating heart! Derek consoled himself with the mental sarcasm as he took his leave of Doctor Kronenberg. She'd clearly dismissed him from her mind already, turning her attention to a sheet of hardcopy which doubtless concerned her next laboratory specimen.

Afterwards, Derek found he had no clear recollection of the days that followed.

In some ways, it wasn't as bad as he'd feared. His schedule wasn't particularly frantic, if only because of the logjam of people being processed through this fairly half-assed installation—it reeked of new construction, and his bunkroom was like Indoctrination Battalion revisited save for the lack of full-bag inspections. But his free time was so excruciatingly boring that he found himself welcoming the summons to more tests.

At least at first . . .

A lot of it was the same sort of thing he'd gotten at Pensacola, only more so. But the drugs were different, or maybe there were just more of them. At any rate, his sense of time became disjointed. He didn't like that. And he didn't like the dreams . . . especially because he wasn't always sure whether he'd been asleep or awake when he'd dreamed them. Besides, they weren't like normal dreams.

At first, he had trouble putting his finger on what it was that made them different. Then it finally came to him. Most dreams—even the scary ones and the far worse ones that make one feel unclean for having dreamed them—have a certain basic familiarity. One *knows* where they come from, however little one may *want* to know. But these were intruders. Not necessarily bad. Just . . . alien.

These thoughts occupied his mind in the intervals between tests when he was certain he was awake. There was little else to occupy it. He began to suspect that the installation's drabness went beyond the military norm—that it was intentional, designed to reduce extraneous sensory stimulation to the absolute minimum. If so, its designers could congratulate themselves on a complete success. Just about the only distractions were his fellow test subjects.

Not that they were all that distracting. In fact the standard-issue clothes made them, too, as nondescript as possible. He'd hoped to run into Paul Rinnard, but was only able to exchange a single brief wave with the fighter jock across a room. He barely saw his three roommates— their schedules were too different, for the tests were carried out with scant regard for day and night. Despite occasional exchanges of pleasantries, he never really struck up a conversation with any of them. Everyone else made even less of an impression.

Except for a certain tall woman . . .

Derek never actually met her. He saw her exactly once, and they never spoke. But, once seen, she was difficult to forget.

He was fairly sure she wasn't military; her thick hair, of a brown so dark as to look black in most lights, was too long, almost down to the small of her back. And, although her clear olive skin showed no overt signs of aging, something indefinable made her seem older than most of this crowd. He wasn't sure the word "beautiful" fit her—certainly not in the conventional fashion-model sense, for her features, while very regular, were too strong and her straight nose too prominent. But her eyes were a lovely gray, strikingly light under her black brows and against her Mediterranean complexion. Derek got a good look at those eyes at their brief encounter, for she turned and gave him a long, wordless regard. It later occurred to him to feel puzzlement at that serene, unsurprised appraisal from someone he was absolutely certain he'd never met.

But then, he reflected, maybe she was just another of the strange dreams that came in the timeless limbo between sleep and wakefulness. It was so difficult to be sure.

Finally, there came a time when there were no more tests. Derek, headachy and out of sorts, was summoned to Doctor Kronenberg's office. A Navy captain was there, and he ended up doing all the talking. Kronenberg stayed in the background, gazing intently at Derek, her expression unreadable.

"Mister Secrest," the captain began, "I just want to assure you—without going into specifics—that what you've been put through here has been of the utmost importance." He glanced at a sheet of hardcopy, gave Derek an odd look, and exchanged a quick eye-contact with Kronenberg. Then he cleared his throat and resumed. "Otherwise we wouldn't have hauled you up here from Pensacola just before your final week."

Derek believed that the captain, a weathered sea-dog type with short iron-gray hair, was sincere about the last part. "Sir," he ventured, "I've sort of lost track of time here. I don't suppose it's possible—?"

"No." the captain shook his head. "There's no way you could catch up with your class at Pensacola if you rejoined it now. Sorry—I know how much that means. But don't worry, you're still on track for commissioning."

"Yes, sir," Derek mumbled.

"In the meantime, since your training schedule has already been disrupted anyway, and since Doctor Kronenberg believes some R and R is indicated for the participants in these tests, we're giving you two weeks' extra leave."

"Uh, thank you, sir." *Curiouser and curiouser,* thought Derek.

"The only caveat is that we'll need to know where you can be reached during that time. I believe your parents' home is here in Virginia, down in Tidewater."

"Actually, sir, that's my grandfather's home. My parents are no longer living."

"Oh yes, that's right," said the captain, obviously annoyed with himself. "I remember now. Your grandfather . . ." His voice trailed off, and his frown deepened. Derek wondered why. "Anyway, will you be going there?"

"Yes, sir."

"Excellent. Now, I believe you've already been cautioned about the security classification of this entire process. You're not to discuss what you've seen or done here with anyone— including your grandfather."

"Yes, sir. I understand." *Not that I'd be able to tell anybody anything even if I wanted to,* Derek added silently. *The whole thing's a total mystery to me.*

"Very well, then. Here are your leave papers."

"Excuse me, sir, but on my return to Pensacola, who do I report to for reassignment to a new class?"

The captain gave Doctor Kronenberg another surreptitious glance. "I believe you'll be contacted before your leave is over. All will be made clear at that time. If there are no further questions, you're dismissed."

★ CHAPTER TWO

The Hampton Roads Bridge-Tunnel was still a royal pain to get through. Not even the newly inaugurated air-cushion ferry had helped much; people still wanted the sensation of being in control of their own cars, however spurious that sensation was when stuck in endless traffic jams.

Derek knew this full well, and he'd briefly considered trying to hop a commuter flight from Washington Dulles airport. But in the end he didn't regret his decision to rent a car instead—not when he finally emerged from the tunnel into the sunlight at the tip of Willoughby Spit, with Norfolk Naval Base spread out before him and the big carriers tied up at Sewell's Point across the water. He took a deep breath of salt air and knew he was home.

The traffic got no easier as he proceeded. His grandfather, whose adolescence belonged to the near-mythic 1960s, claimed to remember a time when Norfolk and Virginia Beach had been distinct cities, with only innocent-seeming tendrils of sprawl beginning to creep into the countryside between them like the first shoots of some poisonous plant. Derek was skeptical. Was it really possible that everything from Hampton Roads to the Atlantic had gotten paved over in less than half a century? Glenn Secrest had chuckled at the question, and reinforced his grandson's skepticism by asserting that it had taken a good deal less time than that.

The driving got less frenetic after he turned off the main arteries onto Princess Anne Road. By the time he worked his way around to the south of Oceana NAS and caught Sandbridge Road, he was in country that came as close to rural-looking as it got around here any more. He could occasionally take his eyes away from the traffic and cast wistful glances at the F-39s wheeling overhead.

Sheer inaccessibility save by secondary and tertiary roads was probably what had kept Sandbridge so very nearly unchanged. That, and the residents' determination to keep it that way. They hadn't altogether succeeded, of course. But as Derek turned onto Sandfiddler Road and proceeded past the beach houses, it was like driving backwards in time.

Those houses tended to be in remarkably good condition considering their age and the difficulty of keeping them up in the teeth of everything the Atlantic could throw at them. But people who wanted to live here at all were prepared to make the effort. The house that was Derek's destination was typical, built of sun-bleached timber in a low rambling style, with a cathedral-ceilinged great room opening through sliding glass doors onto a V-shaped deck that jutted out over the dunes.

As Derek turned into the graveled driveway, his grandfather emerged, waving. After initial greetings and the removal of Derek's limited luggage to his old room, Glenn Secrest announced that the sun was over the yardarm. They adjourned to the deck, where Derek stood at the rail for a moment and scanned the panorama of beach: sea oats waving in the late afternoon breeze, occasional dilapidated remnants of fencing, the tide ebbing to reveal the flats.

His grandfather emerged with bourbon. They sat down and yielded to the illusion that the deck was that of a ship, with only the ocean horizon showing beyond the bow. The sky began to darken a bit, and Derek's feeling of homecoming deepened. In all his time in the Florida panhandle, he'd never adjusted to the sun setting into the sea. Unnatural.

Glenn Secrest sighed. "It's a sure sign of old age," he

philosophized, "when your grandson can drink with you legally!"

Derek snorted, disinclined to fulsome sympathy. At sixty-nine, his grandfather was in even better condition for his age than was the house: tall, erect and active, with hair that was still offensively thick. (Derek had already detected, under bright direct lighting, the first slight but undeniable thinning at the upper corners of his own temples, and had felt an icicle stab through his gut.) Save for a lightening of that hair's shade of gray against his darkly weathered skin, Glenn seemed practically unchanged since the day a certain orphaned thirteen-year-old had arrived at what was to be his new home.

"You'll probably last long enough to be a bad influence on your *great*-grandchildren," Derek predicted, sinking deeper into his deck chair and letting the ocean breeze wash over him. "Hey, listen, I'm sorry I couldn't give you any more notice."

"Forget it. This visit is like a bonus. I wasn't expecting to see you until I flew down to Pensacola."

"For my commissioning ceremony," Derek added, avoiding his grandfather's eye.

The older man noted, but did not comment on, the undertone of bitterness. He spoke in a carefully neutral tone. "I must admit I was surprised at where you said you were calling from. What were you doing up there in northern Virginia? You mentioned something about tests."

"I'm not supposed to talk about it."

"Oh. Classified, is it?"

"Top secret." Derek instantly wondered if he should have said even that much.

Glenn raised his eyebrows, and stroked his gray mustache reflectively. "Well, then, I won't try to pump you. But just for purposes of airline reservations, how does this affect—?"

"I'll have to join another class after I get back to Pensacola. I can't give you an exact date." The mention of airline tickets brought Derek to a sudden realization, and intensified his misery. "Oh Christ, Granddad, it must be too late to cancel your reservation! I'm sorry."

"Again, forget it. I'll just deduct it from your inheritance. Seriously, what the hell use have I got for money anymore? But that's not really what's bothering you, is it?"

"Well . . . I'd sort of hoped that the next time you saw me, I'd be getting my commission." Derek avoided his grandfather's eyes, staring fixedly out to sea.

Glenn Secrest gave an unseen smile. "I know you did. I also know what you've been through down there. I went through it myself, a long time ago, and I understand they've somehow managed to buck the trend and avoid watering it down too much. Believe me, Derek, I'm already so proud of you I can barely see straight. So what if some boondoggle causes you to miss graduating with your class? Believe me, nobody in the fleet is ever going to give a damn about it. And *I* don't give a damn about it, for whatever that's worth."

"Actually, Granddad, it's worth quite a lot." The winter that had settled over Derek's soul melted in a smile, and they clinked glasses.

"Of course," Glenn resumed with a nonchalance that might have fooled some people, "I must admit you've piqued my curiosity. Blame it on my background—"

"About which I've never been entirely clear," Derek interjected pointedly. He knew his grandfather had gone through Pensacola four and a half decades ago, but in the Intelligence offshoot of the flight officer pipeline. After that . . . Well, one wall of the study—the "I-love-me wall" as Glenn called it—held the plaque and group pictures of a squadron to which he'd been assigned at the tail end of the Vietnam war. But after that he'd somehow departed from the conventional career track, never having served as Intelligence officer for an air wing, much less a carrier. What *had* he spent his time doing? He'd always been a master at smoothly deflecting questions about it.

He displayed that same mastery now, letting Derek's interjection slide away into oblivion as though it had never been uttered. "I know you can't tell me any actual facts. But guesswork, speculation and scuttlebutt have never been classified and never will be. Have you heard any of those? Or generated any yourself?"

Derek considered. The ban of secrecy, as he understood it, applied only to what had happened in the nameless installation just outside the Washington beltway. He recalled the connection Lieutenant Rinnard had drawn with some of the odder elements of the physical he'd undergone as a poopie. Nobody had said anything about *that* being classified.

"Well, I don't know if it means anything, but some of us were wondering about the stuff that got done to us in connection with our induction at Pensacola—and, apparently, to other people as well." He described it, appeasing his conscience by sticking to generalizations.

As he spoke, his grandfather's reactions were interesting to observe. First came a flash of startlement that would have been imperceptible to anyone who didn't know the old man very well indeed. Then, after the merest shutter-click of time, the bogus blandness was back in place, possibly even more bogus—at least to someone with years of experience at looking for the signs.

"Well," Glenn finally chuckled, "that's something new—especially that helmet you said they put over your head. In my day, the worst part of the physical involved the *other* end! But now it's time to get started on dinner. I was deep-sea fishing off Hatteras earlier this month, and I've got some tuna salted away. Come on inside. I can use all the unskilled kitchen help I can get."

The last days of the perfect spring fled past, like a final afterglow of Derek's youth.

He felt oddly at peace, for he implicitly believed what he'd been told: the Navy had his immediate future mapped out for him, and would tell him the details in its own good time. His life would resume its expected course after an annoying but not catastrophic postponement.

So he helped his grandfather around the house, rode the waves on the somewhat elderly but still functional Chris-Craft moored at Rudee Inlet, paid ritual visits to some of the old night spots, looked up some of the relatively few old friends still in the area . . .

And, most of all, he took long walks on the beach.

He'd always enjoyed that. But now it held an added element, something resembling urgency, for this would be his last opportunity for he knew not how long—his last opportunity, indeed, before his life changed in many ways. Besides, it gave him a chance to sift over the things that still puzzled him about what had passed in northern Virginia.

His grandfather's house was well situated for such solitary walks—uniquely so, near the southern end of Sandbridge itself but north of Sandbridge Beach with its limited and inoffensive commercial development. At low tide, one could walk out onto the sandbars and, gazing north into the hazy distance past the Atlantic Fleet Combat Training Center, glimpse the towers of the Virginia Beach resort strip—the southern end of the nearly unbroken battlement of high-rises that the Tidewater area presented to the sea. Here, there was nothing behind the dunes and the occasional beach house save the marshes fringing Lake Tecumseh and the northern reaches of Back Bay.

On a certain breezy day, though, Derek found himself wanting more solitude than even that familiar stretch of beach afforded. So he drove south through Sandbridge Beach to the Little Island recreation area.

There were surprisingly few people about. Soon Derek was alone with the sea-birds and a group of dolphins in the middle distance. He smiled as he observed those cavorting cetaceans—the smile that the sight of them always seemed to awake in his species. It was as though he had passed backward in time to an age when all the Atlantic seaboard was like this. For an instant, he allowed himself to imagine that if he stared at the eastern horizon intensely enough he would spot the topsail of the very first English ship to raise this coast.

Then, even as he stared at it, the horizon began to waver. . . .

Derek blinked, and felt his skin prickle with something he didn't yet recognize as fear. He became aware that the wavering was really between him and the horizon—only a short distance offshore, he knew without really knowing how he knew. And it was confined to a circular area, no more than a few yards in diameter if his estimate of the distance to it was correct.

Some kind of heat inversion, Derek told himself.

But then the circle somehow solidified, and behind it the ocean and the sky dissolved into—what?

There is a single, tiny corner of the mind that insists on calling up trivial bits of useless knowledge at the most inappropriate moments. Standing rooted to the sand, suspended in unreality, Derek found himself taking refuge in that corner. And he recalled having read, God knew when or where, that when Magellan's ships had first appeared off Patagonia, the local Indians *couldn't see them.* Not because there had been anything wrong with their eyes, but because their minds had been unable to process what their eyes were reporting. Their Stone Age reality-structure had simply not included anything like those ships.

Derek wondered if that was why he couldn't comprehend what he was seeing through that circle.

All at once, the solidifying process came to abrupt completion—and an explosion of light swept out from the circle's rim. It was a silent explosion; but in place of sound came something worse than a thunderclap, on a level and of a nature for which Derek's native language had no words. It battered not his eardrums but the inside of his brain. He staggered backwards, dazzled and stunned.

Then the light died away, leaving only a glow. As Derek watched, blinking away the cartwheeling galaxies of stars that filled his eyes, a black silhouette appeared against that glow: a female figure running toward him with long hair flying.

With a final leap, the figure came through the circle like a dolphin soaring through a hoop. She landed with a mundane splash in the shallows, and collapsed to her hands and knees.

Other running silhouettes appeared behind her in the strange, perspective-defying depths of the circle.

With obvious effort, she heaved herself partially erect and turned back to face her pursuers, as Derek somehow knew them to be. Her body seemed to convulse with some terrible effort, although she took no apparent action.

Derek's paralysis shattered. Plenty of time later to worry about his sanity. At this instant, all that mattered was coming to the woman's aid. He sprang toward her, splashing through the waves.

There was another outflowing of light from around the circle's circumference. Once again, something that was not sound sent Derek reeling back. This time he lost his balance and fell backwards into the surf.

As he was falling, the circle vanished, along with the figures that hadn't quite made it through.

All was as it had been before, with the addition of the woman—the only concrete evidence that it had all really happened. She sagged down into the water and lay there, motionless, the surf washing through her long, streaming dark tresses.

Derek stumbled to his feet and splashed the rest of the way to her side. He knelt beside her and turned her face-upward lest she drown in a few inches of water.

She was wearing nondescript clothes—jeans, sneakers and a checked shirt—but Derek noticed nothing of that. All he saw was her face. It was a face he'd seen before, just once. Her eyes flickered open. They were a luminous light gray, as he'd known they would be.

Her mouth opened, but speech seemed to require an effort presently beyond her. Whatever she'd just been through must have exhausted her beyond common conception.

"No hospitals," she finally managed to breathe.

Derek blinked. Was she in trouble with the law or something? "I know you—or at least I've seen you. What . . . what . . . ?" He found he couldn't even frame a coherent question about what had just happened, or seemed to happen, on this lonely stretch of coast. "Who are you?" he finally settled for asking.

Incongruously, her lips trembled into the ghost of an amused smile. "Sophia," she whispered. On that less-than-informative note, she lost consciousness again.

For a few moments, Derek knelt in a limbo of futile

indecision, looking up and down the beach for someone he could ask for help. Then he pulled himself together. He slid one arm under her back and another under her knees, and picked her up—not without difficulty, for she was not a small woman and she'd gone unhelpfully limp. Carefully keeping his footing in the surf, he carried her toward the beach and his car.

"Who *is* she?" asked Glenn Secrest as he helped maneuver the unconscious woman inside.

"Says her name's Sophia," gasped the exhausted Derek. "That's all I know—except that I saw her last week, up in northern Virginia."

"So what's she doing here?"

"I don't know. It's . . . well, it's kind of a strange story."

Glenn lifted an eyebrow, but didn't pursue the matter. "I guess we'd better call the rescue squad."

"No!" Derek surprised himself with his vehemence. "She said she didn't want to go to a hospital."

"Why not?"

"I don't know, I tell you!" Derek took a deep breath and lowered his voice. "Look, can't she just stay here for a little while?"

"Hmm . . . Listen, Derek, if the police are after her—"

"I don't think that's it. But she's in *some* kind of trouble— a kind I don't understand." Derek drew another breath. "Please, Granddad?"

Glenn sighed. "You owe me an explanation of what you *do* know, and how you happened to show up with her. But in the meantime, the first thing we need to do is get her out of these wet clothes and into bed." The sight of Derek's expression brought another sigh, this time one of exasperation. "Come on and lend a hand! I doubt if you'll be seeing anything you haven't already seen."

"Of *course* not!" Derek declared with the indignation of the post-adolescent male.

There were no women's clothes in the house—Derek's grandmother had died while he'd been in college. But they wrapped the gray-eyed mystery woman in a bathrobe and put her in the guest bed. Glenn examined her with what he cheerfully admitted were long-rusted first aid skills.

"Well," was his verdict, "she doesn't seem to be suffering from anything more than *really* extreme exhaustion. Let's just let her sleep—best thing for her. You, on the other hand, look like you could use a drink."

Glenn started a fire, partly because the evening was turning unseasonably chilly but mostly as an excuse for giving Derek time to collect his thoughts. Then they settled into the great room's leather-upholstered chairs and sipped their drinks in silence.

"Well?" Glenn finally inquired.

Derek took a fortifying pull on his bourbon. "As I told you, I saw her up in northern Virginia, apparently involved in the same stuff I was going through. We never spoke. But she seemed to know me. And . . . I haven't been able to forget her."

"Isn't she a little old for you?" Glenn inquired with a twinkle. "But on second thought, maybe she's not. It's hard to tell just how old or how young she really is. Funny."

"Yeah," said Derek shortly. Women were a mildly sore subject. Jane Craddock had proven unreasonable about his upcoming months-long absence at Pensacola, to be followed by even longer overseas deployments, and since the breakup he'd been unattached. He dragged his mind back to the task of explaining himself in a way that didn't cause his grandfather to have him committed to the rubber room.

As matter-of-factly as possible, he recounted what had happened earlier that afternoon. "And before you even ask," he concluded hastily, "the answer is: no, I am *not* on any kind of drugs!"

"Actually, I wasn't going to ask," his grandfather said mildly. "I don't believe I need to, in your case."

"Thanks, Granddad," said Derek, ashamed of himself for his defensiveness. But then the unpleasant alternative occurred to him "So do you think I'm crazy?"

"Of course—but no more so than is to be expected at your age."

"Be serious, Granddad! I *know*, with absolute certainty,

that I saw what I've just described to you. But it makes no sense! What conclusion can I draw from that?"

"Well," his grandfather said judiciously, "nobody can say that the whole thing was purely a figment of your imagination. The lady giving out ladylike snores in my guestroom is proof that *something* happened. But it's hard to know what to make of her. I went through her pockets after we undressed her—hey, I never claimed to be a gentleman— and there was no ID in them. We'll have to wait until she wakes up to find out who she is. Maybe she can shed some light on what you saw." (Not, Derek noted gratefully, "what you *claim* you saw.") "In the meantime, though, I can't help wondering if there's some connection with whatever super- secret stuff you—and, according to you, she—were involved in. It reminds me of—" Abruptly, and without his usual smoothness, Glenn clamped an iron gate down over his past.

This time, however, Derek was resolved not to let him off the hook. "Granddad, what *did* you do in the Navy that I don't know about? And . . . did it have anything to do with what happened to Mom and Dad?"

For the first time in Derek's memory, Glenn Secrest looked every day of his age. "Derek, let me take that second question first. As you know, I'm not a conventionally religious man. But I swear by everything that is—if you insist on the word—holy to me that your parents died just as you've always been told they did, in a tragic but perfectly normal auto accident. You must believe that."

"I do, sir," said Derek in a small voice.

"And as for your first question . . . You're a smart boy, and you've probably noticed that what you told me about what you've recently experienced struck a chord in my memory. A long time ago, when I wasn't too much older than you are now—" Glenn shook his head. "No. I can't talk about it, even now—any more than you can talk about what happened to you last week. And I don't even know, really, if there's a connection. I will say two things, though. First, the technology seems to have gotten more sophis- ticated since then, judging from what you did tell me. And second . . ." He gave his grandson a long look. "There's

an old saying that inherited traits tend to skip a generation."

Derek blinked. Was the old guy finally entering his dot-
age? He tried to drag the conversation back to something
relevant. "Aside from what I said earlier about drugs . . . Well,
I can't help wondering. I *did* get a lot of them last week.
Could there, well, be some kind of delayed reaction?"

"You may find out soon."

"Huh?"

"In all the excitement, I forgot to tell you. While you were
out, I got a call for you—a Captain Morrisey. He's coming
here tomorrow to see you, on official Navy business. He's
also bringing a civilian named Doctor Kronenberg. He
indicated that you've already met her."

CHAPTER THREE

The woman who called herself Sophia more than slept the clock around. It was well into the following morning before Derek heard her stirring.

He knocked hesitantly on the door frame. "May I come in?"

"Of course." She sat up in bed, holding the covers modestly across her body but otherwise displaying no self-consciousness. She also showed none of the grogginess that might have been expected of one just awakening from a long sleep of exhaustion. Her gray eyes were clear and alert, and her speech was precise.

"I'm Derek Secrest—"

"I know."

"Uh, I brought you here—this is my grandfather's house, by the way—and . . ." *And just how the hell does she know who I am?* Finding himself at a loss for words, Derek sought refuge in practicalities. "I, ah, imagine you'll want to use the bathroom. It's down the hall to the right, first door on the—"

"That won't be necessary."

Derek blinked. How could it not be necessary? "Well, er, how are you feeling?"

"Not badly." She spoke with a faint accent, one which Derek couldn't place. "I've been through a very trying experience, but I believe I'm fully recovered by now."

"Yes, well, ahem, I've been meaning to ask you about that 'experience.'" Derek mustered his forces. Where to begin? "Yesterday afternoon—"

"Good morning, young lady!" Glenn Secrest's cheerful greeting boomed from the doorway. "Sophia, isn't it? You're looking better today."

"Yes. Thank you for letting me stay here."

"Don't mention it. I took the liberty of laundering your clothes—they're over there. We'll be putting breakfast together—come on down whenever you're ready. Come along, Derek, let's go downstairs and let the lady get dressed."

I never even got to ask her what her last name is! Derek thought through gritted mental teeth as he stood up to follow his grandfather.

But Sophia whatever-her-name-was grabbed his arm. She had quite a strong grip for a woman. But that wasn't what rendered him motionless. No, it was a feeling that some kind of energy flowed through the point of physical contact between them and made it impossible for him to even consider focusing on anything but the depths of those unusual gray eyes.

"Listen, Derek, I don't know how long I'll be able to stay here. So listen carefully."

"Huh? Oh, don't worry, you can stay with us as long as you want to." *Could it be the INS she's in trouble with?* he wondered. *She does look and sound kind of foreign.*

Only . . . illegal aliens don't generally arrive the way she did yesterday.

"Listen, I said! Very soon, your life is going to change in an unexpected way. Your first impulse will probably be to rebel against what fate is forcing you into. But you must not resist. You are at the center of something extremely important—far more important than you can possibly understand. You must—"

The irritation that had been building steadily in Derek ever since he'd been ordered to the super-spooky installation in northern Virginia finally reached critical and erupted. "Jesus H. Christ on a crutch! Can't *anybody* say *anything* to me anymore without talking in riddles?" He shook off Sophia's hand and stomped out of the room and down the stairs, aware of how childish he was being but unable to bring himself to care.

Well, now I at least know what she does for a living, he fumed. *She works in a fortune cookie factory!*

Then, as he reached the bottom of the stairs, he heard his grandfather's voice from down the hall, toward the front door. "Why yes, Captain Morrisey. We didn't expect you so early. Come on in."

Derek cast an alarmed glance—not even considering why he was alarmed—up the stairs to assure himself that Sophia was out of sight. Then he stepped into the hallway.

As he'd more than half expected, it was the same Navy captain he'd met the week before. Doctor Kronenberg came behind him, dressed in civilian clothes about as fashionable as the lab coat in which he'd last seen her. Morrisey advanced, hand outstretched, and Derek—for all that he was on leave and out of uniform—came more than halfway to attention. Normally, an NAOC didn't even come into contact with officers this senior, much less have them come to call on him.

He managed to shake hands. "Good day, sir."

"Good day, Ensign Secrest. And no, that's *not* a slip of the tongue. Obviously, some explanation is in order. Perhaps your grandfather will let us have the use of a room where Doctor Kronenberg and I can discuss certain matters with you."

They sat in the study, and Derek stared at the paper Captain Morrisey had handed him.

The signature at the bottom certainly carried conviction—unless, without Derek noticing it, someone else had been elected President in the last week or so.

"Congratulations, Ensign," he heard Morrisey say, as though from a great distance.

Derek lifted glazed eyes from the commission. "Sir, this . . . this isn't right."

"I assure you it is, Ensign. A little untraditional, I admit, but entirely legal. And, even in my notoriously conservative opinion, not at all improper. You've earned it. You're simply being presented with the paper here and now instead of a week or two later at Pensacola."

"But, sir—"

"And now," Morrisey continued inexorably, reaching into his briefcase and sliding another paper across the desk, "here are your orders. You will note that they are stamped 'Top Secret.' This is because the existence—indeed, the very name—of the unit to which you are being assigned is classified at that level."

Derek studied the paper, and his bewilderment turned to stupefaction, and then to horror.

"Sir, this doesn't say anything about going back to Pensacola for flight officer school."

Doctor Kronenberg's exasperation had been waxing visibly. "For God's sake, Mister Secrest, what *are* you complaining about? Correct me if I'm wrong, but I think you just got handed your precious commission on a silver platter, without having to go back down to Florida and participate in some archaic, time-wasting ritual."

"But, ma'am, I'm in the RIO pipeline, and have been all along!"

"Secrest, don't be ridiculous! Is that really all you can think about—playing your silly little macho games with your silly little airplanes? *Anybody* can do that. You, on the other hand, now have a unique opportunity to do something *important*."

Captain Morrisey, reading the signs, raised a surreptitious warning hand before Derek could say the unsayable. "Doctor Kronenberg," he said suavely, "would you excuse me and Ensign Secrest for a few minutes? I believe I can clarify the situation for him."

"I certainly *hope* you can!" Muttering under her breath, Kronenberg stalked from the study.

Captain Morrisey turned to Derek with a smile. "Doctor Kronenberg is a very brilliant scientist—a major national resource, in my opinion. Unfortunately, she is not what I believe is called a 'people person.' And she is, of course, quite mistaken. You and I both know that not just anybody has what it takes to be a United States Naval aviator. *You* do, and of that you can be justifiably proud."

"Thank you, sir. But—"

"Nevertheless, in a general sense Doctor Kronenberg has a point. The particular combination of abilities and character traits that Naval aviation requires is uncommon . . . but not vanishingly so. Certainly not as uncommon as certain attributes which the tests you underwent last week revealed."

Desperately, Derek sought for the precise combination of words that would make this man, evidently the arbiter of his fate, see what a horrible, inexplicable mistake this all was. "Sir, the Navy has invested a lot of money in preparing me for flight officer training. Won't that all go to waste if I'm assigned to this, uh—" he ran his eyes over the orders again "—this JICPO outfit to do something else?" His resolve to avoid any appearance of pleading began to crack, and so did his voice. "Sir, isn't that why the Navy wanted me in the first place?"

Morrisey's sea-blue eyes hardened. "Naturally, we always seek to make the optimum use of our people's abilities, which is why you were accepted for Aviation OCS. But the Navy did not thereby place itself under any sort of contractual obligation to make you a flight officer. We could send you out to the fleet to chip rust off anchor chains for the rest of your hitch if we wanted to. We won't, of course—but only because that would be a flagrant waste of human resources."

"Precisely the point I was trying to make, sir," said Derek stiffly.

"Ah, but you need to understand something. Employing you as a RIO would be almost as wasteful as would the example I just gave. Not quite, of course. But for what you're going to be doing at JICPO, you possess an . . . aptitude which is equaled by not more than *one in every hundred thousand people*. That figure should be considered minimal, as Doctor Kronenberg is cautious by temperament."

Before Derek could form words, another voice did it for him.

"So it *is* true!"

The study had two doors. The one through which Doctor Kronenberg had exited led to the hallway. The other, in the opposite corner, connected with the great room. Derek's grandfather now stood in that door, glaring at Morrisey, who stood up and glared back.

"Mr. Secrest, I requested privacy because your grandson and I are discussing highly sensitive matters for which you are no longer cleared. Your indiscretion could have grave consequences."

"Spare me that crap. I'm not in the Navy anymore, as you yourself have just emphasized by not even giving me the courtesy title of 'Commander' to which I'm technically entitled."

"You are, however, as subject to criminal penalties under the National Security Act as everyone else. We may be forced to investigate—"

"Investigate *this*!" Glenn Secrest pointed in the appropriate direction on his own anatomy. "What are you going to do to me? Not even prison scares me all that much anymore; it's well known that for older men on the inside, homosexuality is pretty much consensual. Fact is, the only threat you can make that really worries me is a threat to the life and sanity of my grandson—and you're doing that anyway!"

Morrisey exerted self-control with a visible effort. "Of course I know your background, and so I can understand your concern. But by the same token, you of all people ought to be able to appreciate the importance of this—and the importance of your grandson." A wintry smile. "You were quite willing to see him go into aerial combat, so don't try to tell me you're excessively protective."

"Hell, no. When he decided he wanted to fly for his country, he made me prouder than I have the capacity to express. But he made that decision knowing more or less what he was getting into. I'm damned if I'll let you con him into a commitment he *doesn't* understand!"

During this entire exchange, Derek had sat in a state of silent passivity. Now, all at once, his confusion crystallized into a single, very clear realization: he resented being discussed in the third person as though he wasn't even in the room. Resented it like hell. Resented it so much that his mouth was open and the words out of it before he recalled that he was addressing his grandfather and an officer astronomically senior to him.

"Will somebody *please* tell me just exactly what the hell this is all about?"

"Tell him, Captain," Glenn grated. "You might as well, because if you don't, I will. You can start by telling him what the acronym JICPO stands for. I'd like to know myself—although I have a pretty good idea what the letter 'P' means."

Captain Morrisey sighed—perhaps with resignation, perhaps with a kind of relief—and turned to face Derek. "It stands for Joint Interservice Command for Psionic Operations. And you're being assigned to it because you happen to be a very powerful latent telepath."

Derek's next clear recollection was of staring across the desk at the three older people—Doctor Kronenberg had evidently come back into the study at some point. He became aware that she was speaking. Maybe it helped that her voice was so irritating.

"—And, of course, the calibration techniques are still lamentably crude. Not as much so as in your grandfather's day, of course. But we're still not in a position to measure your full potential."

Derek found his voice. "Uh . . . Doctor . . . Captain . . . Granddad . . ."

"Yes?" Kronenberg leaned forward.

"This is *crazy*! I mean . . . *telepathy*? That's nothing but a lot of mumbo-jumbo that stage magicians use!"

"So it is generally thought." Kronenberg sounded well pleased with herself. "The only people who believe in it are the sort of people who are taken in by those very stage magicians. Their belief discredits it. This allows us to explore the phenomenon's military potentialities in secret. No investigative reporter takes it seriously enough to pursue it."

"One of the government's more successful exercises in

disinformation," Morrisey put in. "It dates back to the 1970s, when we first awoke to the potentialities."

Derek turned to his grandfather. "So *that* was what you were doing in those . . . missing years."

Glenn nodded gravely. "Yes. I was recruited, much as you are being recruited now. I was a little older, though, and your father was an infant. It was hard. Very hard. And it didn't come to anything."

"Naturally it didn't," Kronenberg resumed. "Even though you exhibited great power. At that time, we were still essentially in a prescientific stage. We didn't have a unification theory that related psionic phenomena to matter and energy. Now we do." The smugness of her tone left little doubt in Derek's mind as to the identity of that theory's author. "Also, the technology wasn't up to systematically testing large populations for the trait. It was a matter of sheer chance—as in the case of your grandfather."

Derek groped for a handhold on reality. "But, Doctor . . . you're *wrong*! At least about me. I swear to God, I don't go around reading everybody's thoughts, or anything like that."

"Of course not." Kronenberg settled into lecturing mode with what was obviously practiced ease. "That's the pop-culture fantasy of telepathy—and it's one of the reasons for the long-term disinformation campaign Captain Morrisey mentioned. If people knew there were actual telepaths functioning among them, there'd be a panic and hysteria that would make the witch hunts of the seventeenth century look tame. But in reality it doesn't work that way. Indeed, it normally doesn't work at all."

"That's why it came a cropper in my case," Glenn put in, drawing a withering glare from Kronenberg for the interruption. "Although a few times . . . well, the glimpses I had . . ." He shook his head slowly and subsided into a reminiscent silence.

"Nowadays," Kronenberg continued after a glacial pause, "we know that telepathy—and also the other psionic phenomena that are as yet less well understood—are subject to limitations just like anything else. We also know that in all but a very few sporadic cases they are latent, and require artificial stimulation. We're also learning how to supply that stimulation. But even when it does become active, the ability is as controllable as any other. Can you imagine receiving *all* the mental output of each passerby—all the random thoughts, all the constant bombardment of sensory stimuli, and all the subconscious backdrop—without being able to shut it out? And try to imagine walking through Times Square and multiplying all that by *all* the passersby! You'd go mad, of course."

"Still," Derek's grandfather insisted, "a telepath, properly stimulated out of latency, *can* receive the consciously organized surface thoughts of anyone not trained or equipped to counter the power, within a certain range. Isn't that so?"

"Yes, it is," Morrisey admitted forthrightly. "Otherwise it wouldn't be of any military use, would it?" He turned to Derek with a smile. "It might interest you to know that *I* am a telepath. Not as powerful as you potentially are, by a long shot, but powerful enough to receive your thoughts right now." His smile broadened at Derek's expression. "But I'm not doing so."

Kronenberg was less amused. "Oh, *think* about it, Secrest!" she snapped in her winning way. "Look, every infantry grunt in the U.S. Army is issued extremely deadly weapons and trained to use them. If you ask me, that's scarier than psionics. In theory, they could go around blowing the heads off all the civilians they see. So why don't they?" She paused as though she actually expected an answer.

"Well . . . that is . . . I mean . . ." Derek struggled with something too obvious to put into words.

Kronenberg smiled. "Precisely. It would be immoral and illegal, and in practically all cases they'd have no motive. Get it through your head: We're *not* talking about something supernatural. It's simply an aspect of the universe that isn't as well understood as most of the others. In fact, it hasn't been understood at all until very recently. But it's like any other source of power: subject to being abused, no doubt, but also amenable to social controls."

"And," Morrisey added, leaning forward significantly,

"uncommonly useful in the present world situation! Since the Cold War ended in the last decade of the twentieth century, the national security problem has changed. We still can't ignore conventional forms of aggression, but for the last twenty years we've pretty much checkmated that threat. No one in the world can realistically hope to overcome us *that* way, and no one has seriously tried. So the military's emphasis has shifted to countering the more subtle threats of terrorism and insurgency. If anybody ignored the problem of counterterrorism before September 2001, you can be sure nobody has since! For this type of mission, multi-megaton nukes are about as appropriate as using a pile driver for swatting flies. What we need are means of applying force in a very precise, very controlled manner. And, above all, *really* accurate intelligence information on the enemy's intentions. And, of course, undetectable and unjammable communications are always useful, especially in covert ops."

"Also," Kronenberg took up the theme, "means of 'force projection,' to use the militarese term, that are undetectable and instantaneous. Remember what I mentioned about other applications of psionics, about which we're still groping for an understanding? We think you may possess some of those, in addition to telepathy. You'll learn about them at JICPO."

Derek's eyes darted from one authoritative face to another, finally resting on his grandfather's. "Granddad, you're the only one I can turn to for advice—the only one I *know* has my best interests at heart. What do you think?"

"Derek, they've done as I asked and laid their cards on the table. I can't deny that they have a point: you're in a position to do your country a unique service. At the same time, all this talk of 'artificial stimulation' tells me you'd be entrusting your mind to new and untried technology."

"What if they'd had that technology back in your day? What if it had been possible to prolong and repeat those 'glimpses' you talked about earlier? Would you have gone for it?"

"Damned straight I would have! But it has to be your decision. And don't let them bullshit you into thinking they can order you to do this." Glenn briefly exchanged glares with Morrisey, then turned back to his grandson. "As you know, nobody can be ordered to fly an airplane; a pilot can plunk his wings down on the skipper's desk any time. That may not officially be the case with this stuff, but as a practical matter I guarantee you it is."

Glenn fell silent, and no one else spoke. Derek was alone amid the swirl of his thoughts.

Then, in that chaos of indecision, came a remembered female voice.

"... *Very soon, your life is going to change in an unexpected way. Your first impulse will probably be to rebel against what fate is forcing you into. But you must not resist. You are at the center of something extremely important—far more important than you can possibly understand...*"

How did she know?

Abruptly, Derek stood up, and spoke in a voice whose firmness surprised him. "I'm in no condition to think very clearly just now, and I have to ... Well, you'll just have to excuse me for a few moments." Without waiting for leave, he stepped out into the hallway and bounded up the stairs three steps at a time.

Sophia was still sitting on the guest bed. She hadn't resumed her clothes, but still had the sheet draped across her body in a way that seemed oddly precise, almost formal.

"Are you a telepath?" Derek demanded without preamble.

"No."

"I don't believe you." The rejoinder was automatic. Oddly enough, he really *did* find himself believing that she'd told the truth. He just wasn't sure it was the entire truth.

"I assure you that I am not. I do know more or less what has just transpired downstairs, but only as a result of some perfectly mundane eavesdropping."

"Then how did you know in advance that this was going to happen?"

"I didn't—not in detail. In general, though, it was easily predictable."

"And what about that little display I saw on the beach south of here yesterday afternoon? Was that some kind of psionic manifestation?"

"No. Not really. Not in the sense you mean."

Derek gripped his temper with both hands. "As usual, you're not making sense. Look, I want you to come downstairs with me and tell the people down there what really happened on that beach, and we'll get all this resolved. I'll step outside for a minute while you put on your clothes."

Derek stood outside the door for the stipulated minute, then another. Finally his patience snapped. "Come *on!*" he demanded. Bidding good manners be damned, he stepped back into the guestroom.

Sophia was gone. The sheet that had covered her lay on the bed as though it had fluttered down from shoulders that were suddenly no longer there.

Derek ran to the window. It was closed. He opened it, stuck his head outside and scanned the beach to the left, Sandfiddler Road to the right, and the adjacent beach houses. There was no running figure in sight.

Then he noticed that Sophia's clothes were still there, neatly folded.

For a while, he simply stood at the window, not seeing the view, thinking hard. Then he squared his shoulders and headed for the stairs.

★ CHAPTER FOUR

This time, Derek rated a helicopter ride from Andrews AFB to the installation in northern Virginia. Viewed from the air, that installation was even more unprepossessing than it had been at ground level. It seemed an incongruous setting for a super-spooky outfit like JICPO.

Once on the ground, Derek was ushered into one of the nondescript government-issue buildings and through a door on which "No Admittance" was stenciled. He found himself in a small, empty room walled in some composite material. With a faint whirr, a segment of the same gray stuff slid over the doorway, leaving the room a featureless cube. Then there was a sensation of the floor falling away beneath Derek's feet, and he decided the chamber wasn't so small after all . . . for an elevator.

Presently the descent ended, and the door slid aside to reveal a harshly lit corridor. A guard wearing camo fatigues and a sidearm met Derek as he emerged. "This way, sir. I'll direct you to Processing, where you'll be assigned quarters." Derek hoisted his sea bag and followed.

There were a few other new arrivals in Processing. Only one wore a Navy uniform. He turned as Derek entered, and his dark face split in a familiar easy grin.

"Well, well! Congratulations, Ensign!"

"Thanks . . . Lieutenant Rinnard," said Derek. For no reason he could define, he wasn't surprised in the least to see the fighter jock here.

"That's 'Paul'—we're both officers and gentlemen now. It's Derek, right?"

"Right . . . Paul." Derek's eyes went to Rinnard's left breast. "I see you're still wearing your wings."

"Hell, yes! I'll be back to driving F-39s after we're through doing . . . what we're going to be doing here. And," added Rinnard with a sensitivity not generally associated with fighter pilots, "you'll get back to flight officer training. This is just a kind of temporary detached duty."

"You really think so?"

"Sure I do. When I was ordered up here, I was pretty mad at first. Then they told me why, and I . . . well, I just couldn't accept it at first. But the skipper set me straight."

As he was probably under orders to do. Derek dismissed the unwelcome thought. "Hey, I was meaning to ask you something. When we were up here before, did you happen to meet this tall woman—a civilian, I'm pretty sure—with long dark hair?"

"I think I know who you mean. Not exactly what you'd usually call pretty, I suppose, but . . . something about her that I couldn't get out of my mind. And I could never decide what her age was."

"That's the one."

"I never got to talk to her. Too bad; a couple of times she looked me straight in the eye like she knew me from somewhere . . . or maybe *wanted* to know me." Rinnard's cocky grin immediately faded into regret. "I would have been only too glad to oblige! But something always seemed to come up before I could introduce myself."

"Sounds like you saw more of her than I did," Derek mused.

"Anyway, let's get checked in. We're all supposed to report for orientation at 1600. Doctor Kronenberg—remember her, the tight-assed old biddy?—is going to give us an introductory lecture. Maybe we'll see what's-her-face there."

Somehow, Derek doubted it.

✧   ✧   ✧

"As most of you have probably been able to figure out for yourselves," said Doctor Kronenberg, "what you've been through was a winnowing process. The preliminary tests, which everyone in the armed forces has been getting, eliminate those with no latent psionic power whatsoever: about nine hundred and ninety-nine out of a thousand. The remaining one-tenth of one percent—minus those who were, for any reason, not granted Top Secret clearance—were the ones brought here recently for more intensive assessment. This enabled us to further eliminate everyone whose power was deemed too low to be useful. Then we eliminated everyone who was married or otherwise attached." She ran her eyes over the little auditorium. "You're what's left. We don't expect to get many more, if any. The armed forces are just about tapped out."

Small as it was, the auditorium wasn't nearly full. There were only a baker's dozen of variously uniformed people, three of whom were women. They sat giving their undivided attention to Kronenberg, who stood behind the podium on the slightly raised dais. Morrisey—who, it turned out, was the Commanding Officer of JICPO—sat behind and to her left.

"Naturally," Kronenberg continued, "we would like nothing better than to expand our recruitment. Unfortunately, civilians can't be ordered to submit to the testing. Also, we'd have to co-opt a wide range of research facilities—and that would be the end of any hope of maintaining security." Kronenberg smiled, briefly so as not to hurt her face too much. "Incidentally, the reason for the low percentage of women here is that you're a cross section of the military, not of the general population. There is no conclusive evidence of any linkage of psionic aptitude to gender—or to ethnicity, for that matter, even though the trait is clearly genetic.

"And now, before turning the podium over to Captain Morrisey, I'll open the floor to questions."

For a few heartbeats there was an uncomfortable silence as people who were still trying to come to terms with the powers they'd been told they possessed cast nervous glances at each other, each one willing someone else to speak first. Finally, one of the women, an Air Force first lieutenant, raised her hand and spoke hesitantly.

"Uh, Doctor Kronenberg, you must understand that this is all very difficult for us to accept at face value. You're talking about things which we're accustomed to regarding as . . . well, as claptrap. I suppose the very existence of this installation proves that's not the case. But still . . . well . . ." Abruptly, her diffidence vanished. *"Please* tell us what we're dealing with here!"

It was as though a dam had burst, for the silence was no more. Above the rising hubbub, the voice of a Black Marine staff sergeant rose. "You heard the lady, Doctor! We want to know just what the fuck's going on here!" Drilled-in military propriety reasserted itself with an almost audible clank. The man came to a seated position of attention and faced Morrisey, trying not to look appalled at his own lapse. "Excuse me, sir. But we need . . . well, we need to know, without any . . . any . . ."

Morrisey smiled. "Without any jive, Sergeant?"

The Marine smiled back. "That's right, sir."

"Well, Doctor?" said Morrisey. "Without any jive?"

Kronenberg looked nonplussed. "You're all scheduled to receive a series of lectures on the theoretical basis of psionics in due course, with full mathematical—" A renewed tumult from the floor drowned her out.

Paul Rinnard raised a lazy hand and spoke up in an equally lazy drawl. "Doctor, if I might make a suggestion, perhaps a brief, simplified introduction to the subject would be in order at this time." He flashed his trademark disarming grin. "And no math, please! It always makes my poor ol' head hurt."

Joining in the general chuckles, Derek realized that those chuckles were breaking a silence. The vaguely ugly rumbling in the room had ceased the instant the fighter pilot had spoken. He wondered why. Granted, the two silver bars on the collars of Rinnard's short-sleeved khakis made him the most senior person this side of the dais—this was a young group, and mostly enlisted. But there was more to it than that.

If any further evidence of the pilot's unique, indefinable quality had been needed, it would have been supplied by the look he was now getting from the Air Force lieutenant.

Derek had noticed her before. She was of medium height, with a sturdy but very female figure and wheat-blond hair. Her face was wide across the cheekbones, with a short nose and wide-spaced green eyes. He told himself he had no business feeling resentment over the fact that those eyes were quite obviously seeing nothing in the room but Rinnard.

Doctor Kronenberg huffed and puffed for only a few seconds. "Well, the theory can't be presented meaningfully without the mathematics. Ordinary language is simply not structured for it. In essence, however, the facts are these.

"There is an underlying sub-quantum level of reality which determines the nature of the universe which we observe—the universe which conventional physics, chaos theory and so forth describe tolerably well. Any disturbance on this very fundamental level can alter observed reality in ways not readily explainable by established science, nor accountable for in terms of causality.

"It now appears that conscious decision-making above a certain minimum threshold number of neural interconnections somehow provides the energy needed to create just such a disturbance. The mechanics are still improperly understood. But we have inferred the existence of massless particles—'psionitrons' is our convenience-label—which interact in a domain where time and causality become very problematical concepts. Psionics is the exploitation of this energy to . . . shape reality. Or, perhaps it would be more appropriate to say, predispose outcomes."

The Marine sergeant leaned slowly forward, eyes wide. "Whoa, Doc! Are you telling us that somebody who's using psionics is *changing the universe* every time he does it?"

"In very small ways, very subtle ways . . . yes, I suppose that's one way of putting it," Kronenberg allowed judiciously. Then she took up where she'd left off, speaking briskly into the stunned silence. "All neural activity constantly produces these particles—or, at least, it does in the brains of all the animals we've studied. However, in them it's just an irrelevant byproduct. Only human neural processes are complex enough to rise above the threshold I mentioned." Kronenberg's face took on a faraway look that seemed out of character. "It will be interesting to see how the world's religions react to these findings when we finally go public with them. In a sense, we seem to have proven that the human race really *is* unique and not just another member of the animal kingdom, the status to which Darwin relegated us. On the other hand, it could be argued that even this difference is one of degree, not of kind."

A Hispanic-looking Army corporal, clearly uncomfortable with this train of thought, cleared his throat. "Doctor, I don't get it. Earlier, you told us only one in a thousand people have this . . . stuff, and that even fewer, by a long shot, have enough of it to amount to diddly. But now you seem to be saying that *everybody's* got it!"

"You misunderstand, Corporal Estevez. The quantum energy of which I speak is, indeed, inherent in all human neural activity. But the ability to exploit it—loosely, psionic power—is restricted to a rare genotype, which we're now learning to isolate."

The woman in Air Force blue spoke up—a little truculently, Derek thought. "But even if this power is limited to a small fraction of one percent of the human race, the fact remains that there are a lot of human beings—and we've been around a long time! Why hasn't somebody *done* something with it? And I mean something impossible to ignore or rationalize or explain away. Something as inarguable as Hiroshima!"

"Remember, Lieutenant Westerfeld, the power is normally *latent* in human beings. This limits it to the unconscious, low-grade manifestations that we label 'luck' or 'intuition' or 'a sixth sense' or the like." Kronenberg squeezed out another brief, tight smile. *She's getting downright giddy,* thought Derek. "Haven't you ever noticed that some people always seem to drive up to the traffic light just as it turns green? Or that some people seem to know when they're in danger a split second in advance—the proverbial 'tingle between the shoulder blades'? I imagine a great many of the more elusive human qualities will prove to have such an explanation. But only occasionally do certain individuals spontaneously emerge from latency and become 'operant,' as we term those who can make conscious, purposeful use of psionics."

"Like my grandfather," said Derek, as much to himself as to Kronenberg.

The scientist gave him a sharp glance. "Precisely, Ensign Secrest. For reasons we still don't understand—probably just coincidence—there was a rash of such cases in the late 1960s and early 1970s, including Glenn Secrest. *Especially* Glenn Secrest, for he manifested greater power than anyone else who was recruited at that time. But psionic phenomena were not understood at that time—the research was still on the level of Rhine cards. And the emergence into operancy was always brief. The subjects lapsed back into latency, and so the experiments were unrepeatable. The project went pretty much belly-up.

"But things have changed in the four decades since then. Using recombinant DNA, we've been able to tailor psi-reactive drugs. Some of these you have already experienced: the ones which effectuate testing for the trait. But there are others, which stimulate latent powers into operancy. You'll be getting those presently. And still others, which we believe will *enhance* those same powers, are now in the research stage. Using the knowledge gleaned since the completion of the Human Genome Project, we hope to eventually tailor genetic retroviruses which will *confer* psionic powers on those who have none. But that's a long-range dream; I don't really expect to live to see it."

Lieutenant Westerfeld spoke with the same hint of disbelief, which Derek now recognized as a defense mechanism. "Surely you can't believe that you're going to be able to keep this a secret forever. Anything that's discoverable by science—"

"No, not forever. Eventually, we're going to broaden our recruitment, let certain selected scientists in on it. But we're going to be very cautious about it. And now let me turn the briefing over to Captain Morrisey, since I believe I've gone as far as I can in explaining the theory without giving Lieutenant Rinnard a headache." She bestowed one of her almost imperceptible smiles on the fighter pilot as she relinquished the podium.

Jesus Christ! thought Derek. *Even she's not immune!*

"I'd like to welcome you all here," Morrisey began, "and tell you a little about this command. Doctor Kronenberg was correct just now in her remarks on the subject of secrecy. But while the secret *does* last, we're going to explore the military applications thoroughly. This is at least as much a research outfit as an operational one. And we're going to make it our business to see that the secret lasts as long as possible.

"For example, in her discussion of the selection process Doctor Kronenberg mentioned that only single people were considered. It shouldn't be difficult for you to figure out why. Can you imagine family quarters, complete with nursery, in this place? And don't think you're going to get a housing allowance and turned loose to find an apartment in the Washington suburbs! No, you're going to be under conditions of *very* tight security here." Morrisey essayed a pleasantry. "As you were told, you'll be getting hazardous duty pay. But your opportunities for spending it will be somewhat limited.

"Now, I won't go into detail as to the organization chart. That's in one of the handouts you've gotten. I just want to make a couple of remarks about the nature of JICPO as a military outfit—a very unorthodox one.

"First of all, as would be obvious even without the name, it is an interservice command. I will tolerate no rivalries, feuds or animosities that interfere with the accomplishment of our mission. In turn, I assure you all that there will be absolutely no favoritism based on the branch of the service to which anyone belongs." Morrisey accompanied this last with a meaningful glance at Derek, Rinnard and the three enlisted Navy types present. "The only naval custom that I'm going to impose on everyone is that of not saluting when below decks. I think the reasons why that makes sense aboard a ship apply equally to this environment.

"Secondly, what you've just heard from Doctor Kronenberg should make clear that you are *extremely* scarce human material. If it didn't, you need only look around you in this auditorium. You must therefore be prepared to do whatever is needed at any given time. You've already had to adjust to being taken away from the jobs you were trained or in training to do, simply because people with psionic power are so rare that we can't afford *not* to make use of any of them. Flexibility must be your watchword. To put it bluntly, most of your skills have just become irrelevant.

"Furthermore, while I expect ordinary standards of military courtesy and decorum to be observed at all times, the fact is that this outfit is going to have to be function-based more than it is rank-based. Reality dictates this, despite my personal preference for a more traditional military structure. In this, also, we're going to have to be flexible. And—" a wintery smile "—if I can do it, you can do it."

Morrisey looked at his watch. "All right. It's 1800, so let's adjourn to the canteen. Afterwards, I suggest you spend the evening settling in, reading the handouts . . . and getting some rest. There'll be precious little of that in the next few weeks."

★ CHAPTER FIVE

The installation, it turned out, dated back almost sixty years, to a time before the psionic research had commenced or even been conceived.

"The government built quite a few underground facilities around that time," explained Captain Morrisey one day to Derek and a few others who'd expressed curiosity at the place's well-concealed existence. "The Cold War was at its height then, you see. Some of those places were a lot more extensive than this—especially the one in West Virginia that was supposed to be a refuge for the Federal government in event of a nuclear attack."

"But that one's been declassified, sir," observed Sergeant Tucker, the Marine.

"Since before the turn of the century," Morrisey nodded. "Big tourist attraction now. But there was, it was felt, no pressing need to go public with *all* of them. You never know when a bolt-hole like this may come in handy."

And, indeed, the Hole—as they soon came to call it— certainly provided privacy and adequate living quarters for JICPO, whose non-psionic support personnel naturally out-numbered the psis by a considerable factor. Its lack of luxury merely provided subject matter for that griping that is the

45

natural and healthy background noise of every military organization, and whose absence is sufficient to set off alarm bells in the mind of any canny CO. Paul Rinnard was philosophical about it; he assured Derek that the room they ended up sharing was more spacious than a two-man junior officer stateroom aboard an aircraft carrier, and lacked the hellish noise.

"That's the part Hollywood never gets right," he explained cheerfully. "It's like you're living under an airport, with high-performance jets landing right over your head day and night—except that the landings are really controlled crashes."

"But how do you get any sleep?" wondered Derek.

"Human beings can adapt to amazing things. In fact, I think we're pretty amazing creatures all around." Rinnard gave his roguish grin, accompanied with a lift of one peaked black eyebrow. "I guess the fact that we're here proves that."

It was hard to argue the point. But Derek still found it hard to really take the whole business seriously.

Until he awoke—or, to be precise, was awakened.

He'd more or less assumed it was going to involve something like the vaguely scary high-tech caps that had been put over his head at both stages of the selection process. Doctor Kronenberg disabused him of that.

"Those were for purposes of *detecting* psionic aptitude," she explained. "We'd like to be able to stimulate latent talents into operancy by some application of electronic induction. But to date, it's defeated our efforts. As far as we know, the only way that works involves the psi-reactive drugs I mentioned previously."

"Like what we got before?" Derek couldn't keep the distaste out of his voice.

"Not exactly. Those were merely aids to identifying psionic talents. In the preliminary screening—what you got as part of your induction physical—we used a drug that produces the disorientation you noticed in, and only in, those with latent powers. Your fellow-inductees felt no such aftereffects, which made for a crude but effective way of eliminating them. Later, when you were brought here for further testing, we administered a more complex agent, which increased your receptivity to that testing. It had certain side effects: a confused time sense, and a breakdown of the walls that keep out the general telepathic 'background noise.' "

"The dreams that aren't really dreams," Derek half-whispered.

"It gives that impression, yes . . . or so I'm told."

"But Doctor, back at my grandfather's house you said that telepathy was controllable, that you don't constantly get this 'background noise.' "

"That's true of *operant* telepathy. What you experienced was a blurring of the barriers to operancy. Your abilities were still latent, and hence uncontrollable. What we're going to do now is dissolve those barriers altogether. This will result in the same side effects, in a more intense form but lasting only a short time."

"How short?" asked Derek. "And how . . . intense?"

"The duration varies with the individual, but it is measured in minutes. I won't deny that it is, by all accounts, highly unpleasant while it lasts." Doctor Kronenberg took on a look of scientific detachment which, Derek thought sourly, she could well afford. "I have a theory—you'll find I have a lot of theories—that this is why human psionic powers have remained latent. The occasional cases like your grandfather and Captain Morrisey show that the barrier *can* be broken without chemical aids. But the human psyche shies away from it.

"However," she continued, with her very best effort at offering encouragement, "as I said, it's brief. And now, let's see just how brief it is in your case."

The human memory will not retain extreme pain. This forgetfulness serves the species well: without it, no woman would willingly bear more than one child.

It also served Derek well.

What he experienced was not, in the strict and narrow sense, pain. It was the distilled essence of nightmare. The dreams-that-were-not-dreams that he had experienced before had been the most fleeting and veiled glimpses of a monster's

face. Now that alien monster invaded his mind, and his mind
had no capacity to resist nor to flee. For what he was later
told was eight minutes, he was nothing more than a vessel of horror.

Afterwards, he lay in the recovery room, his mind bliss-
fully empty of everything save his own thoughts. He grew
aware of Doctor Kronenberg's presence.

"So my grandfather went through that?" he asked her.

"Not really. Spontaneous awakening into operancy entails
these hallucinatory experiences to a certain degree; that's
what enabled the researchers back in the early 1970s to
identify your grandfather and others, who had the experiences while on active duty. But the partial nature of such
awakenings makes them less severe. Unfortunately, it also
means they're only temporary."

"What about Captain Morrisey? His 'spontaneous awakening' seems to have lasted."

"No. It was fading like all the others. He had to go through
this. It's brutal, but it's also believed to be permanent. And
it could have been worse. You reacted to it as well as anyone
has—and better than some." Kronenberg looked uncomfortable, and bit her lower lip. "Corporal Estevez . . ."

"What about him?"

"He's still in a coma. *Not* permanent, we're pretty sure,"
the scientist hastily added. "In fact, we expect him to come
out of it any time. And even in his case, it *worked*. That
'barrier' of which I spoke earlier is now dissolved."

"Or dynamited," Derek muttered.

"Whatever. Congratulations, Mister Secrest: you're now
operant."

"But . . . but I don't *feel* anything!"

"You're not supposed to. Your abilities are no longer latent,
but you haven't learned to use them. That's next."

The training involved nothing even remotely comparable
to that access of horror. But it took far longer. And it was
tedious.

But then came his first establishment of contact.

He had some notion of what to expect, from Doctor

Kronenberg's lectures. "First of all," she pontificated, "every-thing you know about telepathy is wrong."

"But I *don't* know anything about it!" came a plaintive voice from somewhere in the little audience.

Kronenberg gave a quelling glare and resumed. "It's not like in movies—carrying on a conversation in voice-over without moving your lips. Admittedly, I'm told that the input is perceived as something analogous to sound, prob-ably because this is the way our minds are set up to process it."

Lauren Westerfeld, the Air Force lieutenant, raised her hand. "Doctor, I've noticed you use terms like 'I'm told' and 'as I understand' a lot. Am I correct in inferring—?"

"You are, Lieutenant," Kronenberg cut in evenly. "Like ninety-nine point nine percent of the human race, I have approximately the psionic capability of a rock."

Could that be why you've got such a large, hairy bug up your ass? wondered Derek silently. *Or why you get that dreamy look when you talk about the possibility of some kind of genetic goo that will bestow psi on people who don't naturally have it?*

"And now, if I may resume," said Kronenberg, "what you're going to be doing is picking up thoughts—or, as I suspect is more accurate, *intentions*. This requires focus and concentration. The closest you'll come to conversing this way is by consciously projecting them as well, so another telepath—a friendly one, presumably—will be able to pick them up more easily. Remember my introductory remarks about the nature of psionics. Telepathy is the most subtle of all its manifestations."

Later, they were introduced to some of the less subtle ones.

"The powers other than telepathy can be categorized as follows," Kronenberg told them in a later class. "First, there's what is traditionally called extrasensory perception, compris-ing such abilities as clairvoyance and precognition. These are the talents that most often manifest themselves in the low-grade, unconscious ways I mentioned in the introduc-tory lecture. But, paradoxically, they are very difficult to make conscious, volitional use of. This may be just as well.

Widespread ability to foretell the future might have disturbing philosophical implications.

"Then there is psychokinesis: the direct manipulation of matter and energy. Levitation, for example, and telekinesis. This is far rarer than telepathy, and we're only just starting to understand it.

"Beyond that, things start to get *really* weird."

An uneasy shifting and throat-clearing suffused the room. Kronenberg ignored it. "There are two powers which we tend to bracket together. One is teleportation—loosely, the power of instantaneous physical displacement to another location, without crossing the intervening distance."

There was no more noise in the room. Everyone was too stunned for that.

"The other is projection. This is the least understood of all. In some manner, it detaches the user's consciousness from his or her physical body. That consciousness becomes an invisible, disembodied viewpoint that can roam and observe at will, subject to definite limitations.

"The reason we associate these two is that they both appear to involve some form of extradimensional movement, physical or otherwise. Physicists have long speculated that more dimensions than the four we know may have existed immediately following the Big Bang, only to collapse into nonexistence as the metrical frame of the universe established itself. This speculation now stands confirmed—except that in order to account for teleportation and projection it is necessary to postulate the survival of at least one of the 'extra' dimensions. For us, this dimension is only accessible via psionitron interactions. Actual physical access to it is evidently impossible; a teleported object spends zero time in it before being 'ejected' into some other locus of the normal physical world. The disembodied consciousness, on the other hand, seems to experience time at the normal rate.

"We know," Kronenberg went on, oblivious to her audience's glazed look, "that some of you have certain of these powers in addition to the more common telepathy. We mean to explore their possibilities in due course."

Lauren Westerfeld shook herself and thrust her head

forward in a way that seemed defiant—almost angry. "Doctor, I'm trying my best to accept all this, and discard all preconceptions. But teleportation . . . Look, even accepting that someone can, uh, flick himself to somewhere else, what about the matter—air, if nothing else—that's already occupying his new location?"

"That's a fallacy," said Kronenberg, not troubling to disguise her irritation. "Remember what I keep telling you about the fundamental nature of psionic phenomena. Teleportation isn't 'transportation' any more than telepathy is a 'conversation.' What's happening is that one volume of observed reality—the one occupied by the teleporter—is changing places with another volume, including the air in it. Theoretically, the same ought to apply to anything else that was there, even rock—"

"Instant statue," Rinnard muttered to Derek *sotto voce.*

"—but as a practical matter, there seems to be a psychological block against teleporting into a mountain, say, or even water . . . or, for that matter, to any location the teleporter can't actually see." She made a dismissive gesture. "Or so it seems from the very limited research we've been able to conduct. We hope to learn more—from you."

"May I join you gentlemen?" asked Lauren Westerfeld rather diffidently.

Derek and Rinnard looked up from their table in the club. Of necessity in an outfit like this, it was a combined club, open to all ranks. The Hole's builders had intended it to be an oasis of fake wood paneling and indirect lighting in a desert of bleak utilitarianism. They hadn't altogether succeeded. Still, it was the best—and, just incidentally, the only—place for relaxing over a drink when off duty.

The Air Force lieutenant's words had clearly been directed to Rinnard, and he half-rose from his chair with a courtliness that somehow avoided seeming either affected or old-fashioned. "Why, certainly, Lieutenant. Lauren, isn't it? I'm Paul." Derek mumbled his own first name, silently cursing himself for not coming up with something suave.

"Thank you." Westerfeld sat down. She held a mug of

beer whose level her nursing had barely lowered. Her gaze went from Rinnard to Derek and then back to Rinnard, and stayed there. "I've been hoping for an opportunity to introduce myself. You two are together a lot. I suppose it must have to do with being the only two naval officers here."

"Besides," Rinnard grinned, "we Southern boys have to stick together."

Westerfeld blinked—understandably, Derek thought. Neither he nor Rinnard spoke Hollywood Southern. As a Tidewater Virginia native, his pronunciation of words like "out" and "about" usually got him tagged as a Canadian. And as for Rinnard . . .

"Louisiana, right?" Westerfeld asked him.

"Yep," the pilot confirmed. "Sort of an advantage in this place. We Creoles are a superstitious lot. Makes it easier to accept what's going on here. I mean . . . what's new?"

Westerfeld laughed—dutifully, it seemed. Then she settled back into her usual earnestness. "Seriously, it makes you wonder, doesn't it? Maybe what we're working with here is the reality behind all the old stories of—"

"Magic."

The voice that finished her sentence for her was that of Captain Morrisey, who'd appeared behind her. He gave an as-you-were gesture and sat down. Things were informal in the club. "That's very astute, Lieutenant, but it's not new. And you yourself shot it down with the argument you made back at the introductory lecture."

"Sir?"

"There was this science fiction author back in the 1970s— *not* one of those that were co-opted for the disinformation program; he was too close to the truth. Anyway, he made the same point you did, but he applied it to magic as well as psionics: If it's real, then all the attempts to make it work over the centuries should have produced *something*."

"But, sir," Westerfeld persisted, "maybe some of what Doctor Kronenberg calls 'spontaneous awakenings' occurred in the past."

Morrisey smiled at the argumentative junior officer. "But you run into the same paradox. If those awakenings lasted no longer than the ones that have been covertly studied over the last forty years, they wouldn't have made such a deep and lasting impression on the human memory. And if they lasted, then they should have gotten into verifiable historical records."

"So what's the answer, sir?" asked Derek, beginning to warm to the bull session.

"Well, writers like the one I mentioned came up with a theory to explain it. Seems that magic requires something called 'mana.' The world started out with a fixed supply of this stuff, and magic depletes it. And once it's depleted, it's *gone*. It can never, ever be replenished. Back in legendary times, the sorcerers used up all the mana doing magic. So now magic won't work any more. No 'fuel,' so to speak." Morrisey gave a self-deprecating laugh and finished off his highball. "I was born in the nineteen sixties, and I used to be a nut on classic science fiction. Anyway, the idea made for some good stories."

Westerfeld wore a look of deep thought. Presently, she shook her head. "It won't work," she stated emphatically

"What won't work?" asked Derek.

"That 'mana' theory. It contains a major fallacy. If no new mana can ever be produced, then *where did it come from in the first place?*"

Rinnard snapped his fingers. "Yeah, good point! And how come magic won't work in orbit, and on the Moon, where ol' Merlin and those guys never did any of their tricks? Ought to be oodles of mana left out there."

Morrisey joined in the laughter, and held up his hands as though to stem the tide. "Hey, people, it was just a fictional device! Sorry I brought it up."

"Fun to play with, though," Rinnard smiled. "Buy you another drink, Skipper?"

"Better not, thanks." Morrisey stood up, and the mantle of command descended invisibly. "Busy day tomorrow. I advise all of you to make an early night of it."

★ CHAPTER SIX

To Derek's relief, their emerging telepathic abilities resulted in none of the nightmarish loss of mental privacy he'd feared. It turned out that anyone, given the proper training, could neutralize it by consciously willing one's thoughts *not* to be received. In effect, a telepath could only read minds that were unaware or, better still, cooperative. Everyone in the Hole soon learned to erect such a block as a matter of routine. Ordinary socializing remained ordinary.

Derek found himself doing more and more of it with Lauren Westerfeld.

He wondered how much she reciprocated his growing attraction. Her earnest seriousness was daunting at first. But eventually her stiffness dissolved to the point where he could tease her about it ("Typical Yankee!") and get away with it. In fact, he was fairly certain she liked him.

What he couldn't be certain of was how she felt about Paul Rinnard.

When the three of them were together, she seemed to have eyes only for the darkly handsome fighter jock. That was the bad news. The good news was that look she gave Rinnard seemed ambiguous, mixing fascination with . . . something else. Afterwards, with Derek alone, she behaved differently: less intensely attracted but more relaxed, as though she felt somehow safe.

Derek wasn't sure how to take that.

At any rate, the three of them found themselves increasingly in each other's company, and not just in their off-duty hours. Not even Doctor Kronenberg's verbal parsimoniousness could any longer disguise their emergence as the three most promising psi talents in JICPO.

"We have a couple of potentially more powerful telepaths," she admitted to them in a moment of what passed with her for effusiveness. "But your mastery of the techniques of focus and concentration have enabled you to receive thoughts with greater range and clarity than anyone else. Furthermore, those other telepaths are narrowly specialized, while it is increasingly clear that all three of you possess a wide range of other powers."

"What powers are those?" asked Rinnard with uncharacteristic seriousness.

"I prefer not to go into specifics until I have more definite data. And so far, telepathy is the only psionic manifestation that we're even close to being able to reliably quantify. The other powers are still maddeningly elusive" Kronenberg's frustration was so transparently heartfelt as to almost make her sympathetic. "If we could only isolate those powers to the same extent, I firmly believe we could develop them in you, just as we've been honing your telepathic skills. As it is, however . . . Well, we know it's there, and that's about it. Actually, Lieutenant Rinnard, in your case . . ."

"Yes, Doctor?" Rinnard prompted.

"No. Anything I could say at this point would fall into the category of loose talk." And that was all they got out of her. But she continued to look at Rinnard strangely.

Then came a day marked by something out of the ordinary for the Hole: new arrivals, who appeared in a self-important swirl of VIP-ism. Later the same day, everyone was summoned to the auditorium.

This time Captain Morrisey and Doctor Kronenberg shared the dais with an older civilian-suited man whose hair's grayness seemed to have seeped into his skin. Kronenberg, Derek noted, looked even more disapproving than was her wont, and Morrisey wore a carefully neutral expression as he stood at the podium and introduced the suit.

"From the beginning, I've urged all of you to cultivate flexibility. That quality will stand you in good stead now. It turns out that our training schedule is going to have to yield to the press of events. In other words, we're going to have to go operational sooner than we expected. Mr. Collins of the National Security Agency will now explain the reasons for this new urgency. I stress that this briefing is Top Secret."

Derek, seated beside Rinnard, could sense something like the smooth awakening of tension that runs through a hunting dog whose leash is about to be slipped.

Collins took Morrisey's place at the podium and ran clearly nervous eyes over his audience. Derek grinned inwardly and savored a moment's temptation—but only for a moment, for they'd had a very rigid code of ethics drummed into them. Then the NSA suit cleared his throat and proceeded.

"Ladies and gentlemen, first of all let me express the government's appreciation of your value as . . . a unique strategic resource. The original plan was to withhold you from actual field operations until your potentialities had received a full scientific assessment." Collins cast a hasty glance behind and to his left, then flinched away from Kronenberg's glare. "Despite . . . strongly worded advice that we continue to adhere to that original schedule, it has been determined at the highest levels that the present world situation requires that you be utilized now.

"Much of the background of what I'm about to tell you is common knowledge. I refer specifically to the state of affairs in the Balkans—the region where, ominously enough, the First World War began exactly one hundred years ago.

"The former Yugoslavia was a federation of ethnic groups which the Serbs dominated—without being overly tactful about it. They never really reconciled themselves to the breakup of that federation in the early 1990s. Indeed, they styled their own ethnic successor-state 'Yugoslavia,' and continued to do so until 2003. Their feelings have been exacerbated by NATO's policy of eastward inclusiveness.

"More recently, certain extremist groups have taken these feelings beyond the realm of mere rhetoric."

Yeah, yeah, yeah, Derek found himself thinking. Everybody knew that the Balkan tribes of ragged-assed goat stealers, with their unfathomable feuds, had always caused trouble far beyond their negligible intrinsic importance, and now shared with diehard Islamic fundamentalists the dubious distinction of embodying world terrorism for the delectation of the media. Everybody also knew the Serbs had their undies in a bunch over the admission of Croatia to NATO. *So what's new?*

"Now," Collins droned on, "a new terrorist organization has arisen: the Sons of Dushan. The reference is to Stefan Dushan, a fourteenth-century Serbian prince who after a series of military successes had himself crowned 'Emperor of the Serbs and Greeks.' It all fell apart the instant he died. Nevertheless, these people have persuaded themselves that they are reasserting a historical claim to a Serbian empire over much of the Balkans, including Greece—in opposition to both the Western and Islamic worlds, which they hate about equally."

Sergeant Tucker gave a slow head-shake of disbelief. "Sir, these folks need to get a life! I mean, this is the twenty-first century!"

Collins smiled bleakly. "That observation, Sergeant, is demonstrably correct. Unfortunately, it also demonstrates that you know very little about the Balkans.

"At any rate, these hotheads have the covert support of certain elements in the Ukrainian military, who see a future Greater Serbia as a potential ally. It now appears that, despite the efforts to keep the CBW arsenal of the former Soviet Union under control at the time of its dissolution, the former Ukrainian SSR quietly retained a stock of nerve agents. And . . . I imagine you can guess where this is heading."

Derek could, and his conclusions were not pleasant. *Oh my God! Neanderthals with nerve gas!*

"We have learned that the Sons of Dushan plan to release

these agents against the civilian populace somewhere in Greece, possibly Athens or possibly one of the islands like Rhodes that are filling up with German and Scandinavian vacationers this time of year. In addition to destabilizing the Greek government, the objective is, by typical terrorist logic, terror itself—simply to make an impression, to be taken seriously. Like all terrorists, they know they can count on the cooperation of the Western media toward this end." Collins' long, lined face momentarily looked as though he'd bitten into a bad pickle. "We have learned that Dragoljub Cvetkovic, a high-ranking Sons of Dushan operative, is now in Athens."

Rinnard flipped up a hand. "Excuse me, sir. This isn't exactly my line of work, you understand, but I can't help being curious. If we know about this guy, uh, whatever-vich, why don't we simply pick him up?"

"Or," Lauren Westerfeld put in rather primly, "share the information with the Greek authorities so *they* can pick him up—with our help, if they want it."

"I guess that might be a little more proper," Rinnard allowed. Then he snapped his fingers and grinned. "Oh, I get it, sir! He *is* going to get picked up . . . and afterwards, you want us to get his plans from him."

"Not exactly, Lieutenant. You see, what we *don't* know is where the nerve gas is, or how they got it into Greece. If we apprehend Cvetkovic, the rest of the organization will be alerted. They'll abort the plan, move the nerve gas . . . and whatever information we get from him, even with you people's help, will be obsolete and useless. We'll be back where we started when they try again, using a different plan.

"No, you're going to extract Cvetkovic's plans from his mind—*without him knowing those plans have been compromised.*"

Lauren Westerfeld's eyes widened. "Then he'll go ahead . . . and we'll be ready. We'll be able to make a clean sweep, including the nerve gas!"

"Precisely," Collins nodded. "And now perhaps you understand why the government has been so very interested in Doctor Kronenberg's research." He let that sink in, then resumed briskly. "As I understand, it will be a matter of getting you physically close enough to Cvetkovic to be within the range of your . . . abilities. Even if he knows we're up to *something* in his vicinity, you'll be doing nothing that will arouse his suspicions. I am confident of success, as Captain Morrisey assures me that he is providing me with his two most capable people."

Collins sat down, and Morrisey resumed the podium. "Thank you, Mr. Collins. Now, this is to be the first actual test of this command's capabilities under field conditions. I needn't emphasize its importance." He cleared his throat. "Two of our personnel are being assigned to temporary detached duty with the NSA for this operation: Lieutenant Westerfeld—"

Well, I guess I'm out, thought Derek with a nerve-twinge of disappointment.

"—and Ensign Secrest."

Once again Derek, sitting next to Rinnard, felt the latter's reaction as unmistakably as though they'd been in physical contact. This time, it was a stiffening of surprised resentment.

"The two of you," Morrisey concluded, "will report to my office at 0800 tomorrow for further briefing by Mr. Collins and Doctor Kronenberg. You will also be prepared to depart promptly after that, as time is of the essence. For now, you're all dismissed."

As he filed out with everyone else, Derek noticed that Rinnard wasn't with him. He looked over his shoulder and saw the fighter pilot hanging back, waiting for the auditorium to empty of everyone save Morrisey.

It cast a shadow over his excitement, for he found he wanted—badly—to hear the word "congratulations" from Rinnard.

"Sir, may I have a word in private?"

Rinnard's uncharacteristically formal tone of voice got Morrisey's full attention. He sat down and motioned the younger man toward another chair. "Certainly, Lieutenant. I think I've got a pretty good idea of what's on your mind."

Rinnard lowered himself stiffly into the chair. "Skipper, not for the world would I begrudge Lauren and Derek the recognition they richly deserve. But I'd gotten the impression . . . That is, Doctor Kronenberg has given me some reason to believe—"

"That you're the best," Morrisey finished for him with a smile. "And nobody can expect a Navy fighter pilot to not be competitive! Well, Paul, you can relax. I probably shouldn't be telling you this, but your potential is, indeed, the greatest Doctor Kronenberg has uncovered to date. In fact, you might say you're off her charts. You have a range of potential powers which her theories simply don't allow for. She doesn't know quite what to make of you. I think you frighten her a little."

"Then why—?"

"When Rosa Kronenberg heard about this operation, she went ballistic. As far as she's concerned, what she's learning from studying you people is so important that a trifle like stopping a nerve-gas attack on a city of three million people doesn't even weigh in the balance. She didn't want to let *any* of you be sent out! When Collins arrived this morning, he ran into a cross between a fanatical researcher and a frustrated Jewish mother. He'll probably be a while recovering." Morrisey chuckled reminiscently, and Rinnard tried to imagine the scene.

"In the end," the CO resumed, "a compromise was reached. Rosa grudgingly agreed to let two of her most powerful talents go into the field, on one condition: *you* stay here."

Rinnard's changeable hazel eyes flashed. "Damn it, Skipper, does she think that's all I'm good for? To be kept here and *studied*?"

"It's not that," Morrisey assured him gravely. "Remember, your two friends are going into very real danger. Forget all the self-serving bullshit that terrorists feed their media groupies about their assorted 'causes.' The fact is, they're nothing but murderous, psychopathic human sewage."

"I'm not afraid, sir." Rinnard was only too aware of how

stuffy, if not hokey, that probably sounded, but he was beyond caring.

"Of course you're not afraid, Paul," said Morrisey gently. "You are, however, too valuable to be risked—at least for now."

"'For now?'" Rinnard echoed hopefully.

"Absolutely. Don't think for a minute that you're going to be stuck here forever. The very purpose of conserving you for now is to develop your potential to its fullest, with a view to . . ."

"Yes, Skipper?" Rinnard prompted, when the other seemed disinclined to continue.

Morrisey ran his eyes over the auditorium as though to verify its emptiness, then spoke more softly. "I've got no business telling you this, really. But it's my considered judgment that upholding your morale is worth doing even if it means . . . Well, sometime in the near future, all of you are going to officially learn what Doctor Kronenberg and I and a very few others already know: there've been some, well, peculiar things going on in the solar system."

"Sir?"

"Inexplicable things. Things the government can't allow to become general knowledge."

"Uh, Skipper, you aren't . . . well, of course you're not talking . . . UFOs?" A nervous laugh escaped Rinnard.

"Not in the sense of all the ersatz mythology that's been around for the last seventy-odd years, starting with the 'foo fighters' in World War II and the Roswell nonsense shortly thereafter. No, I'm not talking about mutilated cattle or artsy-fartsy designs in wheatfields. Nor about saucer-shaped vessels doing things like instantaneously reversing direction. But lately there has been some activity in orbit which we cannot account for. And our intelligence is pretty damned good when it comes to space launches around the world. It should be; that sort of thing is hard to conceal.

"Not that anybody seriously thinks there's any paranormal explanation. But something doesn't have to be paranormal to constitute a national security concern. Accordingly, we're trying to ascertain what the hell's going on up there.

Our lack of success so far means we're going to bring to bear additional information-gathering resources . . . *all* of them."

Rinnard's eyes had gradually widened. "You mean—?"

"And here's one more thing I'm not supposed to tell you yet: The spaceplane—yes, the one that's been in development as long as your generation can clearly remember—is very nearly ready to fly." Morrisey hastily raised a hand to check the rising tide of exultation he saw in Rinnard's eyes. "Now, I haven't told you anything official. But I think you can put two and two together. I also think you can now see the importance of maximizing your abilities."

"Yes, *sir!*"

Morrisey smiled the way a middle-aged man smiles at the living reflection of his own younger self. Then he summoned sternness. "I want to caution you that I've spoken in reliance on your discretion. You're not to mention this to anyone—including, and especially, Derek and Lauren."

"Understood, sir."

"Very good. You can, however, wish them the best before they leave for Greece. And you should."

CHAPTER SEVEN

It wasn't exactly how Derek had imagined his first carrier landing: seated facing backwards in a mail plane. But
that was how he and Lauren Westerfeld arrived aboard
USS *Theodore Roosevelt*, on Homer's wine-dark sea—now
un-Homerically polluted—north of Souda Bay in Crete.

One of Collins' people, a lean dark-haired NSA operative
named Bordelis, took them in hand even as they were being
hustled below decks. "We'll get you to Iraklio Airport on
Crete. From there you'll take Olympic, the Greek national
airline, to Athens. I'll be meeting you there. You brought
casual civilian clothes, right? Good. Neither of you would
make a convincing Greek even if you spoke the language.
So you're American tourists." He handed them passports and
airline tickets.

"Mr. and Mrs. *Smith?*" exclaimed Lauren as she flipped
through the papers. "You've *got* to be kidding!"

"Hey, what do you want? Creativity? We're just lucky they
made things simple by assigning us two people who can
easily pass for a honeymooning young couple."

The two of them exchanged a quick, awkward look, then
looked away. *Please, God, don't let me blush!* prayed Derek
even as he felt his ears warming up.

Bordelis made it worse by grinning. "Don't worry. If everything goes according to plan, you won't be there long enough that maintaining your cover gets . . . complicated. You see, we know where Cvetkovic is staying, and it's a highly public area."

"Sounds kind of reckless on his part," Derek opined.

"He's a cocky bastard, no question about it. He's also a fanatic. But he's not stupid. Remember, he knows as well as we do the reasons—which I'm sure Mr. Collins explained to you—for us not to pick him up. He's taken all the usual precautions against conventional forms of surveillance. He's never dreamed that the kind you two are going to bring to bear even exists."

As Bordelis spoke that last sentence, something wavered behind his eyes, and Derek recognized the kind of reaction he'd previously observed in Collins. He'd come to think of it simply as *The Look,* and he decided it had already worn thin. *Better get used to it, though,* he told himself.

"Any chance of a side trip to Knossos while we're in Crete?" Lauren asked. "No, of *course* I'm kidding," she added hastily at the sight of the NSA man's expression. "I know time is of the essence. And, of course, we don't need to make our cover story any more difficult to sustain than it has to be."

Irritatingly, Derek found himself wondering if she would have considered that a problem if he'd been Paul Rinnard.

Jet lag finally caught up with Derek just after landing at Elleniko Airport. Maybe that was why the seven-mile taxi ride northward along the Saronic Gulf to the center of Athens made only a confused and not very deep impression.

Or maybe not. He wasn't exactly the first visitor to the rather seedy modern city of Athens to react that way . . . at first.

But then they were following Syngrou Avenue as it neared their destination, the area known as the Plaka. Derek was seated on the right side of the taxi—it reminded him of some he'd ridden in the West Indies, save that the driver's inexhaustible volubility was Greek-accented, his assortment of religious knickknacks was Eastern Orthodox, and his radio was blaring *bouzouki* rather than reggae. Looking out the window beside him, he saw the few remaining tall Corinthian columns of a temple that looked vaguely familiar, standing in lonely pride in a large open area. ("Temple of Zeus," the driver called out.) Then Lauren jabbed his left arm to get his attention, and wordlessly pointed out the window on her side.

Above the confusion of red-tiled roofs, a rocky hill loomed, its uppermost crags sheathed in massive, buttressed, obviously ancient walls. Derek leaned past Lauren and craned his head up to see that which crowned those walls in marble perfection.

"Acropolis," said the driver—unnecessarily. Enough late-afternoon Mediterranean sun penetrated the chemical haze to make the Parthenon glow with a red-gold inner flame.

All at once, the realization hit Derek, as it had so many millions of others before him, of just exactly where he was, and what it meant.

They continued on past the Arch of Hadrian and, turning left, plunged into a noisy, colorful confusion of winding streets. The Plaka, Derek recalled from his hasty pre-departure briefing, was Athens' old city. Nineteenth-century European philhellenes like Lord Byron—who had a nearby street named after him—had been disillusioned to find a few thousand wretched refugees there, huddling in the shadow of the Acropolis and rejecting with holy horror what little they knew of the pagan greatness towering above their hovels. Those peasants' descendants had learned how lucrative tourism could be, and the Plaka had become largely pedestrianized by the height of its late-twentieth-century reign as Athens' nightlife center. Since then it had grown somewhat less fashionable, and the automobile had wormed its way back as it generally did. But the location was still matchless, and the area had matured gracefully. It still had its share of *tavernas*—now beginning to move to the buildings' roofs with the onset of summer—but accommodations of the *pension* type had also staged a comeback, using the fine old houses with their flower-filled courtyards. Just the sort of area, in short, for affluent newlyweds like the Smiths, in search of authentic ambience.

Bordelis was waiting for them in the sitting room of their suite. "You look pretty wiped out," he observed. "Fortunately, there's no immediate urgency. Cvetkovic is laying pretty low, and there's no indication that any action is imminent. From what I understand, you can't . . . do what you do just standing on the sidewalk outside the place where he's staying."

"That's right," Derek affirmed. "We need to be able to identify the specific subject, not just vaguely cast about in the direction of a whole building. In fact, while it may not be necessary in any absolute sense to actually see the subject, it's the only way we've done it so far. Also, we can't suck out the entire contents of his memory. He has to be actively thinking about his plans at the time we make contact."

"So I was given to understand." The uneasiness was back, but quickly smoothed over. "So you may as well relax, eat, and get settled in. Then stroll around and take in the sights. We've got Cvetkovic under surveillance, and you'll be informed when he comes out. Then we can follow him, and bring you two into a situation were you can . . ." Bordelis' voice trailed off, and he compensated by resuming with official briskness. "The Greek security types have agreed to give us a free hand for the time being—we've agreed to turn all the information we get over to them, as long as they don't ask how we got it. But their political bosses are becoming understandably jittery about the arrangement."

"Doesn't that make it urgent for us to—?" Lauren's question died in a jet-lag yawn she could no longer suppress.

"Yes, but there's nothing you can accomplish tonight. So go ahead and do the Plaka, just to stay in character. I know I don't need to tell you to make an early night of it!"

"What about you?" asked Derek.

"I'm going to go and touch base with the Greek cops. I may be back here later tonight—you two will probably be asleep by then." Bordelis gave an eloquent wave that took in Lauren and the door to the bedroom, then patted the sitting room's sofa. "Derek, I can personally testify to the comfort of this sofa. I'll just crash on the floor if I do come back here tonight."

The blubbery arms of fatigue-induced sleep weren't nearly ready to loosen their grip on Derek when Bordelis shook him into unwilling semiconsciousness.

"Wake up, Derek! Things are happening!" The NSA man walked over to the bedroom door and pounded on it, calling for Lauren. The noise he made wasn't even in the same league as that from the neighboring *taverna* rooftops the night before, and Derek slipped effortlessly back into sleep.

Bordelis unceremoniously tipped the sofa to a forty-five-degree angle and dumped him onto the floor.

"Wake *up*, I said! It's mid-morning, and we've intercepted a call to Cvetkovic. In code, of course, but we think today may be the day."

The bedroom door opened, and Lauren staggered out wearing an extra-large Air Force Academy T-shirt. "But . . . but you said nothing was imminent!"

"Sue me! We've got to act fast." Bordelis' cell phone beeped from his belt. He listened for a few seconds. "Okay, that tears it. Cvetkovic is on the move. Get dressed quick. You'll have to skip breakfast—but believe me, a Continental breakfast is no loss."

In the end, Bordelis relented long enough for them to grab coffee. It was Turkish coffee. Derek decided he'd probably recover. They piled into one of the little fuel-cell cars that were beginning to catch on in Europe, and set out. The crooked streets lacked the crowds and noise of the previous night but were starting to see the day's first influx of tourists. They turned right onto the Dionysiou Areopagitou and drove parallel to the south slope of the Acropolis, past the ruins of the theaters of Dionysos and Herodes Atticus. Above and to the right, the Parthenon gleamed a cool pearl-white in the late-morning sun. All the while, Bordelis kept the cell phone glued to his ear, taking reports from the people who were very cautiously shadowing Cvetkovic.

"We don't want to spook him," he explained. "So we might as well stay in the car until he lights someplace where we can get you two close to him without being obvious about it. . . . Hey, wait a minute, I think this may be our chance. Pull over," he ordered their driver.

They got out near the ticket office at the base of the zigzag ramp up which the Panathenaea procession had once carried a new robe for the marble- and gold-sheathed statue of the goddess Athena each year. Grimly ignoring the swarm of souvenir sellers, they followed Bordelis due west toward the Pynx hill, which held the seating for the nighttime Acropolis sound-and-light shows that had been causing Classical purists to gnash their teeth for almost half a century.

At the foot of the Pynx was the Dionysos restaurant, an institution since at least the 1980s. It was only just starting to fill up with the more conscientious tourists—this was too early for Greeks to even be thinking about lunch. Bordelis paused outside for a muttered colloquy with a man who had the look of a Greek security officer, then turned to Derek and Lauren.

"All right: this place isn't crowded, so we can play it cagy. You two got to study photos of Cvetkovic in the course of your stateside briefing, right? Good. Go in and find seats from which you can observe him—but without paying any obvious attention to him! Major Marinakos here has got a plain-clothes cop in there to keep an eye on you in case things go sour. As soon as you've got the info, come back out here and report to me—but without seeming too rushed. Got it?"

Derek bristled, feeling that Bordelis was spelling things out in unnecessary detail. But then he recalled that the NSA man was a pro saddled with a couple of pristine amateurs for whose lives he was responsible. He decided he ought to make allowances. "Got it," he affirmed quietly. Lauren nodded in agreement.

They entered and looked around—without seeming to, of course—and soon spotted a table where a man in non-touristy clothes was seated in an unmistakable attitude of waiting for someone. His longish hair was graying-brown, and a drooping mustache made his face look even longer and more hollow-cheeked than it was. His high cheekbones seemed to squeeze his eyes into slits.

They found a suitable table and ordered Coke. Derek exchanged a quick look with Lauren. Then he emptied his mind of everything except Dragoljub Cvetkovic.

First there came the establishment of contact. It was like perceiving the subject on a second level: a kind of halo that reflected the contours of the actual man his eyes were focused on. Once that was done, he closed his eyes, for sight had become a mere distraction. He commenced the focusing mental exercises he'd been taught.

His eyes snapped back open, and he grasped the edge of the table to steady himself against a psychic recoil of almost physical force. He again made eye contact with Lauren, and no words were necessary. She'd felt it too.

They'd done this in the Hole with each other and with non-psionically-talented volunteers, and Derek had begun to fancy himself an old hand. But this was his first sociopath.

It was a mind which danced along a giddy precipice in a strange universe of its own where actions had no real consequences and other people felt no real pain. A mind deterred by none of the "social controls" of which Doctor Kronenberg had once spoken to him. But a mind that was, nevertheless, enslaved, for it was held to a predetermined course by inner imperatives of its own, which Derek's own brain interpreted as an incessant rhythm.

Derek had half-expected to enter a seething cesspit of barely controlled bloodlust and sick hate, but this was somehow worse.

He drew a breath, exchanged another glance with Lauren, and plunged in again.

After a time he chugged his Coke and stood up. Lauren didn't look quite as ready to depart, but she followed him outside.

"It's the sound-and-light show," he reported to Bordelis, with a sense of urgency that banished his original intention to be more circumspect in Marinakos' presence. "Up here on the Pynx."

"Tonight," Lauren added even more succinctly.

"Oh, God!" the NSA man muttered. "Like the Aum Shinri Kyo cult all over again, but in a city with no subways—just crowded tourist events."

Marinakos was so horrified he forgot whatever curiosity he'd felt about where the two young Americans had gotten their information. "Their objective is obvious. The news of such a thing would send all the tourists fleeing in panic. Do you have any idea how important tourism is in this country? It would destroy the economy, and bring down the government."

"But where have they got the nerve gas hidden?" demanded Bordelis.

"That was less clear," Lauren admitted. "There was no clear identifying symbology to go with the location."

"Still," said Derek, "I got a sense that it's very nearby—and underground."

Marinakos thumped his forehead with Mediterranean fervor. "Of course! These hills are honeycombed with caves. And, having no real historical significance, they are not much frequented." He whipped out his own cell phone and spoke rapid-fire Greek. "I have ordered in teams, to give the caves a thorough—"

Derek was no longer hearing him.

Deep below the level of any senses ever named, he felt that which he had felt on Sandbridge Beach: a wrongness, a distortion of the probabilities that ruled humanity's familiar reality.

And, behind Marinakos and Bordelis, he saw something begin to happen against the side of the Acropolis.

"Derek, what . . . ?" Lauren's concerned voice trailed off. For she, too, was facing east, and now she could see the circle of wavering distortion.

Then the circle attained definition, with the pulse of light and the soundless mental blow he remembered. That psychic blast stunned him and Lauren—but not, it seemed, anyone else, for Bordelis and Marinakos and the scattered bystanders merely whirled to stare at the visual apparition, speechless with nothing more than amazement.

As they stared, black-clad figures began emerging from the immaterial circle. They held weapons of some kind.

People began screaming.

Derek came out of his stunned immobility faster than Lauren, who had never experienced this before. He grabbed her by the arms and shook her violently.

"Hit the dirt!" yelled Bordelis. He and Marinakos went to their knees and reached for their armpit holsters.

The intruders fired first.

Only, "fired" was the wrong word, for the noise was not that of any firearm Derek had ever heard. Indeed, there was very little noise at all—just a kind of snapping, or crackling.

At the same instant, something scythed through Bordelis' neck and left shoulder, practically decapitating him in a spray of blood.

Marinakos was next. The sleet of death went lower, through his heart, and instead of a spray there was a crimson fountain.

Derek discovered that it was possible to be too stunned and terrified to vomit.

He and Lauren were already prone, and suffered nothing more than a spattering with blood. They waited for death as the black-clad figures advanced on them.

Then, out of the corner of his eye, Derek saw her.

Amid the running, screaming figures, Sophia stood serene and tall, wearing a tasteful charcoal-gray pantsuit. Her expression of abstracted concentration seemed insanely out of place in the scene of terror-stricken chaos around her.

Then, just as Derek remembered from that beach on the other side of the world, the impossible hole in the universe vanished.

The attackers came to a shocked halt. Then they swung their incomprehensible weapons toward Sophia.

Derek, his brain still reeling from the second psychic buffeting, looked wildly in her direction, opened his mouth to shout a warning . . .

But she wasn't there anymore.

Derek didn't even have time to think about that, for all at once he and Lauren were engulfed in a wave of running, stumbling bodies from the restaurant behind them. Doing exactly the wrong thing, the customers had stampeded through the door, straight toward the black-clad killers.

He staggered upright and dragged Lauren to her feet. "Come on!" he yelled, and dragged her back toward the restaurant, fighting his way through the struggling crush of flesh and panic. They got inside the door and took cover just as the sound of the enigmatic weapons resumed, and the crowd's screams took on an added note of agony.

But then came the bark of weapons as Derek knew them. He risked a peek around the door frame. Greek security men were running in from two sides, firing as they came. Whoever the strangers were, they at least weren't bullet-proof, for one of them was already down. They turned their attention to the new threat, and the Greeks began to die— but continued to stand and return fire, with a courage Derek knew he shouldn't find astonishing in the heirs of Marathon and Thermopylae.

The reprieve couldn't last long, though. Derek's eyes met Lauren's. There seemed nothing to say.

"Come with me. Quickly!"

The totally unexpected female voice from behind him brought Derek's head snapping around, to meet Sophia's clear gray eyes.

"How . . . how did *you* get in here?" he demanded.

"Never mind that. Do you want to live? Come on back, through the kitchen. I have a car nearby."

Even at this moment, Derek met her eyes stonily. "A car? Don't you have better ways than that of getting around?"

Sophia smiled slightly. "Actually, I do. But *you* want to come along as well, don't you?"

There seemed no good answer to that.

Lauren spoke in a voice charged with bewilderment. "Derek, do you know this woman? Who is she?"

"Lauren, this is Sophia—and she has some explaining to do. Especially to me. Right now, though, I don't think we have any choice but to follow her."

Afterwards, Derek could never clearly remember the flight Sophia led them on through the unfamiliar environs of the Pynx and Aereopagus hills—it was too unreal. Finally, they reched Sophia's car. She hustled them in—Lauren into the back and Derek into the front passenger's seat—and then started to sit down behind the wheel . . . but then she paused and gazed eastward, where the Acropolis was visible. The haze must have momentarily parted, for the Parthenon gleamed the whitest Derek had yet seen it. Sophia's gaze lingered—reminiscent or wistful, it was hard to tell which

"What are you waiting for?" Derek demanded.

Sophia gave her head a shake and seemed to return to the present. She drove west, out of central Athens, with the ululating sound of European police sirens receding behind them.

"Where are you taking us?" Lauren demanded.

"Somewhere safe," Sophia replied over her shoulder. "Once we're there, I'll answer all your questions. It's not really far as the crow flies, but crows don't have to drive on Greek roads. Why don't you two get some sleep?"

"*Sleep?*" Lauren demanded indignantly. "After . . . after *that?*"

"And what about our mission," added Derek. "We've got to get in touch with—"

"Your findings have already been passed on to Greek security. It will be taken care of. You might as well rest."

"But . . . but . . ." Incredibly enough, Derek actually *did* find himself getting sleepy. *I must have never really gotten over my jet lag,* he thought. He turned to Lauren for support—but she was already asleep.

His last recollection was of Sophia's smile.

CHAPTER EIGHT

Sophia shook Derek awake from a sleep made fitful by the bumpy ride.

After an initial blessed instant of forgetfulness, the impossible events in Athens invaded his mind like the recollection of a nightmare—except that he could have awakened from a nightmare.

He blinked the gummy residue of sleep from his eyes and looked around him. So far, his only glimpses of Greece had been in greater Athens. Now they were driving through a landscape of starkly rugged beauty, mountainous but not in an overawing way, with the slopes lightly cloaked in cypress, fir, myrtle and fig trees and the dells dotted with poppies. Much was terraced, and tiny whitewashed villages clung to the crags. Away from Athens and its pall of pollutants, the air held the almost startling clarity he'd been told to expect in Greece—but with no harsh glare, for the sun was low in the west, ahead of them.

"Where are we?" he asked.

"The Peloponnesus. You missed the Corinth Canal. Too bad—it's a pretty impressive sight when you drive over it."

"Where are we going?"

"We're almost there," Sophia responded obliquely. "You've

been out for a while. I stopped at a village near Corinth and got some food—you must be starving."

Derek belatedly remembered that he and Lauren hadn't eaten since the previous night. "Yeah, you might say that."

"I also got wine." Sophia handed him a straw-bound bottle. "Here—something to get you going."

"Thanks." Derek accepted the bottle gratefully, took a swallow, and nearly gagged. "What are you trying to *do* to me?" he gasped. "That's not wine, it's *turpentine!*"

"Oh, come now! *Retsina* grows on you after a while." Sophia's face took on a judicious look, and she shook her head. "Actually, it doesn't."

"That's quite an admission, coming from a Greek."

Sophia took her eyes off the road momentarily, and they twinkled as she gave him an enigmatic smile. "Who said I was a Greek?"

"What *are* you, then?" came Lauren's voice from the back seat—as cold as Derek had ever heard it.

He turned around. "Oh, hi. I didn't know you were awake." He started to offer her the wine bottle, then pulled it back hastily. Instead, they shared coarse bread, *stefado* stew and *peponi* melons as Sophia drove on into the westering sun.

By the time they'd finished the food, Derek had reached a decision.

At JICPO, they'd all received a thorough indoctrination on the ethical gudielines for using telepathy against an unconsenting party. Those guidelines boiled down to *don't,* except under lawful orders from a superior officer or in response to a clear and present danger to the national security of the United States.

The first exception clearly didn't apply here, and the second didn't seem to. As far as Derek knew, Sophia had never menaced anybody with anything more than a lot of highly irritating mysteriousness. In fact, she had just saved the bacon of two United States agents.

Nevertheless . . .

He reached out.

Nothing. It was like sliding off a surface so smooth as

to be friction-free. Annoyingly—no, infuriatingly—Sophia showed no awareness that the attempt had ever taken place.

"The Plain of Argos," she announced presently as they rounded a curve and saw spread out before them a wide valley in whose center rose a craggy hill crowned with the broken remnants of a stone fortification.

They followed twisting roads—sometimes leaving those roads, although the change was hardly noticeable—toward that ancient citadel, winding past little farmsteads and grazing goats. Sophia finally parked in the neighborhood of some of those goats. They walked across what seemed to be a rough parking area, just in time to see a couple of rickety buses pulling out in a cloud of reddish dust. "Good," Sophia said. "The last of the tourists are leaving. Still, we'll avoid the ticket office, just in case anyone's still there."

They walked up the hill slope toward the fortress, avoiding the pathways, past a wire fence that enclosed a series of what looked like the foundations of very old buildings, keeping to the right of a pair of oddly symmetrical hillocks. Derek began to feel a complex mix of uneasy sensations, the uppermost of which was that he ought to recognize this place. Then, as they rounded it, the hillock to their left stood revealed as artificial, for a sloping stone-walled ramp led deep into it as though a slice had been removed by a giant's cake-cutter. At the bottom of the ramp stood a stone entrance, impressive and of unguessable antiquity.

"Is this Mycenae?" breathed Lauren.

With those words the amorphous half-familiarity crystallized in Derek's mind. From his childhood and adolescence there came rushing back the Greek myths, and the maddening parental assurance that there were yet more tales, but only for "when you're older." That, of course, had drawn him to those tales as surely as a red cloak draws a bull to matador. He'd read voraciously of the self-destruction of the House of Atreus, cursed from the outset by its founder's deeds. But that initial spasm of betrayal, incest, child-murder and cannibalism had been merely the prelude to a rising crescendo of butchery. Atreus' son Agamemnon, who led the Greeks to Troy, had made a blood-sacrifice of his own daughter Iphigenia, for which his wife Clytemnestra and her cousin-and-lover Aegisthus had murdered him on his return home, leading in turn to the madness of his daughter Electra and the blood-drenched matricidal vengeance of his son Orestes . . . all at a place that had merely been a name to Derek before.

Now he looked around at the stones and the soil and the *tholos* tomb to their left and the hilltop citadel above, like something raised by giants when the world was young— which was precisely what the ancient Greeks had thought it was, for it had been ancient history to *them*—and the tininess of his own lifespan shook him.

"Very good, Lauren," said Sophia with a smile. She gestured down the stone ramp leading into the bowels of the *tholos* tomb. "The archaeologists arbitrarily labeled this the 'Tomb of Clytemnestra.' By sheer coincidence, they didn't miss by much. In fact, it was Agamemnon who was buried here."

"Oh," Lauren said, poker-faced, and nodded solemnly. She and Derek exchanged a meaningful look. "*The* Agamemnon. Himself. So *you* know this, right?"

"Yes." Sophia evinced no reaction to, or even awareness of, Lauren's arch tone. "Their *really* lucky guess was the 'Treasury of Atreus,' as they named a *tholos* just south of here because of all the grave goods that, amazingly, escaped the tomb robbers until the Classical age. Atreus really *was* buried there." Continuing to ignore the other two's looks, she led the way onward, past the second *tholos,* which was partially fallen in. "This one got named the 'Tomb of Aegisthus.' Not even close. It dates back three centuries earlier, to the late sixteenth century B.C., and the man buried in it was—"

"I suppose," Derek cut in, "you know all this by some application of telepathy."

"I told you before, I'm not a telepath. In fact, I have no psionic abilities of any kind."

"Oh, come on! You don't really expect me to believe that anymore, do you? After what I saw back on that beach in Virginia—I'll tell you about it later, Lauren—and what happened in Athens this morning, and—"

"I remember you now," Lauren broke in. Her voice held the same note of cold dislike as everything she'd said to Sophia so far, and it stopped Derek's flow of indignation in mid-sentence. "I saw you in the crowd while we were undergoing our screening."

"And I suppose we shouldn't be surprised that you were able to get in there," Derek put in. "Not after the way you left my grandfather's house, to say nothing of what you pulled off this morning."

The tall woman—now somehow even taller—turned around to face them, silhouetted against the stronghold of unmortared stone atop the hill. Again, she smiled her enigmatic smile. "Let's walk a little further," she said, "and I'll tell you a story."

She led them further up the hill, past a bastion of the massive Cyclopean walls. Turning right, they faced a monumental gateway whose lintel was surmounted by a colossal triangular stone slab carved into a relief sculpture of two rampant lions rearing up to face a column from opposite sides. The lions' heads had been worn away by the millennia, but the vivid muscularity of their bodies still stood out with an artistry that the megalithic crudeness of the walls emphasized by contrast.

"The coat-of-arms of the House of Atreus," Sophia remarked, gesturing at the sculpture. She led them through the Lion Gate and past some ancient foundations. To the right, they came to a shallow circular pit almost a hundred feet in diameter, surrounded by a low stone parapet. Derek saw a sign—in English, for the benefit of the tourists—reading "Grave Circle A." Beyond, they could look out westward over the walls and the valley below, to mountain ridge whose outlines resembled a reclining, bearded man against the reddening sunset sky.

As Derek looked around, amid the silence and the inconceivable ancientness, a shudder ran through him. There was something sinister about this place—an oppressive sense of unspeakable evil. Even if he'd never read the tragedies of Aeschylus, he would have *known* that dark and bloody deeds had occurred here.

"Yes," he heard Sophia saying. "You can almost hear the screams if you listen hard enough."

Derek glared at her. "And you *still* insist you're not a telepath?"

"It doesn't take telepathy to know what you're thinking. Mycenae has the same effect on all but the terminally insensitive." Sophia sat down on the parapet and regarded them levelly, and Derek wondered why he'd never thought of her as beautiful. He decided it was because the austere perfection of her features transcended the ordinary standards by which beauty was judged—it was *sui generis*. But here, in this haunted place as far outside mundane human experience as she herself was, such standards no longer applied. Here, she *defined* beauty—but the definition was not an altogether human one, and the beauty held a quality of awesomeness. He began to understand Lauren's instinctive hostility to her.

But now Lauren took one step forward and, with a visible effort, spoke in a tone that was not only civil but almost supplicating. "Will you *please* tell us what's going on, and why we're caught up in it?"

"First of all, tell me something: how much do you two really know about psionics?"

Derek and Lauren exchanged a glance, and the latter responded with a summary of what Doctor Kronenberg had told them.

"She's right as far as she goes," Sophia nodded. "Of course, she's forcing things into the concepts and terminology with which she's comfortable. For example, 'neural activity' is really just a particular instance—the human one—of a generalized abstraction. Intelligence doesn't have to be carbon-based."

"I believe," Derek reminded her pointedly, "you mentioned something about telling us a story."

"I was leading up to it. Once upon a time, in the 'dimension' Doctor Kronenberg has postulated to account for teleportation and projection, intelligence came into existence as a pure energy pattern. It was a very low-probability event, I suppose—but it only had to happen one time. Once established, the new entity could manipulate the energy flow to sustain itself. Others of its kind followed it.

"But their environment was one in which nothing existed except themselves—the ultimate in 'sensory deprivation,' except that they had no experience of sensation and therefore couldn't even feel deprived. And so it went for uncounted aeons, for time was as meaningless as everything else in such a featureless immaterial void. In fact, from now on I'll call it the Void for convenience.

"Then, finally, in another low-probability event, one of those beings—energy patterns held together by will—stumbled onto a way to enter the material universe.

"It was a revelation. Never had they experienced such things as form, solidity, substance and, above all, sensation. It gave them something they'd never had: a sense of reality. It was intoxicating, in a way and to a degree which you can't begin to imagine.

"They organized their energy patterns into material forms—matter, after all, is simply a particular energy-state. But they could only imitate what they found in your world, for nothing they'd known before enabled them to imagine anything else. Thus began a history of interaction with the human race, which was only just beginning to grope its way toward civilization and, being in its cultural infancy, was highly impressionable. For those primitive humans, the newcomers became what we may as well call them from now on: gods.

"And *don't* give me that look! I'm not being blasphemous. I'm only trying to make you understand the origin of many of the ancient legends you've read all your lives."

"Not *all* ancient legends, surely," insisted Lauren in a skeptical tone that didn't quite last to the end of the sentence.

"No, of course not. Humans, unlike the gods, have imagination and creativity coming out their ears. They can dream up fantastic supernatural beings without any help—which is precisely what they did over most of the world outside western Eurasia and the Mediterranean basin, the gods' principal stamping ground. But within that area, the gods—"

"I *wish* you wouldn't call them that!" Even as he blurted the protest out, Derek wondered why it bothered him so much. *It's not like I was religious or anything. . . .*

"I could use any of a number of names they've been called, Derek, but to you those names would be meaningless noises. They wouldn't have the same impact for you, and therefore wouldn't convey the same understanding. You see, while the entities I'm describing may not really be gods in any theological sense, and certainly not omnipotent or omniscient, they are *very* powerful beings. And many of them abused their powers flagrantly in those early times. Eventually, there was war among them."

"War?" asked Lauren. "Over what?"

"I don't know if I can make the issues clear to you. But I've already hinted that the gods became dependent on the primitive humans' creativity. It provided the raw material, so to speak, for the material manifestations that they assumed, and to which they became addicted. You might say they molded themselves into what the humans *expected* gods to be like.

"Gods . . . or monsters.

"Remember, it's a short step from dependency to resentment and overcompensation . . . and hatred. The earlier generation of gods—these beings are effectively immortal, you understand, but they do occasionally reproduce themselves—told themselves it was easiest to rule by terror. Soon, terror became an end in itself. You dimly remember them in many guises . . . the animal-headed deities of Egypt, for instance, and the truly horrible entities the Sumerians worshiped—or, more accurately, tried to placate. But as a convenience-label, let's call them the Titans, the name by which they were remembered in the myths of this country.

"To the younger gods, though, the Earth and the humans who inhabited it were part of their accustomed world. They didn't share the need to punish and hurt that world. They seized power. War began.

"That war was so devastating that it left scar-tissue of memory on the human psyche. And this country's myths retained a very crucial element: to defeat the Titans, the gods needed the help of a mortal."

"Oh, yes, I remember," said Lauren, nodding. "Hercules."

A smile played across Sophia's lips. "Yes, all sorts of mythic elements ended up sticking to *him,* didn't they? But in fact, it wasn't muscle the gods needed humans for. No, it was an ability unique to humans and denied to the gods: magic."

"Magic?" echoed Derek and Lauren in unison, faintly.

"It's another word I can't avoid using, like 'gods.' You see, Doctor Kronenberg is right about the essential nature of psionics: the use by humans of what she calls 'quantum energy' to reshape reality on a fundamental super-subatomic level not subject to the ordinary laws of physics. And that's also the basis of magic. The difference is this: a psi is using his or her own 'internal' or 'personal' quantum energy, while magic involves the collection and exploitation of 'ambient' or 'background' quantum energy."

Lauren leaned forward, eyes alight. "Yes! We've talked about this. That theory about magic being based on something called 'mana,' which magic-use depletes? So 'mana' is really the same thing as the quantum energy that Doctor Kronenberg has discovered!" Then her face fell. "But you still come up against the same paradoxes. If we're still producing it, then why doesn't magic work any more?"

"Neural processes on the human level produce *only* the kind of 'internal' quantum energy that a few humans like you two can exploit in the ways that are labeled 'psionics.' The gods, on the other hand, generate it on a higher level, so as to suffuse their vicinity with it. Only in their presence does the 'ambient' quantum energy necessary for magic exist. And, yes, the practice of magic does deplete it."

"Now wait a minute!" exclaimed Derek angrily. "You just said that the . . . uh, the gods needed humans to do magic for them. But now you're saying that—"

"Yes. Ironic, isn't it? The gods create the *possiblilty* of magic, but they can't use it themselves."

"But . . . but from everything you've told us about the gods' powers—"

"Oh, yes, the gods have very formidable powers. Indeed, their first conscious acts of will—what your Doctor Kronenberg characterizes as 'neural activity'—created the quantum energy by which they stabilized their own existence in the Void. Almost, if not quite, 'auto-creation.' But the gods are locked into certain rigidly defined powers. Only humans, whose entire existence—no, entire evolution—was spent in the infinite variety and riotous changeability of the material word, were capable of the *creative* use of background quantum energy called 'magic.'

"Humans first discovered the art in the area where the gods had been most active, with its high level of background quantum energy. It was a group of islands that no longer exist, to the southwest of the British Isles and west of—"

"Oh no, not Atlantis too!"

Sophia smiled at Derek's wail. "No, that was just Plato lecturing his fellow Athenians through the medium of fiction—although he drew on various sources of inspiration, and it's conceivable that one of those was a very dim racial memory of the land I'm talking about, whose inhabitants called it Rhysqarye. There, the first magicians arose. They made possible the defeat of the Titans, placing the gods under a debt of gratitude. But the Rhysqaruo, as they called themselves, paid a high price. The forces unleashed by magic in that war had weakened the geological foundations of their land, and it began to sink."

"But," protested Lauren, "the whole idea of a sunken Atlantic island like Atlantis has been flatly disproved by geology!"

"The foundations of Rhysqarye were removed by means outside ordinary geological processes," said Sophia with an edge of impatience. "It gradually collapsed into what your geographers know as the West European Basin. The gods, as a reward for the Rhysqaruo's help, offered them a new home, on another world."

"Another world?" breathed Derek.

"You must understand, the Void is infinite, and all parts of it are congruent with all parts of the material universe." Sophia frowned as she sought for words. "Imagine that you were two-dimensional beings living on the surface of a sheet of paper. Now, in the third dimension, crumple up the paper. Similarly, the actual physical universe is crumpled up in Doctor Kronenberg's additional dimension. The Void is what's in the folds.

"The gods can create portals from the Void into the physical universe at any point—it's one of the powers I spoke of before, and it also has its uses in the material world. Also, they shaped the void's energies into constructs based on what they'd found in the material world. They let the Rhysqaruo through portals into that world of theirs, and then back out through other portals which led to a world they knew of, suitable for humans but far away. *Very* far away— in a different galactic spiral arm, in fact. They named it Khron.

"Not all of the Rhysqaruo accepted the offer, though. Some chose to stay on Earth. They abandoned their sinking homeland and sailed east. Some worked their way up the Atlantic coast of Europe as the Megalith Builders, leaving the stone circles to mark their passage. Others passed into the Mediterranean, mingling with other peoples and even- tually reaching their highest cultural flowering as the Minoans of Bronze Age Crete—the 'Linear A' people. As time went by, they saw less and less of the gods, who were spend- ing more and more of their time on Khron. Thus Earth's background level of quantum energy diminished, and magic grew less powerful and reliable.

"Then, in the seventeenth century B.C., came the explo- sion of the island of Thera, ninety miles north of Crete— *not* a result of magical tampering, as far as I know, but a perfectly natural seismic event. Egyptian records of it may have been another source Plato drew on for the Atlantis story. It was one of the most cataclysmic natural events in the lifetime of humanity, and it blighted the Minoan civi- lization. The Rhysqaruo descendants began more and more to blend with the Indo-Europeans who were spreading south and west. But the gods' offer remained open: The portals would still admit any who wished to pass through to Khron."

Well, we finally know where you *come from, don't we?*

The thought sent a chill sliding up Derek's spine to prickle his neck hairs as he looked at the woman whose origin he'd never been able to place. *And I guess we'll find out what you're doing here when you're good and ready to tell us.*

"Finally, in the twelfth century B.C., came the death agony of the Bronze Age." Sophia looked around her, and—in what Derek assured himself was only a trick of the last lingering sunlight—her eyes seemed to reflect the flames of burning Mycenae. "In that nightmare chaos of barbarian invasions, the last few people who remembered their Rhysqaruo heritage—not that they were 'pure-blooded' by any stretch of the imagination, or even went by that name—called in the ancient debt. They departed through the portals to Khron . . . and the portals closed behind them. The gods no longer came to Earth, except for occasional visits. The magic went away."

With Sophia's final words, the sunlight went away too, and she sat silhouetted against the afterglow of sunset, in a silence violated only by the thin keening of the wind across the Plain of Argos. Derek dared not break the moment.

Lauren, however, shook herself and stepped forward in the twilight to face Sophia from across a few feet. She planted her feet wide and spoke as though she was sending each word out to do battle. "I suppose you're telling us, then, that the stuff we saw, and that Derek says he saw back in the states, is a result of magic. But you just said that Earth's supply of 'background' quantum energy dried up after the gods stopped coming here more than three thousand years ago! So how can magic be working here now?" She pointed a theatrical finger at the perfectly straight bridge of Sophia's nose. "Answer me *that!*"

Sophia stood slowly up to her full height. She looked down at Lauren and softly spoke four words.

"The gods are back."

CHAPTER NINE

Afterwards, Derek's next clear recollection was of Sophia leading them back down the path under the first emerging stars of twilight, through the Lion Gate. She spoke with a new briskness. "Let's go. It's getting dark. I'll explain as we walk.

"All you need to know for now is that there is war in the Khron system. The Titans have stirred it up. They have allies among the humans there—the nation of Qurvyshye."

"The Titans?" Lauren queried as she struggled to keep up with her longer-legged companions. "But you said they'd been defeated thousands of years ago."

"Defeated, but not killed. It is almost impossible to kill any of the gods, at least not permanently. The physical bodies can be destroyed, but the energy patterns just reconstitute themselves in the Void. That takes time, though, and it is . . . traumatic. Remember the constructs I mentioned before, the domains the gods can shape in the Void? Well, the defeated Titans withdrew to a domain of their own. They were still capable of creating portals back into the material universe, but instead they sulked—until recently."

"Hold on!" Derek struggled to throw off the last clinging remnants of mental shock. "You're telling us they sat around and sucked their thumbs, or whatever it is they do, for *thousands of years?*"

"Immortals have a different time-scale," Sophia explained succinctly. "Still, there is a grain of truth to what you are thinking. In the course of those millennia, they turned inward on themselves, growing ever more embittered as their embitterment fed on itself. And they were thrown back on their own resources for the sensory environment they were creating out of the Void, cut off from the wellsprings of human creativity they had tapped. It left them in a conceptual 'endless loop.' By now, on any reasonable standard, they must be considered insane. But they've acquired a kind of psychotic cunning. They've learned to restrain and dissemble their loathing of humanity, and *use* humans rather than just killing and tormenting them. In fact, humans have proven quite capable of killing and tormenting their own kind on a scale that satisfies even the Titans."

Their progress down the hill through the gathering dark had led them past a now-deserted guardhouse. From somewhere, Sophia produced a small flashlight. Ahead, in its flickering beam, was a hillock whose caved-in top revealed it to be a *tholos* tomb. Sophia led them down the ramp into that ruined stone beehive, and turned to face them. "So," she resumed, "the old war has resumed—and your services are required."

Lauren shook her head slowly. "Lady, I don't know where you get your ideas, but listen carefully. By your own description, this war is halfway across the galaxy. It isn't *our* war! I mean, it's too bad about the people on this planet of Khron, but why should we get involved?"

Sophia gave her a cool regard. "Because you're next."

"Huh?" they chorused.

"Do you know how the Titans acquired their human allies? They did it by pandering to the human lust for power. They taught their human proxies, the rulers of Qurvyshye, the one exception to what I've told you about magic: a way the internal quantum energy of thinking beings can be tapped for quick magical results. It's not like the way you apply that energy for psionics, though. It's dangerous—exhausting at least, often fatal. But that doesn't matter when *another* thinking being is used, and the user doesn't mind killing him." Sophia took on a cold, remote expression. "It's the ultimate origin of the practice of sacrificing animals found in so many of your early-historical religions. They were dimly groping for a source of magical potency. It never worked, though. You have to kill a human. The Mesoamericans had the right general idea—the ancestors of the Mayas and Aztecs had come under the influence of the Titans—but they'd forgotten the technique. Mass murder had become mere habit for them."

Derek began to see where this was leading. He didn't like it.

"Furthermore," Sophia continued inexorably, "the energy tap becomes even more efficient when the victim's total quantum energy is released all at once by violent death. In fact, an *intense* death—a painful, horrifying one—seems to enhance the effect by a kind of positive feedback. All the more so when you're using victims especially defenseless against pain and horror: children, for example."

"No!" Lauren's voice cracked. "You're lying! Human beings would never—"

"Oh, don't be a silly little twit! After the last century of your own planet's history, you know as well as I do that there is *nothing* human power-junkies won't do to support their filthy habit."

"But surely," Derek protested, "the people who're doing this—these, uh, Qurvyshyians—"

"Qurvyshuo," Sophia corrected.

"Whatever. Surely they can see that they're just being used by the Titans!"

"The only thing in the universe that is truly infinite is the human capacity for rationalization and self-deception. As usual, they have formalized it into a religion. Now they are processing victims on an industrial scale. At the present rate, they will run up against a shortage of human bodies soon, and need a new source to harvest. And . . . they remember Earth.

"Furthermore," Sophia continued into the dead silence,

"the Titans have become interested in Earth again for the same reason the gods have: you."

"Us?" said Derek and Lauren in unison, shooting each other a glance.

"By 'you' I mean humans with psionic abilities. It is a potential source of power which has never been exploited."

"I don't get it," said Derek. "Why don't the gods—including the Titans—just recruit among the local home-grown human psis on Khron?"

"There aren't any." Sophia smiled at her listeners' look of incomprehension. "It seems the gods' abandonment of Earth for Khron at the end of the Bronze Age had an unanticipated evolutionary consequence. With no background quantum energy left on Earth, magic was impossible—except by the kind of tapping I mentioned earlier, which is remembered as 'necromancy' in your darkest legends, and was rejected as an abomination. So, in the absence of magic, psi talent—which Doctor Kronenberg is correct in regarding as a genetic trait—evolved to exploit the internal quantum energy inherent in humans.

"Khron, where the gods remained active, was rich in ambient quantum energy, so there was no such evolutionary pressure. Indeed, psionic ability is so dangerous in such an environment as to be actively contra-survival, and is therefore selected out of the gene pool."

"Why is it dangerous?" Lauren wanted to know.

"For the same reason it is so tempting to both sides as a source of power. You see, there is reason to believe that psionically talented people can use the 'tapping' technique for magic—use it on *themselves,* without the dangers I've described. But only up to a point. There are limits, of course, beyond which the dangers suddenly catch up with the unwary. A magically unskilled psi has no way of knowing those limits, and is likely to end up practically tearing himself apart, or destroying himself with magical side-effects that he cannot control."

"Why haven't we psis on Earth done that?" demanded Derek.

"Living as you do in a world where magic is regarded—

correctly, for the most part—as mere fantasy, the temptation to overreach in this manner never arises. The possibility simply never occurs to you. But in the Khron system, where magic is a familiar, matter-of-fact concept . . . well, is it any wonder that any psis thrown up by genetic accident kill themselves off early?

"Now perhaps you can see why your world has become important again."

"Actually," said Lauren coldly, "we've always thought of it as rather important."

Sophia had the grace to smile. "Point taken. But now it has attracted the attention of the gods—both factions of them. This is the cause of the recent activity in the Solar system."

"What are you talking about?" asked Derek. "What 'activity'?"

"Oh, so you're not aware of it? I thought you might be—your superiors assuredly are. At any rate, you will be officially informed soon. Your government has been forced to the conclusion that extraterrestrial alien spacecraft are present in Earth orbit. They're right about the 'extraterrestrial' part, but not about 'aliens.' In fact, the spacecraft carry humans from the Khron system."

Like you, thought Derek with a mental nod. *So now we know. Only* . . . "How can that be, if Khron is in another part of the galaxy? Are you saying there's a way to exceed the speed of light after all?"

"Not in the sense you imagine. The Khronuo are perhaps two centuries ahead of you technologically, having had their scientific revolution earlier, but they are as subject to fundamental relativistic limitations as you are. Actually, your physicists have arrived at a pretty accurate description of the observable material universe on the supra-quantum level, much as Newton accurately described what could be observed in the seventeenth century. But remember what I said about the gods' ability to create portals from the Void to anywhere in the material universe?"

"Ah!" Lauren nodded. "So they can provide a portal for the, uh, Khronuo to pass straight through from Khron to here without crossing the intervening distance in Einsteinian space."

"It doesn't quite work that way. Oh yes, magic-users can, with great effort, create portals like that over planetary-scale distances—a shortcut through the Void not unlike the psionic teleportation you've been experimenting with. That, by the way, is what was happening this morning in Athens, and back in Virginia. The Titans' Qurvyshuo agents use the technique to move about on Earth." Sophia's face clouded. "I don't know whether they've been using traditional magical techniques to do it, or tapping the quantum energy of victims obtained locally. I suspect the latter—the quick and easy way. Incidentally, the Titans can't do it for them. None of the gods can create portals within the material world—only from the Void.

"At any rate, for interstellar distances, it won't work. One has to go into, and then out of, the Void—meaning, practically speaking, through one of the domains I described earlier. So the gods shaped a domain which is simply an expanse of vacuum, and created portals from it to the Khron system and also to the Solar system. Portals, once created, can be opened or closed either by the gods or by humans using magic."

"Why go to all the trouble of generating this special 'domain'?" wondered Lauren. "Come to think of it, why bother with spaceships at all? Why not just let the Khronuo walk through portals on the surface of Khron to existing domains, then through other portals to the surface of Earth? Or is there some practical problem with that?"

"No, there is no such problem. But . . . the gods like their privacy."

Uh-huh, thought Derek. *Can't have the help trampling the flower beds.*

"Not that the gods themselves can't and don't use the approach you've described," Sophia continued. "You must understand that portals, once created, remain in existence until closed. There are quite a few very old ones still in existence on Earth. No one here has been able to use them since the gods and Earth's last magicians departed for Khron. But . . ." She looked around at the collapsed *tholos* in which they sheltered, and in the flickering illumination of the flashlight her expression was complex.

"This dates back to the fourteenth century B.C.," she said in a voice as remote as that almost meaninglessly ancient time. "The archaeologists named it the 'Lion *Tholos*' simply because it's so close to the Lion Gate. As a matter of fact, though, it was the tomb of somebody you've heard of: Perseus."

"Perseus?" Lauren emitted a splutter of laughter. "Now wait a minute! You're not going to tell us *he* was real, are you? As I recall, he put on sandals with wings on them and flew off to kill some monster or other."

"The Gorgon Medusa," Sophia supplied with a smile. "The sight of whose face under its 'hair' of writhing snakes could turn you to stone. Yes, yes, I know. But at the heart of all those stories lies a kernel of truth: the legend that he founded Mycenae. Actually, it already existed. But he was the king who fortified it with these walls, although Atreus extended them to their final form a century later. He was the conqueror who made it the predominant power on the mainland and even Crete. He was . . ." Her eyes took on a faraway look. "He was also one hell of a man."

Derek exchanged a quick glance with Lauren. All at once, the realization of what he'd been listening to finally caught up with him, and he felt silly. He understood now: outrageous experiences, followed by being abruptly snatched away to this eerie place, had left him in a susceptible state of mind where *anything* seemed reasonable. He balled a fist and struck one of the stones of the *tholos*, roughened by the aeons. Not unexpectedly, it hurt. But it hurt the way any other stone would hurt any human who punched it in the ordinary course of events.

Time to take charge, he told himself.

"Look," he said to Sophia carefully but firmly, "I'm sure you're completely sincere in your beliefs, and I can't deny I've seen some, uh, phenomena that are going to take some explaining. And we appreciate your having gotten us out of danger. But we shouldn't be wasting time out here in the Greek boonies! We need to report in. I must insist that you get us to a phone so we can contact the U.S. embassy in Athens and arrange to be picked up, and—"

"It was hardly to be expected that you would accept all this on my unsupported word," Sophia cut in. She didn't raise her voice in the slightest—but Derek stopped dead. "That is why I brought you here to Mycenae . . . and to this tomb."

"This tomb?" echoed Lauren.

"Yes. As I mentioned, there are still a number of ancient portals on Earth, in certain significant but out-of-the-way places." In the glow of the flashlight, Sophia's face became a spectral thing of flickering illumination and dark shadows, and the shadows deepened as it took on an expression of intense concentration.

Before Derek could frame a question, the uncanny glow he'd seen twice before appeared behind Lauren.

The Air Force lieutenant leaped away from it with a startled yelp, and whirled around to stare at the immaterial circle of light. Her eyes, and Derek's, widened still further as the wavering within the circle resolved itself into the unfathomable vistas Derek remembered.

"I know of the psychic shock that affects the telepathically sensitive at the opening of a portal," said Sophia, "but I will suppress it." She stepped froward, and as she entered the circle the outflowing of light Derek remembered washed outward—only this time he and Lauren didn't stagger backward in stunned disorientation.

Sophia passed through the circle and became a silhouette, for it was daylight beyond the portal—a transcendent daylight of extraordinary brilliance and clarity. Her voice seemed to come from a very great distance. "Come."

The possibility of not following her never even occurred to them.

They stood on a semicircular terrace of darkly gleaming, silvery-veined marble. Derek walked unsteadily forward and leaned on the exquisitely carved alabaster balustrade. He looked out over a vista that seemed to cover thousands of square miles, for there was something strange about perspective here, and the horizon seemed farther away—much farther away—than it was in the world of mundane human experience. The view extended out into sunlit infinity.

It was a mountainous landscape of stunning drama, with low gold-tinted clouds drifting through the crystalline air between awesome crags and cypress-clothed slopes. Rivers meandered through upland valleys, to plunge over precipices in thundering, misting waterfalls that cascaded into gleaming lakes from which slow streams wended their ways through Arcadian meadows. In the remote distance a fjordlike body of water stretched away between mountain battlements to a sea that gleamed like molten gold under the afternoon sun.

But for all its natural grandeur, the panorama seemed crafted into artifice. Efflorescences of architectural fantasy clung to every slope and crowned every peak. On a sudden impulse, Derek turned around. The terrace on which they stood was cantilevered out of just such a structure, which rose in indescribable colonnaded grandeur.

The architectural motif was unfamiliar to him. It wasn't Classical Greek, although it aroused somewhat similar emotional responses. From somewhere, he recalled artists' conceptions of the palaces of the Aegean civilization that had preceded the Classical Greeks. This, he thought, was what that tradition might have become had it evolved in another direction, and acquired the arch and the dome and, with them, a kind of transcendent lightness and airiness. For all their monumentality, these edifices seemed to float among the clouds.

"It isn't *real*, is it?" he heard Lauren ask.

"Real? Of course it is. Remember, matter is just a particular energy state. Granted, this was consciously shaped by the gods out of the Void, rather than being a byproduct of the random fluctuations set in motion by the Big Bang in the material universe. But I don't advise you to test its reality by jumping off the balustrade!"

So, thought Derek, *this is one of the "domains." I guess that would account for some peculiarities. She said they had to mine our world for concepts of physical reality to shape their surroundings into. So naturally this is like Earth, only . . . more so. For instance, the gravity seems normal—*

"We can only stay for a short time," Sophia said, breaking into his thoughts. "And we can proceed no further. I received grudging permission to bring you this far, so you could see for yourselves. No one has been allowed even this far since the Bronze Age—and only a few even then."

And those few must have told stories, Derek reflected. *Stories that got passed down. Now we know where the Classical Greeks got their ideas about Mount Olympus.*

Sophia gestured them back toward the portal: a circular smudge of darkness as viewed from this side, for beyond it lay the nighted interior of Perseus' tomb. She spoke matter-of-factly. "Soon, you will hear from your superiors of the 'alien' activity in Earth orbit. The very purpose of allowing this activity to be observed has been to induce your government to send psis into orbit, where they can make contact with the Khronuo. After that . . . Pay attention!"

"Sorry," muttered Derek, to whom the last two words had been directed. For a fact, he'd heard nothing else after the words *psis into orbit.*

"We are confident that the two of you will be included. But in the meantime, it is crucial that you recruit one other, who will almost certainly be selected for the mission: Paul Rinnard."

"Paul? Why?" wondered Lauren.

"He is *important.* His psionic potential is simply impossible to estimate at this time, nor can its full implications be foreseen. All I can say is . . . No, I'd best say no more at this time. But he may well be the fulcrum around which incalculable events revolve. You *must* recruit him!"

"Why don't *you* recruit him?" Lauren's coldness was back in full force, even in this place.

Sophia's tone, by contrast, was one of remote coolness. "I would be only too happy to do so. But you two were the ones who were deployed here to Greece and thereby became accessible. I could penetrate the Hole, as you call it, but my presence there would be impossible to disguise from your security people. There is no crowd of examinees for me to lose myself in as I did before.

"But now we must hurry. Your superiors are, of course,

in a panic of uncertainty as to your whereabouts. I must return you to Athens. In the course of the drive, I will supply you with an acceptable cover story to account for your absence today."

"The *drive*?" Derek stared, incredulous. "Why don't you just create a portal so we can step from here to Athens?"

"I can't do that, within the material universe. Only magicians can."

"Oh, come on!" exploded Lauren. "All right, you've explained why you aren't, and can't be, a psi. But don't try to tell us you're not a magician! For God's sake, you just opened this portal from Earth to . . . here. And I distinctly remember you telling us—don't deny it!—that nobody can do that except magicians and the gods."

"I do not deny it. That is precisely what I told you."

"Well, then?" snapped Lauren. Then, one lineament at a time, her expression changed from one of irritation to . . . something else.

For a heartbeat or two, Derek didn't get it. Then he, too, thought about Sophia's exact choice of words. Then he ran his mind back over everything she'd said to them. And he finally understood.

She never actually told us she was a human from Khron, did she? We just took it for granted. After all, what else could she possibly be?

Sophia looked from one of them to the other, and smiled her serene smile. "As I explained, gods are limited to certain fixed, inherent powers. Creation of portals from the Void, and opening or closing portals anywhere, is one of them. There are others. One is shape-shifting—including the ability to take on an incorporeal form that can pass through physical barriers—although one adopts a kind of 'default' or 'rest' form, out of sheer habit. It is generally easier to use yet another power—that of influencing perceptions—to create an illusory form instead. Here again, there is a tendency to settle on one such illusion except for special purposes."

And, as she spoke, Sophia began to change.

It was hard to say how tall she grew, for no matter how tall it was she *seemed* even taller. And a dazzlement that had nothing to do with actual light made it almost impossible to look at her. But it was *absolutely* impossible to look anywhere else.

As Derek's eyes adjusted, details began to emerge from the blaze of Power. She was—or seemed to be—wearing something almost but not quite like a Classical *chiton* and carrying a spear and great round shield whose bronze was wrought into reliefs of combats with monstrous opponents. Her features—still recognizably hers, but with their austere regularity transfigured into something beyond perfection— were now framed by a visored bronze helmet, its cheek-guards turned upward in a way that made them resemble horns. A lofty crest surmounted that helmet, flanked by rearing, similarly crested bronze horses.

The warhorses that were sacred to you, thought Derek in some sheltered corner of his skull where he cowered.

At the precise moment when he and Lauren felt they could no longer endure the sight, it vanished. Once again, what stood before them was only a tall, handsome brunette of youngish but indeterminate age, dressed in the businesslike charcoal pantsuit she'd been wearing when she'd appeared that morning in the city named after her.

But now you go by Sophia, thought Derek as he managed to meet her gray eyes. *I suppose it fits as well as any other name . . . the name they gave you when they turned you into a Greek Orthodox saint.*

"Well," he heard himself saying, "now I know why you paused, just before leaving Athens, to look back at the Parthenon in that reminiscent sort of way."

Incredibly, her smile was one of almost girlish embarrassment. "It really was such a *flattering* statue!"

★ CHAPTER TEN

A hero's welcome awaited them at the Hole.

"And in the morning," Derek concluded his narration to the group that had gathered in the club after the hoopla had died down, "we reported in to the U.S. embassy. By that time, the Greek security forces had finished off the last of the terrorists and scoured the caves in the Pynx and Aereopagus hills until they'd found the nerve gas."

"Yeah, you'd been gone all the rest of the day, hadn't you?" said Sergeant Tucker. He looked a little puzzled.

As well he might be, Derek thought wryly.

"Right. We'd gotten separated from our people in the fighting. One of the Greek cops hustled us away. But then he got killed, and we were lost—you can't imagine what a spaghetti-plate of winding, narrow streets that town is! With Bordelis dead, we thought it best to lie low for a while."

"And you were absolutely correct," Captain Morrisey stated firmly. "You were in a strange city where you didn't know the language or even the alphabet. You had no way of knowing who you could trust, or where the terrorists might turn up."

"Yes!" agreed Doctor Kronenberg. She took a pull on an

unaccustomed drink. "You are far too valuable to risk yourselves in a fire fight, for which neither of you is trained."

"Damn straight," agreed Paul Rinnard. Of the shadow that had fallen between him and Derek before the latter's departure for Greece, no visible trace remained. "Leave that small-arms stuff to the specialists, I always say. It's *dangerous*! Oh, by the way, about those terrorists . . . Did anybody ever figure out just how they'd mounted that attack at the restaurant? We've heard some pretty wild rumors."

"Yeah," Tucker chimed in. "Like them appearing out of thin air in a flash of light, with weapons that were beyond cutting-edge. What really happened?"

Derek exchanged a quick glance with Lauren. But this wasn't even part of their personal cover story—it was the party line the Greek and American authorities had agreed on. "Well, it's hard to be certain of how they achieved such complete surprise. They died to a man, so there was nobody to question. But as for some of the wild stories you've heard, the official explanation is that the attack was so sudden and brutal that it inspired a kind of mass hysteria."

"Having been there," Lauren added, "we can tell you that it was pretty shocking."

"I can well believe it," said Morrisey in what they'd come to know as his subject-closing voice. "You've been through quite an experience, and I imagine you're pretty much done in."

"Yes, sir, what with jet lag on top of everything else."

"Of course." Morrisey set his glass down with a decisive click. "But before I can let you go and get a well-deserved rest, we need to get the debriefing out of the way. Please report to my office in fifteen minutes."

Everyone took the hint, and the party broke up. Derek and Lauren entered the CO's office at the stipulated time, to find Morrisey and Doctor Kronenberg and, more surprisingly, Collins, whom they hadn't even known was in the Hole.

"First of all," Morrisey began, "I meant every word I said back there in the club. You two have brought credit to this command, and you can be sure that the classified addenda to your fitness reports will reflect it."

"Thank you, sir," they mumbled in unison.

"However, there are certain matters that I could not raise back there—matters that Lieutenant Rinnard and Sergeant Tucker were getting uncomfortably close to—concerning the terrorists."

Derek and Lauren didn't dare meet each other's eyes. They'd known this was coming.

"The examination of the bodies yielded no passports or other documentary evidence, as was only to be expected," Morrisey continued. "And those black outfits they were wearing were completely nondescript—and, incidentally, made of a synthetic fabric we haven't been able to identify. But afterwards . . . Well, Mr. Collins, perhaps you could elaborate."

Collins cleared his throat in a dusty way. "The bodies were naturally examined for forensic evidence. Nothing was found that the Greek government could link to any known terrorists. Nor did anything about those bodies—dental work, for example—yield any clue as to their origins. So we downloaded fingerprints and other data to Interpol. Again, no linkage."

Uh-huh, thought Derek. *The Qurvyshuo are just a little outside Interpol's jurisdiction.*

"Pressure was brought on the Serbian government—behind the scenes, but at the very highest levels—to cooperate," Collins went on. "Again, no record of any such persons turned up, and no preparations for any such attack as that which occurred at that restaurant in Athens had left any traces.

"However, the real reason the Greek government has given us full access to everything connected with this case is that they simply don't know what to make of the captured weapons. We do, to a certain extent." Collins leaned forward portentously. "The two of you are probably aware, if only in a general way, of the R and D into magnetic linear accelerator weapons—'railguns' in popular parlance. Experimental prototypes are undergoing tests, and they may well arm the next generation of main battle tanks and naval surface combatants. But the sheer mass of the capacitors they require is still a problem. I assure you that no one in the world is seriously researching the possibility of scaling the technology down to small-arms size! And yet these terrorists you encountered . . . well . . . ."

Collins shoved a sheaf of photos across the desk. Derek and Lauren looked at the curious-looking weapons they'd last seen spitting death with the evil crackling sound that Derek now decided must have been that of streams of very small projectiles breaking mach.

Why, he wondered, *did the Qurvyshuo bring along their own stuff? Seems like it would have been smarter, from the security standpoint, to use local off-the-shelf pieces.*

Sheer overconfidence, probably, he answered his own question. *They didn't expect somebody to be there who could slam their portal shut behind them, leaving them stranded in a city full of understandably pissed Greeks.*

Collins gave them a moment to stare at the photos, then resumed. "Our people in Athens have been trying to test-fire these things—thus far without success. They're evidently identity-locked in some way, so that they won't fire without an authorized person's hand on the grip. We've had similar technology ourselves for the last decade or so. But when our experts tried to work around it, we lost one of the weapons . . . and one of the experts. The power source—which, by the way, is a complete mystery to us—went critical on being tampered with."

That might also help explain it, thought Derek. *That, and the fact that they probably expected to be able to simply shoot their way out of any trouble they encountered.*

And they weren't far wrong. He'd seen the final report of the toll the Qurvyshuo had taken with their futuristic weapons before dying. It still shook him—all the more so because the attack's purpose had been to seize him and Lauren. He told himself he wasn't to blame, by any rational concept of ethics. He kept on telling himself that.

Morrisey cleared his throat. "I need hardly tell you that this is all classified at the highest level, and that *no one* has a need to know it—except you, and one other."

" 'One other,' sir?" Lauren queried.

"And why us?" added Derek, already knowing the answer.

Morrisey touched a buzzer. A side door of the office opened, and Paul Rinnard entered, looking uncharacteristically abashed. "Skipper, I'm sorry I opened that can of worms back in the club."

"Never mind. Judging from what Sergeant Tucker said, you could hardly raise the general level of loose talk if you tried." Morrisey motioned Rinnard to take a seat alongside Derek and Lauren. "What's happened has brought certain matters to a head—matters that Paul has known about since shortly before you two left for Greece." He proceeded to tell them what he'd told Rinnard before concerning the sightings in orbit.

As he listened, Derek strove to act as though he'd never heard this before. It wasn't really all that hard. This was still too unreal, for all that Sophia—as he'd decided to continue to think of her—had told them to expect it.

"Up to now," Morrisey concluded, "we've thought we had time to consider at our leisure what to do about these sightings. But now it appears that the ball is in our court."

"Sir?" queried Lauren.

"Think about it, Lieutenant." Morrisey indicated the photos. "These weapons—advanced beyond anything that could be produced in this world—force us to the conclusion that whoever it is that's been operating in Earth orbit has moved beyond mere observation, to a more . . . active role. Not directly—"

"Of course not!" Doctor Kronenberg interrupted angrily. "The one thing we *do* know from postmortem examination of the bodies is that the terrorists were ordinary *homo sapiens sapiens*. The idea that the same species—no, subspecies— could evolve independently on another planet is too preposterous for discussion! I hope, Mr. Collins, that even you people in the Puzzle Palace have better sense than that."

The NSA man winced. "Rest assured, Doctor, that we haven't entertained such a notion for an instant. A few people did suggest the possibility of aliens altered by advanced biotechnology to pass for human—"

"Oh, give me a break! They'd have to rewrite the entire genetic code!"

"—but that theory has pretty much fallen into disfavor. So we're left with only one conclusion: the ETs—I suppose we have to call them that—are acting through human proxies."

Paul Rinnard frowned. "Sir, are you telling us that space aliens are arming the Sons of Dushan and using them as goons?"

"Not necessarily, Lieutenant. The fact is, we have no idea where the ETs are recruiting their 'goons,' as you put it. The physical characteristics and blood-groups of the bodies are compatible with—but do not require—a Mediterranean origin. The genetic testing now underway may give us clues as to their ethnicity. But in the meantime, nothing we've gotten from our Serbian sources suggests the Sons of Dushan are involved. And, at any rate, it's hardly likely that they would have killed Cvetkovic, one of their own—and his body was found among the dead at the restaurant."

Lauren spoke up, so demurely that Derek worried she might be overdoing it. "You'll have to excuse me, Mr. Collins—this has been quite a lot for us to take in. But I don't quite understand. If these people weren't Sons of Dushan, then what were they doing there?"

"A good question. The short answer—the cop-out, as we used to say in my youth—is that we don't know. But personally, I can think of only one reason the ETs would have for intervening at that particular time and place." Collins' eyes flicked from Lauren to Derek and back again. "You."

"Us?" they chorused.

"It's hard to imagine the ETs would concern themselves with Balkan politics. But they might view the emergence of human psis with interest—or even concern."

Derek and Lauren stared with a surprise that was completely unfeigned, for Collins had grasped a critical element of the truth: that they themselves had been the targets of the Qurvyshuo. *Come to think of it,* Derek told himself, *he's also hit on another element, for he knows we're dealing with human agents of . . . others. He can't possibly dream who those others are. Extraterrestrial intelligence is something he can accept; it's part of modern mythology.*

Morrisey cleared his throat. "This hypothesis, if true, lends an even more sinister dimension to the fact that the ETs have begun to take direct, violent action on the surface of Earth. These considerations have led us to decide to accelerate the schedule for—"

"A decision taken over my objections!" snapped Doctor Kronenberg. "It's simply too dangerous! Look, for these ETs to be aware of human psionics at all they must have some kind of ranged psi-detection capability. God knows, a society capable of crossing interstellar distances—which is what we seem to be postulating here—is by definition capable of things beyond our technological horizons."

Paul Rinnard took on a thoughtful expression he seldom wore when he knew anyone was looking. "You know, Doctor . . . Skipper . . . something just doesn't add up here. I mean, if these little green men are so advanced—and you're right, Doctor, they *have* to be or they couldn't have come here—then how come we've been able to detect them up in orbit? Seems like they ought to be able to avoid being picked up on radar. Even us hayseeds here on Earth have been getting a pretty good handle on stealth technology over the past generation!"

He's figured it out, Derek thought into the ensuing silence, which he didn't dare break. *He's gone straight to the heart of the matter, as he so often does—never mind the good-old-boy affectation. Sophia was hoping nobody would come to this realization, because from here it's just one step further to the conclusion that they've* let *us detect them, and that their whole purpose is to manipulate us into making precisely the decision we're about to hear announced.*

The look on Rosa Kronenberg's face showed that she was taking that step. She opened her mouth to speak—

"This discussion is all very interesting," said Collins primly, "but the decision is irrevocable. And yes, Doctor Kronenberg, your objections will be noted in the record as you requested earlier. Please don't take this as a reflection on the regard in which your scientific judgment is held. Rather, it is as Captain Morrisey said earlier: the recent events have made it imperative that we use every intelligence-gathering resource at our disposal to obtain information on what appears more and more to be a grave threat to the national security."

Kronenberg subsided into silent, fuming disapproval. Rinnard went poker-faced. And Derek recalled an expression from his grandfather's reminiscences. *NMH—short for "not made here." That's what this is all about, really. Collins isn't going to give Paul's insight any more weight than the zero he's given Kronenberg's arguments, because neither of them is a member in good standing of the Intelligence Community. They don't know the secret handshake.*

Funny, the way the right thing sometimes gets done for the wrong reasons.

Morrisey cleared his throat and spoke in a carefully neutral voice. "Now I'm going to lay to rest the curiosity I'm sure you're feeling—although this isn't going to come as a complete surprise to Paul. You all know about the testing the new spaceplane has been undergoing. What you—and the general public—don't know is that it's been checked out for a classified mission: to take psis into orbit in an attempt to draw the ETs' attention and take advantage of any intelligence-gathering opportunities that present themselves. You three are those psis."

Rinnard's expression, indeed, wasn't one of stunned surprise. Rather, what Derek saw there was a deep, triumphant exultation that banished any and all suspicions or misgivings. Lauren was doing her best to look floored, and Derek tried to follow suit.

Morrisey handed them each a sealed folder with "Top Secret" stamped across the front in scarlet stridency. "This contains the specs of the spaceplane, and also an abstract of the ET activity we've detected to date. Get some rest tonight and then familiarize yourselves with it thoroughly. Tomorrow afternoon, we'll set up a series of briefings—a *short* series. The schedule for this operation, which you'll also find in the folders, reflects the gravity with which the

ET situation is viewed in high places." His sea-blue eyes gentled a bit, as though sunlight had broken across the water. "I don't need to tell you how important this is. I hope I also don't need to say I have complete confidence that you'll do this command proud."

They mumbled their thanks while Collins uttered a few words of pompous agreement. Doctor Kronenberg said nothing. Indeed, she seemed to be exerting a physical effort to *not* speak, and her expression puzzled Derek. *She must be afraid she's going to lose some choice lab rats,* he decided. *There's no other possible explanation for that look in her eyes—as if she's worried almost to the point of desperation. No, it can't be anything else. Not her.*

Morrisey dismissed them, and barely were they out the door when Rinnard clasped Derek by the shoulders and dazzled him with a grin. "All fuckin' *right*! The *spaceplane*! Man, we are going into *orbit*! Can you believe this, Derek?"

"Yeah. It's incredible." Derek found himself grinning back. It was impossible to be unaffected by the intensity of Rinnard's excitement—a kind of apotheosis of cockiness.

And yet he and Lauren exchanged a look of shared understanding. In the crowded schedule that lay ahead for the three of them, this might be their only chance to get Rinnard alone.

"And you know what?" continued the fighter pilot, oblivious to what had passed between the other two. "After this mission, I'm going to put in for training to *pilot* the spaceplane! The next mission, I intend to be checked out to actually *fly* that baby! And I want you in the second seat, Derek! And don't you worry one little bit, Lauren; I'll think of a way to deal you in. They'll have to agree—it makes sense, doesn't it? They won't have to bother with a flight crew of non-psis. Hot damn! Who would have dreamed that we—"

"Paul," Derek broke in, "let's go for a walk up topside."

"Huh? Oh, yeah, sure. I guess we could all use a little fresh air."

They rode an elevator to the surface. The night was almost cloudless, lacking the usual haziness of Virginia summer, and myriads of stars sparkled overhead with winterlike clarity.

The sight seemed to sober Rinnard. He gestured upward. "I guess we'll never be able to look at those stars the same way again, will we?"

"No, I don't guess we can." Rather desperately, Derek wondered how to approach a moment he'd been dreading. "Paul, we learned some things in Greece—things we need to tell you about."

Rinnard gave him a sharp glance in the dimness—the moon was a mere sickle, and there were few lights in this *faux* base which existed merely to mask the Hole. "Hey, Derek, you know me. I'm not chickenshit about all that spook stuff. But I don't want you to get in trouble by telling me things I don't need to know."

"No, that's not it. What we're going to tell you isn't classified." A nervous laugh escaped Derek. "Nobody's had a chance to assign it a security classification, because we haven't revealed it to anybody until now."

Rinnard's gaze grew more intense, and he ran it over Lauren as well. They both felt the elemental impact of . . . whatever it was about him. "This obviously matters a lot to the two of you. Well, if it's important to you it's important to me. Spill it!"

"First of all," said Lauren, "our story about the Greek cop who got us away from the fighting was a lie."

Rinnard blinked once, but no words were spoken. None were needed. They'd placed themselves unreservedly in his hands, and thereby crossed a kind of Rubicon. "So what really happened?" he finally asked.

Derek picked up the thread. "Remember, when we were reporting in here, I asked you if you recalled a certain woman from the time we were undergoing the tests? The tall brunette?"

"Oh, yeah, I do remember. She was kind of hard to forget. But she's not here now—I guess she didn't make the final cut. So what about her?"

"Well—" Derek launched into the tale, starting with Sophia's arrival in the surf at Sandbridge. He and Lauren continued it through the events in Greece and the Void, sometimes finishing each other's sentences. Only occasionally did Rinnard interrupt them with questions. By the time they were done, the sickle moon had moved across a substantial arc of the sky.

"And that's the story," Derek concluded. "Except for one thing. On our way back to Athens, I asked for—and got—Sophia's assurance that what we're going to be doing is not in any way inimical to American national interests. She seemed to think it was self-evident that we'd be acting for *all* of Earth, including the U.S. But she understood that I needed to have that point spelled out . . . and that you would, too."

With those final words, silence descended under the summer stars. Derek and Lauren waited expectantly for they knew not what response.

Rinnard surprised them by saying nothing at all. Instead, he turned on his heel and walked a few feet away. There he stood motionless for a few heartbeats, hands thrust into his pockets. They did not disturb his silence.

Just as abruptly, he turned back to face them, his expression strange in the faint moonlight. "You know, don't you, what this sounds like?"

"I've got a pretty good idea," Derek admitted miserably.

"Or, rather," Rinnard amended, "what it *would* sound like, coming from anybody else. As it is . . ." He took a deep breath. "Assuming this is true, why doesn't this, uh, Sophia go public with this? Go to the President or the U.N. or whoever and explain the situation?"

"That's another point we raised on the drive back. She says it's too dangerous to our world. If the Qurvyshuo—and, through them, the Titans—thought Earth was threatening to become an open enemy, they'd just eliminate it. They'd hate to lose a potential source of victims to 'tap,' as Sophia calls it, but they'd hate to have an aroused enemy even more. And they wouldn't even need magic to saturate our ABM defenses!" Rinnard grimaced with rueful agreement. Not even China's growing delivery capability had ever scared Congress into appropriating enough for more than a rudimentary antiballistic missile shield, advertised as insurance against nuclear terrorism by rogue Third World nations. "No, as far as Earth is concerned this war has got to remain covert."

Rinnard took another deep breath. "Look, can you give me any evidence in support of all this?"

"Hell, no, we don't have any evidence! But think about it: I might go nuts, and Lauren might go nuts, but how likely is it that we'd *both* go nuts at the same time and in the *same way*?" Rinnard looked thoughtful, and Derek pressed on. "And you said it yourself earlier: we wouldn't be able to detect extraterrestrial visitors unless they *wanted* to be detected. Well, they do! The Khronuo have been obvious about their presence in orbit because the whole idea is to induce our government to send us up there."

"And it looks like they've succeeded, doesn't it?" Rinnard's tone was unreadable, his expression barely visible as what little moon there was went behind a cloud. Again, he turned away and stood in a posture of silent concentration.

Well, we tried, ran Derek's dismal thought. *He's going to fob us off with some conditionally encouraging half-promises, and then he'd going to go and get us sent to the rubber room. It was hopeless from the start.* Rinnard turned to face them. *Yep, here it comes. . . .*

But then the moon reappeared, to reveal the fighter jock's patented grin. "Well," he drawled, "we'll find out soon enough, won't we?"

Derek raised an eyebrow.

"We're being sent into orbit," Rinnard explained patiently. "Just like you say our government has been maneuvered into doing. So I don't guess it matters whether I believe you or not. Once we get up there, according to you, it'll be settled. So till then, I'm just going to go with the flow. Besides . . . Jesus, the things we'll get to see if this is really true!"

Lauren spoke then. "Uh, remember, there may be one problem. Sophia said we need to do some telepathic 'broadcasting' in order for the Khronuo to pinpoint us. But as we tried to explain to her, telepathy is short-ranged. Space is awfully big."

Rinnard's grin widened. "You two have missed out on a few things while vacationing in the Med! Doctor Kronenberg has been working with several of us on what she calls a 'concert.' When it works at all, it gives a kind of enhancement that the Doc is still trying to come up with a theory to account for. I guarantee that you'll be getting the details in those briefings the Skipper mentioned—and that we'll be trying the technique out in orbit."

Derek and Lauren looked at each other. "Sophia didn't say anything about this," Derek remarked dubiously.

"No, she didn't," said Lauren. "But why should she even know about it? Remember, by her own account psionic talent arose on Earth after the gods left. They've only recently become aware that such powers exist."

"Yeah, you did mention that, didn't you?" Rinnard looked thoughtful. Then his face took on another look. "Sort of makes you wonder, doesn't it? How much else do they *not* know about the ultimate potential of psi?"

In the minimal moonlight, it was hard to make out the exact nature of Rinnard's expression. So Derek couldn't say why he found it disturbing.

★ CHAPTER ELEVEN

The X-63 trans-atmospheric vehicle—the "spaceplane" except in official paperwork—had never flown, as far as the general public knew. Further advances in metallurgy, the media were assured, might eventually make its pulsed detonation wave engine concept an engineering reality.

In fact, those advances had occurred. It was a fuel hog, though. The venerable jet-assisted takeoff concept had been resurrected to help with that, and Derek, Lauren and Rinnard had been pressed back into their seats as auxiliary strap-on engines had thrust the sleek craft off the ground. Then the integral engines had engaged, in turbojet mode. Afterwards, the G-forces had increased again as the engines had switched to scramjet configuration for hypersonic velocities. Then had come the orbital insertion phase, and the air intakes had closed as the X-63 had become a rocket.

Getting into orbit this way was so fuel-intensive that "payload" was a rather laughable concept. The X-63 held four seats—including those of the pilot and copilot—in a small space, and that was it. To make the present mission viable, Rinnard had been given a crash course and now sat as copilot beside Major Craig Jackson, USAF.

"This way, spaceflight finally makes sense," Rinnard remarked as Jackson disengaged the engines. "To picture the economics of it back in the early days, you'd have to imagine buying a new car every time you drive to work!"

"Right," said Jackson, whose reservations about a squid—and a hastily trained squid at that—as copilot had been laid to rest by Rinnard's performance. "With the space shuttle, it was a little better: you only had to buy a new *engine* every time you drove to work. But now—or, at least, once they get the fuel-efficiency equations favorable enough to build a cargo hauler . . ."

"Yeah, I know what you mean. During the briefings for this mission our CO, Captain Morrisey, quoted some classic science fiction writer who said, 'Low Earth orbit is halfway to anywhere.' "

"Yeah, I've heard that one too," chuckled Jackson. "But now I've got to report to ground control that we've achieved orbit. Meanwhile, why don't you start computing the orbital transfer to Skybase."

Rinnard turned his head slightly and exchanged an unobtrusive glance with Derek and Lauren, who sat in the rear seats coping with weightlessness and staring through the curved viewport at the diamond-hard stars and the blue-marbled curve of Earth. The mission profile called for them to match orbits with the Skybase space station. There they would perform Doctor Kronenberg's new "concert" exercises in an attempt to attract the attention of whoever was haunting orbital space. Once the rendezvous was complete, Jackson's work would be done.

He didn't know that rendezvous was never to take place.

The shared glance ended. The three of them emptied their minds of the awesome view, the unaccustomed sensation of free fall, their own ethical qualms, and everything else except the establishment of concert.

Derek and Lauren had had time for a few introductory sessions. Rinnard was far more practiced, and so acted as the "director," to use Doctor Kronenberg's terminology. They opened their minds to him. A moment passed and Derek felt nothing. A curious mixture of disappointment and relief began to rise in him.

But then he sensed—"heard" was altogether the wrong word—Rinnard's wordless command. They focused their minds on Jackson, who had finished his report . . . and Derek began to feel the surge of augmented power.

They'd tried this kind of telepathic attack on each other in the Hole. No targeted individual had ever suffered more than a momentary wavering of concentration. But no one had ever been the target of a concert, as Jackson was now. The pilot wore a bewildered look for an instant, then slumped into unconsciousness.

Rinnard broke the concert. "I don't mind telling you, I don't like this part."

"It's necessary, Paul," Lauren reminded him. Derek thought her tone more tender than the circumstances absolutely required. "He can't be allowed to know what's about to happen. He'll come to after we're gone, with no lasting harm . . . and they'll have another mystery on their hands."

"I know, I know," admitted the fighter jock irritably. "I still don't have to like it. Although . . . God, did you feel that sensation? That flow of power? It was like—" Rinnard cut himself off with renewed irritation. "Well, let's get on with it. You say they're going to be shadowing all orbital flights."

"That's what Sophia told us. They just need to be certain this is the one with us aboard."

They reestablished the concert. Then they began to broadcast.

It was a truism of telepathy that a specific individual—the closer the better—had to be targeted for reception of thoughts. Normally, the same was true of the sending of thoughts to another, which in any case was an altogether chancier proposition, especially when the intended recipient was a non-telepath. It was, however, possible to project thoughts in "broadcast" or "global" mode, to anyone and everyone within range. But that range was reduced by an order of magnitude, as was the reliability. Carrying such a price tag, the technique had always seemed one of theoretical interest only, with no practical use.

But, then, no one had ever tried it in concert. . . .

They continued for a time that Derek could not measure precisely, for eating, drinking and use of the zero-gee toilet facilities were out of the question lest they disrupt the concert.

Just as Derek was beginning to feel impatient, Rinnard looked up from his trance of concentration, and the concert vanished. "We're starting to register an intermittent return," he said matter-of-factly.

Derek leaned forward and looked over Rinnard's shoulder at the radar screen. The fighter pilot had been sparing a small, tightly compartmentalized fraction of his attention from directing the concert and keeping half an eye on that screen. They hadn't expected a strong return, for whatever ECM technology the Khronuo used would be cranked up to maximum lest the ground-based radars tracking the spaceplane should detect the rendezvous that was about to take place. Nor were their expectations disappointed. Derek was amazed that Rinnard had been able to spot the blip, so faint and flickering it was. No long-range radar would have a prayer of picking it up.

"You were right Paul," breathed Lauren. "All the previous radar sightings took place because they allowed it."

"Yeah," Rinnard acknowledged absently. "Look at the range. They're matching orbits with us, smooth as silk."

The blip still hadn't firmed up when Derek, staring through the viewport, caught sight of something among the star-fields that didn't belong there: an artificial construct that did not come from the blue planet curving below. Unable to speak, he touched his two companions and pointed. They, too, fell silent.

It was hard to tell, in the absence of familiar nearby objects for comparison, but the object was clearly several times the size of the spaceplane, though too small for an interplanetary craft. Just as clearly, it was not designed for atmospheric transit—it was a stubby round-nosed cylinder. Derek decided it must be some kind of interorbital shuttle. It approached closer and closer with a series of short burns of its maneuvering thrusters. As the three of them crowded together to stare, it drew near enough for them to see that its bulbous nose was partly transparent . . . and to glimpse movement through it. Human movement. And what could only be human faces. The silence deepened as they continued to wait.

"Well," Derek finally got out, "at least they haven't got countermeasures against the Mark One Eyeball."

"Or maybe they're just not using them," Lauren cautioned.

The exchange seemed to break a spell, for they became aware that the radio was squawking demands for acknowledgment from Jackson. Rinnard switched it off. The silence resumed, and stretched. Rinnard broke it. "So now the problem becomes one of communication with . . . them."

"Sophia said that would be taken care of," Lauren assured him.

"But you said there are no telepaths among the, uh, Khronuo."

"No, just—"

Derek became aware that something wasn't right. He was still trying to analyze the sensation, or array of sensations— a disorientation beyond that of mere weightlessness, an odd quality to the lighting—when reality began to go wrong on a level below what could be described in the ordinary vocabulary of the senses.

"—just magicians," Lauren finished in a voice that frayed out into a near-hysterical quaver.

Then none of them could speak, or even think, for a state of dreamlike unreality took hold of their minds. . . .

Then it was gone. And so was the spaceplane.

They were still bunched together as they'd been in the cramped confines of the spaceplane, and still weightless, but now they floated in the center of a somewhat larger open space. To one side, a raised dais held a curving instrument panel—an oddly sparse-seeming one—and a semicircular transparency. It was, Derek knew, the transparency he'd been looking through from the spaceplane, across a few hundred meters of space. He knew because now he could look out through it and see the spaceplane among the stars.

To the other side was a double row of deeply cushioned

seats. The overall effect was one of high-tech austerity, as was only to be expected aboard a space vessel. Then, as one looked, the eye was drawn along curves and arcs and parabolas that didn't really have to be there for any utilitarian reason but which were *right* in a sense that transcended artistic conventions.

But, to be truthful, none of the three noticed any of this until later. All they saw were the people seated at the instrument panel and in the chairs.

They included both genders. Each was dressed in a form-fitting coverall, light tan or cream-colored, with a kind of sleeveless tunic—black, edged with various rich shades of brown, longer for the men than for the women—worn over it. Also common to men and women alike was long hair, generally dark, worn in a fairly elaborate style with braids hanging down in front of the ears and behind the head (two very long ones for the women, one thick ponytail for the men). The oldest-looking of the men—gray-haired, rather portly, and an altogether unlikely looking figure aboard a spacecraft—had a full beard, likewise gathered into a braid. And he wore a different style of clothing over the bodysuit: longer, with multiple folds, in lighter shades. That man stood up, stepped forward—evidently these people's footwear had magnetized soles—and spoke slow, careful English with an accent that did not belong to the repertoire of those familiar to twenty-first century Americans. "Welcome. My name is Urquiashqua. I apologize for any distress I may have caused you by the . . . calling. The entity you know as Sophia told us it is a spell with which you are not familiar. But a physical joining of our two craft would have taken time, and it is necessary that we depart for high orbit without delay."

"Why?" asked Lauren faintly.

"The ground-based telescopes tracking your craft could detect this one, but for a . . . distortion zone we have set up."

"Which our craft is inside, I suppose," said Rinnard with an insouciance Derek could only marvel at. "Otherwise we wouldn't have been able to see you."

"Yes. But it is not completely reliable. So we must not waste any more time. Please seat yourselves, and—"

"Wait just a goddamned minute!" Derek demanded. "How did you bring us here? We've experienced passage through the portals you can create, but what happened to us just now was nothing like that."

"You used the term 'calling,'" Lauren prompted.

"All to be explained in due course, by self and colleagues." Urquiashqua's English began to deteriorate as he ventured beyond his prepared speech. "But now must insist you departure prepare for."

"Let's do it," Rinnard said, and moved toward one of the chairs, accepting the assistance of the Khronuo personnel in zero-G maneuvering. The other two followed suit. A warning tone sounded, and the two men seated at the instrument panel—the pilot and copilot, Derek supposed—lowered openwork helmets over their heads.

Derek wondered what those helmets were for; they obviously provided no protection, and no one else donned them. The puzzle deepened when the Khronuo took up cables connected with their instrument panels and plugged them into sockets in the helmets.

It deepened even more when acceleration began to push him back into the cushions, without either of the crewmen touching anything. In fact, what they'd assumed was an instrument panel actually contained nothing but readouts.

He met his companions' eyes. They were obviously wondering too.

The mothership—Derek decided there was no alternative to calling it that—appeared in the forward wraparound transparency, and grew to a size impossible to estimate. It was shaped like a long, unbalanced dumbbell. What were obviously engines and their fuel tankage occupied one end. At the other was a sphere whose equatorial belt rotated slowly—a spin habitat, Rinnard speculated, mimicking gravity by angular acceleration.

The fighter jock's theory was confirmed after they boarded—by conventional means, this time—and passed through a hatch into a curving passageway that slid along past like a moving walkway in a large airport. There, the concepts of "up" and "down" reasserted themselves. They were ushered to a surprisingly spacious compartment that had the look of a lab or workroom. Urquiashqua proffered three small disc-shaped objects with adhesive backing, and three hearing-aidlike devices. At his direction, they attached the discs to their chests and inserted the earpieces—as he himself did with a fourth set. He then spoke in a wholly unfamiliar language.

"Is this better?" was what Derek heard in his left ear. In spite of himself, he jumped.

Urquiashqua smiled at their reactions. "It picks up the speech of whoever is wearing it, and transmits the translation," he explained, pointing at the disc on his own tunic. "I daresay everyone you'll be dealing with will be wearing them. We've been here long enough to program the interpreter software, but not long enough to actually learn the language ourselves . . . as I'm sure has been painfully obvious from my attempts."

Lauren took a deep breath. "Now maybe you can explain how you brought us aboard that shuttle."

Urquiashqua pursed his lips. "You were correct in surmising that it was not the kind of movement involving transdimensional portals which, once opened, must then be physically passed through. No, what you just experienced requires an altogether different spell, which entails bringing entities into the presence of the caster. Qualitatively very distinct, I assure you."

Just when I was getting used to this futuristic, ultra-high-tech setting, Derek groaned inwardly, *he has to go and say something like that!* Actually, to be precise, the interpreter device had said it. Presumably it had been programmed by people who assumed, as Sophia did, that words like "god" and "magic" and "spell" were required to convey the full freight of connotation.

"So you're the . . . magician around here?" Rinnard queried.

"Correct: the mage." Only a monosyllable of Urquiashqua's

native language had passed his lips. Clearly, the software was correcting Rinnard's usage on its own initiative.

"Then explain something. How come you made us wait so long before, uh, 'calling' us. Why didn't you just flick us over as soon as you got within range?"

It immediately became obvious that this was the wrong kind of question to ask Urquiashqua, for the mage visibly settled into lecturing mode. "Ah, well, the answer to that is inherent in certain fundamental theoretical considerations—"

"Which you can expound at another time, Urquiashqua," came a new voice from the interpreter earpieces—a different voice from the mage's, Derek noted, wondering how many voices the tiny disk could generate. It was a deep baritone that suited the man who had just emerged from a hatchway.

The new arrival was tall and powerfully built. He had a full beard, gathered into a ring like Urquiashqua's, but it was deepest black—he was somewhat younger than the magician, although Derek wasn't sure his familiar assumptions about apparent ages were applicable to these people. He was dressed in the same style as everyone else, but his tunic held a more formidable array of insignia. Indeed, the word "formidable" seemed functionally apt when describing him.

"I am Rhykhvyleshqua, captain of this vessel, the *Ergu Nervy*, and in overall command of our units in this system," he began. "And you are . . . ?"

As they introduced themselves, Derek wondered if he'd be able to get used to these names. He was later to learn that among the mainstream Khronuo cultures personal names were compound words, rather than combinations of discrete surnames and given names—a bit of knowledge that didn't make them any easier to deal with.

"I welcome you," said Rhykhvyleshqua when the introductions were complete, "in the name of Erkhedzye and its allies."

"Erkh—?" Rinnard began.

"Our nation, on Khron. One of the nations that have formed an alliance to resist the aggression of Qurvyshye.

But politics, like magical theory, can wait. We must depart at once."

"May we watch that, Captain?"

"Certainly, Lieutenant Rinnard." The interpreter software had already taught itself the name and rank, flawlessly overlaying Rhykhvyleshqua's halting pronunciation. "We anticipated that you might be interested, so seating was made available on the bridge."

They departed the spin habitat and proceeded forward to what the interpreter software termed the "bridge" to the delight of the two Navy men. A railed balcony overlooked an array of instrument panels, facing a hemispherical visual display which made the bridge seem open to the starfields. Already those stars were drifting past as the ship aligned itself. Alarms whooped, and a vibration ran through the decks as the spin habitat aft of them stopped spinning. They strapped themselves into cushioned seats.

"Captain, something we were wondering," said Rinnard, indicating the operators at the panels below. "What's the story on those helmets your people wear?"

"Our controls are based on direct neural interfacing with the ship's computer. Those helmets provide the connection. In effect, one simply *thinks* commands."

"Like the ship was your own body," said Rinnard, softly. His eyes held a faraway look.

"That is one way to describe it. It is a technology about which I believe your people have speculated."

"That's true," Derek acknowledged, "although to date speculation is all it's been."

Then the alarms took on a new timbre, and warnings filled the air. (Those warnings, Derek observed, were not interpreted by the device in his ear; the intercom, after all, did not wear one of the little discs.) Then acceleration commenced, and Derek had to fight down an odd feeling in himself as the blue curve of Earth began to fall away.

The bridge was so aligned that the deck was "down" when under acceleration. So they were able to move around normally in what seemed little more than one G. But it went on and on. "Captain," Lauren ventured, "we can't help being surprised at the duration of this high-thrust burn. We've always assumed that interplanetary drives would be characterized by low thrust to maximize fuel efficiency. Of course, I'm sure your drives are far more advanced than ours."

"So they are," Rhykhvyleshqua allowed. "In fact, they are based on mutual annihilation of matter and antimatter. But aside from that, at present we can afford the reaction mass. The portal is not far."

"So," said Rinnard quietly, "you're taking us directly to Khron?"

"Yes. As you have repeatedly heard, time is of the essence. We want you out of this system and under high security before the Qurvyshuo are aware of your presence among us. They, too, are very interested in your . . . unique abilities."

The Look again, Derek thought with an inward sigh, as he caught Rhykhvyleshqua's quick glance. "So we were given to understand," he said aloud.

"Yes, of course. Sophia would have told you."

Derek was beginning to master the trick of listening to the cybernetic interpreter while simultaneously hearing, with his other ear, what was actually coming out of the speaker's mouth. The name Rhykhvyleshqua had spoken sounded nothing like "Sophia." It was a little closer—but not identical—to what she'd been called, and worshiped as, when the Parthenon was new.

"I assume," the burly captain resumed, "she also explained to you what is at stake here."

"She did. That's why we consented to all this, despite the possible consequences. We are, after all, now AWOL." Derek trusted to the software's ability to handle that. "Granted, Sophia assured us that you would take us up under circumstances which were arguably not our fault, and inarguably beyond our power to resist—and you certainly did that."

"Still," said Lauren in a troubled voice, "even if our superiors never know that the 'abduction' was really done with our connivance, *we'll* still know it."

"I can respect that. Nevertheless, from what Sophia has

told you it must be clear to you that you are, in a larger
sense, acting to stop an ultimate threat to your own nation—
one it does not yet know exists."

"Yes, that's why we're here."

"Yeah," Paul Rinnard chimed in with an easy grin. "There's
an old saying: if you've got to fight a war, the place to do
it is somebody else's real estate."

His two companions sucked in their breath and held it.
But Rhykhvyleshqua's stern face slowly opened up into a
smile, like dark clouds parting. "Well put, Lieutenant. I
believe I like you. But now we need to prepare for transi-
tion. Urquiashqua is readying the necessary spell."

They strapped in as the big ship flip-flopped and began
to decelerate. Rhykhvyleshqua explained that this was necessary for precise control as the ship approached the portal into the Void domain the gods had provided for interstellar
transit. The hemisphere under which they sat continued to
display the view-forward. As they watched, a circular opening
appeared in the universe, defined by outflowing light as the
ship's mage opened it. It approached at a velocity that was
still several miles per second, a glowing hoop through which
the great ship was to jump.

Then they were through it. . . .

And stared madness full in the face.

Rhykhvyleshqua hastily barked a command, and the
viewscreen went dark. "I apologize," he said contritely to
his three badly shaken guests. "I forgot, because we ourselves have grown used to it. Are you all right? I will send
for medical personnel and—"

"No, no," Paul assured him, recovering first and straight-
ening out from the crouch of instinctive self-protection into
which he'd curled. "We're all right. It's just . . . just . . . ."

"Do not try to describe what you saw. It is indescribable
in any human language. This void domain is, in effect, a
universe of its own—a small infinity. The human mind is
unaccustomed to the presence of such a close event horizon. It is disturbing, on a very deep level. Do not be
embarrassed. Everyone reacts the same way at first. But are
you sure your companions are recovered?"

"Yeah . . . yeah . . ." Derek gasped, fighting to control the shudders that still ran through him. Lauren was still silent, hugging herself tightly. "We're fine."

"Good. We will be emerging shortly. The domain is not large."

The viewscreen now showed a comfortably abstract tactical display. Presently, a circle appeared on it, and grew. Then, as they passed through it, the visual display was restored and the universe reappeared—the universe as it was meant to be, with its starfields receding into illimitable sable depths. And dead ahead gleamed a blue marble such as the earliest moonflights had first revealed to Earthly humanity.

Derek half-opened his mouth to exclaim that something had gone wrong, that they had come full circle and returned to Earth.

But then he noticed, off to the side, the two small moons.

"Khron," said Rhykhvyleshqua. The interpreter earpiece remained silent.

CHAPTER TWELVE

Khron's similarity to Earth seemed remarkable, until one recalled that this very similarity was what had caused the gods to choose it as a reward for their human allies. It was almost identical to Earth in size and mass and, therefore, gravity. It orbited only a little closer to a sun only a little dimmer than Sol. (Lauren, who knew something about descriptive astronomy, spoke of a "late G-class star.") Its rotation period was only fractionally longer than twenty-four hours, nothing that couldn't be adjusted to. It was even cloaked by a lush biosphere with human-compatible chemistry—a truly rare coincidence, and the real reason the gods had needed to search so far afield.

There were, of course, differences. Some, like the presence of two small moons rather than one large one, were little more than matters of scenery. Closer to home, it possessed no polar ice caps, as Earth had not for most of its history; neither of its poles was covered by land or surrounded by it, as Earth's south and north poles respectively were in the present epoch, so the water circulated freely. Other dissimilarities were less agreeable. About half the total land area was locked up in a single vast continent called Loboye, filling almost a third of the tropics and extending far into the south temperate zone, its interior mostly deserts where the winds roamed for thousands of miles in a vain search for moisture. To the east of it, the smaller continent of Emetulye sprawled southeast-to-northwest from the middle latitudes of the south to those of the north. Northwest of Loboye, across a couple of thousand miles of water, lay Qurvyshye, a continent comparable to North America in size and latitude. The three major continents defined what was called the Central Sea, whose clockwise currents and prevailing winds brought southerly breezes and abundant rainfall to the islands that dotted its eastern half. Those islands, the dozen largest of which ranged from Sicily- to England-sized, had been the destination of the original Rhysqaruo arrivals—the closest thing to paradise the gods could provide. Today, they were still the destination of those in search of romantic ruins, dark mysterious old cities, haunted houses, the ambience of antiquity, and general "character." But over the millennia, economic and political power had migrated away to the continental land masses. Qurvyshye, for example—a continent now coterminous with a nation by reason of conquest. And a whole cluster of nations had grown up around an inland sea, the Nernere, near the northwestern end of the eastern continent of Emetulye. One of these was Erkhedzye, leader of the coalition that exchanged glares and snarls with Qurvyshye across the Central Sea.

"I've been wondering about that," said Rinnard in the shuttle taking the three new arrivals from Earth down to Bozemtoum, Erkhedzye's capital city. "Nukes must be old hat to you people—hell, I remember Rhykhvyleshqua saying something about antimatter. So how is it that your conflict here hasn't reduced this planet to a cinder?"

The question was addressed to Urquiashqua, who'd turned out to be a very highly regarded member of one of the institutes into which magical practitioners organized themselves, and was accompanying them down. "The question contains its own answer. The very destructiveness of the weapons precludes their use within the planet's atmosphere. Not even the nominal winner could escape devastation as long as both sides have a viable presence in orbit. So here on Khron, the conflict remains a low-grade one of espionage, subversion and minor proxy wars."

"Sounds familiar," said Derek. "Earth went through a stand-off like that in the last century, after the invention of nuclear weapons—the Cold War, it was called. The deadlock remained stable long enough for our own country's totalitarian opponent to die of sheer corruption and inefficiency."

"Regrettably, our 'Cold War' is inherently unstable. Both sides maneuver incessantly for advantage in space, for if either gained uncontested control of near-Khron orbit the other would have no alternatives other than surrender or extinction. And here the Qurvyshuo have an advantage."

"What advantage is that?" Lauren asked.

"As your own people have doubtless begun to understand, the key to a self-sustaining presence in space is making use of the resources that are available there—living off the land, as the military people would put it. From the earliest days of space flight, we have dreamed of utilizing magic for this purpose—spells powerful enough to demolish asteroids and moons for easy mining, or even alter their chemical composition. It has remained impractical, though, due to the limited amount of ambient quantum energy available in any given region. But the Titans have taught the Qurvyshuo rulers a way around this limitation. By their willingness to tap the internal quantum energy of others on a vast scale they are able to employ magics of an equally vast scale, providing the powerhouse of their space-based industrial and military machines."

"So," said Lauren bleakly, "magic has the effect of making totalitarianism a viable proposition."

"Sad but true—at least the way they practice it. Their system provides victims in abundance: political dissenters, conquered populations, ethnic undesirables, and all the rest that the totalitarian regimes of your own world have exterminated with such relish during the last century. The Qurvyshuo have found a *use* for mass murder."

"But," protested Rinnard, "they can't just go on killing everybody off! They'll run out of slaves!"

"At our technological level, slave labor is largely redundant. But in a sense, you are correct. They *are* beginning to come up against limits. They have had to implement various measures for . . . resource management. Forced overbreeding, for example, of the traditional sort. Human cloning is too expensive."

Derek felt ill in a way that had nothing to do with the bumpy reentry. Lauren looked even sicker than he felt. He though he heard an odd, low sound from deep in Paul's throat.

"Indeed, they have begun drawing more and more on their own people: voluntary sacrifices, driven by religious fanaticism. But this approach has obvious built-in limits. So they have begun to lose the momentum their ruthlessness initially gave them, and the struggle is settling into stalemate."

Which you're hoping we'll help you break, thought Derek.

Just then they passed through a final thin cloud layer, and Bozemtoum lay before them in the hazy afternoon sun, spreading crescentlike around the concavity of a bay at the foot of a range of hills. Soaring towers clustered near the bay, surrounded by suburbs nestled amid foliage, extending up into the hills. The shuttle banked in that direction, up a valley, and presently a landing field appeared.

Disembarking, they were taken in hand by people dressed in the style they'd observed aboard *Ergu Nervy* but with the addition of various weaponry and sensory enhancements. They hardly noticed as they stepped onto the soil of an extrasolar planet and let its wholeness take them. Nothing so gross as differences in gravity and air pressure and distance to the horizon—those were actually so slight as to be imperceptible. No, it was a subtle difference in the quality of the light, a very faint pervasive aroma that wasn't really like honeysuckle at all but could be compared with nothing else, a faint bluish overlay in the green of some but not all of the vegetation. . . .

The security types conducted them to a vehicle clearly related to the wingless vertols that Earth's more affluent military forces were beginning to employ for specialized tasks—although Rinnard opined that the relationship was like that of an F-39 to Von Richtofen's flying circus. It whined aloft and shaped a course for a hill seemingly standing sentry duty at the mouth of the valley. The top of that hill was flatter than nature could account for.

Urquiashqua pointed out a sprawling collection of buildings that crowned the hill, ringed by what were obviously weapon emplacements despite the unfamiliarity of the weapons they mounted. "It is known as the Citadel—the headquarters of the Erkhedzuo military," he informed them as their carrier settled onto a circular landing pad.

The hilltop commanded quite a view—the towers of Bozemtoum were visible in the eastward distance, with the Nernere Sea beyond, while in the opposite direction the westering sun hung over the gently rounded ridgeline of a low mountain range. But they were allowed no time to appreciate it before being hustled inside. A bewildering route, including a long descent by elevator, brought them into a vast chamber lined with work stations and view screens, evidently a command center.

A daunting array of VIPs awaited them. Many were dressed in what was evidently the Erkhedzuo military style, like what they'd seen aboard the spaceship but without the skintight body suit, which they'd learned was a light-duty vac suit. Others wore uniforms similar in style but differing in color and insignia; these proved to be officers of allied nations like Lodye, Kherye, and various islands of the Central Sea that Erkhedzye had taken under its wing. Still others wore civilian garb like Urquiashqua's, which differed only minimally by gender.

But Derek noticed none of this after spotting one particular tall female figure in civvies.

"Sophia!" he exclaimed, and began to step forward—only to stop short as it occurred to him that he might have committed a *faux pas*. The name, after all, might not be the appropriate one by which to address her in this place. *And besides,* he thought, *with her I should maybe act a little more . . . well, formal.*

But then he noted that none of the Erkhedzuo seemed to be displaying any awe or unease in her presence—they must be accustomed to gods walking among them. And Sophia herself favored him with her serene smile.

"Greetings Derek, Lauren. And you must be Lieutenant Rinnard. I am glad to finally make your acquaintance."

"Likewise," Paul mumbled, uncharacteristically short on badinage. He knew what Sophia was, and hadn't had his companions' opportunity to adjust to it.

"And now, let us finish the introductions," said Urquiashqua briskly. He seemed even less intimidated than his compatriots by Sophia's presence. "We have much work to do. Using direct neural interfacing technology, we should be able to study your abilities to a far greater depth than your own researchers have been able to plumb. In particular, we want to investigate a possibility of which those researchers have never dreamed: the degree to which psionically talented individuals can tap their own internal quantum energy for magical purposes without the usual hazards."

More studies, Derek thought grumpily. *Am I going to spend the rest of my life getting poked and prodded? It's getting pretty damned—*

"Here is my assistant Nydierya," continued the mage, ushering a young woman forward, "who will be taking an active role in the tests."

—pretty damned interesting, all of a sudden, Derek completed his thought, gawking.

Nydierya was unexpectedly young, and unusually fair for a Khronuo human, with wavy dark-blond hair whose color was matched by her eyes of deep, glowing amber. You could lose yourself in those huge, perfectly shaped eyes—indeed, they could almost make you ignore the perfection of the rest of her features. They could not make you ignore her figure.

The great golden eyes remained on him while Urquiashqua was introducing him, just long enough for him to receive their full impact. Then they swung away, settled on Paul Rinnard . . . and stayed there.

"Ah, Lieutenant Rinnard!" The English-language contralto the interpreter generated for Nydierya was pleasant enough, but her own natural voice turned her native language into a symphony of background music for it. "I have requested to be assigned to work with you on an individual basis. Closely."

Rinnard was immediately himself again. He gave his copyrighted lazy grin. "I'm deeply flattered, ma'am. I hope not to disappoint."

"I'm sure you won't." Nydierya's smile went up to what surely had to be full power.

Why am I even surprised? Derek sighed inwardly.

He stole a glance at Lauren. She didn't seem to be taking it quite as philosophically as he was.

Over the course of the next few weeks, they learned something of magic, and how it worked.

"You talk about 'spells,'" said Derek on one occasion. "And yes, I know, that's just what the interpreter software is programmed with. But do you really, well, say some kind of magic words, and draw pentagrams in the dirt, and burn incense?"

"Not as often as we used to," smiled Urquiashqua. Derek and Lauren were sitting in his office in the Citadel, deep within the bowels of the hollowed-out hill. A wall that was a 3-D screen that let them view the valley and the distant city by the sea as though the hill hadn't been there. "Nowadays, we tend to be more intellectualized about it. But ritual activity in the broad sense is still essential, even if it has come to take more abstract forms. It is a way of inducing a heightened mental state."

"So there's nothing, uh, magical about any one particular style of doing it?"

"No, there isn't," admitted Urquiashqua after a perceptible pause, "although many of my colleagues would be scandalized to hear it. You see, tradition is *very* strong in the Institutes, though intellectually every mage knows that the same sort of effects can be obtained in various ways. It's all a means to the end of creating conditions under which the ambient quantum energy can be organized and focused for a particular purpose."

"'Whatever works,' as people say," observed Derek.

Lauren ignored his attempt at flippancy. She leaned forward

in her earnest way. "Does this relate to why it took so long for you to 'call' us from the spaceplane?"

"Very astute, Lauren. Yes, magic takes an extended period of concentration. And the more complex, difficult and spectacular it is, the longer it takes. Actually, that didn't take long at all; it involved only three subjects, whom I could see through the canopy of your craft, and the distance was not great, and—"

"Still, we tend to have this mental picture of a sorcerer just pointing his hand and—*zap!*"

"No, it doesn't normally work that way. There is, however, one exception. Quick magical results of the sort you envision can be obtained by employing the tapping technique—immorally if tapping others, or dangerously if doing it to oneself."

"Yes, Sophia has explained it to us." Lauren looked even more thoughtful. "So I begin to understand why you're so interested in us: you think we can 'tap' ourselves without danger."

"Without unacceptable danger, yes." Derek silently noted Urquiashqua's qualifier. "We mean to explore this possibility—with great care, of course, to avoid endangering you by . . . by . . ."

"Pushing the envelope," Derek supplied.

Urquiashqua nodded, leaving Derek struck anew by the interpreter device's flexibility. "Precisely. After all, it is only by sheer coincidence that a psi will also possess inherent magical talent."

"So this 'magical talent' is a genetic trait, like psi power?" Derek queried.

"It is, but with this difference: *anyone* can learn magic. Anyone, that is, with the intelligence, motivation and self-discipline to pursue a highly demanding field of study. Those who lack the inherent gift will do so at a considerable disadvantage, which is why in practice hardly any of them ever try—but it can, in theory, be done. Not like your psionic abilities, which absolutely require the genetic predisposition. Actually, it is those psionic abilities that I am most interested in."

"Oh?" Lauren cocked her head.

Urquiashqua leaned back in his chair and settled into lecturing mode, as he often did when there wasn't some practical type like Rhykhvyleshqua around to bring him up short. "As you seem to already understand, magic and psionics both involve the exploitation of quantum energy to alter reality. It is therefore no surprise that there is a great deal of overlap in the effects they can achieve. Not complete overlap, of course, but considerable. And while magic can, given time, tap far greater power, there is a flexibility about your ability to attain quick results."

"But," Derek ventured, "how useful can it be? According to Sophia, the aptitude simply doesn't exist among your people."

"For perfectly sound evolutionary reasons," Urquiashqua confirmed with a nod. "Regrettably, that is true. Still, I believe there is much to be learned from studying the . . . interface, if you will, between psionics and magic. Particularly interesting are the psionic power of telepathy and projection."

"We've never been able to do anything with those," Lauren cautioned.

"Using our neural induction technology," said Urquiashqua complacently, "it should be possible to gain a more complete understanding of their nature than you have heretofore—and, perhaps, put them to practical use."

"Paul will be excited," said Derek. "He's always been eager to try those out."

"Yes," said Lauren. "Too bad he's not here to be hearing this."

Derek gave her a sharp look, for her voice seemed to hold an undercurrent of something indistinguishable from resentment. It was true, though: they hadn't been seeing much of Rinnard lately. He was almost always with Nydierya.

CHAPTER THIRTEEN

At least there were none of the drugs Derek had grown so sick of at JICPO. Instead, there were the neural induction helmets, painless and noninvasive.

And it had the effect Urquiashqua had hoped for. He soon confirmed Doctor Kronenberg's belief that all three of them possessed powers beyond telepathy. Armed with his findings, they were able to bring the mental techniques they'd learned to bear on those powers.

Derek's first teleportation wasn't too bad. It was only a few yards. But instantaneously, without even the passage of the proverbial split second, he was looking at the room from a different angle. And then came his first jump from one room to another. To his eyes, the first room simply vanished, to be replaced by another. That took some getting over.

Lauren muttered darkly about conservation of energy, and predicted dire consequences if they were to teleport any distance on the surface of Khron or any other rotating planet. Urquiashqua pooh-poohed it, saying that the Void acted as a sump for the energy differentials involved. He only made the observation offhandedly, though; he was far too excited about the theoretical implications of what was coming to light.

He grew even more excited after their first successful attempts at projection.

To Derek, it was less startling than teleportation but even more unsettling.

He wasn't even aware it was happening, at first. But then he saw himself, sitting in the comfortable chair he'd been provided for the experiment. And then he yielded to something like vertigo, before snapping back into his accustomed corporeal housing.

Afterwards, they learned to deal with being a disembodied viewpoint, able to observe the material world whose denizens could not see them, moving at the speed at which their physical bodies could walk or run—apparently because that was the rate at which their minds were programmed to handle the sensation of personal movement. So, at least, ran Urquiashqua's theory.

By then, Urquiashqua had quite a few theories.

"The degree of overlap between psionic and magical effects is becoming clearer," he told an attentive audience in a large, circular chamber atop one of the towers of central Bozemtoum. "And we now have a sufficiently large statistical universe for us to venture some generalizations."

His listeners leaned forward expectantly. Their average age was greater than his, for these were elders of the Lokhyoum Institute, to which he belonged—and also of other magical institutes, invited here in a rare gesture of inter-institutional collegiality. (Mages, it seemed, were a prickly lot.) Derek had quickly given up trying to remember their names. They sat at a long crescent-shaped table, at whose focus Urquiashqua stood at a lectern facing them. The three Americans sat behind him, wearing Erkhedzuo uniforms with the insignia of the courtesy ranks they'd been granted—equivalent, they were assured, to their U.S. ones. Nydierya sat with them—beside Rinnard, naturally.

During the preliminaries, Derek's attention had wandered to the wide-curving windows behind the table, around two-thirds of the room's circumference. Those windows overlooked the awesome cityscape of mile-high towers, rainbow-tinted from the artificial diamondlike structural materials that enabled them to soar so impossibly. This was the first time Derek and his companions had been brought to the city itself, and his ability to absorb unfamiliar sights was suffering from overload. But now that Urquiashqua was getting down to business, he perked up along with the dignitaries at the table.

"To begin, there is no magical equivalent of telepathy or extra-sensory perception—although there are any number of spells aiming at alteration of others' thought-patterns, as the Khorum Institute is well aware," Urquiashqua added with an inclination of his head toward a gaunt woman representing that institute, which specialized in mental control. "At the same time, psionics encompasses nothing comparable to the spells dealing with such matters as temporal distortion and transmutation of elements." Further nods to other big-deal mages. "No, the overlap of which I speak occurs in the areas covered by the psionic powers of telekinesis, projection and teleportation. Here, magic and psionics can produce the same results, albeit by different means.

"There are, however, curious differences between teleportation and instantaneous transit via the portals with which we are familiar. The former involves the exchange of that segment of reality containing the teleporter with another segment of equal volume somewhere else. And it can be used *anywhere,* although we have yet to learn its maximum possible range. On the other hand, the equivalent magical spell—and the comparable power possessed by the gods—opens a portal through which one must physically pass . . . although *anyone* can so pass as long as the portal remains open. And, as we are all aware, the actual *creation* of new portals is difficult. The Qurvyshuo have been doing so from one point of the material world to another, enabling them to move about on Earth; presumably they have been tapping local victims to provide themselves with the quantum energy to do so. Equally difficult is eliminating one." Derek nodded unconsciously, remembering the visible effort slamming a portal shut had cost Sophia. "And, of course, creating a new portal from the Void is possible only for the gods, while creating a portal *to* it from the material world, while theoretically possible for an extremely powerful mage, has never actually done and is believed to be, as a practical matter, impossible."

A rustle of shifting and throat-clearing ran around the table. Once Urquiashqua got up a head of lecturing steam, he saw no reason to deny himself the joy of imparting information just because his audience happened to already know it. The Grand Pooh-Bah (or whatever) of the Lokhyoum Institute cleared his throat with especial loudness. "This is all very interesting, Urquiashqua. But as to the 'generalizations' you mentioned earlier . . . ?"

"Ah! Well, the full statistical abstract of my team's findings is available for everyone's perusal. But in plain language, I believe psionics is inherently *personal* to the user in a way that magic is not. This should come as no surprise, given its essential nature; and it accounts for the fact that psis do not require the kind of highly structured mental ritual that is, as a practical matter, essential to magic. But the peculiarities—from our standpoint—of psionic teleportation confirm it.

"However, what is *really* interesting is the insight our research has given us on the nature of the Void. We have been able to build on the work of . . . What was the name of your chief researcher again?"

"Doctor Kronenberg," Derek supplied.

"Yes, of course. I wish it were possible for me to meet her!"

"You'd like her," Rinnard said, deadpan.

"I'm sure I would. But now, let me turn the presentation over to my assistant."

Nydierya rose from her seat and took Urquiashqua's place at the lectern. Derek noted with amusement the reaction of the mages . . . at least the male ones. *No surprise,* he thought. *In fact, in her case the* lack *of that reaction would have been a surprise. These guys may be old, but they're not dead!* Lauren was being studiously expressionless.

"Doctor Kronenberg has correctly deduced that teleportation involves transference through the Void," Nydierya began in her subliminally thrilling contralto, "although she doesn't call it that, and indeed knows nothing of its nature. For her it is simply a mathematical abstraction—something whose existence she has had to infer in order to account for the observed facts. She has also groped at the connection between the Void and projection. But we, unlike her, have been able to observe the technique in actual operation—in both its magical and psionic manifestations. This has enabled us to confirm and refine certain hypotheses.

"Briefly, it appears that projection—whether achieved by psionic or magical means—involves a kind of interface zone between the Void and the material universe, which we have labeled 'the Outer Void' for convenience. It can be psychically entered in realtime, being closest to the material universe. This psychic presence is difficult to maintain—again, we believe, because of the same proximity. Of course, 'proximity' in this context is a question-begging term. The dimensional interrelationships involved require a special mathematics to describe them—"

"A mathematics in whose development Nydierya has been instrumental," Urquiashqua interrupted in an effusion of something resembling parental pride.

Beauty and brains both, thought Derek wistfully. *Not to mention a name with only three syllables!*

"In contrast to the Outer Void," Nydierya resumed, "is the 'Inner Void,' to which the gods are native. Time and distance are essentially meaningless there—except in the gods' domains, where they have imposed those concepts along with so much else. Hence the instantaneous nature of teleportation.

"No one has been able to reach the Inner Void by psionic projection . . . not even Lieutenant Rinnard." Nydierya turned briefly and flashed Rinnard a dazzling smile over her shoulder. "There are, however, recorded cases of extremely powerful mages entering it. Once there, the psychic presence can be sustained indefinitely. But there is little point in doing so, as the material world cannot be observed from it. And the projected consciousness apparently cannot access the domains; only the amorphous 'undeveloped' regions of the Inner Void can be so entered. The disembodied viewpoint finds itself suspended in an infinity of what the human mind interprets as swirling, glowing chaos."

An exceptionally old mage cleared his throat and addressed Urquiashqua directly, bypassing Nydierya, who presumably was too young and too junior—and, maybe, too female, although they'd seen no evidence of gender discrimination among the Khronuo. "These remarks on what you have labeled the 'Inner Void' merely restate the conventional wisdom."

"So they do," Urquiashqua admitted. "But they form a necessary foundation for certain conclusions we have reached regarding the Outer Void. In particular, we believe we have obtained new insights into certain attributes of the gods."

That got everyone's attention. Derek found his own interest stirring as well, for he'd never been entirely clear on the nature of the relationship between the gods and their human protégés on Khron. It must, he thought, be one whose terms were set by the gods. And the gods, as Sophia had remarked, liked their privacy. But the Khronuo bore the genetic heritage of Earth's insensately curious primates. The eager way the mages now leaned forward spoke eloquently of that.

Urquiashqua resumed the lectern, now even more in his element. "As we are all aware," he began, oblivious to winces and sighs and low groans, "the gods lack the human ability to perform magic. Rather, they possess certain fixed, innate powers—formidable but strictly delimited—which exploit quantum energy in ways that seem magical. Most of these can be best understood within the contest of the gods' fundamental nature as beings of . . . of . . ."

"Quantum energy with attitude," Rinnard suggested.

Some of the mages looked scandalized—whether at the interruption or the irreverence was impossible to tell. Others seemed to be suppressing smiles with difficulty. Urquiashqua started out in the first camp, then defected to the second. "That is one way to put it. I am thinking specifically of the ability to seemingly assume an insubstantial form, in which they can move in a manner analogous to levitation, and pass freely through material barriers." Derek recalled his grandfather's empty guest bedroom, and Sophia's sudden appearance at his shoulder in the beleaguered restaurant in Athens. But then Urquiashqua resumed.

"We have always believed—a belief the gods have never confirmed or denied—that this is a specialized variant on their shape-shifting ability. Our remote ancestors on Earth assumed that they took on 'bodies of mist.' More recently, we have had to come up with increasingly tortured rationales to sustain that theory, which requires interpenetration of matter. Now, however, we have concluded that 'insubstantiality' is a misnomer, and that what we are really seeing is a *physical* entry into the Outer Void, of a sort which cannot be achieved by either magic or psionics. In essence, a god who appears to be passing through a wall is in fact going *around* it via the additional dimension that is the Void. Likewise, the levitationlike phenomenon can be best understood as a sustained succession of very tiny teleports which—unlike psionic teleportation or displacement via portals—involves the Outer Void. And finally—" Urquiashqua paused to savor the sight of his audience collectively leaning even further forward "—it appears that this same power is what enables the gods to open portals. Presumably it is also related to their ability to create new portals from the Void; why it will not function in this manner in the material universe is a question that must await the accumulation of additional data."

After a moment, the head of Urquiashqua's institute spoke ponderously. "You have certainly given us food for thought—you and your lovely assistant. We will need time to digest these findings. I propose that we reconvene tomorrow at the same time. In the meantime, I hope our guests won't mind remaining here in the city overnight."

Rinnard exchanged a glance with Nydierya. "I think we can manage it, sir," he said, all noble resolution.

Just north of central Bozemtoum, and separated from it by a low ridge like a Swiss cheese of tunnels, was the district of Quire, a place of specialty shops, taverns and restaurants, suffused with a flavor that Paul Rinnard thought of as "Bohemian" although the word was of course unknown on Khron. It was a flavor that, to him, stood in appealing contrast to the overpowering techno-wonderland that was

Bozemtoum. At Quire's northern margin the land rose again, and there tall modern towers had begun to encroach.

The restaurant Nydierya had suggested was atop one of those towers. They ate at a private table on a southward-facing balcony, in the warm evening. The view, thought Paul, was magnificent. Their balcony overlooked the narrow crooked streets and colorful plazas of Quire, with a seawall and a small beach off to the left. To the south rose the slender towers of Bozemtoum; beyond them, the coast curved away, dwindling into the haze of distance, while the Nernere Sea extended to the eastern horizon.

The Rhysqaruo who'd passed through the gods' portals to this world had brought some of their familiar plants and animals, and most of these had found niches in Khron's friendly ecosystem. One result was a cuisine which combined ingredients familiar to Paul but prepared in unfamiliar ways, and the wholly exotic. Their meal was no exception . . . or, rather, was exceptional only in its superb quality. As they ate, the city lights began to twinkle to life with the onset of twilight. By the time the after-dinner drinks had arrived, the few clouds had lost the pinkness of sunset and the stars were beginning to appear, along with a sickle of moon. They lingered over the brandy as the cityscape became a blaze of light that couldn't quite banish the strange constellations above— stars never even glimpsed from Earth, more light-millennia distant than anyone had ever calculated. Among them were swiftly moving artificial intruders: satellites, many of them armed. The thought of those armaments reminded Paul of what he'd been able to forget for a time, as he often did in Nydierya's company. The second moon rose, but now he thought not of a sickle but of a scimitar-blade.

He drained his snifter—oddly but pleasingly shaped, to his eyes—and leaned back with a sigh. "It seems so peaceful. Perfect, even. Hard to believe there's a war on."

"A very low-grade war, here on Khron . . . so far." Nydierya frowned. She even did *that* beautifully, Paul thought. "If all-out fighting ever comes to the surface of Khron, then all this will die."

Paul shivered in the warm evening as he imagined a

lifeless hell under a sky dark with radioactive ash, and evil mushroom clouds looming on the horizon—the chiliastic vision that had haunted his culture throughout the last half of the last century, and which had yet to be altogether exorcized. He touched a glowing finger-tab on the tabletop to signal for another round. It soon arrived, brought by a live human waiter—this was an expensive place. "What is it about this nation of, uh, Qurvyshye anyway? Why are they working for the Titans?"

The tabletop lamp's soft light was insufficient to make out Nydierya's expression. "Qurvyshye has a distinct identity—a somewhat eccentric one. You see, this world was settled gradually. The first wave, which left Earth before Rhysqarye had sunk, established the basic cultural template. They had thousands of years in which to increase their numbers, spread over the planet, and assimilate the later arrivals who came incrementally."

"I suppose that's why, even though you have a lot of distinct nations and ethnicities by now, you've still got one common language."

"Precisely. But then came the final wave, at the very end of Earth's Bronze Age, a little over three thousand of your years ago."

"Yeah, this has all been explained to me. After that, the gods slammed the door."

"Yes. Those people were the last group of humans on Earth who had any realization of their ultimate Rhysqaruo heritage. But their ancestors had mingled with the Indo-European invaders in the Aegean area, giving birth to the tribes you know as the Achaeans who sacked Troy, and the Sea Peoples who tried to sack Egypt and, failing, settled in the Levant and became the Philistines. So read the Iliad and the Old Testament, and you'll get an idea of what kind of people came out of that cauldron of blended blood: warlike, brave, ruthless and proud. Very, very proud."

"You know a lot about our history," said Paul. "A hell of a lot more than I do, I have to admit. Not that that's saying much."

"Most of us don't. It is only recently that we have, you

might say, rediscovered Earth. I just happened to have made a study of our expeditions' findings."

"To prepare yourself for working with us, right? Very professional."

"Yes, it was that way at first. Now, of course, I have more personal reasons."

Paul had gotten so used to the interpreter software that a second passed before he realized Nydierya's last sentence had been spoken in charmingly accented English. He reached across the table, touched her hand, and spoke certain words of Khron's common tongue that she'd taught him in bed. She drew back with a smiling demureness that neither convinced nor was intended to convince.

"As I was saying," she resumed with an attempt at seriousness, "that last wave were assimilated like their predecessors, at least to the extent of adopting the common tongue. But there was something different about them—everyone recognized it, including themselves. They gravitated toward the thinly settled northwest continent, where they became the Qurvyshuo. They never entirely lost their distinct character over the next three thousand years. They've always had a reputation for being . . . well, militaristic and humorless, but efficient and generally formidable. I'm sure you have national and ethnic stereotypes on Earth as well."

"God, yes! Even regional ones, within the nations. Remind me to tell you about it sometime. I'm from the southern United States, you see, and—"

"But you must understand, they've never considered themselves evil."

"Nobody does."

Nydierya seemed to sense his sudden seriousness. She gave him a cool regard. "Would it surprise you to know that I am one-quarter Qurvyshuo on my mother's side?"

Paul paused only momentarily, then reached for his brandy. "Frankly, it would, a little. Partly because you couldn't be less like this image of grim fanaticism, but mostly because you're in such a highly sensitive position with the Rhysqaruo government. Just as we've got stereotypes on Earth, I'll bet you've got security clearances on Khron!"

Her expression showed that the software had conveyed his, thus confirming his assumption of the concept's familiarity. "Yes. But Urquiashqua wanted me on the project—I'm a protégée of his in the Lokhyoum Institute."

Paul kept forgetting that she was a magician—no, a *mage*. It seemed incongruous that she should be—except, of course, in the immemorial female way of magic. . . . He applied the brakes to that train of thought. "Well, I owe him one big one for bringing you in! Hey, speaking of which, do you think you could put in a word with him about my request?"

"Request? Oh, yes, I remember: you want to be allowed to pilot an aircraft using direct neural induction."

"Yeah! It must be beyond anything . . ." Paul's voice trailed off, and his eyes focused somewhere beyond the horizon. But then, with a sudden intensity that had ceased to surprise Nydierya, he leaned forward in a way some people thought was premeditated and done for effect. Actually, it wasn't. He really didn't know how much, with his dark curve-nosed features and peaked black brows over light-hazel eyes, he suggested a bird of prey. "Say, you remember what I told you about the psionic technique Doctor Kronenberg calls a 'concert'?"

"Why, yes. It's the way you and your friends were able to signal our ship in orbit around Earth."

"Right. Well, this talk about your direct neural induction technology got me to thinking. . . ."

"Yes?"

Paul seemed to be arranging his thoughts. "The technique permits levels of power beyond that of the most psionically capable member of the concert—the 'director.' This suggests to me that individual psionic power isn't an absolute upper limit. Doctor Kronenberg agrees—she keeps fiddling with the drugs used to awaken latent psi powers, trying to come up with variants that can *enhance* those powers, or even confer them on non-psis." He stopped suddenly, and gave the self-deprecatory grin that, Nydierya thought, was so practiced it had actually become sincere. "Not that I know anything about the underlying theory of course—never could cope with math, you know. But

I can't help thinking . . . if those helmets you people use can allow direct electronic—or 'psychotronic' we should maybe call it—interaction with the brain, maybe they could be modified to—"

"Yes!" With an abruptness that startled him, Nydierya leaned forward and grasped his left forearm in a grip of surprising strength. Her amber eyes gleamed in the flickering light. "Of course! A psionic amplifier! It's so obvious! Why hasn't anyone thought of that before?"

"Well, you people have only just become aware of psionics, and our psionic researchers have never dreamed of psychotronics," Paul said reasonably. There was something unsettling about her excitement—a febrile quality. He wasn't sure he liked it. "So of course it never occurred to anybody on either side. It took—"

"It took *you.*" The amber eyes now held a softer glow—one Paul knew well. *That's more like it,* he thought. But the quivering, trembling undercurrent was still there.

"Hey, I don't know if this will even work," he cautioned.

"We'll find out soon enough, now that we can put the specialists to work on it. And if it does . . . Paul, I know enough about neural induction technology to know it's not subject to many of the inherent limitations of the biotechnic dodges your people on Earth have experimented with. If it works at all—and I have a strong feeling that it will—then there are, at least in theory, no limits."

"No limits," Paul repeated softly. All at once, he caught her vison, and they were one in a way they had never been even in the most exalted intertwinings of their bodies. "No limits," he repeated, and grasped both her hands.

It was fully dark now, and despite the city lights the night was ablaze with an infinity of stars. In unspoken unison, they looked up and surveyed the universe.

CHAPTER FOURTEEN

Derek stood on the balcony overlooking the lab, leaning on the rail and watching Paul Rinnard pop back into the universe, still wearing the silvery headpiece.

Urquiashqua stood beside him, staring intently at a set of readouts and frowning. Derek stole a peek over his shoulder, and his jaw dropped.

"That far? He teleported *that* far?"

He wondered why he was so shocked. It was merely the usual sort of results Rinnard had been getting with the psionic amplifier. The usual teleportation ranges, the usual telepathic precision . . .

"Yes." Urquiashqua's frown intensified. "This has become . . . unsettling. For now, at least, the power-damping feature must remain in place."

"Paul will be disappointed."

The tests had been run on all three of them, of course. But—equally of course—Rinnard himself had provided the most precise calibrations and the most spectacular results. So much so, in fact, that the experimenters had soon built in some highly restrictive safety cutoffs.

Derek gave the mage a quizzical look. "Are you still disappointed, Urquiashqua?"

"Disappointed?"

"That the psionic amplifier can do nothing to enhance innate *magical* aptitude." That point had been settled almost at once, after the first working model of the device had been put into operation.

"Actually, I never was all that disappointed. Oh, granted, the possibility occurred to me the instant I had Rinnard's idea explained to me—"

"Yes, I remember. It was the argument you used to sell the idea to the establishment."

"True," Urquiashqua smiled. "In the end, though, I wasn't too surprised when all attempts to use the device as a magical amplifier came to grief on the fundamental nature of magic. The talent for using disciplined mental effort to harness the quantum energy that pervades any area where the gods are active is an all-or-nothing proposition: either you have it or you don't. It's really more an intellectual predisposition than anything else."

And, thought Derek, in his heart of hearts the mage was more pleased than not by the confirmation of his own theory about the impersonal nature of magic, as opposed to psionics. And the chimerical hope of enhanced magical empowerment had served its purpose by securing the kind of blank-check backing which got the fighter pilot's brainstorm transformed into hardware in record time.

"Psionics, though, is intensely personal," Urquiashqua went on. "*That* aptitude is a specific genetic complex, integral to the interrelationship of a psi's brain and its own self-generated quantum energy. And the very first time a surge of power was sent through a neural-interface helmet that was specific to that particular neural function, the accuracy of Paul Rinnard's intuition stood confirmed."

"Especially in the case of Paul himself."

Urquiashqua smiled, correctly interpreting the undertone in Derek's voice. "You've participated in the tests as well, to the not inconsiderable best of your ability."

And so he had. He'd felt the indescribable surge, physically manifested in longer teleports and more spectacular teleki-netic manifestations, even at the stringently damped-down levels at which he knew the device was being operated. Of course, he understood that the enhancement represented a factor of the psi's normal powers, so he still couldn't expect to equal a psionic Godzilla like Paul Rinnard. Only in projection was he even close to being the fighter jock's equal. But he'd accepted this, and done his best to appreciate the rapid intensification of his own powers—powers that were already close to the maximum of the human race.

In the meantime, he's been coping as best he could with the change in Lauren's attitude.

Around her, he'd always felt himself locked into a frustrating, almost humiliating second-best status. Oh, she'd always been comradely, even friendly. Indeed, she'd even seemed to find him attractive . . . whenever Paul wasn't around. These days, Paul was hardly ever around. But her behavior was beyond that which the fighter jock's mere absence could normally account for. Now, for the first time, she was . . . well, coming on to him, and in a way that was so awkward as to suggest something like desperation.

Derek wasn't really unsophisticated, at least for his age. He was not unacquainted with the concept of "rebound romance," nor was he so high-principled as to be above taking advantage of the phenomenon when the opportunity—dare one say it?— reared its head. He was, if the truth be known, no less sexually opportunistic than most other men in their early twenties. It goes with the territory, as does being a closet romantic, and only idealogues see a contradiction between the two.

He was, nonetheless, capable of finding Lauren's behavior disturbing.

He finally got up the courage to ask her about it, one night in their quarters in the Citadel.

They were in a post-coital languor which, he thought, would insulate their new-found intimacy against any defensiveness she might feel. For once, this was not an illusion. Her rather stocky but pleasingly curved body stiffened only slightly in his arms, and she voiced only the most perfunctory denials before turning away and speaking in a low, toneless voice.

"I'm frightened."

It was perhaps the last thing he'd expected to hear. "Frightened? Of what? Of *Paul*?"

"No . . . Well, yes, in a way. Of what Paul is becoming." She rolled over to face him in the dimness. "Haven't you noticed that we hardly ever see him any more?"

"Well," Derek ventured, "I know he spends a lot of time with Nydierya these days—"

"That's *not* what I mean!" Her protest was, he thought in the wake of the Bard, just a little too vehement—but he decided no useful purpose would be served by saying so. At any rate, she seemed to sense it herself, for she took a deep breath and spoke in a self-consciously quieter voice. "It really is not that. In fact, I'd feel better if I thought they were spending all their time . . . doing what you're thinking. No, I believe he's being seduced in another way."

It wouldn't, Derek thought rather sullenly, have taken all that much effort on her part to say it didn't matter to her—not *now*. She could even have summoned up a rapturous tone of voice if she'd really tried. But no such avowal—rapturous or otherwise—seemed forthcoming, so he contented himself with a simple "What do you mean?"

"Remember what we've been told about how the Titans turned the Qurvyshuo into their pawns?"

"Oh, yeah." Since coming to Khron, they had learned the details of the generalized tale Sophia had told them in the magically-charged ruins of Mycenae. "The Qurvyshuo leader, uh, Lokhvyrgashqua, who allied himself with the Titans, was trying to unify the continent of Qurvyshye. They offered him the means to do it." Sheer revulsion stopped Derek short of mentioning the nature of those means. "Anyway, he seems to have been the kind of clever guy who was so used to manipulating everybody around him that he was sure he could manipulate the Titans. In the end, of course, it was the other way around. But what does all this have to do with Paul?"

"Haven't you sensed it? He's getting intoxicated with the rush that enhanced power gives him. I could see it even when we were acting as a concert with him as director. But now, with this amplifier . . ."

"Hey, that's just the way he is! Remember, he's a jet pilot— a *Navy* jet pilot, and they've always been a special breed. And anyway, to repeat, what does the history of Qurvyshye have to do with him? He's working for the good guys!"

"Yes, yes, I know." Lauren turned away again, in an irritable way that Derek could not interpret. "I'm just frightened, that's all."

"Uh . . . have you mentioned your concerns to anybody? Like maybe Sophia?"

"Sophia hasn't exactly been available lately." It was true; the goddess had been off on her own unimaginable affairs. But there was, Derek knew, more to it than that. He couldn't see Lauren's face, but something in her tone told him she'd never entirely gotten over her instinctive initial dislike of Sophia.

"Somebody else, then?"

"I don't know who to talk to. Oh, it's not that I exactly distrust anybody. I just feel . . . lost here, sometimes. Honestly, Derek, don't you feel it?"

"Yeah, I know what you mean. All the similarities to Earth sometimes just seem to bring the alienness into sharper relief. And it's so hard to really open up to the people . . ."

Lauren rolled over and met his eyes in the semidarkness. "I suppose that means that we ourselves are even more important to each other."

It was still a good ways short of rapturous. But Derek decided to be satisfied with it.

With nightfall, everyone had gone home and all was quiet in the research lab that Lokhyoum Institute operated in conjunction with the Erkhedzuo military. There weren't even any guards nearby; this was so deep in the Citadel that no one could possibly be present without having long since passed numerous layers of security, including the magical defenses that made the creation of a portal into the mountain's interior impossible even for a mage who knew the layout well enough to attempt it.

So Paul Rinnard was quite alone, as he sat gazing at the gleaming openwork headpiece and tried to come to terms with his own feelings.

He was still trying when a figure appeared in the doorway, silhouetted against the lights still glowing in the outer office.

He knew at once who it was. He'd never used telepathy on Nydierya, of course. For one who'd undergone JICPO's training regimen, the notion was—to use a term he would never have dreamed of employing—obscene. No, his awareness of that silhouette's identity arose from something more basic than psionics.

She entered the dim lab, whose only illumination was focused on the workbench which held that webbed helmet. She met his smile with her own and settled onto his lap. "Working late?" she asked archly.

"Not working at all—as usual." But then the moment of sexual playfulness was over, as though it had never been, and once again Rinnard's consciousness was as focused on the psi-enhancing helmet as were the lights.

Nydierya sighed. "I wish I could fully know what it is you've been experiencing. I want to share it with you, if only vicariously."

"I wish I could describe it," he said, face-to-face with a familiar problem. "I've tried my best to verbalize what psi feels like. Well, this is like the same thing but with a . . . well, a power surge. Like the lights burn brighter."

"I envy you," she said quietly. "It's something that is forever denied to me."

He laughed with a sudden harshness. "Don't be too envious. They won't even let *me* crank it up to full power!"

He realized how childish that sounded almost before it was out of his mouth. Here he was, whining that he wasn't being allowed to experience in supercharged form something Nydierya would never experience at all! He lowered his eyes in embarrassment.

Which, probably, was why he missed Nydierya's shrewd look, instantly smoothed over as she spoke briskly.

"Yes, it's typical: the overcaution of old establishment

farts." The interpreter software had been steadily expanding its English vocabulary. "So I suppose we have to expect it, and live with it. Only . . ." She slid lithely off his lap and stood contemplating the helmet for a moment before turning to face him eagerly. "I have a sudden urge—"

"You usually do."

"No, no, not that! What I want is . . ." She turned to face him, leaning down with her hands on the armrests of his chair and bringing her face close to his. "Let me see you do something with it! I've seen some of the things you can do unaided—telekinesis, levitation, and all the rest. Let me see what you can *really* do, with the amplifier on!"

"Uh, seems kind of flashy, don't you think?" he temporized, taken slightly aback.

"Please?" The earpiece did its best, drawing the English word out to three syllables.

"Hey, you know we're not supposed to use it except under controlled laboratory conditions, under full observation by—"

Abruptly, Nydierya's tone changed from wheedling to something very much like scorn. "I can't believe who I'm hearing this from!"

Paul blinked, stung. "Well . . . What the hell? I don't suppose it can do any harm."

"Of course not!" Her eyes ignited, and she drew his head to her and kissed him fiercely. "Come on—I'll handle the controls."

He moved to another chair, in the angle between the workbench and a console to which the amplifier was connected by slender cables. This experimental model required an external power source, and a remote operator—a role in which Nydierya was qualified. She gingerly took up the silvery helm and lowered it over his head with a care that was almost ceremonious, as though it was a crown and this was a coronation. Then she seated herself at the console.

From his chair, Paul could look over her shoulder and see the controls. He watched as she activated the system. Then she placed a slender right hand on the power-setting lever, which moved horizontally from left to right along a series of settings marked in the common Khronuo script. About a quarter of the way along those settings was a red line whose meaning somehow transcended language. Should the lever pass that line, the system would automatically shut down.

"Okay," he said. "Gimme the juice."

Nydierya's head turned, and she looked at him over her shoulder—a look he could not interpret. Then, quickly as a striking snake, her left hand grasped a cluster of leads and yanked them out of the side of the console.

Before Paul had time to react, her right hand slid the lever rightward, past the red line, which had gone dim with the disconnection of the safety cutoffs. She slid it all the way to the highest setting.

His brain exploded.

He'd tried to describe the sensation of artificially enhanced psi powers in terms of a power surge. This was more like a supernova.

He didn't know whether he screamed or not. Indeed, he wasn't aware of anything at all at that moment except a transcendence for which no words existed, or could exist, for human words could only describe that which lay within the realm of the familiar human senses.

But then, like the fading afterglow of a supernova, that indescribable supra-sensory effulgence began to fade. Gradually, he became aware of his physical surroundings again, taking note of things one at a time.

Oddly enough, those things were floating in midair.

It puzzled him at first. Then he became aware that they were commencing to float when he noticed them.

Then he realized that he himself was at least three feet off the floor.

In the corner of his eye, he saw Nydierya standing openmouthed. He ordered himself *not* to think of her, and concentrated on bringing his powers of telekinesis and levitation under control. Objects began to settle toward the floor—objects he'd been lucky to move mere inches before, with a teeth-clenching effort. Now he had only to wish them to move, and against his wish gravity was powerless.

He felt a strange calm, as though he inhabited the eye of a hurricane of power. Very deliberately, he decided to experiment with other powers. He concentrated on a far corner of the lab and organized his mind to teleport. At once, he was surveying the lab from that corner.

A kind of serene recklessness took hold of him. Ordinarily, it was considered hazardous to attempt to teleport oneself somewhere out of sight . . . not that anyone was likely to do so, at the dinky ranges they'd managed. At the very least, it was deemed essential to be able to visualize the specific target location, as in the experiments that had been conducted with TV images of a room on the other side of a solid wall. But now he merely thought the single concept *up*, and willed himself to the nearly ultimate recklessness of a random teleport, seeking maximum range to the exclusion of every other consideration.

In a stunning agony of cold and suffocation, he hung below the stars and above the kind of dark panorama he knew well from high-altitude night flights. To one side was the valley with its landing field; to the other spread the sea of lights that was Bozemtoum, with the inky blackness of the actual sea beyond.

Freezing and gasping, knowing with stark certainty that he had only seconds of consciousness left, he desperately focused his remaining reserves of concentration. He visualized the lab, and willed himself there.

Gravity, warmth and thick air smothered him in their blessed embrace. Consciousness fled.

He awoke in Nydierya's arms.

She was kneeling on the floor, cradling his head in her lap. That was so distracting that an instant passed before he noticed that his head was no longer encased in the helmet.

"It's all right . . . it's all right. . . ." Her voice gradually entered his consciousness. He struggled up into a sitting position. Then slumped back down as the universe—or was it his head?—began to spin.

"Rest, darling," Nydierya urged. "You're exhausted, after what you've done. Rest now."

It was what Paul himself most earnestly desired—to let unconsciousness take him again. But some inner imperative made him try to frame a question. "What . . . ?"

"Do you understand what we've done?" Nydierya demanded breathlessly. "We've proven that there really are no theoretical limits to psionic powers! You can surpass mages, whose powers cannot be artificially enhanced. Yours can—and if you're allowed to use those enhancements without limit, you can defeat the Titans!"

Her vision seduced him in a way beyond anything her body could do. And yet . . . He looked her in the eye, disturbed. "You had no right to do that."

Her unflinching eyes challenged him. "Would you rather that I hadn't?" she demanded.

His own eyes slid away as he remembered. "No," he whispered.

She gave an unseen smile. "Rest now. It will be better when you've learned to control and focus the levels of power you now know you can command. But there will be plenty of time for that. Rest now."

He obeyed, and let absolute exhaustion take him. His sleep was roiled by strange dreams.

The streets of Quire were deserted in the small hours of the morning, save for a few furtive figures that kept to alleys and entranceways as though shunning the moonlight. Nydierya, cloaked against a damp chill in the air, paid them no heed. Magic was ill-adapted to self-defense, given the time and concentration needed to use it. But Nydierya carried a small, highly effective and very illegal weapon, so vicious in its effects that the mere sight of it was more than sufficient to deter any attackers.

The street ended at the seawall; beyond, the moons glistened on the waters and the soft sound of breaking wavelets could be heard in the traffic-free silence. Nydierya turned right, walking along a row of narrow-fronted houses until she came to a certain doorway flanked by a vine-burdened trellis. She brushed aside the vines and felt for a familiar concealed lens, an incongruous bit of smooth high-tech set in the rough stucco. Locating it, she brought her right eye close enough for it to recognize her retinal pattern. The door clicked open.

As was usual in these meetings, the man she was to meet sat behind a desk; a lamp behind him was the room's sole source of light. She had never gotten a clear look at him, only heard his reedy voice.

"Well?" he asked without preamble.

"It succeeded."

"I assume you mean the approach you suggested after it appeared that Rinnard's notion of a psionic amplifier would prove practical."

"Yes!" Nydierya gave a brief account of what had occurred in the lab. "The results were beyond our wildest expectations," she concluded breathlessly. "And I cannot over-emphasize that what occurred was little more than a random set of uncontrolled psionic manifestations. I simply can't imagine what he'll be capable of when he learns how to focus his enhanced powers. Furthermore, the amplifier was only an experimental prototype. Later, when he's using the technology in its mature form—"

"But will he be using it for *us*?"

The question brought Nydierya to a startled halt, for it was not asked in the thin voice of her control. Instead, it was a deep rumble like that of thunder on the western horizon. There had never been a third person present here before—or, at least, no such person had ever revealed his presence.

But now, the darkness in one of the room's dim corners seemed to shift, and a figure entered the fringes of the light. Nydierya could make out no details. But it was a male figure—brutally so, in its thick massiveness, which went with the heavy voice. The slighter form of Nydierya's control seemed to shrink to even smaller dimensions as he cringed like a dog in the presence of its master.

But none of this was at the forefront of Nydierya's mind. For she possessed a certain extremely rare talent.

A few human beings had the ability to sense the presence of a god, whatever the god's outward semblance. No shape-shifting or illusion availed. Nydierya, and the few other humans so endowed, saw the god's "default" human appearance—and *knew* that what they were looking at was a god. The sensation was old hat to Nydierya by now, for Sophia was often present at the Citadel.

But what she was feeling now was subtly different. The difference was partly qualitative, for she felt an undercurrent of inescapable malevolence similar to that which sometimes surfaces when one awakes early and the desperations of the human condition suddenly come crowding in to banish sleep. But the real, the stunning difference was quantitative. Never had her god-sense been so overpowered by sheer, pompous intensity.

She forced herself not to wonder about the nature of the entity that faced her from just outside the circle of light, lest her will and intellect be paralyzed by terror, reducing her to the disgusting level of her control, whose whimpering was now audible. For she had to keep her wits about her and exploit the stupendous prize that was now hers to offer her clandestine employers, squeezing the last quantum of bargaining advantage out of it.

"What do you mean . . . sir?" she got out.

"You know perfectly well what I mean," came the stormy reverberation that served this being for a voice. Nydierya could almost smell the ozone. "All you have demonstrated so far is that this Rinnard creature was correct in believing that psionic powers can be artificially amplified to unprecedented levels. It was this possibility that has caused me to take personal charge of this operation, which clearly can no longer be entrusted to underlings—least of all the underlings whose incompetence allowed these psionically gifted humans from Earth to be brought here and placed under the aegis of the Erkhedzye-led alliance. Does it not seem likely that Rinnard will simply use his new-found power in the service of that alliance?"

"To the contrary, sir," said Nydierya, surprising herself with her boldness, for by now she had a pretty good idea of the identity of him to whom she was speaking. "Rinnard is *ours* now. After what he has experienced, he will be utterly dependent on the need to repeat it—and the Erkhedzuo establishment won't let him. All we have to do is exploit that need, by . . ." A phrase she'd heard from Rinnard came to mind. "By being his enablers."

"You, of all people, should know of the effectiveness of this approach."

Nydierya felt her face go hot, but she dared not venture an angry retort to the contempt in that basso voice. *Besides,* said the stubborn inner whisper she wished she could rid herself of, *it's true.*

"However," continued the voice that seemed to presage summer cloudbursts, "I believe you may be placing too much reliance on it. We require, as the old saying goes, a second string to our bow."

"Sir?"

"You are doubtless correct about the strength of Rinnard's addiction to the sensation of power that the uninhibited psi-amplifier gives him. But we must make it possible for him to rationalize his dependency. This will require some further play-acting by you."

"Of course, sir," said Nydierya, lowering her eyes with a demureness she couldn't quite sustain. Avidity won out, and she looked up boldly. "I trust that any additional services I perform will be remembered when—"

"Do not presume to try and hold us to what you imagine to be obligations." The cold contempt was back in full, and Nydierya thought it best to incline her head again. "Still, your efforts will be remembered. We keep our bargains, even with such as you."

Nydierya looked up, eyes alight. Self-disgust had lost its power to dampen her eagerness. It had lost it the very first time she had watched the children in their artificially prolonged death-agonies, and felt the flood of magical power that those agonies had fed. Now there was nothing left inside her but her need to experience that flood again Yes, she truly did know what Rinnard was feeling now, and what lay ahead for him.

"What you must do," the inhumanly deep voice resumed, "is convince Rinnard that you are playing a dangerous double

game—a different game from the one you are actually playing. A *triple* game, in fact."

"I will do as instructed, sir. I must caution you, however,
that he isn't stupid. Immature and headstrong, yes, but not
stupid."

"We are aware of this. However, we have a plan which
does not require stupidity on Rinnard's part, only the kind
of impulsiveness and overconfidence to which you have
alluded. Fortuitously, it also involves putting an end to a
worrisome problem: his two companions from Earth."

"Sir?" queried Nydierya, surprised.

"As long as they are with him, they will always serve as
a kind of anchor for him. Their very presence reminds him
of his original loyalties. They must be removed."

"Rinnard will never agree to harm them."

"Not knowingly, no. Still, he must be our instrument for
placing them in a position where they can be dealt with.
It will be part of your task to persuade him to become that
instrument."

CHAPTER FIFTEEN

Paul Rinnard and Nydierya soon found a getaway spot.

They went there whenever they could manage time off from the routine at the Citadel. It wasn't hard to convince Paul's handlers that he needed frequent R&R, after the batteries of strictly regulated tests they ordained for him. And they didn't even know of his surreptitious explorations of the outer limits of his enhanced abilities, conducted with Nydierya after hours. Indeed, it was only by applying those powers to the problem of restoring his own fatigue-ravaged physiology—an ability he'd stumbled onto by accident in the course of exploring his inner psionic frontiers—that he was able to keep going at all, and conceal his secret double regimen that would otherwise have broken him.

He'd begun to allow himself to wonder if he could use the technique to extend his lifespan. . . .

Still, traditional restorative techniques were more fun— especially when applied in Nydierya's company. So he was careful not to keep himself *too* chipper, lest the powers-that-be grow too complacent about his condition. Thus they escaped often to the special place they'd discovered.

South of Bozemtoum, the coast curved away in a crescent of sandy beaches behind which rose a range of low hills, dotted with seaside villas amid groves of trees where native and Earthly species mingled. Seaward spurs of that hill-range interrupted the dunes with occasional rocky headlands. One of those promontories, far enough to the south that the sandy bluffs were nearly empty of villas, sheltered a grotto that could only be entered from the sea. Rinnard, whose powers seemed to have been growing even without artificial amplification—or perhaps it was merely a growing awareness of what he could do, a receding of limits—would levitate the two of them out to the cavern-mouth, and from there they would swim into the watery blue-glowing darkness, among stalactites as old as time. Sometimes they made love on an expanse of flat rock in the dim blueness of the grotto. More often, seeking the sun, they emerged onto a stretch of beach whose isolation would probably have assured their privacy even without the spell of illusion that Nydierya laid on. There, on what to the non-magically-talented observer would have seemed a deserted stretch of sand, they joined in the shallows, amid the gentle but complex tides wrought by two small moons.

It was there, late one afternoon, that Nydierya spoke the revelation that would change their relationship—and so much else—forever.

Rinnard goggled at her. "You're . . . you're a double agent?"

"At least that," she smiled. The ruddy westering sun had already touched the bluffs above the beach, and they'd wrapped towels around their nakedness against the evening breeze blowing in off the Nernere waters. Now, even though it was really no cooler, she hugged her knees tightly. "Hear me out, Paul. This isn't easy for me, you know."

"Why not?" he demanded, with the anger that is often a side effect of emergence from shock. "Why would it have been so hard to be honest with me from the first?"

"Do you realize you're the first person I've ever told all of this to, after years of holding it inside? Please don't make it even harder than it has to be!"

"All right, all right," he said, suddenly contrite. "I'm listening."

Nydierya stared out at the darkening gray horizon and spoke in a monotone. "Remember I told you my mother's family was partly of Qurvyshuo extraction? Well, one day Qurvyshuo agents contacted me, showed me undeniable identifying information concerning some of my blood relatives in Qurvyshye, and made it very clear what would happen to those relatives if I didn't cooperate. Sickeningly clear."

She paused and gauged the effect of her words on Paul. It was as she'd hoped. And this had been the easy part, so far. It was even *true*. It really had been that way . . . at first.

But now came the veering off into the fiction her handlers had prepared.

"Later, some family friends in Qurvyshye managed to get word to me. The people Qurvyshuo intelligence had been using to blackmail me were already dead. The evidence I'd been shown that they were still alive was faked—computer simulations and the like.

"My first impulse was to tell the Qurvyshuo what to do with themselves. But that would have accomplished nothing except my own death, the first time I ventured outside the Citadel. So instead I quietly approached the Erkhedzuo counterintelligence people. I admitted what I'd been doing, and offered to act as a double agent in exchange for immunity from prosecution."

"So you've been walking this tightrope ever since?" Rinnard shook his head slowly, and reached out and took her hand. "You poor kid!"

Nydierya returned the pressure of his grip, while surreptitiously reflecting that his reaction was, once again, as per expectations. He was a pilot of hydrocarbon-burning atmospheric aircraft, the most advanced his world's technology could produce, with a single subordinate to handle specialized targeting systems, but basically an individual warrior. It was a type that the industrial era had, paradoxically, allowed to reemerge after centuries of human automatons firing their muskets in volleys on command—just as, more than a millennium earlier, the invention of the stirrup had brought it back after the blight of phalanx and legion, allowing it to live as it had not since the Bronze Age.

It was, she decided, really a matter of economics. Whenever the weapons of decision were so expensive as to be the weapons of an elite—bronze chariots, or supersonic launching platforms for fire-and-forget missiles, or whatever—then that elite unfailingly reappeared to wield them.

Rinnard, like all his ilk through history, lived and breathed an ethos centered on the straightforward application of maximum violence. It was a mentality to which the twilight world of intelligence work—"spook stuff" as he called it—was utterly foreign. Nydierya would have to overcome that hostility. To her advantage, though, was the naïveté that went with it.

"I can't even imagine what you've been going through," he continued. "But now I at least understand why you couldn't talk to me about it. Only . . ." His brows drew together in perplexity. "Why are you telling me now?"

"Because things have changed. A new opportunity has opened up, but to seize it I'm going to have to act strictly on my own—and I'll need your help." Nydierya hastened on before Paul could interrupt, once again lapsing temporarily into partial truth. "Until now, I've dealt with ordinary human agents of Qurvyshuo intelligence. But now the Titans themselves have begun to involve themselves directly. I've come face to face with one of them, and I have reason to believe that he's their leader, the one people usually call the High Lord because they can't bring themselves to pronounce his name—any of his names." She smiled without humor. "Have you ever encountered evil, Paul? Well, I've encountered Evil."

Rinnard's eyes were round. "But . . . but why has this, uh, High Lord suddenly decided to get into the action himself?"

Nydierya leaned forward urgently, and without apparent intention her beach towel slid off her right shoulder and revealed one perfect breast. "Do you really need to ask, Paul? *You're* the reason! The High Lord understands your transcendent, no, *cosmic* importance, as our side unfortunately doesn't. You're a new factor in the equation, one that makes everything that has gone before meaningless!"

Rinnard tried to haul his wits together—not easy, between Nydierya's words and her bare breast. "Well, uh, have you passed this on to the good guys? You know, the people in Erkhedzuo intelligence you're now reporting to."

"Them? They're nothing but bureaucrats in uniform, Paul. They can't possibly grasp the opportunity this presents. Surely you're familiar with limited mentalities like theirs, from your own world?"

"Oh, sure, you bet! Remind me sometime to tell you about . . . Uh, what 'opportunity' is that?"

"Don't you see, Paul? This is a chance that will never come again! We can *trap* the High Lord himself! Or, to be exact, *you* can."

"Me?"

"Yes! You see, not even the High Lord has grasped the full extent of your potential. It's a weakness of the Titans. They can't see past their contempt for humans. Well, you can use that weakness against them. They know about you and me, and they want me to persuade you to go over to them. Very well: we'll pretend that I've succeeded!"

"You're saying you want me to . . . string the High Lord along?"

"Exactly! But we'll have to act on our own. No one must know."

"Huh? Not even Urquiashqua?"

"Especially not Urquiashqua! Yes, I know: he's an old dear, and I owe him a lot, and I truly respect him. But he's like all the rest of them: a—" Nydierya sought for the English expression "—fuddy-duddy. He and the others would never allow it. They're old and conservative and over-cautious. And besides . . . the scheme's chance of success rests on what the two of us have learned about your true potential. If we went to the authorities, we'd have to admit what we've been doing."

"Hmm . . . There is that."

"After which, of course, we'd no longer be able to get away with letting you use psi amplification at full power after hours." Nydierya let Rinnard chew silently on that for a heartbeat or three before resuming earnestly. "Besides, Paul, we don't *need* them! We can act on our own, lead the Titans on. Only . . ."

"Only what?"

"It will take a gesture from you. A *major* gesture, to convince them you've truly turned."

"What . . . gesture?" Caution appeared in Rinnard's eyes, and Nydierya reminded herself of what she'd told the High Lord: this man wasn't stupid. As a matter of fact, he was far more intelligent than he usually allowed himself to seem. But he knew it all too well, having spent most of his life among the less clever. And, like most such men, he had few defenses against flattery with a basis in truth—the kind of flattery she'd been laying on with such a lavish trowel.

"Well," she began carefully, "after I convinced the High Lord that I can turn you, he immediately began to get even bigger ideas. He wants you—in his service, of course—to have a monopoly of psionic powers in this world. This, of course, would require removing Secrest and Westerfeld from the board. And we're in a position to—"

"Now wait just a goddamned minute!" Nydierya recoiled physically from Rinnard's rage, which needed no psionics to amplify its impact. "Derek and Lauren are my friends, and I will *never* harm them, or allow anybody else to. No convoluted spy games are worth that. I don't care what stakes you're playing for, you will *not* play with their lives! Is that clear?"

"Oh, of *course* not, darling!" said Nydierya hastily, frightened that she might have gone too far too fast. "Nobody said anything about killing or even hurting them. I'd never do that, and I know you'd never have any part of it. No, we can satisfy the High Lord by merely *isolating* them—and, unknown to the High Lord, it would only be temporary."

"What do you mean?" The lambent glare in Rinnard's light hazel eyes died down a little, and the fire and fury ebbed from his voice, leaving a residue of sullen suspicion.

"The High Lord has created an empty void domain like the one you passed through in your journey here, but with only one portal to the material universe. That portal opens in the outer regions of this system. I have a plan to induce your friends to go through that portal, along with Urquiashqua."

Rinnard's remaining anger collapsed into bewilderment. "But . . . but I don't get it. Maybe Derek and Lauren will be alive, but they'll be stranded in this extradimensional pocket universe. And won't this be playing into the Titans' hands by robbing our side of the services of two very capable psis?"

Nydierya donned a look of vindicated cleverness that she was fairly sure Rinnard would identify with. "Ah, but remember I said Urquiashqua will be with them! And he knows how to open portals. Indeed, he's one of the acknowledged masters of that particular area of magic. Now, it takes a little while to locate a portal. But once they find it, Urquiashqua will be able to bring them back."

Rinnard's perplexity deepened. "But doesn't the High Lord know all this as well as you do?"

"Yes—except that we won't let him know Urquiashqua is with them. He will think your friends are permanently banished from the material universe—and your credibility will be established."

"And where does my 'credibility' go when they reappear? Straight down the toilet, that's where!"

Nydierya had to order herself not to smile, for she knew she'd won. Rinnard had begun nit-picking the plan, a sure sign that he'd accepted it in its essentials. "We'll claim we didn't know Urquiashqua was aboard. The High Lord won't be happy, but he'll have no reason to doubt our good faith. After all, our story will make sense; there will have been no real need for Urquiashqua or any other mage with his abilities to go along on a voyage intended to be strictly in-system. We'll be able to plausibly claim it was just an unforeseeable circumstance."

Rinnard remained stubbornly dubious. "I don't like it. Sounds to me like you're being too clever by half, as they say. It's awfully risky."

"I tell you Paul, there is no real danger to your friends. And besides, even if there were some element of risk to

them . . . well, the fact remains that it is *you* who is crucial. Derek and Lauren are valuable to the alliance, no doubt,
but they're simply not in the same league as you. And
remember, this is war. Certain risks must be taken. You can
understand that, being a military man."

"Derek and Lauren are military, too. They can also understand it. Why don't we bring them in on this?"

"*No!*" Nydierya backed off immediately from her vehemence and spoke with studied reasonableness. "They must
under no circumstances be told. One or both of them might
tell higher authority, and the plan would be aborted. You
know how conscientious your friends are, how—"

"—Straight arrow," Rinnard supplied. "Yeah, I understand
what you're saying. But it gripes me that they're going to
think I've betrayed them." He stared moodily out to sea,
thereby missing the triumphant smile that finally broke
through Nydierya's reserve.

She quickly smoothed it out into another sort of smile.
"I believe the plan can be modified in such a way as to
allow you to explain things to them when it can no longer
do any harm."

She outlined the plan, and Rinnard listened in acquies-
cent silence. But his face wore a troubled expression.

He was wearing the same expression several weeks later,
out beyond the orbit of the Khron system's innermost gas
giant. Derek found it puzzling and a little disturbing.

They were standing on the bridge of Rhykhvyleshqua's
Ergu Nervy. The big ship had still been in low Khron orbit
after its extended tour of duty in the Solar system, and
therefore available to transport them into deep space on short
notice. The burly captain didn't look entirely happy about
having been thus pressed into service. He was off to one
side even now, muttering to Urquiashqua about it. Derek
was close enough for his interpreter earplug to pick up their
conversation.

"Explain this to me again, Urquiashqua," the captain was
grumbling. "We're going out into nowhere because you think
certain psionic abilities—"

"Teleportation and levitation," the mage interjected. "And, possibly, projection as well."

"—will function better outside the sun's gravity well?"

"That's appallingly imprecise terminology," said the mage with pained pedantry. "To be more accurate, Nydierya has demonstrated mathematically that those abilities should operate at the equivalent of a far higher power level—an order of magnitude higher, in fact—in an insignificant gravity field. Specifically, a field of less than approximately .000001G."

The interpreter software didn't have to change the value, for it was only approximate and Khron's gravity was very close to Earth's. Rinnard had explained that it was the equivalent, in terms of the Solar system, of going out almost to the orbit of Neptune. It didn't involve quite so long a voyage here, where the local sun was less massive than Sol. Still . . .

"Well, I go wherever I'm ordered," Rhykhvyleshqua said fatalistically. "But considering the cost of operating this ship, it seems like an awfully high investment in a mere mathematical model." He shot an apologetic glance at Nydierya, who stood demurely by.

"But you must admit it makes sense," she argued with a smile. "Teleportation and levitation both employ quantum energy for purposes of spatial distortion. It stands to reason that they would be easier where gravity—which, after all, shapes space—is weak."

"Just so," said Urquiashqua with a nod that set his wattles jiggling. "Of course, the case is less clear with projection. But Nydierya's mathematical projections suggest—"

Derek turned away. He was familiar with this line of argument. It was why he and Lauren were along: he continued to hold his own as a strong second-best projector among them, and Urquiashqua had wanted Lauren for a statistical control. The mage himself hadn't wanted to come at first, insisting—correctly—that he was getting too old and fat for space travel. But he'd yielded to entreaties by Nydierya, who had protested her inability to evaluate the findings in the absence of his wisdom and experience.

Derek walked over to join Rinnard—carefully, as the ship was maintaining a steady acceleration of a quarter G and he still wasn't entirely accustomed to low-weight conditions. He had, however, gotten over being disconcerted by the visual display, with its illusion of openness to the empty vacuum of space. The fighter pilot was standing at the railing, staring fixedly out at that star-blazing infinity, as though he was expecting to see something.

"Won't be long now," said Derek, making conversation.

Rinnard looked startled, but recovered immediately, turning with a smile that seemed somehow less easy and spontaneous than usual. "Oh, yeah, not long at all. We've nearly reached the point where the gravitational value will be low enough for us to strut our stuff." The smile flickered and died. "Hey, Derek, in case I don't have time to tell you later, I just want you to know something. . . ."

"Yes," Derek prompted as Rinnard's voice trailed off into uncharacteristic indecisiveness.

"Well, it's really you and Lauren both. I just want to make sure the two of you understand that—"

"There you are, Paul!" Nydierya appeared at Rinnard's elbow. "Derek, you'll have to excuse us. I need Paul to come and help me do some calibrations of my instruments." She looked at Rinnard and added, with an odd emphasis, "It's time."

"Uh, yeah, sure. Catch you later, Derek." He departed in Nydierya's wake. On the way out, he passed Lauren and waved a distracted greeting.

"What's the matter with him?" Lauren asked Derek, joining him at the rail.

"I don't know. He started to tell me something, but . . . Oh, well, not much longer now."

"No." They stood in silence for a time. The bridge murmured around them as *Ergu Nervy* drove on.

The alarm klaxon came utterly without warning. At effectively the same instant, acceleration ceased and they were in free fall.

Derek was out of practice—not that he'd ever really been in practice—for weightlessness. For an instant of sickening disorientation, he clung to the rail and struggled to bring his now-activated magnetized soles into contact with the deck, as everyone hastened to resume their seats and the air vibrated with loud intercom announcements unintelligible to him.

"What's happening?" he demanded of Urquiashqua as he staggered into his seat and clung to a handhold, fighting down nausea.

"Something has disabled the controls for the matter-antimatter flow. I don't understand the details—not my field. But under such circumstances, the safety overrides automatically shut down the reactor."

"You mean we've lost power?" asked Lauren.

Derek firmly told himself that it was just his imagination, the air couldn't be getting stale this fast.

Rhykhvyleshqua overheard the question. "Only the drive. All the secondary systems, including life support are powered by safe cold-fusion units. But the drive *must* stay deactivated until the problem is rectified. Safety considerations *have* to be paramount. With antimatter, there are no small accidents!"

"But we're in no immediate danger?" Urquiashqua queried.

"No. We simply can't maneuver. We've committed to the hyperbolic orbit we were following." A new report arrived, claiming the captain's attention. He turned back to the others scowling in perplexity. "One of our lifeboats deployed just an instant after we went into free fall. Communications!" he called out. "Try to raise that lifeboat."

The term "lifeboat," Derek recalled, was one of the interpreter software's less apt vocabulary choices. The things were small auxiliary spacecraft, powered by fusion drives and capable of interplanetary flight. And, of necessity, they could be launched by their occupants without the need for clearance from a bridge that might no longer exist.

"I don't understand," Rhykhvyleshqua was muttering. "Even assuming that somebody panicked when the drive shut down, they couldn't have gotten to that lifeboat and detached it in so short a time." He glared at a small radar screen, which Derek could glimpse over his shoulder. The lifeboat was curving away, its drive overcoming the momentum it had inherited from the mothership and sending it into a new orbit that would take it back insystem.

The communications officer—who didn't wear the interpreter gear—reported to Rhykhvyleshqua in what was to Derek gibberish. The captain started, then turned and gave Derek an odd look. "The lifeboat has responded to our hail. But the message is for you."

"*Me?*" Derek was mortified to hear his voice emerge in a squeak of incredulity.

"You and Lieutenant Westerfeld." Rhykhvyleshqua motioned him toward the comm station.

Moving through a haze of unreality, they crowded around the comm screen. The unreality became concrete as they stared at the face on that screen.

"Paul!" they gasped in unison.

Rinnard looked out at them from against the backdrop of the lifeboat's tiny control room. "Derek . . . Lauren . . . listen to me, because I haven't much time. I'm sorry about this. I'm even sorrier that I couldn't take you into my confidence about it. But I'm going to ask you to believe me when I tell you that what I've done is necessary. And I give you my word that you'll be returning soon."

Lauren found her voice before Derek did. "Paul, what in God's name have you done? What was 'necessary'?"

"The sabotaging of *Ergu Nervy*. It was done in such a way as to assure that no one would be killed. You're just going to have to . . . go away for a little while. But it's only temporary. I would never have consented to it otherwise. Urquiashqua is with you, and he'll be able to bring you back."

"Bring us back from *where*, Paul?" Derek demanded. His voice broke in his bewilderment. "What are you talking about? I don't understand any of this!"

"You'll soon know. Just trust me for now, okay? I'm telling you, it had to be done this way in order for me . . . I mean, for *us* to defeat the Titans."

Behind Rinnard in the screen, Nydierya appeared, wearing

an impatient expression. "Paul, sign off! We haven't any more time."

"Gotta go," said Rinnard. A ghost of his old easy grin awoke. "So long for now, guys. Best of luck." The screen went dead. Derek stared for a long time into that blackness, feeling nothing but dull hurt.

Ergu Nervy plunged on.

Presently, Rhykhvyleshqua received another report. He muttered a few words to Urquiashqua, then ordered the activation of a screen which showed the view dead-ahead at extreme magnification.

"Derek," said Lauren, arousing him from his misery and gesturing at that screen.

He stared at it. No explanation was necessary. He's seen often enough the kind of glowing ring of luminsescence that appeared against the star-fields, enclosing a circle of something that wasn't really blackness. And he knew, without knowing how he knew, that this one was large enough to admit a capital ship of space.

"Can we avoid it?" he heard Urquiashqua asking nervously.

"No." Rhykhvyleshqua's deep baritone was somber. "All we've got are attitude-control thrusters. They can't alter our course significantly."

"But," Lauren protested, "when we went through a portal on our way to Khron, you said the ship had to decelerate, because precise navigational control was necessary to get through it."

"That was when the ship was seeking out and traversing a portal of fixed location, which Urquiashqua had to open for us," explained the captain patiently. "Here, the situation is the other way around. *This* portal was obviously created especially for us, directly in our path."

"An extraordinary, if not unique, occurrence," Urquiashqua put in.

"I'm flattered," Rhykhvyleshqua said. "And, to continue, it's already been opened by whoever—or, more likely, whatever—created it."

"But where does it lead?" Lauren asked him.

"We are about to find that out."

Derek turned to Urquiashqua. "Can't you close it?"

"In theory, perhaps. But that spell would take time—more time than we have."

Derek saw what the mage meant. The ring of light was growing, looming ahead of them.

"Like a net for a butterfly," he heard Lauren say. She was reading his thoughts without benefit of telepathy.

"Or a hoop for a dolphin to jump through," he murmured.

"At least they get fish for it," she observed.

The growth of the portal seemed to accelerate. To their eyes, it swept up to enclose them. At the last split second, Derek and Lauren could glimpse what lay beyond it, and felt the onset of madness.

Then they flashed through it, and madness took them for its own.

Nydierya bent over Rinnard and put her arms around his hunched shoulders. "There was no other way, darling."

"You're sure?" he mumbled, is search of reassurance.

"Yes! Our cover story is intact—the ship was lost to accident, and we alone were able to escape. And the High Lord will be convinced. And remember, it's only a matter of time before they locate the portal and Urquiashqua opens it for them."

"Yeah, you're right." Rinnard stood up slowly—the life-boat was accelerating at almost one and a half gravities—and walked toward the Spartan living quarters.

Nydierya sensed that this was a time to leave him alone. So she remained in the control room, flopping down onto one of the acceleration couches and staring at the viewscreen. Motivated by an obscure impulse, she adjusted the screen to show the view-aft.

She couldn't have seen *Ergu Nervy* even if it had still been in the material universe. Still less could she have seen the portal that had swallowed that ship . . . even if it had still existed.

She imagined, however, that she could see the heavily stealthed Qurvyshuo warship that had transported the High Lord out to that region of space, shadowing *Ergu Nervy* until it had vanished into the portal, then remaining there long enough for him to do what only the gods and few very powerful mages could do: slam a portal shut forever, erasing its existence as though it had never been.

As far as the material universe was concerned, *Ergu Nervy* was now as nonexistent as it would have been if their cover story was true and it had been reduced to subatomic plasma by a freak antimatter reactor accident.

Inevitably, Paul would find out. But, she assured herself, he would get over it in time.

Anything could be gotten over. She knew that well enough.

CHAPTER SIXTEEN

It soon became apparent that the mini-universe in which they found themselves had no exit.

That was the essence of Urquiashqua's report to a meeting consisting of Rhykhvyleshqua, Derek, Lauren and some senior ship's officers. "We have," he began, looking around the circular table in the briefing room just aft of *Ergu Nervy*'s bridge, "entered an empty Void domain—"

"Urquiashqua," growled the captain in tones of dire warning.

"Ahem . . . ah, yes, I suppose that is self-evident, isn't it?" The mage glanced nervously at Derek and Lauren. They had recovered, more or less, from their unprepared emergence into this pocket infinity, but they were clearly in no mood to listen to him state the obvious about it. "Well, after passing through it at a far higher velocity than we customarily make such transits, we lost track of the portal. Nevertheless, our instrumentation is quite up to the task of reacquiring it. But all our efforts to do so have been unavailing. We must conclude that the portal no longer exists, that it has been closed from its opposite terminus in the outer system of Khron, presumably by the entity which originally created it."

"Created it specifically for the purpose of capturing us," Rhykhvyleshqua added grimly.

"Indubitably. It was precisely in our path, into which we were locked by the disabling of our drive." The mage's voice went dull with misery. Nydierya's treason had left him devastated. "The positioning was too exact for coincidence."

"Well, at least the drive is back on line," said the captain briskly. "We just have nowhere to go, in . . . what's out there."

A strong shudder ran through Derek as he recalled their emergence, unprepared, from the portal into "what's out there." He had stared full in the face of that which he'd gotten barely an eye-blink of before, in their journey to Khron, and he wasn't sure he had fully recovered, or that he ever would. He pulled his whimpering mind back from the rim of that bottomless hell-pit of persistent memory, and ordered it to concentrate on the subject at hand. That proved to be not an altogether good idea, for, like Urquiashqua, he found himself reminded of a hurtful and inexplicable personal betrayal.

At least, he thought, he was dealing with it better than Lauren seemed to be. She'd said little since their last glimpse of Paul Rinnard in the viewscreen, and her expression reflected a complex intensity he hadn't dared probe with questions.

"Uh, let me make sure I'm clear on this," he ventured. "There's no way you can create a new portal for us?"

"Of *course* not!" snapped the portly mage. "I've *told* you—" Urquiashqua stopped short, at least as taken aback by his out-of-character outburst as everyone else was. He clutched his braided beard nervously and resumed in an embarrassed mumble. "Creating portals is very difficult even under the best of circumstances. For it to be possible at all, it is necessary for the mage to be able to clearly visualize both his own location and the location at which he wishes the portal to open. This is one reason why the creation of portals within the material world to another locale within that world is relatively easy, as such things go. Creating one from there to a Void domain would be harder by orders of magnitude, and there is no reliable record of any human mage actually doing it. Such a mage would have to be intimately familiar with the domain he was targeting, in addition to possessing unprecedented power. But as for creating a portal *from* a void domain to the material universe . . . No. That is asking too much. It isn't even a theoretical possibility for anyone but a god. The gods, you see, are native to the Void. They can . . . orient themselves there. Humans are inherently incapable of doing so."

"All right, all right," Derek muttered. He couldn't claim to understand the theory, but was prepared to accept Urquiashqua's professional judgment. And yet he felt a sense of dissatisfaction, as though something about the mage's exact choice of of words—something he couldn't put his finger on—had left an elusive and irritating loose end.

Lauren emerged, shakily, from the place to which her mind had withdrawn. "We seem to have established what we can't do. So what *can* we do?"

"Nothing!" The exclamation came from Zhezum, who was probably best thought of as *Ergu Nervy*'s executive officer, although "flag captain" might have come closer inasmuch as Rhykhvyleshqua was normally in command of an entire task group and was therefore describable as a commodore in traditional wet-navy terms. Anyway, he was Rhykhvyleshqua's second in command, and Derek had been amazed to encounter an Erkhedzuo with such a short name. He'd later learned that Zhezum was not a native of Erkhedzye, but had arrived there as a child-refugee, a bubble in the human wrack that had washed in from Qurvyshye's forcible unification of its continent. By sheer guts, ability, and hatred of the Qurvyshuo leviathan that had swallowed his parents along with the rest of the small nation into which he'd been born, Zhezum had clawed his way up from the refugee camps to commissioned rank. And he had an outsider's resentment and distrust of *different* outsiders.

"Nothing," he repeated, glaring at the two Americans. "We're hopelessly stranded here, by of the treason of your friend!"

"Now just hold on!" flared Derek, forgetful that Zhezum was at least the equivalent of a full commander. "I don't know why Paul did what he did. But Lauren and I had no part of it."

"No? Then why that special message for you, at the last? What did it mean?"

"I don't know, I tell you! But Lauren and I are still here. And *we,* at least, aren't going into fetal position and giving up hope!"

"Then you're fools! We're as isolated from the rest of the human race as completely and irretrievably as we would be by death. In fact, for all any of us can prove to the contrary we *are* dead!"

"All right, that will do." Rhykhvyleshqua raised his voice only slightly, but the depth, resonance and, above all, steadiness of his deep baritone halted the incipient ripping apart of frayed nerves. The massive captain was the only one aboard *Ergu Nervy* who had remained rock-steady through everything. His imperturbability had seen them through, and now it did so again. He spoke more quietly, into the silence he'd created. "Bickering among ourselves accomplishes nothing. Neither," he added with a stern glance at Zhezum, "does wild speculation about our present circumstances."

That's for damned sure, though Derek, shuddering. Zhezum's words had summoned up images best not thought about: ghosts, trapped for eternity aboard a ghost ship in a limbo beyond the reach of normal imagination. Even the Flying Dutchman had at least roamed the honest seas of Earth. His mind quailed from what lay beyond *this* hull, here in a dimension where mortals did not belong, and from which only the gods could find their way. . . .

Yes! Of course. That was it. Now he knew what had been bothering him about what Urquiashqua had said. It was the mage's automatic qualifier to the impossibility of creating a portal from the Void: " . . . *for anyone but a god.*"

He leaned forward, reining back his excitement. "Look, people, maybe I'm missing something, but the solution seems obvious to me."

"Oh?" said Zhezum archly. "Perhaps you'll condescend to share it with us."

"Gladly," Derek shot back. "Creating a portal from the Void to the material universe is possible only for the gods, right? Well, then, what we need is . . . a god."

The facial expressions around the table ran the gamut from puzzlement through pity to—in Zhezum's case—disgusted contempt. Urquiashqua spoke gently. "But, Derek, we have no god with us."

"Damn it, we're in the Void—specifically, what you've termed the Inner Void—aren't we? It's where they live, whenever they're not soaking up the sensory novelties on Khron. They're out there." Derek waved in the general direction of the bulkhead.

"But what good does that do us?" demanded Rhykh-vyleshqua.

"I can contact them," Derek said quietly.

All the faces, without exception, now wore the same, unmistakable expression. Derek decided he'd better hurry on before the men in white suits with nets—or the Khronuo equivalent thereof—were summoned. He also decided he'd better speak persuasively. "Urquiashqua, you've told us that psionic projection in the Inner Void is theoretically possible. Well, I'm second only to Paul Rinnard as a projector. And we know that the projected consciousness can employ other psionic powers while detached from the corporeal body. I'll find Sophia and signal to her telepathically the way we signaled to you in Earth orbit."

Urquiashqua shook his head sadly. "Derek . . . my dear young man . . . I wish with all my heart that this gallant and very original idea of yours could work. But I hardly know where to begin enumerating the impossibilities. First of all, none of our experiments in psionic projection have ever actually succeeded in entering the Inner Void."

"But we're *already* in the Inner Void!"

Urquiashqua opened his mouth to speak, then halted. After a moment, he closed his mouth and assumed an expression of deep thought. No one disturbed him.

"All right," he finally allowed. "You may have hit on an interesting point. And, historically, a few supremely powerful mages are alleged to have projected their minds into the Inner Void, although Qyloeshqua himself was the only one whose experience is actually verified."

"Yes, so you've told us, as I recall," said Derek, pressing what he perceived to be an advantage.

"Ah, then you'll also recall that none of those mages ever claimed to have entered the gods' domains. Rather, they found themselves in the formless chaos that is the Inner Void in its natural state. What makes you think you could succeed where they failed? And assuming that you could, what makes you think you could locate the particular domain in which Sophia resides? And even assuming that you could do all these things, what makes you think that you, individually, could contact her by the kind of telepathic broadcasting which, on the occasion to which you've referred, required a psionic concert directed by Paul Rinnard?"

Derek drew a deep breath. The idea had come on him like a sudden epiphany, and he was making up the details as he went along. But as he did so, he felt less and less self-doubt. Indeed, by now he felt none at all. And when he spoke, his voice held an absolute assurance that, had he but known it, communicated itself to his listeners—all of them older than he and full of the unconscious assumption of superiority that went with being products of a more advanced civilization—and silenced them.

"Urquiashqua, the answer to all these objections lies in your lab. We have with us the new model of the psi amplifier—the compact one, with an integral power source. You brought it along to use in the experiments we were going to conduct, subject to the usual safety cutoff. Well, I think the time has come to disengage that cutoff."

Now everyone was staring at him—especially Lauren, with a horrified intensity which puzzled him. Then he recalled what she'd once said, in the privacy of the bedroom, about what the psi amplifier was doing to Paul Rinnard. He thrust the unwelcome association out of his mind and resumed in the same doubt-free voice. "I believe the problems you've raised are not fundamental ones. They're nothing that can't be overcome with more psionic power. I'll have other things in my favor as well. For

example, I know Sophia. I'm convinced that this relationship has created a kind of mental resonance which will
make it easier to establish contact with her when I've
reached her domain. Speaking of which, I've visited that
domain; I'll recognize it. And the usual limitations on the
speed and range of movement by the projected consciousness shouldn't apply in the Inner Void, where you've told
us time and distance are effectively nonexistent."

"But, Derek," the mage protested, "your only experiences
with projection have been in the Outer Void, from which
your disembodied consciousness could observe the material
world and simply 'snap back' into your corporeal body at
your pleasure. In the Inner Void, without this essential
element of connectedness, how will you be able to . . . find
your way home?"

"The answer, of course, is that I don't know. But this,
uh, Qyloeshqua must have gotten back. Otherwise his
experience wouldn't be so well documented. If he could do
it, I can do it."

Derek stopped and held his breath. He had a pretty good
idea that he'd come across sounding like someone who'd
used those last nine words in connection with Mozart and
Classical composition, or Tiger Woods and golf. But he
couldn't back down now.

Zhezum spoke—and, to Derek's surprise, his sarcasm and
hostility seemed muted. "Have you considered the possibility
that your consciousness will, at first, find itself in this empty
Void domain where we now find ourselves rather than
roaming at large in the Inner Void?"

Urquiashqua spoke up. "Yes! I consider this an eminently
possible contingency. In a Void domain, the Inner Void has
been organized into a small analog of the material universe.
Under these conditions, an extradimensional interface comparable to what we call the Outer Void quite probably exists."

"And," Rhykhvyleshqua spoke up sternly, "you know the
effect an empty Void domain like this has on the human
mind—especially on an inexperienced one like yours."

"Yes, I know. I'm hardly likely to forget." Fleetingly, he
recalled that first intolerable sight, with no stage scenery

to mask the naked walls of a small infinity. He suppressed the memory.

"So," the captain continued inexorably, "can you imagine what it would be like to be a floating viewpoint outside the ship, not just glimpsing this domain through a viewscreen but totally surrounded by it?"

"I have indeed thought of the likelihood that I'll find myself in such a situation. But I believe it may work in my favor. You see, such an environment will be so totally intolerable that my consciousness will flee, out into the generalized environment of the Inner Void, with a kind of, uh, momentum."

"Won't your consciousness be more likely to snap back to your body in terror?" asked Lauren. Her color wasn't very good.

"That would certainly seem the most obvious refuge for it to seek," agreed Urquiashqua.

"Well, then, like so much else about psionics it becomes a matter of *will*. I'll have to keep uppermost in my mind the need to go and get help, and that I can't let myself run screaming back to my own body." Derek looked around the circle of faces. "Hey, instinct—even the survival instinct—can be fought! Have any of you ever shot a carrier landing?" He hadn't either, but saw nothing to be gained by pointing that out. "You have to follow the Landing Safety Officer's orders unhesitatingly, even though your eyes tell you that the goddamned son of a bitch is trying to kill you by making you crash into the stern of the ship!"

"You are assuming," Urquiashqua said gravely, "that you will be able to exert the necessary willpower long enough, before your sanity gives way. If not, your mind will either return to your body or, perhaps, be unable to do even that. And we will be left with your body, either hopelessly psychotic or as totally mindless as though anencephalic."

Lauren was now very white indeed.

"This is nothing but a million-to-one shot," muttered Zhezum. The interpreter software was getting better with idioms.

"All right, maybe it is. But what other chance do we have?

You yourself said earlier that we have *no* alternative except sitting around and watching our supplies run low." Derek looked around the table again. "How about it, people? Does anybody have a nine-hundred-and-ninety-nine-thousand-to-one shot to offer?"

No one answered him, or met his eyes.

"I still say we should both do it," fumed Lauren as they walked along the curving passageway of the spin habitat.

"You know you're not in my league when it comes to projection," Derek reminded her.

"No, but we could set up a concert!"

"Nobody's ever tried to do that while projecting."

"It's worth a try. Other psi abilities work with the consciousness projected."

"Even if it did work, the added benefit wouldn't be worth the risk."

"I could order you to do it in concert with me," she said, tight-lipped. "I do outrank you, you know."

"Excuse me, O Exalted First Lieutenant! By all means, put me on report! But I somehow doubt if Rhykhvyleshqua is going to be too concerned with the distinction between a gold bar and a silver one." Derek halted abruptly and faced her. "Look, you're the only other psi around. We need for you to stay aboard, in reserve."

"You've just got to do it on your own, don't you?" she ground out. "The great big fearless macho man!"

"Fearless? What a joke! I'm so terrified I'm about to wet my pants." He turned on his heel and hurried on before she could formulate a response. She was still seeking words when they arrived at the lab.

Urquiashqua supervised the preparations, with Rhykhvyleshqua and Zhezum looking on. First they strapped Derek into a reclining couch equipped with clamps for securing his wrists and ankles lest he injure himself in the grip of an insane mind that had fled, gibbering, from the regions of madness around them. Then medical personnel attached IV ports so that he could, if necessary, be fed intravenously, for no one knew how long his mind would be absent.

Finally, Urquiashqua summoned the three observers forward, for whatever farewells they felt the urge to make.
Lauren grasped him by the shoulders, and kissed him with
fierce intensity. "I'll be with you," she whispered into his
ear. Then she stepped back, stood trembling for a moment,
then composed herself to wait.

Zhezum stepped forward, wearing an unreadable expression. Then he extended his right hand, palm outward.
Remembering the Erkhedzye equivalent of a handshake,
Derek placed his palm flat against the other's. Their eyes
met for a wordless instant, and then Zhezum returned to
his place against the bulkhead.

Rhykhvyleshqua stepped forward in his massive way.
Meeting his somber dark eyes, Derek wondered what had
called forth dim early-adolescent memories of his father,
whom the captain didn't resemble in the least. "One thing
I didn't ask you before, Derek. Assuming—against all the
astronomical odds—that you can actually contact Sophia,
are you really so very sure you can rely on her help?
Remember, the gods are notoriously capricious."

"Oh, yes, I'm sure. She and the rest of the gods have
invested a lot of effort in this scheme of enlisting the psionic
powers that have evolved on Earth in their absence; they
won't want to let it go to waste. Besides, I think I know
her well enough to be sure she doesn't look on humans
as worthless pawns."

"How can you be so sure of that?"

Derek hesitated, suddenly wary of seeming foolish. "She's
remembered in my culture, by another name, through myths
that have come down to us from Earth's Bronze Age."

"Ah, yes." Rhykhvyleshqua nodded slowly. "I've heard of
those legends, from just before the last of the Rhysqaruo
descendants were allowed through the portals to Khron. The
Heroic Age, it was called."

"Right. Well, one consistent theme in all those stories was
that she helped deserving mortal heroes. Bellerophon,
Odysseus, Perseus . . . she mentioned him in particular, once,
at a place on Earth called Mycenae, where he ruled."

"Yes, I know those tales. And I also know this, Derek:

if those heroes of your boyhood stories were all here today, you would belong in their company. Succeed or fail, you have earned a place among them by what you have dared." The captain gave his shoulder a quick squeeze, then joined Zhezum and Lauren and waited with folded arms.

Derek became aware that the medics were attaching IV tubes and securing the clamps that immobilized his arms and legs. Then Urquiashqua approached, bearing the psi amplifier. It was the operational prototype, intended for shipboard deployment. There were three of them aboard— or had been, for Paul Rinnard's was missing. This was the one he'd spent the trip out practicing with, so the preliminary step of attuning the device to a particular user was long since done.

"I have disengaged all safety restraints," said the mage portentously. "Quite simply, I do not know the factor by which it will enhance your powers. I also do not know what the effect on your mind will be. If your ability to control your unaccustomed level of power fails, it is possible that you could experience a kind of negative feedback, resulting in irreversible brain damage. Were it not for our desperate circumstances, I would refuse to participate in this incredibly rash experiment. In short, if you continue on your present course you will do so without benefit of my professional counsel. Do you wish to continue?"

Derek stared at the headset in Urquiashqua's hands. Bits of folk wisdom about the inadvisability of riding a tiger flitted mockingly through his mind. He tried to swallow, but his mouth was too dry for that, or even for speech, so he only nodded. The mage placed the absurdly light framework over his head and sat down at the control console. He fiddled with the controls, then met Derek's eyes. "This model, unlike the earlier experimental ones, can be fine-tuned, as it were, to enhance only one psionic power. It has been so adjusted, for projection; you need not worry about extraneous, distracting psionic manifestations. I have now activated the system. You need only signal me when you are ready for me to give it power. I will do so gradually, beginning with the low setting to which you are accustomed."

Derek permitted himself to meet Lauren's eyes one final time. Then he turned away, for nothing must distract him. He found he could now speak, and he did so. "Ready."

At first it was like his previous projection experiences, roaming immaterially about the room and viewing its occupants, including himself. But then he watched—or, as he decided was more accurate, "perceived"—as Urquiashqua moved the power setting further to the right.

He didn't experience a moment of supra-sensory transcendence, for the mage was upping the power cautiously. But he was conscious, in some indescribable way, of the heightened energies at his command. He willed his disembodied viewpoint to move, and this time it flashed from the laboratory, through the bulkheads and along the passageways of the spin habitat before he managed, like a rodeo rider, to bring it under control. He continued to practice, roaming elsewhere in *Ergu Nervy*, faster than his body could have run, though not nearly at the speed of which he knew he was now capable.

But he didn't let himself unleash that speed, which would have carried him instantly through *Ergu Nervy*'s hull, as meaningless as any other material barrier to a projected consciousness. He wasn't yet ready to face what lay beyond that hull.

He could not delay any longer, though. He gathered himself for that which he'd known there would be no avoiding.

For a split second his surroundings were a blur of relative motion, and then *Ergu Nervy* lay off to the side. But he gave the massive ultra-high-tech dumbbell shape no notice, for he was floating in an infinity only a few thousand miles in diameter, and he had no eyelids to squeeze shut and no mouth with which to scream.

Had he been able to perceive his body, he would surely have returned to it, gibbering as he sought shelter from the intolerable. But he could not, and so was able to cling to his original resolve. There could be no thought of fine control, though. With a soundless shriek, he willed himself out of this mind-destroying place as quickly as his enhanced powers would permit.

He felt a momentary, dizzying disorientation, and the empty Void domain vanished. There was no passing through any barrier or boundary. Presumably, the gods' incomprehensible Void constructs simply didn't work that way.

He didn't have time to think about it, for now he was observing the Inner Void in its pristine state.

He felt no vertigo, and no sensation of falling, because there was nothing to fall toward in this place with no floor, ceiling or walls. He willed his insubstantial identity-locale to move, but there were no reference points in this limitless abyss. Yet he felt, if not the sensation of motion, then an intuition of it. Likewise, he felt an awareness of the passage of time, albeit strangely distorted. He must, he decided, be somehow imposing his own metrical framework on this textureless realm of primal chaos where time and distance had no meaning. Likewise, he must have brought with him the memory of colors and sounds—but, unable to attach them to any physical reality, he perceived the abyss as a slowly swirling infinity of dim colors unknown to mortal eyes, and a deep, mournful sound somewhere between a roar and a howl, wavering eerily up and down an unhuman scale.

He didn't belong here. He wanted to go home.

But he couldn't let himself dwell on his lostness, his utter lack of any notion of how to find his way back to the quiescent body that lay strapped into a reclining couch aboard *Ergu Nervy*. Still less could he let himself visualize a stretch of beach with the breakers rolling in from the Atlantic and the sandfiddlers hopping daintily along just ahead of them, as the seafood aroma from his grandfather's grill blended with the salt air and the low tide. No, he must fare onward, broadcasting a call for help with all the enhanced telepathic power he could bring to bear. This time, he did so without the help of a concert, but at least he had a specific target-persona, albeit a non-telepathic one.

Time passed. Quite a lot of time—or so it seemed to Derek. But he had no way of knowing just how much, for his time-scale seemed to be drifting further and further from its moorings. He wondered if he would return to his body in

Ergu Nervy after what seemed to those aboard her to be a mere eyeblink's absence, or if he would find a dusty ghost ship crewed by skeletons, including his own.

The real question, of course, was how he was going to find his way back there at all. He did not permit himself to contemplate that. He must focus his entire being on the need to continuously broadcast that cry for help.

Finally, something began to happen.

At first it was barely noticeable. The dimly colored chaos that swirled against the infinitely remote twilight backdrop began to take on a semblance of form and solidity. Derek had only just begun to notice those vague planes and angles and surfaces when they began to whirl into a dizzying vortex . . . but only for an instant. Then it was over, and he knew where he was, for he'd been here before.

The clouds, tinted pale gold by the sun of an eternal afternoon, drifted among the palace-crowned mountains and above the Arcadian glens. Derek's disembodied viewpoint surveyed the impossibly vast, heartbreakingly beautiful landscape from the same balustraded marble terrace where his physical body had once stood.

His hunch had paid off. Adrift in the trackless abyss of the Inner Void, his projected consciousness had sought for the familiar like an iron filing in zero gravity seeking a magnet.

He pulled himself together and began broadcasting again.

At the back of the terrace, something stirred in the colonnaded entrance to the soaring palace. A tall dark-haired female figure in Khronuo dress stepped forward. Her gray eyes darted this way and that, and her almost-too-regular features wore a puzzled look.

"Sophia!" The name would have come out as a choked sob of relief had Derek's larynx formed it.

CHAPTER SEVENTEEN

Once before, on a road in the Peloponnesus, Derek had tried to tap into Sophia's thoughts. As he vividly recalled, he'd run into the psionic equivalent of a brick wall.

He had decided no useful purpose would be served by mentioning this when he was trying to sell his idea of contacting her. They all knew humans could prevent telepathic contact simply by the application of a definitely opposed will, so surely the same went double for the gods. And the gods, as Sophia herself had pointed out, liked their privacy.

And so it had proved. Catching her unaware and unprepared, he had been able to broadcast his desperate cry to her. And once that contact was established, she understood what was happening and opened her mind to him.

Telepathic linkage with a god was no more like a spoken conversation than it was with a mortal non-telepath. But Sophia "thought very loudly," making her organized surface thoughts as clear as possible. The disembodied viewpoint that was Derek followed her like a puppy as she swept into the mountainside edifice, through corridors too vast to be indoors and along sunlit fern-hung galleries. Afterwards, he was never able to remember more than fragments of all that architectural fantasy, glimpses that haunted his dreams.

Indeed, his entire incorporeal stay in the gods' domain was itself more than a little dreamlike.

But afterwards, one memory stood out in sharp relief. He was in a large, airy chamber, overlooking through a semi-circular loggia the breathtaking valley below. He watched as Sophia, standing, addressed a group of other figures reclining on couches or seated on marble benches. He could not understand what was being said—even if his consciousness was still linked to the interpreter his physical body wore aboard *Ergu Nervy* in the same unfathomable way it still partook of the psionic enhancement conferred by that physical body's headpiece, the software was of course no help here. So he tuned out the unintelligible colloquy and studied the room's occupants. Like Sophia, they were all wearing Khronuo garments—although he'd now seen enough of such garments to recognize these as formal and exceptionally fine, almost an idealization of the style. This was especially evident in the case of a choleric-looking bruiser wearing a version of Erkhedzuo military dress whose long black sleeveless tunic was edged with a burgundy far richer than the more ususal earth-tones, and was bedizened with a blinding array of decorations. The getup put Derek irresistibly in mind of the opening sequence of the classic old movie *Patton* despite the total unrelatedness of the two styles.

The others were all in civvies. They were of differing apparent ages, but all possessed Sophia's elusive agelessness—particularly a placidly handsome young-seeming man and his athletic-looking twin sister, to both of whom Derek took an instinctive dislike. There were others as well: a blonde who made Nydierya look downright homely, watched with evident jealousy by a stocky engineer type . . . a well-fleshed matronly woman, kindly-looking but with an unmistakable air of melancholy loss . . . a wiry, active young guy with an engagingly mobile face, who had "gofer" written all over him. . . .

There were still others, and it almost hurt the eyes to look at a room full of them, for each had a quality he'd noticed from the first in Sophia: it was difficult to look anywhere else.

But even in this company, there was one who made it very hard to notice the others. Had there been a table, wherever that one had sat would have been the head of it.

He had the semblance of a big, powerfully built man at the zenith of vigorous maturity. His wavy hair and curly beard, iron-gray in color like thick dark clouds, framed strong features that reflected both firmness and thoughtfulness . . . and, occasionally, a lip-quirking amusement as though he was recalling incidents of a very interesting life. He almost defined the concept of masculinity, but with none of the glowering, jut-jawed hostility of the uniformed type.

Derek had a pretty good idea of just who it was he was observing. In fact, he was more and more certain of the identities of most of these individuals—the identities by which they were remembered in his particular culture—even without the occasional, tantalizingly half-familiar names he caught in the otherwise unintelligible conversation. He also had a pretty good idea that the general climate of opinion was most charitably described as irritable—and that his psionic presence here was the reason.

He was glad he wasn't physically present. If he had been, he would have been trying his best to be small and inconspicuous. It wouldn't have been hard. Not here.

The conclave lasted a while, and occasionally grew acrimonious. But then, abruptly, it resolved itself and dispersed. Sophia turned and departed with the deliberate haste of someone who'd won a point and didn't want to tempt fate by waiting around long enough for second thoughts to crystallize. Once again, Derek's consciousness followed her through the corridors, and he put out a mental feeler. He was always careful not to presume on the opening of her mind to him; he made contact only with the mental equivalent of a timid tap on a door frame. And he hadn't even done that during the conference he'd attended; it would, he was mortally certain, have been *very* bad form.

Now, however, she allowed him to tap her organized surface thoughts freely. Indeed, those thoughts were consciously directed toward him, making it far easier. It still wasn't like hearing spoken words—telepathy never was. It was, as Doctor Kronenberg never tired of pointing out, more a matter of reading *intentions*. And in this case, Sophia's intentions were very plain.

She was telling him to launch himself back into the Inner Void.

His mind quailed at the thought of that yawning abyss. Indeed, with the best will in the world he wasn't certain he'd know how to send his projected consciousness out of a domain, without the stark, shrieking horror that had propelled it before. And if he did emerge into the incomprehensible chaos of the Inner Void, how would he find his way? With all the concentration he could muster, he broadcast his fears and his doubts to Sophia's wide-open mind.

What he read there was clear and serene. For once it was almost as though he was listening to spoken words.

Do not worry. I will be with you.

Derek swallowed hard—or would have, had his consciousness-locale possessed a throat with which to do it. He recognized the doomed futility of any protests. And he recalled Urquiashqua's theory that the gods were capable of *physical* movement in the Inner Void—which, on reflection, they must be, for they were native to it.

He didn't waste time on a futile effort to understand. He willed the immaterial viewpoint that was the locale of his mind outward, through the inconceivable corridors and out into the crystalline sky. He soared up and up, above the impossibly dramatic landscape and as he rose higher, he began to notice something wrong about the horizon—or where there should have been a horizon. Something deeply disturbing . . .

Then there was the same dreamlike disorientation he had experienced when leaving the hollow Void domain that was *Ergu Nervy*'s prison. And, just as abruptly as on that occasion, he was in the softly roaring, dimly glowing abyss that was the Inner Void.

As before, he made no attempt to impose any direction on his movement. Here, "direction" was as meaningless as every other concept derived from the orderly universe of matter. This time, though, he was not broadcasting a cry for help like a psionic beacon; even had his friends aboard *Ergu Nervy* been able to receive it, which he doubted very much, none of them—not even Lauren—would have been able to do anything about it. No, he simply willed his projected consciousness onward, holding his purpose firmly in mind and reminding himself that he'd been assured his incorporeal journey would be shepherded. That was all he had to cling to in this realm of no reference points, where he was lost and alone in a way no human had ever imagined it possible to be lost and alone.

And—also as before—time passed. It became more and more difficult to focus on his purpose. So he made that purpose less and less abstract in his mind, until it resolved itself into the memory of Lauren's face.

Then, without warning, form began to impose itself on chaos in the remembered way, and he was momentarily caught in the remembered dizzying vortex. Then he was in that empty Void domain from which his consciousness had fled screaming. But *Ergu Nervy* lay dead ahead, solid black against that backdrop of what humans had no business seeing. He clawed his way toward that silhouette like a drowning man struggling toward the sun glimpsed through the water above. . . .

And he was in his body. His body wept.

Blinking away his tears, he became aware of the commotion around him. The next thing he became aware of was that he was no longer on the recliner in Urquiashqua's laboratory. He was in a bed in *Ergu Nervy*'s sickbay, hooked up to what looked to his inexpert eyes very much like serious life support.

The *next* thing he noticed took longer, because he'd become unaccustomed to the sensations of his body. It felt like lead, after the unfettered freedon of motion the projected consciousness enjoyed—that was to be expected; it was always that way, and he'd never projected for so long a time before. But he could soon sense that all was not well. He felt weak, with an enfeeblement such as he'd never experienced. Also, he was hungry as hell.

Then all that was forgotten as the door opened and Lauren was the first through it.

Even at that instant, he could see the change in her. She was unwontedly pale, and her cheekbones stood out with an alarming starkness. As the others crowded in behind her, he observed the same signs in them—even Rhykhvyleshqua, whom he'd thought as adamantine as bedrock. They also wore a uniform expression of joyful relief, although in Lauren's case it was overlaid with tears.

Then the final arrival came through the door. Derek wasn't too surprised that she was still wearing the same understatedly sophisticated Erkhedzuo outfit he'd seen her in as she'd faced her kin in the chamber of the wide-curving loggia.

They held a meeting as soon as Derek was up to it—or a little sooner than that, in the grumpy opinion of his doctor.

He was sitting up in bed, unenthusiastically spooning up the dietary solution to which he was restricted until he was up to solid foods. It was highly nutritious, and it even filled his shrunken stomach. But at that moment he would have mortgaged his future for a cheeseburger and a beer, and thrown in his soul for a side order of onion rings.

"Four months?" he asked wonderingly. The interpreter software had put it into Earth equivalents.

Urquiashqua nodded. "We had given you up for lost. I was forced to conclude that my gloomiest predictions had come true, and that your consciousness—your soul, if you like—had gotten hopelessly lost in the Void, leaving us with an empty body."

"Glad you didn't dispose of it," said Derek drily.

Rhykhvyleshqua smiled, and glanced at Lauren. "I'd like to have seen us try!"

Urquiashqua was not amused. "My dear boy, your body was still alive, albeit mindless. We were under an ethical obligation. So we moved it—I mean, we moved *you* . . . well, you know what I mean—here where long-term life support was available."

"But . . . *four months?* I mean, it didn't seem that long to me."

"In the Void," explained Sophia, "time passes at a different rate. Rather, it passes at different *rates,* in a manner too chaotic to be understood. One's time-sense is unreliable."

Derek stared at Lauren and the others. *Ergu Nervy*'s life support system, like that of all state-of-the-art Khronuo space vessels, was based on molecular-level recycling techniques, and could keep the occupants alive indefinitely if they didn't mind going on short rations—which they generally didn't, given the unappetizing monotony of the emergency food the nanomachines churned out. And yet . . . he tried to imagine what it must have been like, imprisoned in close quarters without hope for month after month inside these walls of steel. (Oh, all right; it was an artificial composite laminate.) He fully understood why they looked the way they did. Even Rhykhvyleshqua's leadership must have been fully stretched to keep them from killing each other.

So he wondered why they weren't looking happy now.

"Well," he ventured, "better late than never, as they say. Sophia, you *can* create a portal out of here to anywhere in the material universe, can't you?"

"To any definitely known locale, yes." The goddess nodded.

"Which Khron is!" Derek looked again at the faces of these people, who should have been turning handsprings. *Am I missing something?* "Well, uh, what are we waiting for? Why are we still sitting here eating small helpings of tasteless glop? Why aren't we back in the Khron system, or at least on our way there?"

The others looked at each other awkwardly. Lauren finally spoke.

"Sophia arrived here a little before your body reawoke, Derek. She's had time to brief us on what's been going on for the last three months, and . . . Well, there may be nothing in the Khron system worth going back to."

The story came out bit by bit, in its full horror.

Sophia had visited Khron shortly after *Ergu Nervy* had vanished, and like everyone else had accepted the story Nydierya and Paul Rinnard had brought back in their lifeboat: that the ship had died in a flare of antimatter annihilation in the outer system. Through her, this was the story the gods had received.

"So," remarked Sophia, "it was something of a shock to receive a telepathic broadcast from someone we had all believed to be dead. That was one reason your cry for help caused such a stir. The other reason was that you were the first human ever to project his consciousness into one of our domains. We had thought that to be impossible. Some of my . . . relatives were highly upset to learn otherwise."

"Gee, sorry to have been such a bother," muttered Derek with no good grace.

Sophia's serenity was unruffled. "Our assumptions were based on *magical* projection. Human psionic powers are something new in our experience, and artificially enhanced ones are even newer. It is . . . food for thought. Especially coming on the heels of the news from Khron."

"What news?" But Derek found he could answer his own question. He just didn't want to. "Paul," he breathed.

Sophia nodded. "At first, he and Nydierya remained circumspect. To the extent we have been able to piece the sequence of events together, he started out thinking he was deceiving the Qurvyshuo and the Titans who stood behind them."

"Yes. Lauren, remember that last-minute message to us? He said something about that, didn't he? Something about how sabotaging this ship was somehow necessary for the ultimate defeat of the Titans."

"Unfortunately, as so often happens in the realm of espionage, an assumed persona became a real one." Sophia turned grave. "It is easy enough to reconstruct the course of events. There would always have been just one more thing he had to do to establish his credibility with the Titans. Eventually, Rinnard reached a point where he could not turn back—if, indeed, he still *wanted* to turn back. By that time, he had probably been seduced by the power of his psionic abilities.

"In the meantime, he was becoming more and more powerful as he learned to channel and focus the psychotronic enhancements. Also, he had been learning more and more about the potential applications of telepathy. The walls of normal security were now like tissue paper to him. At any rate, before Erkhedzuo counterintelligence had begun to more than suspect anything was amiss, he and Nydierya had surfaced in Qurvyshye with a state-of-the-art psychotronic amplifier.

"It can hardly be mere coincidence that shortly afterwards things started to go horribly wrong."

Derek listened, aghast, for unlike the others he hadn't had time for the shock to dull. The cold war in the Khron system had blown hot, and with sickening rapidity the Qurvyshuo had smashed the allies in deep space. At crucial moments in the struggle, things had happened . . . unexpected things.

"As the decisive space engagement was teetering on a knife-edge, the alliance commanders were led into tactical blunders by large-scale illusions," Sophia explained. "That kind of thing can be done by magic—but magic can also counteract it. Traditionally, in warfare on Khron, the two sides' mages cancel each other out. But psionics is something else.

"Later, Qurvyshuo raiders began appearing in crucial nerve centers. There was a bad firefight in the Citadel itself. Once again, magical countermeasures prevent the opening of portals into sensitive areas. But Rinnard has evidently learned to teleport other people and things with him."

"It is a technique we will want to explore," Urquiashqua put in, with irrepressible intellectual curiosity.

"And duplicate," added Lauren with a more practical appreciation of its potentialities.

"It soon became apparent," Sophia went on, "that these phenomena were only occuring one at a time. Hardly surprising: Rinnard cannot be everywhere at once. This may be why the situation is not even worse than it is. Still, it is bad enough. Even the conventional fighting on the surface of the planet, though limited by tacit agreement, has caused widespread devastation. The alliance is still holding out there. But the Qurvyshuo are the undisputed masters of deep space. The alliance is still maintaining a viable presence in low Khron orbit. When it can no longer do so— and it is only a matter of time—then all will be over."

"Yes, this was explained to us," Derek said dully. "But can't you gods help?"

"We have endeavored to do so. That, incidentally, was another reason your—'appearance' is hardly the right word—was so inopportune. We were in the midst of a war crisis. But, as I have repeatedly told you, we are not omnipotent. Far from it. And the Titans are actively engaged on the Qurvyshuo side. As I previously remarked about the use of magic by the two sides, we and they have canceled each other out."

Lauren, who had been seemingly studying the deck between her feet, looked up. "Sophia, remember when we were at Mycenae? You told us about the real origin of some of our world's myths."

"Yes, I remember."

"Well," Lauren continued, a ghastly smile, "this time, it seems Hercules has joined the Titans."

If possible, the silence grew deeper and gloomier. Rhykhvyleshqua finally broke it. "Our duty is clear. However futile a return to Khron appears, we have no choice. *Ergu Nervy* may have been extensively modified for research purposes before its deployment to the Solar system, but this is still a combatant ship. We may not be able to affect the outcome at Khron, but we have no alternative but to try."

Zhezum looked up, red-eyed. "Yes! If nothing else, we can take some of those Qurvyshuo vermin with us!"

"So be it." Rhykhvyleshqua straightened up as though laboring under a great weight. He addressed Zhezum heavily. "Give the order to—"

"No."

There was a moment of shocked silence. Derek was the most shocked of all, at the realization of what he'd just said to the captain of this ship. But he somehow managed to resume. "Excuse me, sir, but a doomed suicide charge isn't our only option. Look, the balance in the Khron system has been kicked over by Paul's psionic powers, right? Well, we ought to fight fire with fire—and psionics with psionics!"

"This is axiomatic," intoned Urquiashqua. "But, Derek, do you truly believe you and Lauren would be a match for Rinnard?"

"No way. We weren't before, and we're even less so now, given what Sophia has told us about the exponential growth of his powers."

"Well, then . . . ?" Rhykhvyleshqua let the question hang in the air.

"Since we're no match for him, we need more help. Sophia, you can open a portal for us to the Solar system just as easily as to Khron, can't you?"

"I would not precisely call it *easy*," the goddess demurred primly. "But . . . yes."

"And there are more psis on Earth. And *we* have the enhancement technology here aboard this ship." Derek didn't realize how wolfish his grin looked. "That was Nydierya's mistake. She should have sabotaged the hell out of every psychotronic headset aboard except the one Paul took with him. But then, she didn't think she needed to; we were going to be stuck permanently in limbo."

"Derek," Sophia cautioned, "everything I told you and Lauren before about the danger of overt contact with the authorities on Earth is still just as valid now."

"Oh, yes, I know we can't just land on Earth and blurt out the truth. But there are things we *can* do. First of all, I know of one psi JICPO doesn't have squirrelled away: my grandfather."

"Your grandfather?" Zhezum's voice rose to an incredulous squeak that the interpreter tried to mimic.

"Yes. In his youth, he was a latent psi who emerged temporarily into operancy. A number of them did, around that time, but I understand he was an extraordinarily powerful one. In fact, he was part of the reason my nation's military awoke to the potential of psionics."

" 'Temporarily'?" echoed Urquiashqua.

"Yes. It didn't last—it never did in those days. He lapsed back into latency."

"Well, then—?"

"Urquiashqua, with the neural induction technology you've

got, I'm willing to bet you can reawaken his powers. Especially if . . ." Derek trailed off, thinking.

"If what?" prompted Rhykhvyleshqua.

"We need to pay a visit to JICPO. And no," Derek added hastily in Sophia's direction, "not an open visit. But if Lauren and I start working with Urquiashqua right now, I'll bet we can develop our teleportation abilities enough to get in there. Remember, we know the layout. And there's somebody there we need. I'll bet she'll even come willingly."

Lauren stared at him. "Dr. Kronenberg—?"

"Yes, the battle-axe herself." Derek turned to the mage. "Urquiashqua, you have knowledge and technology she's never dreamed of. But she's spent decades studying psionics. Hell, she invented the mathematical basis for quantifying and identifying it! If you and she can be brought together . . . Well, I can't even venture to predict what you might come up with."

"Hmm . . ." The mage took on a faraway look.

"Didn't you once say you wished you could meet her?" asked Lauren innocently.

"Yes, so I did, didn't I?"

"But we don't have time for a side-trip to Earth!" exploded Zhezum. "You heard what Sophia said about the situation in the Khron system. By the time we get there, it could all be over!"

Urquiashqua blinked away his dreamy look and turned to Rhykhvyleshqua. "All the more reason for us to get underway for Earth without delay," he said in a voice as firm as his ever got. "I believe Derek's suggestion may have merit. At least he offers us an alternative to futility."

The debate went on, but Derek knew he would win it. He now had an unshakable ally in Urquiashqua, and no really hard-core opposition. All of them, even Zhezum, wanted to believe there was hope—he could see it in them, and hear it in their voices.

He made brief eye-contact with Sophia. She smiled her enigmatic smile.

★ CHAPTER EIGHTEEN

The blaze in the fireplace roared defiance at the gales of winter. Glenn Secrest nevertheless wore a turtlenecked sweater as he stood at the sliding glass doors and gazed out to sea.

The horizon was indistinguishable; ocean and sky were all one great desolation of gray. Overhead, a few seagulls hung practically motionless as they beat against the wind whose mournful whistling invaded the house through the chimney.

Now I know where the expression "bird-brain" comes from, thought Glenn as he watched the stubborn exercise in avian futility.

His lame attempt at inner humor failed to cheer him. He continued to stare at the scene whose dreariness mirrored so perfectly his spirit. *The good news,* he told himself, *is that there'll be no stars out tonight.* Once, he'd loved sitting on the deck on clear nights and letting his imagination roam the star-studded firmament. But that had been before the cruelly beautiful summer day when the carefully worded letter from Captain Morrisey had arrived. Now the stars just reminded him of Derek.

You made it into orbit, boy, he thought, addressing the

memory of his grandson with silent pride. *It must have been a good way to go.* It was the only thought that still had the power to cheer him.

But the feeling never lasted. A lifetime's steadfast refusal to con himself had left him incapable of denying the truth. And the truth was that he didn't have a clue as to how Derek had met his end. The dead hand of Security had squeezed the life out of Morrisey's narrative, leaving only one dry husk of fact: Glenn's grandson was no more. His efforts to extract the full story from the government had run into the full bureaucratic array of infuriating passive defenses: phone calls put permanently on hold, letters answered with promises to send him forms which in fact never arrived, and all the rest. He'd finally come to the rueful realization that the windmill was winning, and had given up. Now his longevity was a burden, his unabated physical health like ashes in his mouth.

He turned away from the bleak late-afternoon panorama and walked past the fireplace to the bar. The contents of the latter, like those of the former, could warm his body but not his soul. Nevertheless, he picked up a glass. He knew he'd been drinking too much lately. He didn't care.

He was reaching for a decanter when a very slight breeze of disturbed air caused the hairs at the base of his neck to bristle—that, and a knowledge below the level of the senses that something out of the ordinary had just occurred in the room.

"Hello, Granddad."

Glenn whirled around. The glass dropped from his nerveless fingers and shattered on the hardwood floor.

"Good thing you hadn't filled that." The new arrival smiled.

"Derek?" Glenn croaked. Then his voice and face hardened into anger. "No! Derek is dead. Who the hell are you, you son of a bitch, and how did you get in? And what kind of getup is that?"

"Come on, Granddad, you know it's me. I realize I'm a little out of uniform—although it is, in fact, *a* uniform." Derek shook his head, dismissing the uniform of his Erkhedzuo courtesy rank. "But you still know it's me, don't you?"

Strangely enough, Glenn found he *did* know it. The voice, the mannerisms, everything—nobody could have duplicated Derek's persona so perfectly, even had a motive existed. And it would have made no sense for an imposter to wear such an outlandish costume.

But . . .

"But they told me that you . . . that Derek died in orbit! The details were a mystery, they were so vague about the whole thing."

"That's because it was a mystery to *them*. The State can never admit the existence of anything it doesn't understand, because that would mean admitting it isn't omniscient."

"Well, well! I guess I at least managed to infect you with my political philosophy!"

"More like an *anti*-political philosophy," Derek retorted. They exchanged grins, and Glenn's last doubts evaporated.

"But I don't understand any of this!" protested the old man. "Starting with how you got here."

"Teleportation," said Derek succinctly.

"Teleportation! That was just a theoretical possibility back when I was operant—one of the psionic powers other than basic telepathy for which some sort of basis seemed to exist in folklore. A pipe dream."

"It's still largely a pipe dream—or would be except for this." Derek touched the plastic framework that capped the crown of his head.

"And what, exactly, is that?" demanded Glenn.

"It's a psionic amplifier. Field model, with an integral power source."

" 'Integral power source'—inside *that* thing?" In the storm-center at the back of his mind where his sense of reality was sheltering, Glenn couldn't believe he was quibbling about such details.

"Granddad, you have *no* idea! For now, just take my word for it that this can magnify any psionic powers you've already got, even if they're only present on a uselessly tiny level. Even tinier than mine. Speaking of which, excuse me a second while I link with somebody who doesn't know this house intimately and couldn't teleport into it like I could."

Derek took on a peculiar look of concentration that Glenn recognized from long-ago memories. Then, with no warning, another figure was standing beside Derek. A female figure—very female, in fact, although she couldn't have made a living as a high-fashion model—wearing a variation on Derek's outfit.

"Grandfather," Derek began in a formal tone which, intentionally or otherwise, had the effect of calming Glenn's disarrayed nerves, "I'd like to introduce First Lieutenant Lauren Westerfeld, United States Air Force. Like me, she is assigned to JICPO. And, also like me, she is currently on . . . unofficial temporary detached duty."

"A pleasure, Lieutenant Westerfeld," said Glenn with a courtly nod. "And Derek, I presume you have some explanation of those last four words."

Derek swallowed before responding. "There were two reasons they wouldn't tell you or anybody else what happened in orbit. First of all, we were sent up there to investigate something whose existence hasn't been revealed to the public: extraterrestrial activity in near-Earth space. And no, *please* don't interrupt me! The second reason was that the spaceplane's pilot lost consciousness and then regained it to find himself alone. Lauren and I and Lieutenant Paul Rinnard had vanished without explanation. They're probably convinced that the extraterrestrials are somehow involved . . . and they're right. What they don't know is that the extraterrestrials are human. They also don't know what—or who—is standing behind those humans and their enemies."

Derek spoke on, hastily lest his grandfather could formulate protests or questions. Lauren often took up the narrative, which was helpful inasmuch as a Southerner of Glenn's generation wasn't about to interrupt a lady. By the time they were done, all three found they were sitting on the leather-upholstered chairs, without clearly recalling how they'd gotten there, and the fire had died down to dimly glowing embers.

"So," Derek finished, after they'd described the desperate pass to which the Erkhedzuo-led alliance had come, "instead of going back to the Khron system and putting our heads in the lion's mouth, we came here to Earth because we need help."

"Help?" Glenn echoed. "Who, here on Earth, can possibly help?"

"You, for one."

Glenn had held up remarkably well so far—better, probably, than he would have for a story that had been only *partially* fantastic and thus left him a hand-grip on reality. But now, for the first time, his jaw dropped. "Me?"

Lauren leaned forward urgently. "Yes, Commander Secrest. You're the only psi we know of whom the government doesn't have under lock and key at JICPO."

Glenn gave his head a shake of weary sadness. "Lieutenant Westerfeld, my grandson doesn't seem to have made the situation clear to you. The fact of the matter is, I'm not a psi. At absolute most, I'm a *former* psi. I'm a useless, broken-down old fart who, once upon a time before your parents were out of elementary school, had a kind of awakening . . . and then went back to sleep. It was just a fluke."

"Granddad," insisted Derek, "since joining JICPO I've learned that you were the most powerful of all the latent psis who, for whatever reason, emerged into operancy back then."

"You've got it exactly right: *back then.* I'm no damned good any more. Not for anything, least of all that."

"But, Granddad, we've got stuff now that nobody had dreamed of in the nineteen sixties and seventies. Remember, unlike you I never did awaken into operancy on my own. They did that for me at JICPO with psi-reactive drugs."

"And," Lauren addded her voice, "the Erkhedzuo have got stuff JICPO has only dreamed of! Remember the things we were just telling you about? Direct neural induction technology that can—"

"But that's all for people like you—young people, fresh people, people who're like . . ." Glenn waved at the fireplace. "Like firewood waiting to be ignited. I'm like those ashes in there: burned out. You might as well try and get them to burn as—"

"At least it would be *trying,* Granddad," insisted Derek.

"I tell you, it would just be pissing into the wind."

"Even at that, it would be better than sitting here and wallowing in booze and self-pity!"

Glenn looked up sharply, too angry to realize that his anger had, at least for the moment, burned away his despair. "What the hell do you know about it?"

"At least as much as you know about Erkhedzuo technology!" Derek shot back. "And *nobody* knows what the results may be when that technology is put at the disposal of Earth's greatest psionic theorist."

"Which means—?"

"Doctor Rosa Kronenberg. You remember her—she came here with Captain Morrisey last spring. We've got Urquiashqua with us, who's already studied psionics from the perspective of a culture that's been using quantum energy the *other* way, through magic, for its entire history. We're going to snatch Doctor Kronenberg out of the Hole. When those two are brought together . . . well, who knows what they'll be able to produce? So don't give up in advance."

Glenn's face was a battlefield, as his desire to believe what he was hearing warred with his fear of setting himself up for disappointment. *Maybe my last disappointment,* came the unwelcome morbid thought. He'd turned seventy a couple of months after receiving Derek's death-posting, which hadn't helped in the least.

And yet . . .

"Do you really think . . . just maybe . . . ?"

Even as he weakened, Lauren moved in for the kill. She leaned forward again, and took his hands in hers. "We don't know, Commander. We won't know until we try. But we've *got* to try. And so do you. We need you."

Glenn squeezed his eyes tightly shut against the tears he'd been brought up to regard as unmanly, and returned the pressure of her hands as he tried to remember the last time he'd heard those words.

The Hole went to lights-out at 2200, leaving only redly glowing night lights to illuminate the corridors. Rosa Kronenberg had lost track of time while working alone, and was hurrying back to her quarters before the lights dimmed. As always, it took her through an unfrequented stretch of corridor.

She turned a corner and came face to face with a group of figures that didn't belong there. In fact, they were so out of place that at first her mind simply refused to process them.

Working too hard, ran the thought through her shock-dulled mind.

There were four of them. All wore the same kind of utterly exotic outfit: a sleeveless tunic over a coverall, all in various earth-tones except for the tunics' basic black. The two on the flanks—big, dark-complexioned, hard-looking men—wore helmets and various items of exotic but unmistakable combat gear, and carried equally unfamiliar long-barrelled weapons. The man and woman between them had only light openwork headsets. There was something about those two that was familiar. . . .

"No," she heard herself saying. "It can't be."

"Yes, Doctor, it's us," said Lauren with a smile. "The rumor of our death was . . . well, you've heard *that* old Mark Twain line."

For an instant, Kronenberg was struck dumb by the sheer number of questions. "How did you get in here?" she finally managed.

"Teleportation. Yes, Doctor, it really does work, subject to the limitations you've theorized. But we know the inside of this place well enough to visualize the target location clearly . . . and we knew you'd be coming this way around this time of night."

At the mention of teleportation, all of the questions that most people would have thought had more immediacy—how it happened that Secrest and Westerfeld were still alive, how they had vanished from the spaceplane, what they were doing here now, who their companions were, why they were wearing such odd clothing, and all the rest—fled Kronenberg's mind. "*Teleportation?* You mean you can actually do it? But . . . but that must mean . . . are you saying you teleported here from *outside this facility*!"

Derek grinned. The sight of Doctor Kroneneberg rendered

almost inarticulate with astonishment was one he'd never imagined. He found himself relishing it—more than he knew he probably should. "Yes, Doctor. We're not just talking about a few feet or yards. In fact, we teleported from orbit. We don't know yet what the absolute range limitations are for psychotronically enhanced teleportation—or if there are any."

"'Psychotronically enhanced?'" Kronenberg echoed faintly.

"Also," Lauren added, picking up the thread, "on our way back to the Solar system—yes, you'll learn about that—we've had a chance to experiment with what was until recently not even a theoretical possibility: teleportation of objects other than yourself." She gestured at the two enforcer types. "That's how we got these gentlemen here."

A shadow seemed to pass across Derek's face. "The reason we had to bring them, Doctor, is . . . Well, we must insist that you come with us."

"Huh?" Kronenberg blinked once, then dismissed the words she hadn't really even heard. "Let me make sure I understand: you can teleport extraneous objects?"

"Not only that," said Lauren. "It is possible to bring such an object from a remote location, if that location is clearly known—or, if it's a human being, you can establish telepathic contact with him. In fact, if you'll excuse us a second . . ." She and Derek took on an abstracted look that Kronenberg recognized as that of telepaths going into concert. And then, with no fuss at all, another oddly garbed figure was standing there.

This one was a plump elderly gent with a full white beard gathered into a thick braid. He stepped forward, beaming, and addressed her in a stream of enthusiastic gibberish.

"Hold on, Urquiashqua!" Derek handed Kronenberg a tiny adhesive disc and what looked like a hearing aid. "Sorry, Doctor—I forgot. Please put this thing in your ear, and stick the disc to your chest."

It didn't occur to Kronenberg to protest, any more than it had occurred to her to raise an outcry. With the earpiece in place, a running translation began to accompany the oldster's incomprehensible speech. "Doctor Kronenberg, it is an honor and a privilege to meet you at last! My name is Urquiashqua, and you may regard me as a colleague of sorts—at least in a related field."

"Uh—what field is that?"

"Magic. Permit me to congratulate you on your brilliant insights, without which the subsequent work of myself and others in the area of psionic enhancement would have been quite impossible."

The look that had come over Kronenberg's face at the word *magic* vanished with comical abruptness. "What? Did you say 'psionic enhancement'? You mean the things I've just been hearing about?"

"Yes, Doctor. And I cannot tell you how much I am looking forward to working with you on some extremely interesting problems that continue to elude solution, like that of restimulating the psionic powers of an individual who once experienced a temporary spontaneous awakening into operancy."

"We have Glenn Secrest, Doctor," Lauren amplified. "You know about him, of course."

"Yes. Indeed I do. In fact—"

"Freeze!"

The sudden parade-ground bark came from a fatigues-clad MP sergeant as he and one of his men leaped from behind the corner, their Beretta sidearms levelled. At appreciably the same instant, the two Erkhedzuo security men smoothly brought up their weapons. For a heartbeat, the tableau held. Then Captain Morrisey appeared behind the MPs, his eyes wide at the sight of the five figures with Doctor Kronenberg. They got wider still as he recognized Derek and Lauren.

"All right, drop those, uh, weapons and get your hands in the air," ordered the sergeant in a not altogether steady voice. "And Doctor, please get over here behind us."

Derek gave one of the Erkhedzuo a small nod.

The MPs were badly rattled by these impossibly bizarre apparitions in the inviolate precincts of the Hole, but even if they'd been at the top of their form they would have stood no chance. The weapons they were up against struck at the speed of light, and were soundless save for a faint crackle as an electric charge flashed along a tunnel of ionized air created by a laser guide-beam. So before they knew anything was happening they were slumping to the floor, unconscious.

"They're not dead, sir," Derek hastily assured Captain Morrisey. "Not even injured. Just stunned. I'm sorry we had to do that."

Morrisey's mouth opened and closed a couple of times before he could speak. "Secrest . . . Westerfeld . . . I never would have thought it of you two, that you could . . ." His features and voice hardened. "Who are you working for? Who have you sold out to?"

Derek flushed hotly. "I don't suppose I can blame you for thinking that, sir—as much as it hurts, coming from a man I respect above all but a very few others. And lately I've found out what it's like to feel betrayed. I'll just have to ask you to take my word that we're acting out of loyalty to the United States—which, like the rest of the world, is facing a threat you can't possibly comprehend, and which I couldn't reveal to you even if I had the time. We're going to be fighting for this country—among others."

"It is not your place to decide where, when and under what circumstances you are going to fight for this country, Ensign! You, I and the rest of the armed forces are instruments of policy decisions made at a far higher level than ours, by the elected civilian leadership."

"I know that, sir, and I've always believed in it. But I now find myself in circumstances which are, to put it mildly, without precedent. I have to make my own decisions, with nothing to guide me except my own sense of honor, and the examples I've had the good fortune to have set for me by some truly outstanding men—including you. And I know within myself that what I'm doing is necessary. It is also necessary that we take Doctor Kronenberg with us."

"It seems, Captain," said Kronenberg, "that I have no choice but to accompany them." Her voice wasn't quite as indignant and distraught as it might have been. But then she turned to Derek with quite the old frostiness. "You realize, Mister Secrest, you have a *lot* of explaining to do!"

"Uh, yes, ma'am."

"And now, if I *must* go, permit me to pick up a few CDs

and chemical samples." She headed back toward the lab, accompanied by one of the Erkhedzuo.

Morrisey spoke like a father to errant children. "Look, you know you can't possibly get out of here. Don't add kidnapping to the list of charges you're going to be facing. Give yourselves up. You have my word that I'll do what I can for you."

"Actually, sir," said Derek with a smile, "I think we *can* get out of here." Kronenberg returned, and Derek exchanged a nod with her escort, who was lugging a couple of carrying cases. Then he and Lauren concentrated visibly . . . and the two security men were gone.

Derek turned to face the gaping Morrisey. "I know I'm out of uniform, sir, besides being below decks. But . . ." He rendered a salute that Sergeant McManus at Pensacola could scarcely have found fault with. And then Morrisey was alone in the corridor with the two unconscious MPs.

Some people who'd heard a commotion arrived mere seconds later. They found Morrisey wearing an odd smile on his lips, sketching a return salute even though there was no one there.

Ergu Nervy did not return by the old route, the terminus of which the triumphant Qurvyshuo might have under surveilance. Instead, Rhykhvyleshqua took his command back through the portal Sophia had created, into the empty Void domain where they'd been trapped. There, the goddess created another portal, to the outermost reaches of the Khron system.

They had only just emerged, with Khron's sun little more than a zero-magnitude yellow star dead ahead, when Glenn Secrest awoke.

He had lost consciousness in the midst of the hell Derek remembered: the chemically induced dissolution of the barriers that kept latent psionic powers latent. The fact that in his case the barriers had once crumbled on their own and subsequently rebuilt themselves evidently didn't help—not at all. Given his age, they'd had some bad moments as they'd waited for him to come out of the oblivion he'd fled to.

But now they all stood around his bed in Urquiashqua's lab. And, as his eyes cleared, he saw that they were smiling.

"I always knew you were a tough old bird," Derek remarked.

Urquiashqua and Doctor Kronennberg were also smiling, but at the instrument readouts rather than at the patient. "Congratulations, Doctor," said the mage.

"I could never have done it without you," Kronenberg assured him with what passed in her for effusiveness. "Your facilities made it possible to confirm that his powers were still present, even though in a banked-down form—a kind of super-latency."

"Ah, but you correctly identified the modifications to the psi-reactive drugs' molecular structure needed to overcome this."

"But without your nano-constructors, the modification could never have been performed in such a short time."

"But—"

Glenn turned away from the Gaston-Alphonse act. "So . . . I gather it worked."

"Yep," Derek affirmed. "The instrument readings confirm it. Like everybody else, you don't feel anything at first. You'll have to be trained to use your powers—although Doctor Kronenberg has a theory that the process may go a lot faster in your case because it won't be a first time for you."

"That's right," said Kronenberg. "It will be a relearning process. Of course, you'll still need practice, starting with establishment of contact with a cooperating subject."

"I'd like to volunteer for that," said Derek, smiling.

"If you think you can stand it." His grandfather smiled back. "Oh, and by the way . . . thanks for what you've given back to me."

"You psionic ability? You should thank Doctor Kronenberg and Urquiashqua for that."

"No, that's only part of it—and not even the most important part."

CHAPTER NINETEEN

To Paul Rinnard, it bore an obscene resemblance to a vast operating theater.

As he entered the semicircular balcony—enclosed with transparent soundproof plastic to muffle the screams that nothing could completely shut out—he could look down over the serried array of framework beds with their sinister clamps and straps. He knew the significance of their precise arrangement. It was a new innovation: positioning parents so that in the midst of their own torments they could see the things that were being done to their children. There was no absolute proof that it enhanced still further the quantum energies released by the death-agonies of this room's victims, but the mere theoretical possibility had been enough to put the Qurvyshuo mage-priests of the Titan cult enthusiastically behind the idea.

Nydierya was standing at the railing, watching. She was breathing in the rapid, shallow way that Rinnard had come to recognize as she eagerly awaited the rush of power that would be hers for a moment as all the rooms's occupants were brought simultaneously to a death which, though as painful as science could make it, would be a release from what they would undergo first. Staring fixedly at the preparations below, she didn't notice his arrival.

Rinnard studied her. At one time, he'd loved her, or thought he loved her. He knew that for a certainty. He just had no recollection of how it had felt. Indeed, he'd forgotten what it was like to feel anything at all for her but cold disgust.

Not that he could say so openly—at least not yet. He still needed to keep on her good side, because she controlled his access to the psi-enhancement devices. Eventually, of course, those who stood above her would recognize his indispensability—he'd had hints that it couldn't be much longer—and he'd be able to dispense with her. For now, though, he continued to dissemble. He could even make himself perform sexually with her . . . not that he was often called on to do so, for like all addicts she had become little more than a walking vessel for a need that had eaten her away from the inside, leaving nothing but itself.

She heard his approach, turned and gave an abstracted smile. "Paul! You came!" She knew how little he liked this place.

"Why was I summoned here?" he demanded after a kiss on the forehead whose pro forma quality she was still capable of recognizing, and about which she once would have cared. But she gave no sign. Lying to each other had by now passed beyond the merely habitual and become the essential condition of their lives.

His question was not an unreasonable one. His duties had nothing to do with magic. The theory that psis could tap their own internal quantum energy for magical purposes without the usual attendant risks—originally the reason they'd been sought after for this war—had proven quite true. But it had also become irrelevant. Partly, this was because of the flaw Urquiashqua had spotted long ago: only by sheer coincidence would psionic power and magical aptitude occur in the same individual, and given the rarity of both genetic traits the probability of such a coincidence was infinitesimal. But mostly it was because the results had proved so paltry—little more than parlor tricks, even had Rinnard been a natural-born mage and spent years learning the techniques of using such a gift—when measured against the emerging reality of psychotronically enhanced psionic powers. Even the quantum energies the Qurvyshuo could place at the disposal of their mages by the assembly-line abominations that went on in this building and others like it had intrinsic limits. If the geometrical progression of psionic power through artificial feedback had *any* limits, they had not been discovered to date.

If Rinnard had had it in him to feel anything for Nydierya any more, he would have felt pity. She had sold her soul for a dead end.

She turned brisk. "I don't know what it's about—I wasn't told. But *he* wants to talk to you."

"You mean—?"

"Yes. The High Lord."

"He's here?"

"No." Nydierya's businesslike facade began to crack, and resentment glowed through the fissures. "You're to pass through a portal."

"So he's in the Titans' Void domain?" Rinnard's pulse quickened.

"Yes, he is." Nydierya's envy was now open. "You're one of the very few mortals ever to be invited there."

This must be it! Rinnard exulted inwardly. *The Titans have finally decided to give me direct control of the psychotronic equipment. No more having to be your gigolo, you sick bitch!* But prudence kept his voice level and his face expressionless.

"Is that what this is for?" he inquired. "Opening the portal?" He indicated the scene below, where the first glassy-eyed victims were now being led in. They were mostly ethnic Qurvyshuo—the empire's minority groups were largely used up by now—but not the eager religious fanatics who had been used for a while. That supply, too, had dried up. These were convicts. By now, practically *everything* in Qurvyshye was a capital offense under laws deliberately framed so as to be impossible to obey. Those laws were enforced by a vast police establishment that had become a virtual state-within-a-state, its loyalty assured by its members' desperate determination to safeguard their own immune status.

"Oh, no. Remember, opening a portal, as opposed to creating or eliminating one, is relatively unchallenging. We're preparing a *major* spell here." An edge of malice entered her voice, and Rinnard had to force himself not to smile at her pathetic attempt to downplay the importance of his extraordinary summons from the High Lord. "Come; I will attend to it while the preparations are still in progress."

They departed the balcony just as a sound of transcendent horror and despair began to penetrate the plastic, rising from below where the adult victims, now immobilized, saw their children being led in. Rinnard clenched his teeth tightly and kept his face immobile. Nydierya, who had unnecessarily told him to meet her here, smiled.

Their route took them along an open gallery with a view of Zquerte, the capital of Qurvyshye. The weather was dreary and overcast, but even on the loveliest of days Zquerte was hideous—especially this district where fortresslike government buildings squatted. Elsewhere, the kind of modern architecture permitted by Khron's materials technology soared almost as Rinnard remembered from Bozemtoum. But even those towers rose from a base of squalor. That squalor, like a form of pollution saturating the soil, extended underground to the lower levels where criminal gangs—tolerated by the state as long as they kept order in their turf and supplied a quota of victims for tapping—lorded it over an underclass degraded almost below the level of humanity.

They proceeded more deeply into the grotesquely huge building, through dim corridors wide as highways, finally passing through thirty-foot-high doors into a vast, clumsily monumental hall. Like all Qurvyshuo governmental architecture, it had taken leave of the human scale. But in this case there was a reason, for this was where the Titans appeared to their human tools when it suited them to do so.

The hall was currently deserted. Rinnard and Nydierya walked alone, between rows of monstrous basalt columns, to the dais at the far end. The symbol of the Qurvyshuo theocratic state—a rampant lion endowed with human hands, one of them gripping a sword plunged into the vitals of the planet whereon it stood—appeared in bas-relief on the six-storey wall behind the dais. In front of it, occupying the center of the dais, was an oval area marked out by slightly raised stone. Here they paused, and Nydierya took on a look of intense concentration, muttering under her breath in formulas Rinnard did not understand and had no particular desire to understand.

Contrary to Nydierya's bravado, the spell for opening an existing portal to a Void domain required a fair amount of ambient quantum energy. Rinnard forced patience on himself while Nydierya performed the time-consuming procedures required to collect it. He told himself he shouldn't be complaining. At least she hadn't slaughtered innocents simply to provide him with quick transit.

In less time than seemed to him to elapse, the glowing hoop of a portal appeared over the raised oval section of floor. It was several times the diameter of the usual planetary-surface portal. He knew why.

He also knew about the sickening disorientation that affected the psionically sensitive at the opening of a portal, for Derek and Lauren had described it. So he was more or less prepared, despite Nydierya's spiteful failure to warn him. He set his feet wide apart, clamped control on himself, and stared that circle of unreality full in the face.

"Proceed," he heard Nydierya say.

He stepped through and looked around him.

Derek and Lauren had also tried to describe the domain into which Sophia had led them. Quite obviously, the Titans had used other sources of inspiration when molding the chaos of the Inner Void into an imitation of physical reality.

He was atop a blocklike raised platform of extensive size, open to a twilit sky. In all directions, awesome cityscape spread away to the indescribably, disturbingly *wrong* vanishing point that he'd been told to expect. But it wasn't like any city he'd ever seen, because cities contained the full panoply of structures that a living, operating human society shared. Even artificially created capitals like

Washington and Brasilia weren't *all* pompous public buildings. This place was utterly sterile. Wide avenues stretched away from the great block of monumentality on which Rinnard stood, like spokes from the hub of a wheel . . . but no vehicles moved along them. They were there simply because they were required as spacing by the mammoth exercises in meaningless architectural self-aggrandizement that lined them to either side.

It all reminded Rinnard of models he'd seen of what Albert Speer had promised Hitler he would make Berlin into. The architectural styles were entirely different, of course. Speer had been working in early-twentieth-century Totalitarian Neoclassical—like the Supreme Court building in Washington, but with unlimited budgeting and very limited taste— whereas this was what Rinnard had grown accustomed to in Khron's public buildings: the Bronze Age look of Crete and Egypt evolved along a different pathway than that which Earth had followed (for the Titans, like all the other gods, could only mine the creativity of humans). But in a deeper sense, there was a real kinship with Speer's models. This, too, was architecture that existed for no purpose except to assuage its creators' inferiority complex.

On reflection, Rinnard decided there was an even closer parallel than those Nazi fantasies: Hollywood's vision of Pharaonic Egypt. This was a somber necropolis, but lacking even the excuse of departed greatness whose memory deserved to be enshrined. *Zquerte is light and lively by comparison,* he thought.

He spared only an instant for all these observations. The High Lord sucked in his attention like a black hole.

That entity was seated on a mammoth black onyx throne in the center of the raised expanse on which Rinnard found himself. He was dressed in a style that presumably dated back to Earth's Bronze Age and, as such, held resonances for the Qurvyshuo with whom he normally had to deal. His hair and full beard were curly and ink-black. He was, as Nydierya had described, disproportionately broad, thick and short-legged. He was also, Rinnard soberly estimated, eighteen or twenty feet tall standing up.

Which, of course, accounted for the grotesquely squat build. Once a god adopted a "default" form in the material world, he more or less bound himself to the laws of that world. And under a one-G field, bodies as huge as those the Titans had adopted for the purpose of terrifying primitive humans required enough cross-section to support their tonnage. More recently, for purposes of interacting with their relatively sophisticated underlings on Khron, they had tended to scale themselves down to a more convenient humanlike size. But, with the lack of creativity that was their hallmark, they had kept the bodily form that the square-cube law no longer required.

Here, though, without the need to fit through Qurvyshuo doorways and stand up under Qurvyshuo ceilings, they could give their overcompensation full rein. The High Lord's somber black eyes, under their shelf of brow ridge, gazed down from an altitude of almost twice Rinnard's height, even though their owner was seated.

Still, Rinnard observed, he deigned to use human-produced technology. The archaic robe evidently concealed a little adhesive disc, for an English translation in his ear accompanied the the disturbing voice Nydierya had tried to describe, barely above the lower threshold of human audibility.

"You have done well," the being said without preamble.

"I do my best to justify your trust, sir." Had Rinnard but known it, his tone—carefully polite on his standards—had achieved the closest approach to jauntiness ever heard in this place.

The wide face darkened as though from an infusion of thick blood. But the *basso profundissimo* stayed level, although Rinnard could feel its reverberations through the soles of his feet. "Yes. You have convincingly demonstrated the potential of artificially enhanced psionics. Indeed, such is its usefulness that we are considering releasing you from the restrictions we have heretofore imposed, and utilizing you for independent operations, reporting directly to me."

Rinnard's heart raced. This was more than he'd dared hope for. *Not just free from that cunt Nydierya,* he exulted inwardly, *but from the whole disgusting gaggle of fanatics and brass hats that make up the Qurvyshuo power structure!* Involuntarily, he took an eager half-step forward.

The thick, ropy lips in the blue-black beard gave an almost imperceptible twitch of sardonic amusement. "However, there is one matter that needs to be tidied up first."

A twinge of tantalized, frustrated anticipation shot through Rinnard. "Sir?"

"It concerns your friends—or, I should say, former friends—from Earth. Their ship has, it seems, returned to the Khron system."

Rinnard's mouth fell open. "Impossible!" he blurted before he could stop himself.

The shaggy black brows lowered, and the voice grew, if possible, even lower and more menacing. "Things which have actually taken place are seldom impossible."

"Ah . . . yes, sir. But it makes no sense! I can assure you there was no god aboard that ship to create a portal from the Void to the material universe. There was only the human mage Urquiashqua who, naturally, could only open a portal that already existed. And there was no such portal in the Void domain to which we sent *Ergu Nervy.*"

"As you, of course, knew full well at the time." The deep voice became a purr of amusement.

"Of course, sir." Rinnard commanded himself not to flush. Finding out the truth had been the beginning of the end of his affair with Nydierya. But he had come to terms with it, if not with her. It had been unavoidable, as he'd come to understand. And, since it was a *fait accompli* anyway, there was nothing to be gained now by failing to take the credit for it.

The High Lord seemed to tire of his game. He leaned forward, bringing his coarse features a little closer to Rinnard. "At any rate, *Ergu Nervy* has reappeared, on an orbit which indicates a new portal in the outer system—or, at least, a portal hitherto unknown to us. As a result, we did not become aware of its presence until it was already well into the inner system, and no Qurvyshuo heavy units were in a position to achieve an intercept vector. As soon as they became aware that they had been detected anyway, they began sending broadcasts which have already had the effect of stiffening the alliance forces' morale. Nor is that the only reason this unexpected turn of events is of concern to us. Urquiashqua is one of the most accomplished mages in the Erkhedzuo alliance. And Nydierya has given us to understand that the humans Secrest and Westerfeld, while by no means as powerful as you even in concert, could make themselves inconvenient to us—especially if they augment such a concert with artificial enhancement."

"The possibility can't be denied, sir." Rinnard's noncommital reply was verbal camouflage for the complexity that swirled behind his carefully composed face. On one level, he was fascinated by the possibility the High Lord had raised: No one had ever tried to use psychotronics while simultaneously in concert. But his intellectual curiosity was little more than an island in a tossing sea of conflicting emotions. *So Derek and Lauren are alive . . .*

He'd had time to adjust to the idea that they were dead, carefully not letting himself think about the probable details of their demise and assuring himself, over and over again, that he hadn't actually killed them, merely sent them into what he'd sincerely believed to be temporary exile. Now his comfortable structure of rationalization had been kicked apart, levelled to its very foundations, and it was difficult to know just exactly how he felt, or ought to feel.

"You will understand, then," came the High Lord's almost subliminally deep voice, like distant thunder, "that we expect your help in dealing with this nuisance."

"What? Oh, yes, of course, sir." Rinnard's inner turmoil abruptly deepened.

But then, like a break in his clouds of indecision, came the realization that this might, perhaps, offer an opportunity. . . .

"Yes, sir. In fact, I believe I've thought of a way in which I can be helpful to you in this matter."

"I don't think you should have gone." Lauren's voice on the communicator was irritable with concern.

"We've been over that," Derek reminded her.

"I still don't like it."

"You worry too much. Yankees have a tendency to do that, I've noticed."

"It's called considering the consequences! Why do you think we won the war?"

Derek only grinned, and leaned back and contemplated the star-fields beyond the curving transparency. The copilot had let him have a turn in the second seat of the shuttle. It was the same shuttle he and Lauren and—a brief inner hurt at the thought of his friend, grown dull with familiarity—Paul had been snatched by magic from the spaceplane in Earth orbit, seemingly so long ago.

Sophia had created a portal into a region of Khron's outer system far indeed from the usual Erkhedzuo route from the Solar system. From there they'd coasted sunward in free fall, undetected until long after it was too late for the Qurvysahuo conquerors to intecept them—even magic drawing on the quantum energies wrenched from numerous tortured victims couldn't overcome the laws of physics to *that* extent—and Sophia had smiled gently as they'd congratulated themselves on their own cleverness.

Then, as the deep-yellow sun of Khron had waxed in the view-forward and Khron itself had grown from a bluish star into a perceptible planetary disc, the distress call had come . . . only to promptly die.

It had been an Erkhedzuo capital ship of a class even heavier than *Ergu Nervy*—and, unlike *Ergu Nervy*, never modified into a research ship. But even so awesome a tonnage of techno-death had not been immune to the energies that had flamed around Khron and its moons in the final, cataclysmic battles as Qurvyshye had tightened its stranglehold. This ship, even though largely intact, had fallen behind in the great cold darkness as the battle had raged on planetward, for its drive had been crippled by an unlucky hit. In another turn of miserably bad fortune, the secondary radiation effects of particle beam weapons had fried the lamed giant's electronics, leaving it only capable of putting out the faint signal *Ergu Nervy* had picked up in its last expiring moments.

The cries for help from a crew dying out here had been impossible to ignore—they'd been in similar case themselves, not so long ago. And the firepower that ship could contribute to the allied cause, once rendered mobile again by the help *Ergu Nervy* could provide, had been impossible to resist.The problem had been locating the derelict, now plunging helplessly along on a hyperbolic orbit. The brief, feeble signal had provided enough of a fix to approximately infer that orbit. But *Ergu Nervy* could not depart from her own orbit to search along that track without activating her main drive—and even at the technological level at which the Erkhedzuo operated, antimatter was very expensive stuff, and so difficult to contain that even a large ship could carry only so much of it.

A shuttle, however, could be dispatched. And given the cripple's inability to communicate by conventional means, there was only one way to contact its desperate occupants.

"Yes, I know why you had to go along," Lauren resumed, interrupting his thoughts. "Just be careful, okay?"

"I've got it!" exclaimed Leirteshqua, the pilot. He pointed at the radar blip. "I'm surprised we had to get this close, and the return is still surprisingly faint. But there it is."

"Got to go," Derek told Lauren. "Leirteshqua needs to report in." He signed off, then relinquished the seat to the copilot and moved to another, from which he could still observe. He donned the psychotronic headset and composed his mind to begin broadcasting globally.

Once he established telepathic linkage with someone aboard that ship, he'd be able to safely teleport onto her. If neessary, Urquiashqua could probably create a portal.

Presently the cripple became visible, glinting with reflected sunlight. She grew in the transparency, an unbalanced barbell like *Ergu Nervy*, only even more massive and complex.

Derek began to wonder why he wasn't picking up anybody aboard her. At this range, with his telepathic abilities artificially enhanced . . .

He wasn't the only one who was puzzled, for Leirteshqua turned to him with a frown. "Funny. The radar return we're getting is nothing even close to what it should be for a ship that size. And I keep getting little tiny returns from all around us—only there's nothing there." He waved at the transparency, empty of all save the star-fields and the damaged ship.

"Something's not right—" began Derek.

Then, as he watched, the giant ship beyond the transparency began to waver and ripple, and then was gone.

In its place was a much smaller spacecraft: an interplanetary craft, but obviously built for speed rather than cargo capacity: a high-priority personnel transport. Derek didn't recognize it from the cursory enemy-recognition studies he'd had time for. He did recognize the lion-with-sword-on-planet insignia of Qurvyshye.

In the split second wherein he saw all this, the shuttle bucked like a burned animal and a deafening explosion rang through its protesting structure. A glance at the near-stroboscopic display of warning lights that awoke on Leirteshqua's control board told Derek that the shuttle was robbed of the ability to maneuver, as throroughly as they'd believed the nonexistent Erkhedzuo battleship to be.

It was also clear where the shot had come from that had wrecked their drive . . . and what those little radar returns were that had perplexed Leirteshqua.

Derek had never personally encountered powered combat armor in his time on Khron, but he knew it when he saw it. In addition to protecting the wearer with inches of laminate armor and enhancing his strength with their myoelectric "muscles," the suits could be sealed against vacuum. With the addition of extended life-support units and thruster packs, they became one-man anthropomorphic spacecraft. And now they swarmed around the unarmed, immobilized shuttle like flies around a dead dog. The series of faint clangs as they began to attach themselves magnetically to the hull were, in their own way, more terrfying than the explosion that had disabled the drive.

"Seal up!" he heard Leirteshqua yell. Without pausing to see if Derek and the copilot were obeying his order by putting on the gloves and flexible transparent helmets that turned their coveralls into emergency vacuum suits, he turned frantically to the communicator. "*Ergu Nervy*, this is an emergency! We are under attack. The distress call was a hoax. The crippled ship was an illusion, masking a Qurvy-shuo *Khimtevr* class light assault transport, and we are about to be boarded. . . . What's that? No, I don't know how it could have happened!"

Derek knew, though, and the knowledge was misery in him.

Ergu Nervy and her auxiliary craft, like all military vessels, were routinely warded against magical assaults. The effect was of limited duration, and had to be periodically renewed—it was one of Urquiashquas's duties. But he was very conscientious about it. So the pilot's bewilderment was justified. No magical illusion could be imposed from outside on the senses and minds of the shuttle's occupants.

No *magical* illusion—that was the kicker. Urquiashqua's countermeasures had no effect on *telepathic* illusion. Like other forms of telepathic contact, it could be neutralized by a consciously opposed will. But it had never occured to Derek to think that such an effort was necessary.

But now he belatedly remembered what Sophia had told them about the defeat of the Erkhedzuo deep-space fleet. And he knew, beyond all possibility of doubt, the identity of one of that Qurvyshuo transport's complement—someone whose treason he'd never truly accepted, continuing to believe, on a level below that of rationality, that surely in the end some good explanation of everything that had happened would come to light, that it would all turn out to have been some terrible misunderstanding. . . .

With a crash that dwarfed the earlier hit on their drive, the starboard bulkhead blasted inward.

Their seat straps held them in their couches as the air rushed out. Figures like high-tech steel gorillas advanced into the shuttle against that outward gale, held to the deck by powerfully magnetized soles.

"*Ergu Nervy*, we are taken," Leirteshqua continued with heroic persistence. "Get away now!" As he spoke, his copilot twisted around in his seat and brought to bear a pathetically futile-looking handgun.

One of the armored figures aimed a weapon that his

unaided strength could never have handled—there may be no weight in free fall, but there is mass, and therefore inertia. Derek recognized it as a plasma gun. "No!" he screamed. Simultaneously he shut his eyes tightly, lest they be blinded by the bolt of star-stuff the weapon fired along a laser guide-beam. Thermal pulse washed over him and a roar bruised his ears. When he opened his eyes, the control panel was a charred ruin and the two men seated at it were little more than carbonized skeletons.

The snout of the plasma gun swung toward him.

Another armored figure appeared and pointed toward him. Presumably the new arrival was shouting orders into his helmet communicator, for the plasma gun lowered. Instead, another of the boarders aimed a different weapon. Derek knew this weapon well, for it was the one they had used on the MPs in the Hole. He clenched his teeth and braced himself for the sensation of electric shock.

Just before unconsciousness took him, he looked through the faceplate of the newly arrived armor suit, and his eyes met the light-hazel ones of Paul Rinnard.

★ CHAPTER TWENTY

They took Derek to an orbital station at the L-5 point of Zylimi, Khron's outer moon.

He remembered nothing of the journey. Presumably they'd kept him unconscious even after the electrolaser hit wore off. At any rate, he awoke as the assault transport was making its docking approach, too sick, famished and generally miserable to appreciate the sight of the great space habitat with its slowly revolving ring of living quarters.

Weak and groggy though he was, he found he was capable of walking after a single application of a baton comparable to an electric cattle prod, only much worse. They marched him to what was unmistakably a dispensary, where he was given a quick, dispassionate checkup and a drink of some kind of stimulant, and then to what was even more unmistakably a security cell. There he waited, eating the meals that were passed to him through a sliding grate—ravenously at first, then with the lack of enthusiasm the food's quality inspired. There was no one he could communicate with, even had anyone evinced any talkativeness, and he soon gave up the attempt.

He also gave up his attempts to use telepathy against his captors. It quickly became obvious that everyone who would come in contact with him had been told how to prevent that. He could and did let his projected consciousness roam—though only a short distance, in the absence of artificial enhancement—and thus obtained a knowledge of his immediate environs that he could have used to teleport out of the cell. It would have been pointless, though; he couldn't teleport out of the station, having no inclination to try breathing vacuum, and teleporting within it would have accomplished nothing except to annoy his captors.

Finally, the door of the featureless metal cube slid aside and two Qurvyshuo goons entered and gestured him outside with the pain-batons. As they proceeded along the curving passageways the general look of things grew a little less hideously utilitarian, and the occasional touch of needless ornamentation began to appear. *Officers' country,* Derek thought as they stopped in front of a doorway. It slid silently open, and one of the goons shoved Derek through with more force than was strictly necessary.

The sight directly in front of him took his breath away, for the opposite wall of the chamber was a transparency, and the starfields streamed by in silent majesty as the spin habitat rotated. For a moment, he noticed nothing else.

"Hi, Derek."

Derek froze. The mere sound of English was startling, for they'd taken away his interpreter earpiece. But beyond that, he recognized the voice. He made himself turn slowly and face the desk to the right of the door, from whence the voice had come.

"Hi, Paul." He couldn't think of anything else to say.

Rinnard turned to the good-humor men and spoke coldly. "That's all. You're dismissed."

The two thugs gave Rinnard the Roman-like Qurvyshuo military salute in a manner that suggested they weren't certain he rated it—he was, Derek noted, wearing an austere version of Khronuo civvies—but weren't about to take the risk of not rendering it. Then they got out, practically stumbling over each other in a way that would have been laughable anywhere else.

Rinnard shook his head and chuckled. "Cretins! They've

grown up taking magic as much for granted as engineering. But psionics terrifies them—it's something new. They're out there in the passageway now, doing whatever their equivalent is of my ancestors crossing themselves!" Turning serious, he stood up and walked around the desk and the globe of Khron that flanked it. "Hey, listen, Derek, I apologize for the way you've been treated—like some ordinary prisoner. But my status around here is, well, ambiguous. I can exert influence, as you've just seen, but I have no official place in the chain of command. At least I was able to veto their bright idea of keeping you so doped up you couldn't concentrate enough to use psi. That could have eventually turned you into a vegetable."

"Thanks."

"Don't mention it. And don't worry; I'll pass the word among the low-level geeks that if they mistreat you I'll hear about it. They'll be too busy shitting in their pants to give you any grief." Rinnard dismissed the subject with an airy wave, and smiled his old disarming smile. "Anyway, it's good to see you. I'm glad you made it back. How the hell *did* you get back, by the way?"

Derek had been standing mute, paralyzed by a sense of unreality. Now, bathed in the light of that familiar easy grin, he felt himself yielding to a desire to lose himself in relief, to forget that any of this had ever happened, to sink back into the old days.

And yet . . .

He shook himself angrily. "Glad I made it back? What a crock! You *sent* me to that Void domain—me and Lauren and a bunch of others!"

Rinnard looked deeply hurt. "Come on, Derek, that's not fair! I never intended to strand you—that wasn't the plan. I honestly believed there was a portal from that domain, for Urquiashqua to open for you. I was lied to, you see. I was a victim, too."

"Lied to by whom? The Titans?"

"Yes—through Nydierya." Rinnard's face clouded. "When I found out . . . well, that was when whatever I felt for her died. I can pinpoint the moment. Now I'm just faking it

with her until I don't need her any more. God, Derek, there's
no hell like being trapped in a loveless relationship! I've
always read that, but I never believed it until now. Anyway, forget about that bitch! The point is, you *know* I never
meant you any real harm. Remember my call from the
lifeboat, explaining all that?"

"Yes, I remember it. I remember you told me that what
you were doing was necessary to defeat the Titans. I gather
that no longer applies. Or did you ever mean it? Maybe it
was an 'inoperative statement,' as some twentieth century
politician is supposed to have said when he got caught lying
his ass off."

Rinnard winced. "I suppose I had that coming. But you've
got to believe that it really did start out that way." He gave
a laugh that had little humor in it. "I was going to worm
my way into the Titans' confidence like some kind of psionic
James Bond, complete with beautiful female spy!"

"So what changed? Look, Paul, let's say I believe you.
Maybe I really *do* believe you. But that still doesn't explain
what you've been doing since then. For God's sake, Paul,
help me understand!"

Rinnard turned abruptly on his heel and walked over to
the transparency. For at least two heartbeats he stared
outward. Then he turned and faced Derek, arms folded,
silhouetted against the slowly parading starfields in a way
that unaccountably caused a shiver to slide along Derek's
spine.

"I came to a couple of realizations, Derek. The first was
that I—and you, and all of us—had been pissing into the
wind." Rinnard looked at the globe of Khron. He made no
apparent motion, but the globe awoke in colors. Derek saw
at once that red was the color of Qurvyshye. But it had spread
far beyond the shores of its own continent. The islands of
the Central Sea showed like a scarlet rash. The inhabited
coastal fringes of arid southern Loboye were the same color.
And even in Emetulye it was spreading like a bloodstain,
encroaching on the Nernere basin where the green of the
Erkhedzuo alliance crouched at bay.

"You see, Derek, the Qurvyshuo—and therefore the Titans

who control them—are going to win. No one can prevent
it."

"That's nothing but self-serving bullshit! It's only because
of *you* that they're winning! You're just rationalizing."

"No, Derek. They would have won anyway, sooner or later.
Once the Titans accepted the necessity of using human
magic, their victory became inevitable because of their total
ruthlessness. The Erkhedzuo have no defense against magic
drawing on the amount of quantum energy the Qurvyshuo
death-cult can provide. All I've done is hasten what would
have happened eventually."

"Then you at least admit you've accelerated the process.
Why?"

"Isn't it obvious, Derek? The victory of the Titans can't
be prevented, and anyone who tries will be plowed under.
At the same time, people who just stand back and let it
happen will end up passive victims of events they have no
power to influence. So I've chosen a third way. I'm making myself useful—and, eventually, indispensable—to the High
Lord." Rinnard grinned. "I've spoken to him in the Titans'
own Void domain! Very few people have been allowed there."

Derek stared at the man he'd thought he'd known. "So
you've decided you want to be the power behind the throne?"

"You still don't quite understand, Derek. You see, the *second*
realization I've come to is that Doctor Kronenberg and
Urquiashqua are even more right than they know about the
potential of psionics. We had our first inkling of it when it
became clear that a concert was more powerful than its
director. Now psychotronic enhancement has confirmed it. A
psi isn't restricted by the amount of quantum energy that his
own neural processes produce—that's not the limiting factor.
The limiting factor is the psi's ability to suck it out and exploit
it." Rinnard laughed. "Doctor Kronenberg would fry me to
a crisp for being so imprecise . . . but you know me and math!
The point is, there is *no* theoretical upper limit—none that
we've discovered yet, anyway—to how high a psi's powers
can be boosted. It's merely a question of technology.

"Magic, though, *is* limited in fundamental ways. Urquiashqua is right about that, too. Even when you're tapping

other humans, you come up against a point of diminishing marginal returns—the Qurvyshuo are starting to discover that."

"But," Derek protested, "a mage using the traditional way can keep on collecting quantum energy. It just takes time."

"Psionics doesn't. That's a decisive advantage. Besides, there are various limiting factors to that collecting process, even given all the time in the world. For one thing, there are a lot of mages working here in the Khron system, and above a certain level of quantum energy they begin to set up . . . harmonics. Or so it's been explained to me. I don't pretend to understand the theory. Nor do I need to. The point is, psionics is potentially boundless. We can become greater than any mage, Derek! We can become greater than any gods, including the Titans!

"So you see, Derek," Rinnard finished in a voice that had dropped back to the conversational level, "you were considerably short of the truth when you thought I wanted to make myself the 'power behind the throne.' "

When Derek was finally able to speak, he carefully held in check the pleading tone that he knew would enter his voice if he let it. "Paul, this may or may not mean anything to you anymore, but as far as I know nothing has released you from your oath as a commissioned officer in the United States Navy. Do you remember why we came here in the first place? The Titans won't stop here! Don't you know what they've been doing on Khron, through their Qurvyshuo stooges? Or have you closed your eyes to that?"

"Oh, I know about it," Rinnard said, very softly. "As a matter of fact, I know more about it than you do. And the things I've seen . . . No, I haven't closed my eyes. I've learned that there are things so horrible they won't *let* you close your eyes."

"Well, then? Is that what you really want to see happening in the U.S.—or anywhere else on Earth, for that matter?"

"Of course not, Derek! That's the whole point! Haven't you understood *anything*?" Rinnard took a deep, shuddering breath and then spoke calmly with an obvious effort. "Yes, you're right: Earth is next. That's inevitable. With their technological edge, the Qurvyshuo wouldn't even need magic to swab the decks with anybody on Earth, even the U.S. That's the very reason I have to do what I'm doing. In the first place, the whole human-sacrifice perversion will become unnecessary—no, *irrelevant*—because it can't match enhanced psi no matter how many victims they torture to death! In the second place, I'll be in a position to protect Earth."

"Because you'll have become indispensable to the High Lord?"

"That's the way it'll be at first." With another Mercurially sudden mood-switch, Rinnard laughed in a way that was very much like his old self—horrifyingly so. "The Titans have gotten cagier since their defeat on Earth back in prehistory, but deep down they're still blinded by their hatred and contempt for humans. They can't *let* themselves see that their special powers, like human magic, are inherently limited. The High Lord thinks that by letting me enhance my abilities more and more he's just making me more useful to him. So I'm increasing my powers continuously—and also discovering new dimensions to them. For example, I learned to teleport with extraneous objects—"

"Yes, so we heard. Lauren and I have mastered that."

"Ah, but now I've become able to teleport things to remote locations without teleporting myself with them! And I can do it to ranges you wouldn't believe. You see, there's a subconscious built-in safety factor that won't let you teleport yourself further than you can reliably do so. But it doen't apply when you're flicking things of which you don't mind losing a certain percentage.

"So you see? The High Lord just doesn't get it! He's setting himself up to be supplanted. It's like I told you before: we can surpass gods. We can *be* gods. *Real* Gods!"

Derek simply stared.

"So," Rinnard resumed, switching back again to chatty mode, "once I'm in charge nobody on Earth will have anything to worry about. Nobody on Khron, for that matter. I'll do right by everybody."

"But," Derek said quietly, "the fact remains, you'll be Emperor of Khron and Earth."

"Aw, hell, Derek, I don't need any silly titles! And besides, I'm not thinking of some kind of one-man rule. Far from it. I want you with me!"

Derek's sense of unreality became total. "What? You want me to join you?"

"Sure—you and Lauren both. You *belong* here with me. Don't you see? If we stick together, there's nothing we can't do! Come to think of it, I'd like to recruit some of the JICPO people we left behind on Earth. Sergeant Tucker, for instance. And once Earth is secure and there's no longer a need for secrecy, we can start testing the general populace. Start building a—"

"—Psionic ruling class?"

Rinnard frowned. "That's not exactly the way I would have put it, Derek. More like a . . . vanguard, leading the way into what is clearly going to be the next stage of human evolution. And I want to be as inclusive as possible. I'll give Doctor Kronenberg free rein to work on her pet project of developing a genetic virus that can resequence anybody's DNA for the psi trait. The Titans will be left behind in the dust! But first, though, we'll have to build on the psis we already know about, and—"

"Before you get too far ahead of yourself, Paul," Derek cut in, "it might interest you to know that we've already taken *Ergu Nervy* to Earth. You asked earlier how we got out of that Void domain. Well, we established contact with Sophia—never mind how—and she created a portal for us. We went to Earth and recruited my grandfather, who used to be a powerful psi—and now is again, thanks to Doctor Kronenberg."

"Doctor—?"

"Yes, that's right, Paul. We also recruited *her*. She's working with Urquiashqua now, and God alone knows what those two will come up with. We're going to stop the Titans!"

"You can't." Derek had hoped to get a rise out of Rinnard, for anger would at least have been a *human* response, but he just shook his head slowly. "It's hopeless."

"No, it isn't—especially if *you* rejoin us!" The tone Derek had been sternly holding back finally broke through into his voice. "Come back to us, Paul!"

"No, Derek." Rinnard's voice held no discernible expression, and in the semidarkness his features were indistinct. "I've gone too far. And it has to be done my way. Look, don't worry! I can handle the High Lord."

"You only think you can. Can't you see that the Titans are playing you for a sucker? Remember what we've been told about that guy Lokhvyrgashqua, who founded the godawful regime in Qurvyshye with the Titans' help? *He* thought he could 'handle' them, too. But they were just using him—like they're using you now, to expedite their conquest-by-proxy of Khron and, afterwards, Earth."

"You still don't understand, Derek," said Rinnard quietly. "That conquest *must* proceed to its inevitable conclusion. If there's no empire, then there'll be no empire for me— sorry, I mean *us*—to take control of."

"You had it right the first time, Paul," said Derek, just as quietly. "I'll never join you. I guarantee Lauren and my grandfather won't either. To do what you say you're going to do, you'll have to destroy us first."

"I'm truly sorry, Derek." There could be no possible doubt that Rinnard meant it.

Nothing more was said, for there was nothing more to say. After a time, Rinnard touched a key on a pocket remote unit. The two guards came in and led Derek away. His last sight of Rinnard was of a dark silhouette, somehow both more and less than human, with the universe of stars wheeling around its head.

That final image haunted Derek's dreams, after he finally managed to get to sleep on his cell's hard narrow bunk.

Time stretched and stretched, and no one contacted him in any way save to feed him. In the absence of the watch they'd taken away, his only way to tell how much time had passed was to use projection to consult clocks outside his cell. After a while, he found himself losing interest. Time became almost as meaningless as it had been in the chaos of the Inner Void. He began to wonder if it was a ploy, to break him by isolation. If so, it was working. And the dreams grew steadily worse.

It was in the midst of one of those dreams that he felt the touch of another mind.

It brought him bolt upright in his bunk. He had never bothered erecting mental barriers. There was no point. Rinnard's remarks about drugs had only confirmed what he'd assumed from the beginning: they could disorient him beyond the capability of resisting telepathic intrusion anytime they chose. Their failure to do so represented a true if insulting assessment of the information left to be gleaned from him, now that he'd blurted out the tale of *Ergu Nervy*'s stopover at Earth in his misplaced eagerness to get through to Paul and win him over.

But the thought-tendril he now felt inside his head had nothing hostile about it. Indeed, it possessed a quality to which he could unhesitatingly put a name: *Lauren.* And the intent it wordlessly expressed also had a name: *rescue.*

He emptied his mind of its soaring excitement, and everything else that might distract him from putting out one crystal-clear image: his own identity coupled with the layout of his immediate environs as his projected consciousness had observed it.

He hoped his unenhanced power would be enough. Lauren, of course, would be using psychotronics—and, perhaps, be in concert with his grandfather as well. Still, they couldn't be but so far away. He composed himself to wait, hoping that Lauren would give him some warning.

In the event, all the warning he got was gut-shaking noise and concussion, as though a giant had whanged the station with his hammer.

He got to his feet as alarm klaxons began to whoop. He forced himself to clearly visualize the deck-plan around him, picked a location, and teleported out of the cell.

He found himself in the midst of pandemonium. Figures in black-and-maroon Qurvyshuo uniforms were running about in passageways filled with acrid smoke. The smoke was moving in one direction, and there was a thin whistling sound. The Qurvyshuo were slipping clear nanoplastic hoods over their heads. Belatedly, Derek remembered that they'd taken away his emergency vac suit and given him a prison uniform of mere cloth.

He stopped worrying about it when one of the Qurvyshuo, with Security insignia on his upper arm, noticed him and brought a long-barrelled railgun to bear.

Derek flung up his hands, palms outward. The Qurvyshuo didn't look like he particularly cared. . . .

Three figures in powered combat armor came around a corner of the passageway. The Qurvyshuo turned to face them . . . just in time to be practically cut in half by a stream of hypervelocity flechettes.

By then, Derek was flat on the deck, trying to make himself even flatter. He'd glimpsed a plasma gun in the hands of one of those power-armored figures, and surely there were heavily armed Qurvyshuo on the way. Very soon, this passageway was going to become a combat environment in which nothing unarmored could live.

"Derek!"

He recognized the voice despite its artificial amplification. He risked a peek upward. One of the powered-armor suits was bending over him. Lauren's face smiled at him through the faceplate.

She must have gotten checked out on these suits while I wasn't looking, he reflected.

"We've got to get you out of here quick," she said briskly. "Sorry; I know this is a little untraditional, but . . ." With the strength the suit conferred, she scooped him up in her arms and carried him swiftly down the passgeway.

She'll pay, Derek thought darkly. Then the din of renewed fighting behind them buffeted his ears. *On second thought, maybe this isn't so bad after all.*

"Paul's here," he told her, shouting to make himself heard. "I've talked to him."

"Not now. Intelligence has learned that he's gone off somewhere; he must have left just after you saw him. That's one reason we decided to try this raid. We used telepathic illusion to conceal ourselves until we were right on top of this station—your grandfather has gotten very good at that. Ah, here we are."

They came to the breach that had been blasted in the station's skin, now partially enclosed with a transparent flexible bubble. Beyond it, Derek could see the Erkhedzuo assault shuttle from which the attackers had come. "These guys will fight a rear-guard action," Lauren told him, "then get away on the shuttle. But we've got to get you to a special-high-speed courier that's out there in cloak. That's why I came along. Get ready!"

"What? Lauren, I haven't got an enhancer. And even with one, you can't teleport that far with me and that suit!" They'd established experimentally that there was a tradeoff between range and the mass the teleporter was carrying. And the powered armor weighed a quarter of a ton.

"I *am* enhanced. And Doctor Kronenberg has come up with some new stuff. . . . Look, we don't have time to chat! Ready?"

Before Derek completed his nod, they were inside the confines of a small spacecraft, and Lauren was plopping him unceremoniously into a deeply padded acceleration couch. "Strap in!" she commanded. He'd barely obeyed when the courier's drive thundered into life and G-forces shoved him down into the couch. Blackout closed over him.

★ CHAPTER TWENTY-ONE

"So *that's* how you did it!" said Derek, staring at the device in Urquiashqua's lab.

"Aw, and I was hoping you'd think it was all me," Lauren smiled.

Doctor Kronenberg ignored the byplay. "It would have been impossible without Urquiashqua's analysis of my accumulated data on teleportation, applying his work in extra-dimensional physics."

The plump mage gave a hand-wave of bogus self-deprecation. "As you know, I've been fascinated by teleportation, as it is one of the psionic effects that has no precise magical counterpart. It was only after consultation with Doctor Kronenberg that I considered the teleportation-related possibilities of locally stressed space/time—something within the capabilities of our technology."

"*Not,*" Doctor Kronenberg added sternly, "to the extent of producing nonsense like 'artificial gravity' or 'antigravity' or 'reactionless drives.'"

"Of course not," Urquiashqua agreed. "Although eventually . . . perhaps . . ." He shook his head and resumed. "At any event, our expectations were confirmed. The device draws a teleporter to it, reducing the quantum energy requirement—"

"—And thus effectively increasing the range and carrying capacity of somebody teleporting to it," Derek finished for him. "Now I understand your name for it: the 'teleport attractor.' Between that and her enhancer, no wonder Lauren was able to get me and her powered armor back to that shuttle. Good thing it's small enough to be installed in a shuttle and still leave room for the space, right beside it, where the teleporter actually appears." Studying it, he found himself less awed by the pure science—which he couldn't hope to understand anyway—than by the speed with which they'd gotten the actual hardware operational. Molecular engineering, it had turned out, could perform perhaps twenty percent of the miracles breathlessly predicted for it by the enthusiasts of Derek's world, who tended to overlook problems like heat-exchange, fine control and the corrosive effects of free oxygen. Still, in some ways industrial nanotechnology was more magical than magic.

"We are also exploring other applications," Urquiashqua continued. "One in particular. I almost hesitate to mention it, inasmuch as we have only an experimental prototype which has yet to be tested. But I know that Rosa—Doctor Kronenberg, rather—will fail to give herself proper credit."

"It really involves no new theoretical breakthroughs," Doctor Kronenberg demurred. "Basically, it's just an extension of the principles of psychotronic enhancement which you originated." For just an instant, she and Urquiashqua exchanged a look that was almost . . . *No! Impossible!* thought Derek.

"The suspense is killing us," said Lauren.

"Briefly," said Urquiashqua, deceiving no one who knew him, "the device is analogous to a psionic amplifier, but is specialized for teleportation, attaining extremely high levels of enhancement for that one particular ability at the expense of versatility. Also, it is connected with, and attuned to, the *Ergu Nervy*'s central computer, to which it incorporates a direct neural interface. In effect, a psi—or, to make effective use of it, a psionic concert—will be able to teleport *the entire ship,* and do so to unprecedented ranges."

"We don't know what the ultimate limits of those ranges

may be," added Doctor Kronenberg in a subdued voice. "Conceivably, we could be talking interstellar distances."

"And," Lauren asked, just as quietly, "have your experiments confirmed the theory that teleportation is truly instantaneous?"

"Yes." Doctor Kronenberg let the word fall like a coin into a well. Derek tried to imagine what it must be like for her to uncover a challenge to the sacrosanct velocity of light. Probably like a devoutly Christian archaeologist who'd dug up a skeleton which was inarguably that of Jesus of Nazareth.

Urquiashqua's pocket communicator beeped. He spoke into it, and listened to a stream of what was, of course, unintelligible to the others. "We are summoned to the Command Center," he told them, "on a matter of the highest urgency."

They proceeded to another compartment, which held a portal to the flagship. Urquiashqua had created it at the cost of much time and effort. Now, as the mage began doing what was necessary to open it, Derek found himself wishing they were in less of a hurry and could take an inter-orbital shuttle—the scenic route, as he still thought of it, for the sight of the serried ranks of warships with the curving blue vastness of Khron below had yet to pall for him. This was where the alliance had concentrated the bulk of its surviving space fleets, the better to maintain its all-important presence in the planet's orbital space. It was a stunning sight . . . except that Derek now understood the grim military realities behind it, and it had begun to bear a disturbing resemblance to a very large-scale and high-tech circling of the wagons.

The most awesome sight of all was the great orbital fortress known simply as the Command Center, for it housed the central headquarters of Erkhedzye's military presence in space. It had gotten crowded of late, as many functions had been moved to it from the Citadel, whose security could no longer be taken for granted. The greater numbers had somehow intensified the oppressive atmosphere of gloom and despair—it was a palpable presence, an unwanted third party in every conversation. Derek had been glad to escape it

aboard *Ergu Nervy*, where Urquiashqua and Doctor Kronenberg were oblivious to encroaching night in the purity of
their scientific enthusiasm. Now the four of them emerged
into a beehive-swarm of movement, most of it in the
direction of the main conference room.

"Derek!"

"Granddad!" They hadn't seen each other much of late,
for Glenn Secrest had been undergoing evaluation of his
reemerging talents, whose frontiers had never been properly explored before. "Are you on your way to this conference too?"

"Yep. Scuttlebutt has it that the news isn't good."

"It seldom is, these days," Urquiashqua philosophized.

They filed into a large chamber dominated by a long
table in front of a viewscreen. Concentric semicircles of
seats faced the table, at which sat Yqenomumdzashqua,
whose rank-title the interpreter software rendered as "Grand
Admiral," and variously uniformed representatives of
Erkhedzye's allies. Sophia sat to one side, at a slight but
unmistakable remove. They took seats just as the Grand
Admiral—which was how Derek always thought of him,
finding his name even more intractable than most in this
culture—rose to his feet.

"I will be blunt," he began abruptly. "Dzoemrya has
fallen."

Stunned silence enveloped the room. The heavily defended
base on Khron's inner moon had been the alliance's last
toehold in space beyond low orbit. Skilled tactical coordi-
nation of the base's own weapons and the lighter but mobile
ones of warships had held off attack after attack in a series
of desperate actions. But now . . .

"Our defenses," the Grand Admiral explained, "were taken
by surprise by something new. Not to put too fine a point
on it, our ships began taking hits without having tracked
any incoming missiles. Naturally, all standard magical
countermeasures were in effect." He turned to the three psis
from Earth. "That is why you are here. Can you suggest
any explanation?"

Hastily organizing his thoughts, Derek reviewed what he

knew about space warfare as practiced at Khron's technological level.

From his early-twenty-first-century perspective, the limited role played by laser weapons had come as a surprise,
especially considering that the Khronuo had the capability
to produce coherent X rays without detonating a fusion
bomb—something to do with using a free-electron laser to
ionize carbon material, producing a plasma that underwent
a population inversion. But even at X-ray wavelengths, a
laser was still subject to the iron law that tied effective range
to the diameter of the focusing optics. At the distances
involved in space combat, delivering a useful quantity of
directed energy to a target required a dish at least hundreds
of meters in diameter. Even ignoring the little matter of
expense, such a thing would have posed insuperable problems in spacecraft design, and been hopelessly vulnerable.
So missiles were the primary offensive weapons, made all
the more devastating by antimatter warheads.

But *defensive* lasers were an engineering possibility. A
viable spacecraft design could incorporate point-defense
versions, while orbital fortresses—like this one, under whose
weapons the tatters of the alliance fleets sheltered—and bases
on airless moons and asteroids could accommodate larger
ones for area defense. With such lasers striking at the speed
of light, antimatter-tipped missiles—too large and expensive
to be employed in defense-saturating numbers—became less
terrifying. The resultant rough standoff between offense and
defense was yet another reason for the typically indecisive
quality of the struggle in the Khron system.

Now, however, the Qurvyshuo had unbalanced the equation, delivering antimatter warheads without using missiles
for the lasers to fry.

Derek had a pretty definite idea of how they were doing
it.

"It naturally occurred to us," the Grand Admiral continued, "that we might be dealing with large-scale psionic
illusion such as Paul Rinnard has used before, when they
smashed our deep-space fleet. But it seems impossible. Since
then, we have automated our defensive systems to an

unprecedented level, sacrificing human initiative and intuition for security from telepathic influence."

"No, sir, that's not it." Derek instantly had everyone's undivided attention. "Remember what I reported when I first arrived here. During my captivity, Paul told me he's gone beyond the ability to carry extraneous objects along with him when he teleports. Now he can send them to remote locations without going anywhere himself."

The horror in the room deepened as, one by one, people grasped it.

Lauren was the first to put it into words. "You're saying he's flicking warheads into our ships?"

"But," spluttered one of the allied officers, "surely he can't perform that kind of teleportation out to such ranges!"

"He explained to me that the kind of psychic safety cutoff that limits self-teleportation doesn't apply. And besides," Derek added, mostly to himself, "I don't think we can safely assume that *anything* is impossible for him anymore."

The Grand Admiral sat up straighter, visibly imposing military discipline on his soul. "We can form an estimate of what his range is by analyzing the recorded data on how far away the enemy units were at the time—Dzoemrya kept transmitting to us right up to its fall. But at the moment, the crucial question is this: what can be done to counteract this kind of attack?" He looked at the trio from Earth, and for an instant a kind of imploring hope broke through his sternness.

Derek didn't meet his eyes. "Sir, teleportation, by definition, is instantaneous transposition from one point to another without traversing the intervening space. So interception is out of the question, as is any kind of barrier. We can form a concert and try to set up a telepathic illusion to mask the locations of our ships. But, as you yourself intimated earlier, that can't fool instruments under the control of AI."

"Besides," Lauren said grimly, "no illusion, whether psionic or electronic, can help with this station. Its orbital elements are fixed, and a matter of record. It would be absurdly simple for a computer to predict its location at any given instant."

An immaterial but palpable shudder ran through the conference room as the implications sank home. The Grand Admiral remained steadfast. "Yes. That makes sense. Besides, they targeted ships during the reduction of Dzoemrya, and they won't want to be predictable. Yes, the Command Center will probably be the target for any teleported warheads." He did not add what everyone already knew: afterwards, Qurvyshuo control of low Khron orbit would be uncontested, as would the Titan cult of death.

Derek stared miserably at Urquiashqua and Doctor Kronenberg, but saw no help there. He looked at Sophia. Her perfect features reflected a serenity which, he thought with a flash of bitterness, she could well afford. "Listen, Sophia, teleportation involves the Inner Void, to which you're native. Can't you do anything to interfere with it?"

"No." The goddess faced him squarely, and he decided he had misinterpreted what lay behind those cool gray eyes. It was a sadness which, though genuine, was felt within the context of eternity, a perspective which reduced grief as humans knew it to impossible bathos. "Teleportation, like every other manifestation of psionics, lies beyond our understanding. The only thing of which we can be certain is that it takes place on a different . . . plane from that on which we can negotiate the Inner Void. And, at any rate, teleportation is instantaneous. It is a truism that no force or influence of any kind can be exerted upon a phenomenon which persists for zero time."

Derek's head drooped. He stared at the floor, alone with his feeling of inadequacy. Around him, the silence deepened until it grew unendurable.

What broke it was, of all things, a chuckle.

"Hey," said Glenn Secrest, "I'm still a little new to all this, so maybe I'm completely off-base. But . . . Rosa, remember what you were telling me earlier about this 'teleport attractor' you and Urquiashqua have come up with?"

"Yes; I was explaining it to Derek just before we came over here from *Ergu Nervy*."

"Well, one thing I forgot to ask, because it didn't occur to me at the time." Glenn grinned lazily and stroked his mustache. "Does the gizmo only work when somebody is using it like Lauren did to rescue Derek—that is, teleporting to it *on purpose?*"

"Why, of course not. The intent of the teleporter has nothing to do with . . ." Doctor Kronenberg's puzzled expression faded out, and her mouth dropped open.

Suddenly, Derek understood. With a yelp that scandalized the assembled brass, he was on his feet. *"Yes!"*

They were on *Ergu Nervy*'s bridge—so the interpreter named it, and so Derek couldn't help but think of it—when the Qurvyshuo offensive struck.

They'd been willing to await the attack in the Command Center, but the Grand Admiral had decreed that they were too uniquely valuable to risk aboard the presumptive target. Also, it made sense for them to have access to Urquiashqua's facilities. Derek had agreed, with what he'd hoped was a proper display of reluctance.

Sophia was there too. Her presence had at first surprised Derek, who had expected her mysterious comings and goings to be in the "going" phase when the moment of battle approached. He'd subsequently felt ashamed of the thought.

So now they gazed, along with Rhykhvyleshqua, at a tactical display with a blue marble representing Khron at its center. Out toward the display's outer rim, revolving clockwise, the moon Dzoemrya shone with the baleful red of Qurvyshuo occupation. Inward from it ran the dotted red line marking the hyperbolic orbit the enemy invasion fleet was following, curving around the blue planet and terminating at the green dot that marked the Command Center, currently on the opposite side of Khron from Dzoemrya and likewise orbiting the planet clockwise. Near that end of the dotted line, sliding along it like a bead along a string, was a little red icon which, for all its sinister color, seemed a rather banal symbol for the most stupendous tonnage of killing machinery ever deployed in the history of Khronuo humanity.

Derek had read the intelligence tallies, and viewed the computer-generated diagrams of capital ships larger than the aircraft carriers of Earth's oceans. It had all blurred into near-meaninglessness after a while. All that still had the power to appall him were the stricken faces of the Grand Admiral and Rhykhvyleshqua and all the others who fully understood what those inconceivable statistics meant. The Qurvyshuo had called in their victorious fleets from throughout the system and massed them into a kind of cosmic wrecking-ball, now swinging down toward Khron.

The alliance still had enough scout boats in cis-Dzoemrya space to keep tabs on enemy activity around the moon. And the combined burns of all those mammoth space dreadnoughts was hard to miss. As soon as the offensive had gotten underway, the Grand Admiral had sent his grossly out-matched ships accelerating out of low orbit, sweeping ahead of the Command Center and outward into an elongated orbit that, after a three-quarter circuit of the planet, came abreast of the oncoming armada of hostile ships, though somewhat ahead of them, and just close enough for an indecisive running missile duel. Now the battered ships of Erkhedzye and its allies were coming back around and approaching the Command Center. The Qurvyshuo were following them . . . which, under any other circumstances, would have been preposterously reckless on their part.

The planet below was of no consequence from a defensive standpoint. It was axiomatic that military spacecraft had nothing to fear from planet-based weapons; X-ray lasers dissipated in atmosphere, and missiles had to struggle up out of the gravity well. But the Command Center was something else again. The vast space station mounted the kind of area-defense laser dishes that were an engineering impossibility for any mobile platform.

But now the Qurvyshuo were advancing with apparent unconcern, pursuing the Erkhedzuo ships toward the very mouths of those hellishly potent energy weapons. The conclusion to be drawn from their tactics was clear: they expected those weapons to no longer exist by the time they came within range.

"I guess our hunch about their target was right," Glenn remarked. Derek was in awe at his grandfather's *sang-froid*.

His own legs had gone weak with relief at the confirmation of their assumptions, the basis of the defense to which they had already committed themselves.

"Also," Rhykhvyleshqua added, "it gives us a way of predicting when the warheads will be teleported: just before their ships come within the defensive envelope. That would make tactical sense."

"It is also consistent with the range from which Intelligence has estimated Rinnard can teleport them," added Urquiashqua, studying the readouts.

Wordlessly, the captain manipulated a remote. The tactical display seemed to zoom closer, until the big screen held only Khron and its immediate environs, including the Command Center and *Ergu Nervy*, which lay well off to the side. There were also a number of green icons so tiny you had to look closely to see them, as befitted the relatively insignificant mass of the satellites they represented. They encircled the Command Center in a nimbus that was being replenished by a stream from *Ergu Nervy* like a cascade of emerald-dust.

As they watched, the cascade dried up.

"That's all of them," stated the captain.

"It was all we were able to produce in the time we had," Urquiashqua added, a little defensively.

"Seems like quite a lot to me," Glenn commented in an uncharacteristically subdued voice. His formative years belonged to the third quarter of the twentieth century, and he hadn't had as much time as his younger companions to adjust to the capabilities of Khronuo technology.

Rhykhvyleshqua made further adjustments, and the display seemed to recede from them a little, revealing more of surrounding space. "At this scale," he explained, "the screen shows out to a little beyond the range of the area-defense lasers." Even as he spoke, the first of the green icons of the fleeing Erkhedzuo ships appeared at the upper-right-hand corner.

"It won't be long now," Glenn observed, unnecessarily. Or maybe it *was* necessary, to fill the silence.

More of the green icons straggled onto the screen, to a

depressing litany of damage reports. They were in free fall, on the looping orbit they'd been following. So were the Qurvyshuo ships that presently appeared astern of them.

Those ships were not dispersed in a defeated scattering of icons like those they pursued. Instead, a compact formation appeared on the screen with shocking suddenness, like a phalanx of scarlet. A screen of lighter ships—less dense but still well-ordered—streamed back from its flanks. The whole fleet was locked into a single entity, computer-designed to maximize the individual ships' mutually supporting firepower into a flawless latticework of death. Within that umbrella, far enough back to be safe from the highly energetic exhausts of the capital ships, came a single icon which the computer had tagged in the Khronuo script Derek had never learned to read.

"The command ship," Rhykhvyleshqua explained. "Intelligence believes Rinnard is there. And—" He glanced at readouts, and faced the others somberly. "It has come within what we believe to be his maximum range for remote teleportation."

They fell silent, and their eyes flickered back and forth between the tactical display and the outside visual, where the Command Center could barely be seen as a glint of reflected sunlight. Eternity stretched to the snapping point . . . or seemed to. In fact, only a few seconds passed. But the suspense was of the uniquely poignant sort that arises from knowing that what one awaits will come with absolutely no warning.

It did.

The computer polarized the visual just in time to save them from blindness. But even a momentary glimpse of the miniature nova out there left their eyes dazzled. As Derek blinked away the afterimage of that hellish event— "explosion" was a banality—he strained to see the tactical display.

The icon of the Command Center was still there. He couldn't make out the tiny green dots that haloed it, but he knew one of them would be gone. That was what they were for. His grandfather had put his finger on the essential fact about the teleport attractor, which had escaped its inventors. In their fixation on the goal of providing a kind of beacon for intentional teleportation, it hadn't occurred to them that their brain-child would draw to it *any* teleport whose destination was within a sphere defined by its radius of effect.

So they'd seeded the volume of space around the Command Center with satellites mounting attractors, positioned so that those immaterial spheres encompassed the station and overlapped with each other. Anything teleported to the Command Center would, instead, materialize at the nearest of those satellites—as one just had.

Unavoidably, the satellites weren't far from the Center. But in space there is no air to carry a shock wave. And, while there were no space-operatic "force shields," electromagnetic screens that protected crews from the UV rays that had no ozone layer to block them were standard equipment. They did much to protect the Center from the radiation sleeting from those matter/antimatter reactions. For what got past them, the Khronuo had sophisticated antirad drugs.

Almost immediately, there was another sunburst—this time visible only as an expanding, white-fringed violet sphere in the stepped-down viewscreen. Then another. And another. They'd expected it. A single antimatter warhead teleported into the guts of the Command Center would have been enough, but it had been beyond belief that Rinnard wouldn't have others in reserve. They could only hope that he didn't have as many of them as there were teleport attractors out there.

Now the viewscreen seethed with the violet spheres, like the blossoming of evil flowers, one after another. *So Paul still has some limitiations,* Derek thought. *He can only teleport them one at a time.* But the thought occupied only a small portion of his mind—the portion that could think clearly as he stared, in stunned disbelief, at the catclysm raging around the Command Center. He tried to imagine what it must be like out there, but his imagination failed.

Then, all at once it was over.

"Sheer ecomomics," he heard Sophia remark coolly.

"Antimatter warheads are far more expensive than teleport attractors."

"Besides," Rhykhvyleshqua added, "they didn't expect to need many."

In the tactical display, the enemy fleet was still on course . . . right into the range of the great lasers that weren't supposed to be there anymore.

Desperately, the Qurvyshuo began trying to alter their vector. Derek visualized the great ships turning ponderously with attitude thrusters, then burning their main drives at right angles to their orbital path.

It was obviously a panicked effort by individual ship captains, not a smooth implementation of a contingency plan. As Derek watched, their invincible formation wavered and began to dissolve.

But it was far too late for them to skirt the defensive envelope. Inexorably, their insurmountable momentum carried them past that imaginary boundary in space . . . and individual scarlet icons began flickering and, in some cases, going out.

Derek continued trying to visualize the scene.

For once, Hollywood had gotten it right—more right than a lot of printed science fiction. The notion of a weapon-grade laser as a continuous beam, an "energy sword" neatly cutting a spaceship into salami slices, was absurd. Instead, a multi-gigawatt laser like those of the Command Center produced a very short pulse of energy. When that energy was "dumped" into a target, it instantaneously superheated and vaporized the area it had struck, causing an explosion in approved Industrial Light and Magic style and sending shock waves crashing through the body of the ship. Naturally, the capacitors had to be recharged before a second pulse could be generated. But the dedicated antimatter powerplants possible for a construct of the Command Center's citylike size could manage it in seconds.

At the same time, the alliance ships were braking their own velocity. Uninterested in getting out of the range of those hellish lasers, they had turned end-on-end and were applying direct retro-thrust. As a result, the range between them and their erstwhile pursuers closed rapidly, and the ship-to-ship battle resumed. Soon, the remaining antimatter missiles were being launched at "sprint" ranges, making interdiction difficult even for point-defense lasers. The green icons were still heavily outnumbered, but they were fighting under the Command Center's supporting firepower. Perhaps more importantly, they fought with the consciousness of dawning, incredible, unhoped-for victory, against a demoralized, disorganized enemy. More and more of the red icons winked out.

And astern of that maelstrom of battle, the Qurvyshuo command ship, which had been lagging far behind the main formation, was making its its own course-change—which, just barely, averted the death-zone around the Command Center. Its new orbit would bring it curving around Khron.

"It's obvious that our fleet doesn't have anything in position to intercept it," said Rhykhvyleshqua. He ordered a course projection, and studied it. "He's not even going into orbit. The ship is going to do a low pass that will carry it right over Zquerte, the Qurvyshuo capital."

"Rinnard must mean to teleport down there," Glenn opined. "It'd be a lot quicker than riding a shuttle down."

"I imagine," said Lauren in a voice of concentrated and distilled venom, "that he'll have some explaining to do!"

"Yes," said Sophia. "To the High Lord himself."

"That's right," said Urquiashqua. "Intelligence has reported some odd activities in the central governmental/religious building—in Qurvyshye, the distinction is blurred—and my colleagues and I were able to be of some assistance in interpreting it. Evidently, a portal has been created from the Titans' Void domain to a large hall which exists as a setting for them to reveal themselves."

"Hey, Derek," said Lauren, "didn't you mention he'd told you he'd once been invited to that domain? This must be how he got there." Her expresssion grew even more vindictive. "Talk about getting called on the carpet! I'd love to be there to see it! Wouldn't you, Derek? Uh . . . Derek?"

Derek wasn't listening. And he wasn't watching the dimenuendo of the battle on the tactical display. One by one, they all turned to stare curiously at him. He didn't notice. Finally, he turned to face Sophia. His face was very controlled, and when he spoke, so was his voice.

"So we can assume that when Paul gets down there, this portal in Zquerte is going to be opened?"

"Yes," nodded the goddess. "I believe that is a safe assumption."

"Sophia, a long time ago, in Greece, I believe you told Lauren and me that it's practically impossible to kill gods permanently. Is that correct?"

"It is. As I explained at the time—"

"All right, then," said Derek, shocking everyone by interrupting the goddess. He met her gray eyes and held them. "How do you kill gods *temporarily*?"

CHAPTER TWENTY-TWO

For a time, no one moved or spoke.

"Derek," Sophia finally said, "do you realize what you're asking of me?"

"I do. I'm asking you to help me do the very thing you recruited me and Lauren for: end this war and defeat the Titans." Derek took a deep breath. "Hey, why are you so shocked? Wasn't this what you did to the Titans yourselves, in your *first* war with them, thousands of years ago on Earth? And didn't human mages help you do it?"

"Yes. But that was different. The humans of that day were, at most, high-grade Stone Age. We were grateful for their help, as you know; the presence of their descendants here in the Khron system proves that. But their help was . . . well, easy for us to accept. Since then, humans have become so . . . so—"

"Uppity?" suggested Lauren coldly.

Sophia turned slowly to face her. "I am accustomed, Lauren, to being able to finish my sentences." The goddess didn't grow, or seem to grow, any taller, or change in any outwardly visible way. But Lauren flinched back, and they all felt themselves withdrawing inward a little.

But Derek managed to keep his eyes on that perfect face,

and he saw something in it that made him recall snatches
of what Paul Rinnard had said, standing against a wheeling backdrop of stars. *Psionics is potentially boundless. . . . We
can surpass gods. We can be gods. Real Gods!*

And all at once, he understood.

Alone among them, he stood up and faced Sophia squarely.
He spoke in a voice that was strangely gentle but didn't
waver at all.

"I don't think you have much choice, Sophia. What has
happened can't be undone. The human race has outgrown
the kind of relationship you had with it in those days. Things
have . . . escalated since we defeated the Titans for you with
magic. We can do it for you again, this time with psionics.
But you're going to have to deal with us, not as we were
then, but as we've become."

"I know," said the goddess in the softest voice Derek had
ever heard from her. "It is difficult . . . but I know it must
be." The moment passed. She straightened up and was her
old self. "Very well. As you know, we cannot assume physical
bodies without accepting the physical laws of the material
universe—but only in a general way. We appear to perform
your normal bodily functions out of a sense of fitness or
completeness, but we do not *have* to do so. Thus we cannot, for example, be suffocated or starved. Likewise, any
wounds we sustain regenerate promptly—this is related to
the ability you characterize as 'shape-shifting.' However, if
our bodies are *destroyed* on the molecular level—as was done
to the Titans in our first war with them by the magic they've
now taken pains to counteract—our quantum energies return
in the Void as I told you, and reconstitute themselves only
at the expense of much time and trauma."

"That's good enough for me," said Derek. "So basically,
it has to be ground zero. And that's what we can give the
Titans if we can catch them with that portal open. And I
can do it, teleporting down from over that city, just like
Paul plans to."

"No," said Lauren firmly. "Not you. *Us!*"

"But," protested Rhykhvyleshqua, waving at the display,
"look at that! The orbital elements aren't right! Even if we

got underway this instant—and I have no orders to that effect—we couldn't pass over Zquerte until long after they're finished doing whatever it is they're doing."

"Yes, we can, sir. In fact, *Ergu Nervy* is the one ship in the fleet that can." Derek turned to face Urquiashqua and Doctor Kronenberg. "Isn't that so?"

"Surely," spluttered Urquiashqua, "you're not speaking of the experimental prototype we described to you!"

"Why not? You said it's already been installed on this ship."

"To await testing," snapped Doctor Kronenberg. "As you would have heard if you'd been listening." She was quite her old self, and Derek felt an odd relief. He'd been afraid she was mellowing.

"Yes!" said Urquiashqua with the emphatic nod he could never quite bring off. "There is no guarantee it will work at all. And even if it does, it was intended from the first to be used from one point in deep space to another such point. You have not considered the complications introduced into the calculation by conservation of momentum."

"But you've always told us the conservation laws of physics don't apply to teleportation. And our experience has confirmed it."

"That 'experience,'" said Doctor Kronenberg glacially, "has been confined to short distances. At these ranges, we have no way of knowing whether our data still apply—as ought to go without saying."

Yeah, she's back, thought Derek with an inward sigh.

"Just so," agreed Urquiashqua. "The Void can, indeed, act as a 'sump' for the kind of energy differentials involved in, for example, teleporting a few miles in a north-south direction on the surface of a rotating planet, or from one elevation to another. But for the combination of factors involved here—the rotation of Khron, our present orbital velocity around it . . . Well, I simply cannot venture to assess the hazards."

"Yeah, well, those 'hazards' are getting steadily worse and worse while we sit here beating our gums about it! The closer that command ship gets to the surface, the closer to it *we're* going to have to materialize in order to beat Paul down there. Maybe in atmosphere!"

"Preposterous!" Rhykhvyleshqua surged massively to his feet. "*Ergu Nervy* is not streamlined for atmospheric transit. She would burn up from friction. I will formally protest any orders from my superiors to risk this attempt—which, by the way, I have *not* received."

Overcoming all his conditioning, Derek looked the captain in the eye and spoke unflinchingly. "Sir, I can't deny that what I'm proposing involves an element of risk to your ship. But I ask you to consider the opportunity it offers. We've defeated the Qurvyshuo in space, true—but they'll just build back up and try again. We have a chance to put an end to this war by putting an end to what stands behind the Qurvyshuo and their death-cult!"

As Rhykhvyleshqua wavered, Derek caught sight of Zhezum out of the corner of his eye. Seeing the look the XO was giving his captain, he kept his mouth shut, letting Zhezum's expression speak for him and thanking his stars for such an unexpected ally.

The captain squeezed his eyes shut and gripped his beard in a fury of decision. Then the moment was over and his dark eyes met Derek's. "I cannot and will not jeopardize this ship without orders. But I will transmit your suggestion to the Grand Admiral. In the meantime, in anticipation of his decision, I see no reason why you can't be going ahead and making preparations for implementing your idea without delay. In fact, I suggest that you do so."

Derek's "Yes, *sir!*" was barely out of his mouth when he was on the move, grabbing Lauren by the arm and yelling at Urquiashqua and Doctor Kronenberg to follow.

"I still don't understand," Doctor Kronenberg fumed, "why the two of you have to teleport down. Rhykhvyleshqua could send *them*, and more like them, by conventional means, in powered armor."

She indicated the two Erkhedzuo security men waiting unobtrusively in the background of Urquiashqua's lab. They were the same two that Derek and Lauren had taken down into the Hole, so being carried along by teleporters was no novelty to them. They'd also been in on the raid that had rescued Derek. Their names were Qyloashqua and Urysteshqua. That was about all Derek knew about them—which, he reflected, was damned little to know about two quietly reliable men who, just incidentally, had saved his life.

They were in ordinary battle dress; Derek and Lauren could each teleport with another human, but without the help of a teleport attractor they weren't up to the added mass of powered combat armor. Other security types were helping them on with the same getup: a coverall of chemically treated ballistic fabric with chest- and abdomen-protecting inserts of composite laminate armor, and attachment points for assorted gear. The most impressive item wouldn't go on till last: a full-protection helmet whose multiview visor incorporated thermal imaging, light-gathering and anti-glare. Other accessories included a voice-activated communicator and a holographic HUD—and, in the case of Derek's and Lauren's helmets, psi-enhancing circuitry.

Qyloashqua and Urysteshqua were wearing articulated, gyrostabilized harnesses for squad-support weapons their unaided strength couldn't have handled. They carried, respectively, a heavy-duty railgun with an integral grenade launcher under the barrel, and a missile launcher for tactical nukes. The latter's microlaser-triggered deuterium fusion warheads had a "dial-a-yield" feature; they were now locked into the maximum setting of about a kiloton.

Derek and Lauren would carry light railguns—functionally, carbines—for self-defense. They'd only had the most rudimentary training, but the practically recoilless weapons were easy enough to use. And anyway, devastating firepower wasn't their job.

"Rhykhvyleshqua *is* going to send a powered-armor landing force down via reentry capsules," Lauren reminded Doctor Kronenberg. "That's the plan—they'll secure that building. But Derek and I have to be there, to counteract Paul. Besides, the Qurvyshuo can track the capsules with radar; by teleporting down first, we can achieve complete surprise."

"That's right," said Derek, adjusting his harness. "Don't worry about us, Doctor."

"I am *not* worried about you! I simply think it would be regrettable to waste your unique capabilities."

"Of course, Doctor," they chorused, straight-faced.

Glenn Secrest had been standing off to the side, uncharacteristically quiet. Derek was pretty sure he knew why. Now he spoke up rather irritably. "I'm damned if I see why *anybody* has to go down there! If we're going to appear out of nowhere over the Qurvyshuo capital, why not just drop a tactical nuke on that central building and then scram?"

"That might not work, Granddad," Derek explained. "The Titans might have time to slam their portal shut. Even if they don't, the blast effects might not . . . uh . . ." Derek's voice trailed off as he noticed the expression on Urquiashqua's face.

"But, but," stammered the mage, "we *couldn't*. Not even the Qurvyshuo have ever . . ." He stumbled to a halt, as though stymied by the impossibility of putting into words a fundamental cultural taboo.

Which, Derek belatedly recalled, was precisely what it was. Nuclear weapons had appeared on Khron a century and a half earlier than on Earth. Since then, they'd been used in anger from time to time . . . but never, ever against population centers. Even now, in the death-struggle raging on the planet's surface, the Khronuo had continued to abide by that unwritten rule, which they firmly believed to be the reason their civilization had survived its Atomic Age. *They might even be right*, reflected Derek.

Aloud, he spoke carefully, as much to Urquiashqua as to his grandfather. "At any rate, for all these reasons, the plan is to put the tactical missile through the portal into the Titans' domain. And, as Lauren said, she and I have to be down there running psionic interference for the professional combat soldiers while they put it there."

"I ought to be going, too," Glenn muttered.

Uh-huh! Derek nodded to himself mentally at the confirmation of his supposition as to what was eating his grandfather.

"We need to leave a psi in reserve aboard this ship," he said, hoping Lauren would keep her lip zipped about the time he'd used exactly the same line of argument on her. "And you haven't had as much time as we've had to get checked out on Khronuo stuff. And you've never teleported except under laboratory conditions. And—"

"And besides, I'm too goddamned old," Glenn finished for him.

Before Derek could try to answer the unanswerable, the lab's comm screen awoke, showing Rhykhvyleshqua's face against the backdrop of the bridge. "The Grand Admiral has agreed," he rapped out. "Our fleet has been tracking the Qurvyshuo command ship, and we believe it's going to be impossible for us to intervene before Rinnard teleports down. In fact, he may have already done so. We've calculated where this ship is going to have to emerge so as to give you a few seconds to get your helmets on before we pass over Zquerte. I'm downloading it now." A computer screen began to flash with data. The captain looked grim. "It's in the very uppermost regions of the atmosphere. Any lower and I would refuse to consider it. Now move!"

As alarms reverberated through the ship, Derek, Lauren and Glenn took their stations around a device that had the unpolished, cobbled-together look of the experimental model it was. Connected to it by fiber-optic cables were three headsets, bulky by the standards of Khronuo technology, that served a triple function. As he lowered the thing over his head and activated it, Derek experienced a bewildering variety of sensations: the familiar power-surge of psionic enhancement, the less familiar one of direct neural interfacing, and the wholly novel one of psychotronic linkage with the teleport drive. The fact that he was simultaneously establishing a concert with his two companions didn't help.

He imposed steadiness on himself and studied—if that was the word for how he perceived the images indescribably downloaded into his brain from the ship's central computer—the coordinates and visual location of a certain point above Khron's surface. The teleport drive was subject to the general rule that a teleporter—Derek in this case, as director of the concert—had to be able to visualize his destination.

All was in readiness. He thought a confirmation, waited a few seconds to allow the ship's personnel to prepare themselves, and then focused his own mind and those of Lauren and his grandfather on that set of coordinates.

"Now," he said aloud.

Derek had thought himself too old a hand to be shaken by the disorientation associated with teleportation. But this was far worse.

He barely noticed, however. The subliminal sense of wrongness was swamped by the sheer physical impact of noise and vibration as *Ergu Nervy* popped into existence still carrying most of her momentum relative to the planet. At such a velocity, the wispy upper atmosphere around them was like a series of cosmic speed-bumps. For a horrible instant, Derek thought the ship was going to shake itself— and him—apart.

Then a lower, steadier roar joined the din. Rhykhvyleshqua was burning the main drive, bringing the bucking ship under control. At the same instant, Derek grew aware that the security men were removing the headset that had done its job. They then fitted the combat helmet over his head and locked the fasteners that sealed suit and helmet against CBR agents—not that they expected to encounter such in the enemy's capital. He forced himself to concentrate on the image on the lab's comm screen.

It was a download from observation satellites in low orbit over Zquerte's hemisphere. Night lay over that hemisphere, but the light-gathering optical sensors were up to showing the city in ghostly colors as well as extraordinary magnification. As Derek watched, that seemingly endless cityscape zoomed toward him, zeroing in on the gigantic, roughly pyramidal government buildings . . . and one in particular, the largest. Down, down the viewpoint seemed to swoop, until a landing stage near the top of that building filled the screen.

Derek shot a side-glance at a readout. In her mad careen

across Khron's night side, *Ergu Nervy* was hurtling toward Zquerte. In seconds, she would be within what they'd agreed was safe teleport range.

Derek and Lauren hefted their weapons. They looked at each other and at Qyloashqua and Urysteshqua. All four nodded.

Just before he began to concentrate on that landing stage, Derek gave his grandfather a wave. Out of the corner of his eye, he saw the old man wave back.

Before the motion was complete, the lab was gone and they were atop the monstrous building, looking out over the panorama of Zquerte.

The brutally massive government buildings rose like volcanic islands from an ocean of city lights. There were other lights to see by, for here and there the city was burning in splotches of flame. The audio pickup of Derek's helmet brought to his ears a low, uneven background roar like distant surf, compounded of sirens and thousands of rioting voices.

The news from space must have leaked out already, before censorship could be clamped down, thought Derek. *They know the fleet has been smashed. It's like the first crack appearing in a pane of glass. Now the people who live—if you can call it that—in the shadows of these monstrous piles are rising up against their tormentors.*

As he watched, there was suddenly still more light. Far overhead, a blazing meteor streaked across the zenith. Derek knew precisely what it was, and he ordered himself not to go weak with relief at *Ergu Nervy*'s survival. Not that she'd been in any real danger from Qurvyshuo air defenses that must have been caught flat-footed by an interplanetary vessel popping out of nothingness above them. But the heat of atmospheric friction was something else again—he was sure what he was seeing was the glow of the hull as well as the flare of the drive.

And even now Rhykhvyleshqua is firing off ablative reentry capsules containing power- armored troops, who'll descend here and secure this building until our fleet arrives in force.

*Which reminds me: It's time to cut the goddamned rub-
bernecking!*

"Let's go," he yelled, and headed across the stage toward
the entrance to the cliff-face of the building, Lauren and
the two security men behind him. As he ran, he activated
his helmet HUD. A schematic of the building's interior
appeared.

It would have been nice to send his consciousness winging
ahead of him as a disembodied scout. But the great draw-
back of projection was that you couldn't do anything else
at the same time; the physical body was, to all intents and
purposes, comatose. Fortunately, Erkhedzuo intelligence had
obtained the blueprints of this building. The helmet's tiny
brain now held those floor plans—including the cavernous
hall that was their objective. As Qyloashqua's grenade
launcher blasted the door out of their way and they passed
through the blackened hole, a tiny dot representing Derek's
own location appeared on the HUD. He spared a fractional
second for one of his frequent grateful thoughts about
Khronuo technology.

Advancing through that labyrinth of corridors, they held
the same advantage that *Ergu Nervy* possessed above: total
and absolute surprise. Furthermore, they'd appeared in the
midst of other crises, notably the rising in the city around
them. Resistance was sporadic and disorganized, and the
security guards they encountered were armed only with the
light weapons that were all they'd ever expected to need
here in the innermost sanctum of the Qurvyshuo state. Derek
used his carbine several times, but his fire and Lauren's were
largely superfluous. Qyloashqua's death-dealing weapon
ripped any opposition apart with heavy flechettes of
molecularly aligned superdense steel, or blew it into pink
mist with grenades. Urysteshqua, carrying the all-important
missile launcher, stayed in the rear; the expression "a hero's
nothing but a sandwich" might not have translated well into
the Khronuo common language, but combat veterans like
these understood the concept.

And as the moving dot in Derek's HUD worked its way
closer and closer to the great rectangular emptiness at the

center of the display's intricate complexity, a single thought began to gnaw at the edge of his mind: *Where is Paul?*

He was thinking about it when a totally unexpected voice reached his ears through the pickup. "Hey, Derek, slow down!"

He stopped in his tracks and whirled around. Words failed him.

"You didn't really think you were going to get rid of me that easily did you?" asked Glenn Secrest. He was gasping for breath, but still grinning—as could be clearly seen, since he was still in ship dress, with the only light latticework of a standard psi amplifier on his head.

"How . . . how . . . ?" Derek finally managed.

"I made telepathic contact with you shortly after you got in here. Then, through you, I was able to visualize your location, and I teleported down. I . . . didn't bother Rosa or Urquiashqua or anybody else with things they didn't need to know. Anyway, I've been following you ever since."

And, Derek thought, he himself naturally hadn't noticed the sensation—the *tickle* was the only way he'd ever been able to describe it in ordinary sensory terms—of another telepath making contact. He'd had other things on his mind while in combat.

"Urysteshqua," he snapped, not meeting his grandfather's eyes, "you're now officially in charge of this old coot! Keep him back there with you by any means that seem indicated."

"Aye aye, sir."

Derek turned away, seething with fury. *This is all I need! Something else to worry about.* He gestured to Qyloashqua to lead the way, and their advance resumed. The dot in the HUD got closer and closer to the great hall. They encountered no one. Derek began to find the absence of resistance worrisome.

Finally, they stood before an entranceway five times the height of a man. Qyloashqua had been ready with the grenade launcher, but the double doors were open. They stepped through into a dimly lit space that seemed too vast to be indoors but was nonetheless rendered claustrophobic by the squat massiveness of all the architectural elements. At the far end, beneath a towering bas-relief of the Qurvyshuo emblem, glowed the hoop of a portal which, considering the distance, was clearly of extraordinary diameter.

It's open! Derek exulted, his misgivings forgotten. *We made it in time!* He stepped through behind Qyloashqua.

Only then did he notice, not far ahead of them but dwarfed by the hall's giganticism, a slender female figure.

At first Derek didn't recognize her, for insanity can render a face unrecognizable. But then she stepped forward.

"Nydierya," he breathed. And he wondered how he could ever, for even an instant, have thought her beautiful. For now he stared full in the face of that which the ancient legends had recalled as Maenads.

He was still paralyzed by the sight when, with a shriek that would haunt his dreams, she flung out her hands.

Magic was generally not useful in combat, due to the time it took to accumulate the ambient quantum energy it required. So at first it didn't occur to Derek that Nydierya, awaiting them in the hall, had had ample time to charge the spell she was preparing. And thus it came as a complete surprise to him when he began to burn.

Not literally. The spell Nydierya launched at him raised a firestorm that enveloped both him and Qyloashqua, just ahead and to his left. His sealed battle dress saved him from instant death, but the heat seared through it. He fell to the floor, screaming at the intolerable pain as his skin began to erupt with blisters. Qyloashqua was less lucky. He was festooned with bandoliers holding extra grenades for his launcher. He died in a roar of secondary explosions. Above that din rose a shrill sound holding neither mind nor soul— the laughter of the Maenad.

Then, out of the corner of his right eye, through his thickening haze of agony, Derek glimpsed a figure launching itself at Nydierya.

The mage saw it too. She was not too far gone in madness to react in self-preservation, using the only weapon she had. With a quavering scream of hate, she swung toward the onrushing figure. The fireball she was controlling moved with her. Abruptly free from the heat, Derek was able to recognize that figure just before the flames enveloped it . . . and horror temporarily made him forget his pain.

"Granddad!" he cried.

Glenn's light-duty vac suit lacked the flame-resistant quality of Derek's sealed battle dress. It was merely fuel for the fire that engulfed him.

Derek became aware that the screaming that filled his ears was his own.

He heaved himself to his feet and staggered toward Nydierya, gloved hands outstretched. She saw him and, with a smile from which the last vestige of sanity had fled, began to swing back toward him. . . .

Derek never heard the crackling sound of the small-caliber flechettes. But a diagonal row of tiny holes appeared on the front of Nydierya's dress, and a spray of blood from exit wounds misted the air behind her. The needlelike projectiles had practically no knockback effect. The mage simply stood for a fractional second, her features slackening into something almost recognizable as the Nydierya they'd known, then slumped to the floor. The swirling midair flame guttered out.

Derek also collapsed, as the pain he'd been suppressing came back in a rush. He glanced over his shoulder. Lauren was lowering her carbine.

He dragged himself over to that which had been his grandfather. He forced himself to look, and to smell, in a kind of penance. There'd be no dying speech, of course, or any other such thing. Glenn had told him that the true horror of war was the banality of death.

"Derek," Lauren spoke urgently, "lie down. The powered-armor troopers from *Ergu Nervy* should be here soon. They'll have a medic with them, and—"

"No." To move was agony. To *exist* was agony. But Derek stood up and turned his face to Lauren, who recoiled just a bit from the purified essence of murder she saw there. "Let's finish this." He motioned Urysteshqua forward. The Erkhedzuo readied his launcher.

Then, as they all gazed at that glowing hoop beneath the

stone planet-stabbing lion, a man appeared in it, dwarfed. He walked slowly forward, and behind him a figure took shape, looming darkly in the profane halo of the portal—a figure three times his height and blocky even in proportion, a repellant travesty of the proper form of Man. Likewise, the voice that filled the vast hall was pitched too low for any human voice, setting up vibrations at the very bottom of audibility.

"Kill them," commanded the Titan.

The human stepped forward. Derek knew who it would be even before the face became visible in the dusky lighting. And *this* human face was not distorted by mad frenzy. It held . . . nothing.

"Paul," said Derek, beseechingly.

Rinnard might or might not have heard. But he instantly identified the primary threat.

Without warning, Urysteshqua was flung backwards with a force that sent him smashing into one of the columns with a sickening compound noise that included the snapping of his spine. The missile launcher went spinning across the floor.

Before Derek had time to react, he and then Lauren were likewise gripped by the irresistible power of telekinesis and sent skidding across the floor. Derek's blisters were torn open, and he cried out in intolerable pain. He ordered his body not to seek the sanctuary of shock.

But even at that moment, he could understand that he and Lauren had been handled with relative restraint, or perhaps hesitancy—not sent hurtling through the air to die, crushed, on impact.

The High Lord could also see it.

"I begin to wonder," came the rolling thunder that was the Titan's voice, "if you are truly the right choice to be my primary instrument."

Rinnard stiffened. He stepped forward again. Derek gazed full into that handsome face, and saw no hope there. He closed his eyes.

Then, through his tightly shut eyelids, came a glow.

He opened his eyes. The hall was, indeed, illuminated— but not with normal light. He saw at once what had illuminated it.

Sophia was there. Not as he'd become accustomed to seeing her, but as she'd once appeared to him, in the gods' domain— the way she had once revealed herself to those Bronze Age Achaeans who had made her into the goddess of wisdom and of civilization and of the warlike virtues employed in defense of that civilization. It was the last of those roles that was now ascendant as she faced the High Lord.

The Titan had also taken on an Aspect. But he was glowing with a baleful blood-red, and the semblance he had assumed . . . Derek looked away, fighting down his rising gorge, for he had looked on the ultimate source of all depravity—a *wrongness* beyond the reach of even the most diseased human imagination.

A battle was underway.

There was nothing visible to indicate it, for the goddess and the Titan stood immobile. But Derek knew it, and the knowledge nearly immobilized him. Whether a non-psionic human would have been aware of the forces at work he was never to know. But he could feel the very foundations of reality shake. He knew that what was occurring here was a kind of combat that belonged in the howling chaos of the Inner Void, not in the material universe and certainly not in any enclosed space.

Rinnard stood immobilized, looking as stunned as Derek felt.

Then Derek noticed the missile launcher, only a few yards from where he had come to rest.

Forgetful of his agony, he scrambled across those few yards, unnoticed by Rinnard. With a surge of hysterical strength, he lifted the launcher to his shoulders. He struggled to recall the time Urysteshqua had briefly checked him out on the thing.

Let's see . . . get the target in the video scope and squeeze the first trigger, to fix that image in the missile's microscopic, suicidal little brain . . . there! Then the second trigger . . . "Lauren! Paul! Get out of the way!"

Amazingly, Lauren heard him, and rolled across the floor. Rinnard also heard him . . . and his face became a mask of horror.

"NO!" he screamed.

Derek squeezed the second trigger.

The missile roared into life, and streaked toward the portal. The backblast of its passage sent Rinnard staggering. It punched through the High Lord's thick torso as it arrowed through the portal.

It was not even temporarily fatal to the Titan, for a god's physical body could regenerate even such a wound as this one. But a basso cry of pain filled the enormous hall, and the sheer force of impact sent the mammoth form staggering back through the portal and into the domain behind it.

And then, within the portal, there was a sun.

A solid bar of blinding white-hot fusion fire burst through the portal and roared down the hall between the rows of pillars. Lauren had rolled out of its path. Derek, off to the side, felt the torment of renewed heat on his already-cooked flesh, but lived. Rinnard, directly in front of the portal, was instantly reduced to a husk of ash, then only a flake of it, blown away by that roaring thermonuclear blowtorch.

Then, before their dazzled eyes, the portal vanished. The cylinder of flame was snuffed out, leaving only the suffocating, overheated air to remember it by.

As Derek's sight returned, he saw Sophia bending over him—Sophia as merely a tall handsome brunette in a sensible suit.

"What happened?" he rasped, barely able to speak.

"It is a peculiarity of a portal from the Void," she remarked, at her most didactic. "When the god who created it is disintegrated and his energies returned to the Void, it ceases to exist. It is fortunate that this one did so. Once that vent was gone, the entire blast effects were contained in the Titans' domain, with results upon which I am sure it would be superfluous to enlarge."

"Sophia—"

"Hush," she said. "The landing force is arriving. And Lauren is all right." As though on cue, Lauren's face appeared over the goddess's shoulder. Her wheat-blond hair flowed downward as she removed her helmet.

"Sophia," he repeated. "You came. You saved my life."

Sophia smiled. Then, as he watched, she again began to be haloed with what was not really light, and she gazed at him from under the high-crested helmet with the bronze warhorses. But her gray eyes twinkled, and she spoke in an idiomatic Americanese he'd never heard on her lips before.

"Hey, remember those Greek myths you grew up on? I always *was* a sucker for handsome young heroes!"

And Sophia was gone.

EPILOGUE

Dawn was breaking over Zquerte, its light filtered through smoke. Not all the fires had been brought under control.

The troopers from *Ergu Nervy* had expected to have to fight to hold the central building. Instead, they'd been little more than onlookers as Zquerte had descended into chaos. Meanwhile, the Grand Admiral had brought his victorious fleet into low orbit and obliterated the Qurvyshuo presence there. With the alliance in undisputed control of Khron's orbital space, the Qurvyshuo armies on the surface were surrendering everywhere. And Erkhedzuo occupation troops were being airlifted from across the Central Sea, and had restored a semblance of order to Zquerte.

Now, standing on the landing stage to which they'd teleported only a few days before, Derek watched armed vertols crisscrossing the sooty sky, patrolling a city less pacified than stunned.

"Who would have dreamed it?" exclaimed Rhykhvyleshqua. He'd managed to put *Ergu Nervy* into an elliptical orbit around Khron after her hair-raising transit of the exosphere, rather than screaming off into space on the vector she'd retained after her jump via teleport drive. Now he stood off to the side, shaking his massive head with disbelief. "No one could have imagined the Qurvyshuo state would collapse so suddenly and completely."

"I could have," said Lauren. "Remind me to tell you about another overextended totalitarian state that imploded, a little less than twenty-five years ago on Earth."

"Ah, yes," nodded Urquiashqua archly. He and Rosa Kronenberg had come down on the same shuttle with the captain. "The Soviet Union, I believe it was called."

"Right. And unlike Qurvyshye, it hadn't even suffered a catastrophic military defeat; it just had seven decades of corruption, inefficiency and obsolescence catch up with it all at once."

"I suspect," said the mage, "that totalitarian systems always look formidable from the outside until the moment of their actual disintegration, which therefore seems shockingly sudden. And once they disintegrate . . . well, the totalitarian state is, by its own definition, all-encompassing. When it is gone, the collapse is complete because there is no societal 'safety net,' as it were. The state has allowed no other forms of human association to exist."

"Except organized crime," said Derek, speaking for the first time. "It stepped in to fill the vacuum when the Russians gave the Soviet regime the bum's rush. My grandfather used to tell me about it. . . ." His voice trailed off into wretchedness.

"Indeed," said Urquiashqua, oblivious. "That is a problem here, as well. It is one of the things we're going to have to deal with, when—"

"I think," said Rhykhvyleshqua, cutting him off firmly, "that before we complain about the problems of victory we should consider the alternative. I also think," he added with a significant side-glance at Derek, "that we have business which requires our presence elsewhere."

"Ah . . . ahem! Yes, of course." Captain and thoroughly embarrassed mage departed.

Lauren stepped over to Derek and started to lay a hand on his shoulder. She thought better of it at the last second. Erkhedzuo first aid had worked wonders, as had Urquiashqua's healing spell, but his skin was still both stiff and tender.

"Derek," she began hesitantly, "I know how you must be feeling, what with your grandfather—"

"And Paul Rinnard," Doctor Kronenberg interjected suddenly. They both stared at her, dumbfounded by the completely out-of-character sensitivity.

"That's right," Lauren resumed. "I remember now: just before you fired the missile, you yelled a warning to him, as well as to me. Even after everything that's happened."

"I can't forget the man I knew before," Derek said without expression, staring fixedly out over the cityscape and seeing nothing. "What *happened*, Lauren?"

She looked away, helpless.

"There is," said Doctor Kronenberg, "an old saying that power corrupts and absolute power corrupts absolutely. Well, Paul was tempted by *godlike* power."

"He told me," said Derek, almost too softly to be heard, "that human psis had the potential to be *greater* than gods."

"He was quite right," stated the scientist matter-of-factly. "And now, if you'll excuse me, I need to go inside and consult with Urquiashqua on certain matters."

"And that," said Derek a few moments after she was gone, "leaves us face to face with the question of what we're going to do now."

Lauren blinked. " 'Do now'? Well, of course I've thought about it. And it seems to me that now there's nothing to prevent us from returning to Earth and letting people there know what's been going on—and, just incidentally, clearing our names in the process. Or am I missing something?"

"No, not really. You know the reason we've always had to keep all this—" He gave an expansive gesture that took in the world of Khron and its human population, magic, the gods, the truth about psionics, and all the rest of what they now knew. "—from becoming known on Earth. Well, that reason no longer applies. The Qurvyshuo have been defeated, and the High Lord and the rest of the Titans are gone."

"Not gone forever, Derek," Lauren cautioned, falling as she so often did into the role of devil's advocate. "Remember—"

"Yes, yes, I know," said Derek impatiently. "We can't

guarantee that they won't be back to plague our descendants, after re-forming in the Void. As far as that goes, we can't guarantee that there'll be no asteroid strikes, nearby supernovas or mutant viruses either! And last time this happened to the Titans, it was thousands of years before they tried again. That's close enough to 'forever' for me."

"Actually," said Lauren with a certain reluctance, "I was talking to Urquiashqua, and he has a theory that it may take them even longer the second time around. Maybe they're getting a little . . . punch-drunk."

"All right. Better still. So there's no reason not to let the truth out on Earth. Except . . ."

Understanding dawned in Lauren. "Except what happened to Paul," she finished for him.

"We," said Derek obliquely, "were the result of a psionic assay of the U.S. armed forces. There are a couple of thousand times more people than that on Earth. That's a *lot* of potential psis! How many of them are as powerful as Paul was? Maybe there are even some who are *more* powerful." He took a deep, unsteady breath. "It's easy for us to sit around on our complacent butts and say he was tempted beyond his character. But maybe he was tempted beyond *anybody's* character!"

"So," asked Lauren after a few heartbeats, "what do we do?"

"I don't know."

"Maybe," Lauren suggested tentatively, "we could ask Sophia—"

"I don't think she can help us. I don't think any gods can. Not anymore."

After a long silence, Lauren spoke in a troubled voice. "I don't know either."

Their hands sought each other as they stood there, all alone.